Michele du Barry

The Loves

Also by Michele du Barry

Volumes II and III of The Loves of Angela Carlyle:

Across Captive Seas
Toward Love's Horizon

MICHELE DU BARRY

The Loves of Angela Carlyle (Vol. 1)

Into Passion's Dawn

Futura

To my husband

A Troubadour Book

First published in Great Britain in 1986 by
Futura Publications, a Division of
Macdonald & Co (Publishers) Ltd
London & Sydney

ISBN 0 7088 2973 2

Printed in Great Britain by
Cox & Wyman Ltd, Reading

Futura Publications
A Division of
Macdonald & Co (Publishers) Ltd
Maxwell House
74 Worship Street
London EC2A 2EN
A BPCC plc Company

PROLOGUE

Bad Blood

England
1797

I am as I am and so will I be,
But how that I am none knoweth truly,
Be it evil, be it well, be I bound, be I free,
I am as I am and so will I be.
—Sir Thomas Wyatt

The sweetness of autumn was in the air. In the woods the scent of ripe blackberries, damp earth, moss, and dead leaves combined into an elusive fragrance, the harbinger of winter.

Angela had lingered far too long among the flaming trees and now she was late. Running at a furious pace along the leaf-strewn path she could feel her hair slip down her back into a disordered tangle. There would never be time to freshen up before tea and today of all days she should have known better.

The Duke of Brightling, a distant relation of her mother's by marriage, would be arriving at any moment, and it would be her fault if she disgraced her parents. She should never have given in to the lure of the forest today. But the autumn with its cool breezes and splendor of gold, crimson, and purple was Angela's favorite season. Even wet, rainy weather couldn't dampen her enthusiasm for wandering among the trees, and this day had been fine and sunny.

Her brother, Brian, was probably all dressed and combed, waiting for their guest in the sitting room. Angela sighed. Why had she inherited all the wildness of her mother's bad blood? Not that the taint had affected her well-bred mother in any way. It just cropped up periodically among the descendants of the Campbells' and had chosen her in this generation.

Angela had heard over and over again the story of the infamous Clan Campbell. How they had been guests of the Macdonalds' for twelve days, until her distant kinsman Robert Campbell and his troops repaid their hospitality by massacring them. Blood had flowed scarlet and hot, spattering the snow, drenching the earth. The nefarious deed still rang through the annals of Scottish history. Glencoe, Glen of Weeping, that place of bare mountains and gloomy skies would be forever haunted by the vileness of that treachery.

Bad blood never changed and it had left its mark on Angela Carlyle. Where else could her unruly mane of black hair have come from, if not her Scottish forebears? Her parents were both fair and so was her brother. An impetuous, reckless disposition always landed her in trouble over the least incident. In fact trouble seemed to seek her out, taking pleasure in dogging her footsteps.

Flying out of the woods, Angela paused, then ran around to the back of the old timbered cottage her father had inherited from his great-aunt Felicia. If it hadn't been for Aunt Felicia's timely death they would be as poor as church mice. As it was they were only slightly better off. That was the reason for the duke's visit—money.

Angela's mother, Clarissa, was a delicate semi-invalid. One more winter in England, the doctors said, would seal her fate. So her most prized possession, the ancient Celtic necklace that had been in the family for over six hundred years, was being bartered off to the duke. He had had his eye on that piece for years and was about to be granted his wish—another magnificent prize for his vast collection.

If all went well there would be enough money to take them to Italy, a land of sunshine and temperate weather that the doctors recommended for consumptive patients. And if the sunshine didn't effect a cure, perhaps the countless specialists on the continent could help. A secret smile curved Angela's mouth. There might even be enough left over for a horse, her fondest dream.

Peeking into the kitchen, Angela found it empty, but it wouldn't be for long. Cakes and scones were baking and the tea kettle was on the stove. She scurried through and into the hall before Molly, the eagle-eyed maid, could catch her. As she tiptoed past the sitting room a flash of color caught her eye.

The temptation of the empty room was too much. With a furtive glance down the hall she went in, stopping short before the table and the square of black velvet on which rested their salvation. The colored stones winked at Angela in a conspiracy, daring her to touch them. The afternoon sun slanting through the diamond-paned window was a beacon beckoning her on.

Holding her breath she let the tips of her fingers brush gently over the necklace. Growing bolder, Angela carefully picked it up and clasped it around her neck. The old gold felt strangely warm against her skin, as if it were alive. Staring into the mirror the jewelry seemed to spring into motion, moving and swaying.

The ornate spirals and links were intertwined with mythical birds, beasts, and flowers and lay heavily on her chest reaching to her waist. Tiny gems of every color of the rainbow sparkled with fire. In the very center was a huge aquamarine, exactly the same color as her eyes. It glittered with a pale intensity that outshone all the other jewels. The ancient thing would have better graced the neck of some barbarian queen, lost in the dark ages of the past.

With the overactive imagination of the young, Angela didn't see a child of ten with tangled curls and a smudge marring her nose, but a beautiful princess, proud and regal. The worn cotton dress was a satin robe and she smiled, inclining her head graciously to her besotted subjects.

"Angela!"

She gave a choked scream of fright as her mother's voice abruptly ended her daydream. Spinning around, frantically trying to undo the necklace at the same time, she froze. In the doorway were her parents—and the duke! Brian made an impish face at her and clapped his hand over his mouth to keep from laughing. She had been so caught up in her musing that she hadn't even heard the coach arrive.

The catch on the necklace seemed to have locked and now she was caught red-handed. The gold tightened around her neck, cutting off her breath. With flaming cheeks Angela watched in a daze as the duke entered the room, his watery brown eyes glued to her face.

With his advancing bulk, the sunlight disappeared from the room and the atmosphere became chill and damp. An involuntary shiver went up Angela's spine. He was tall and fat, dressed as splendidly as a peacock, with a white-powdered wig perched on his head. Leaning heavily on a gold-headed cane, the duke limped toward her.

"Angela, make your curtsy to the Duke of Brightling, child," chided her mother softly.

She made a jerky little curtsy, staring fascinated yet repelled at the wrinkled face carefully inspecting her from head to toe. Angela had never seen anyone dressed so outrageously with so many different colors and materials.

The duke smiled, revealing broken tobacco-stained teeth. Then he took her hand and placed a wet smacking kiss on it. "Charming, just charming," he said as Angela surreptitiously wiped her hand off on her skirt. "You have a lovely daughter, Clarissa. She certainly makes the perfect setting for those jewels."

But the duke was not looking at the necklace; in fact he had hardly glanced at it. Instead his eyes wandered from Angela's rosy, parted lips to her unusual eyes, gliding over the creamy youthfulness of her complexion. Someday she would be a startling beauty, and already a plan was forming in the back of his mind.

He smiled, well satisfied, and sat down as Molly arrived bearing a large silver tray laden with tea. The others took their places and Nigel looked with distress at his daughter. She needed a firm hand, yet he was always loath to dispense discipline.

"Go to your room, Angela," he told his mesmerized daughter, who was still standing staring rudely at the duke.

"No! Let her stay," boomed the duke imperiously, banging his cane on the floor. "Here, girl, sit in this chair next to me—and keep that necklace on. You'll wear it little enough. Damn! if that stone isn't the same color as your eyes."

He chucked her under the chin with strong brown and white mottled fingers and Angela shrank back into the chair. Her father was looking at her with distress in his anxious eyes and she knew exactly what he was thinking: Blood and breeding always tell, and you my girl are an untamed little savage.

There would be no dinner for her tonight so she concentrated on eating as much as possible, trying to ignore Lord Percival Harrington's lecherous eyes.

As the conversation progressed through tea, Angela learned that Lord Harrington's third wife and Clarissa had been distant cousins. But his duchess had died giving birth to the duke's only son many years ago.

"Yes," said the duke, a wide grin on his raddled face, "they say I'm rough on my women. That's why I've gone through so many wives."

Angela looked in puzzlement at her mother's normally flushed cheeks blazing with scarlet mortification. Nigel cleared his throat nervously, almost upsetting his teacup, his soft eyes casting around, desperately trying to think of something to say.

"And I'll be damned if my son isn't cast in the same mold! That young devil is already cutting a wide swath where women are concerned." A scowl suddenly settled on Lord Harrington's features and he shook his head. Angela sneezed as some powder from his wig wafted her way.

"But that one's a troublemaker. Has been since the moment he was born. Rebellious and arrogant! Too much of that dark Scottish blood in him."

Angela's ears pricked up. So, this anonymous cousin of hers had the same problem she did. She would like to meet him and compare troubles. In a way it was comforting to know that she didn't have the full share of Campbell wickedness—at least she shared it with someone else. A little frown settled on her brow. She wondered what "cutting a wide swath with women" meant. Maybe Brian knew.

She looked at her brother. Yes, he knew. There was a half-suppressed smile on his face and Angela was determined to get it out of him later. Even though he was four years older than she, she knew how to twist Brian around her little finger. She smiled. Sometimes that blood came in handy for boldly finding out things she wasn't supposed to know.

At least having dashing, mysterious ancestors led to some excitement. Life would be very dull without that, and Angela had a feeling she would never be bored with her future.

PART ONE

Shadows In The Night

England
1802-1803

Stay, gentle Night, and with thy darkness
 cover
 The kisses of her lover;
Stay, and confound her tears and her shrill
 cryings,
Her weak denials, vows, and often-dyings;
 Stay, and hide all:
 But help not, though she call.
 —John Fletcher

Chapter One

The golden, sun-filled Italian days were over. The money from the necklace had flowed in an unending stream, but all things must end—and so did that.

Angela sat with her cheek pressed against the cool windowpane watching the ceaseless drip of rain fall onto the beloved countryside surrounding Windy Arbor. They had left five years ago in the fall and had returned to the same season. Everything was exactly as it had been, but different.

She was older and wiser, sadder because Brian had been left behind. Never again would he feel the cold English rain or see the spring flowers. They would not frolic in the snow anymore or pick summer apples. Forevermore he would lie beneath the foreign soil of a sunny land, so far away.

In a moment she would be crying and she couldn't stand that. Springing to her feet Angela threw down her unread book and hastened to the closet. Snatching up a hooded cloak she threw it around herself and escaped into the cool watery afternoon. She would be scolded later for getting drenched but she didn't care. Clarissa had forbidden her to go out in such inclement weather for fear she would get a fever like the one that had taken Brian. But she was made of sturdier stuff than her mother and brother, and rebellion was her second nature.

Angela ran through the orchard and on into the woods. The rain beat deliciously against her hot face and she laughed at a rabbit she startled. The soothing trees enfolded her. She was home.

The years they had spent abroad had a dreamlike quality about them. The tiny villa they rented in the south of Italy, blue sunny days, swimming, sailing, riding, running wild—after three weeks at home it seemed like a fantasy. There had been the trips to Germany and Switzerland, taking her mother to the best lung specialists money could buy and always the same reply: Rest and sunshine, stay away from England. It's too damp, too cold.

She was glad to be home, if only her mother could spend the winter in Italy. Already Clarissa's cough had returned and the bright spots of color on her cheeks too. She was worried and knew there was no way out. Their resources were at an end, the only alternative to live frugally in England and hope for the best.

Angela racked her brain. If there was any way to send her beloved mother to a better climate, anything she could do she would. But what could a fifteen-year-old girl do? She was too young to get a job even if one were available. In a few years perhaps she could become a governess or companion but by then it might be too late.

If only her father were stronger, more dependable; but he wasn't. His poetry was the world to him, his life's work, and if he was practically penniless and unappreciated now, maybe later the fame would come. Clarissa too was weak. Oh, she could manage the house and be a pretty ornament with her blond hair and big cornflower-blue eyes, but that was the extent of her expertise.

In spite of their shortcomings Angela loved her parents with all her heart. They were kind, gentle people and they were all she had. If only Brian were still alive—but that didn't count. *If onlys* didn't make dreams come true; wishing for something, no matter how desperately, couldn't make something happen. Only positive action counted in this world, and unless a person was strong they would be walked over.

Fantastic plans of becoming a highwayman flashed through Angela's mind. She had learned to handle pistols and swords when Brian did and had excelled beyond him. Why couldn't she have been born a boy? That would have solved all their problems. No one would take a fragile girl seriously if she pointed a pistol at them and yelled, "Stand and deliver!" They would laugh and cart her off to jail, or worse send her home to her parents to be chastised for another ridiculous prank.

But she was the strong one in her family. Whatever was to happen would be her doing and she must think of something right away—today. Her firm chin tilted upward, stubbornly determined to find a solution to their problems. Let her wild blood come to her aid now! It must be good for something other than getting her into scrapes.

There was only one answer—the duke. He was their only relation better off than they were. He was rich and powerful. Surely he wouldn't let Clarissa die—not if Angela had anything to do with it.

With a firm step she marched herself back through the trees and into the house. She was drenched but that didn't matter. Her mind was made up as to what she would do and she would do it now.

Without even bothering to remove her soggy cloak Angela sat at her father's desk and drew sheets of paper from the drawer. She wrinkled her straight nose, concentrating on what to say. Mystery was the thing that would lure the duke there so that she could speak to him in person. Not once did she write of their needs, only of an important matter that required Lord Harrington's urgent attention. With a dramatic flourish she mentioned that her whole life and future happiness depended upon him.

With resolution she slipped from the house for the second time that day, intent on mailing her letter. The sooner the duke received it, the sooner their problems would be solved. It never entered her mind that she could be turned down. If she had to get down on her knees and beg, then she would do it.

Two weeks was a long time for an impatient girl to wait but today all Angela's plans would come to fruition. The duke would be calling on her! Excitement was in the air and in her as she prepared herself for the visit.

She was perfect, except for her hair. Clarissa wouldn't let her put it up yet and that would have been exactly the right touch. Angela wanted to look competent, older so she could command the duke's respect. Her glossy black hair had been combed back from the sides of her face and held with a silver clasp, to tumble down her back in riotous curls that no amount of brushing could tame. It would have to do, she thought, with regret. At least the rest of her outfit lent her an air of sophistication.

Her best dress was pale yellow velvet of the latest Empire style. The skirt fell straight to the floor from the black satin ribbon that circled beneath her breasts. New black kid slippers just peeped from the scalloped hem which allowed a delicious glimpse of lace. To Angela's way of thinking it could have been cut lower at the neckline, but again she had been overruled by her mother. Long sleeves were gathered in puffs at the shoulders, tight fitting down to her wrists. Jewelry would have been nice but she didn't own any.

It was more than adequate for a girl living in genteel poverty, and she silently scolded herself for desiring more. As long as her mother was saved that was all she wished for. Anything else would be a luxury. Angela wondered if she could persuade her father to let her handle the money the duke would offer. She had a much better head for figures than he did and was sure expenses could be cut to the bone.

"First get the money!" she said to her reflection. "Then the rest will fall neatly into place."

The weight of the whole future of her family rested on her shoulders, and as Angela made her way into the garden to wait she rehearsed exactly what she would say.

Her parents had been puzzled by the duke's intent to visit again, especially since he made it clear he had business with Angela. They knew nothing of her letter, and she thought that the less they knew the better off they would be. Not that they could stop her. Nothing could sway Angela once she was set on a certain course.

The laughing cry of a rainbird broke off and Angela caught her breath. The noise of the duke's arrival set her heart fluttering nervously and she smoothed her hair, doubts assailing her for the very first time. What if he refused? Dragging a deep gulp of air into her lungs she pressed one hand over her madly throbbing heart. This was it! She must gather all her courage and wits.

Clarissa and Lord Harrington appeared around the corner of the house. He was fatter than ever, his limp more pronounced. A myriad of wrinkles webbed his face but those eyes were as alert as ever. The brown orbs fastened on Angela as she sank into a graceful, much-practiced curtsy.

"Your Grace, how kind of you to come." Her voice fell musically on his ears.

The same wet kiss was placed on her hand but this time Lord Harrington lingered over it and Angela suppressed a shudder. It wouldn't do to let him know how distasteful even his presence was.

The duke stared, an oddly disturbing grin cracking his pale face. She had been a beautiful girl at their first meeting but now she was breathtaking. Angela's full sensuous lips curved into a welcoming smile that set dimples dancing in the hollows beneath her high cheekbones. Her magnificent green-blue eyes fringed with a dense forest of black lashes sparkled mischievously, daring him to reveal their secret, urging him to get rid of Clarissa.

"We would like to speak alone, Clarissa," the duke ordered haughtily.

"But. . .but. . .it's hardly proper," fluttered her mother nervously.

"Come, come. We have business to discuss."

"Please, Mama!"

She was torn, but obeyed the command of the duke's imperious eyes.

"Your Grace, would you care to sit here?" Angela asked in a honeyed tone, indicating a wicker settee.

As he sat down she choked back a nervous laugh,

hoping it would support his bulk. It wobbled dangerously but held. Then Angela sat in the chair opposite him folding her hands in her lap, demurely lowering her eyes.

"Now that all the pleasantries have been gotten out of the way, suppose we get right to the point, my dear." Her aquamarine eyes flew to his face, confused. "I read between the lines of your letter and I know exactly what you want."

He raised a mocking eyebrow and smiled. Angela felt like a pawn being shoved around on a chess board by a master player. How could he know when she had said nothing?

"You—you little minx, want money!" Lord Harrington almost laughed out loud at her surprise. He had her full attention now. It was riveted on him and he proceeded, supremely sure of the outcome. "I'm right—your face has given you away. I may be old but I'm not a fool! Did you think you would get something for nothing? What collateral could you put up for such a loan?"

"Why," stammered Angela, totally at a loss, trying to gather her thoughts. "I have nothing."

"Did you think I would just give you the money to get your mother back to Italy?"

"I suppose so."

"I don't think you are stupid, Angela. I would expect something in return."

There was a sick feeling in her stomach and she hastily swallowed the lump in her throat. Things were not going well at all. She felt like a little girl being manipulated and backed into a dark corner from which there was no escape. Suddenly rage exploded deep inside her and she glared at the duke, her eyes spitting green and blue sparks.

What a magnificent creature! A thoroughbred of spirit and beauty. The duke chuckled as she sprang to her feet. She was perfect, his memory hadn't played him false. The plan crystalized in his mind and he knew that he had to have her.

"You are going to be my wife!"

"What?" Angela sank back into the chair, her legs suddenly unable to support her.

"You heard me, my dear. If you want money, you must marry me. You're getting the best of the bargain—believe me!"

His ugly, old man's face spun before her eyes. Marry him! He was ancient, old enough to be her grandfather. Now she was sure she was going to be sick.

"Look, let's lay all our cards on the table. I need a wife, a young one. You see, I want a son to carry on the family name. All my life I have chosen my wives carefully, with an eye to estates and fortunes. I've had four rich wives and made myself into one of the wealthiest men in England. Now I'm old and can choose what I want—and I want you!"

Her face was crimson and her mouth moved without forming any words. With a connoisseur's appreciation he let his glance play over Angela's small breasts, her tiny waist and curving hips. She would give him fine strong sons! And just the thought of initiating her into the rites of love was an aphrodisiac. Surely she could revive the flagging passions he had struggled to maintain over the past few years. With Angela in his bed anything was possible, and her innocence would add an additional fillip.

"This is outrageous!" Angela finally found her tongue. "You are old. Old!"

"I know my proposal is startling but calm down and think it out. I'm offering you the honorable way out of your troubles. Marry me, give me a son, and you can have anything you want. A title, money, houses, clothes, jewels—anything your heart desires. You will be a duchess and our son will inherit everything! Give me a son, Angela, and I will give you the world!"

"I don't understand this obsession with having another son. You have one already."

"That ungrateful wretch! Damn him to hell!" The duke's face turned red, then purple as he continued, "He hates me, he taunts me by turning down every match I've arranged. He knows I want to see the line carried on before I depart this world and he refuses, bent on revenge for some imagined wrong I did him.

"Besides he's too reckless, gallivanting all over the countryside in the dead of night—he's up to something dangerous that's sure to get him killed. I cut off his allowance and still he has money. There's something underhanded going on and I wouldn't be surprised to find him holding up carriages. Any night I expect the dragoons to shoot him down or catch him and hang him.

"Then where will my good name be? Then where will my heir be?" he shouted pounding his cane on the gravel. "We need each other, Angela. As soon as you give me another son I will disinherit Scott. Turn the tables on that scamp!"

"You're taking a lot for granted," she said coolly, turning the matter over in her mind. He was right, she had everything to gain by his proposition but that didn't make the contemplation of it any easier.

"I know that the only drawback is my age," Lord Harrington went on slyly, "but that will work to your advantage. I'm seventy-two years old! Think—I have only a few years left. I'm a realist and you should be too.

"If I live, say, another five years, you will be only twenty—a young rich widow. You will have wealth, power, an ancient title and your youth. Everything any woman could ever want is within your grasp. All you have to do is reach out and take it! Be my wife and your mother will live. Marry me and you will never have to worry about anything again."

"No! No!"

"Yes—just a few years of your life. You will never miss them. When I'm gone you can have any man in the world. Do you have a choice? Be sensible, girl!"

His urgent voice egged her on. Her common sense said yes and her heart screamed no. The duke was dissipated, grotesque, and he had gone through four wives already. Angela would do anything to save her mother's life—but could she do this? Could she sell herself for money? The idea was utterly revolting and her nostrils flared in disgust at the sight of his eagerly waiting face.

"I. . .would have to have time," she said in a hushed, tremulous voice. "I must think this over very carefully."

"Nonsense!" Lord Harrington heaved himself to his feet, clamping a hand on her shoulder. The fingers were cold and moist, even through her dress. "You have already decided—the only way you could. Wise decision, my dear. You will never regret it!"

"I wonder?" She was setting in motion a whole series of events over which she would have no control. Could she survive marriage to an old roué?

"Then you agree?" His voice was triumphant.

"Yes," Angela answered wearily, feeling her life end with that one word.

"Good—good! Your parents will have objections but I'll take care of them." The duke laughed uproariously. "If they don't agree I will threaten to elope with you. Can you imagine, me, at my age, running off with a little girl of fifteen? You have made one devil of a bargain!"

But Angela knew she had just made a bargain with the devil, selling herself body and soul.

Her childhood was over. Angela had faced up to the hard realities of poverty, and by betrothing herself to the duke, she had left some of her ideals behind. Always when she had thought of marriage it had been a young handsome man she had pictured. Someone that would love her and sweep her right off her feet. That would never happen now. She had made a business deal and in doing so had shoved her own dreams aside.

A tempest had broken their happy household apart when Nigel and Clarissa were informed of her plans. Her mother had cried, pleading with her to stop the tide of events. But when she saw the flecks of blood on her mother's hastily hidden handkerchief, Angela's resolve had been strengthened. To give up a few years of her life in exchange for her mother's was not too great a sacrifice. The bargain had been struck, and no matter what the consequences she would go through with it.

They would be married in one month, in November. So short a time in which to make all the arrangements and to discipline herself for a new role. But the duke's money worked wonders, smoothing over all obstacles, and it flowed freely. Dressmakers descended on the cottage filling Angela's every moment with poking and prodding, turning this way and that, pinning and measuring until she was exhausted. She was overwhelmed in a flurry of dresses, petticoats, negligées, shoes, hats, and jewelry. The choosing of colors and rich materials blurred into an uninteresting ritual that soon lost its charm.

In order to have a little time to herself Angela took to rising early in the morning before the first glimmer of dawn. Hurrying to wash and dress, she would rush outside to meet the first rays of the sun. The long solitary walks she took were her way of bidding farewell to this magical corner of her life, the country garden of Kent. The duke had a house in London and a vast estate in Essex, so it was doubtful if she would see much of the cottage she had been born in, or her beloved countryside. When her parents left a few days after the wedding for Italy, she would be absolutely alone, abandoned among strangers.

The mist was luminous mother-of-pearl, creeping and curling around the trees. Its dampness invaded Angela's green hooded cloak and caressed her cheeks with wet fingers. She strolled aimlessly along the country lanes, saying good-bye to the familiar landmarks she had always known.

A fiery-red guelder rosebush stood like a beacon in the pale fog. Angela touched a scarlet leaf as she passed. It would be one of the last shrubs to shed its leaves. Soon winter would blanket the world and she would have a new life. She paused, examining a bedewed cobweb, like silver lace stretching over the dark-green furze.

A sound caught her attention, muffled, indistinct. It was difficult to tell what direction it was coming from. The fog played tricks with hearing and sight. She stepped off the road onto the grassy verge starred with yellow and white mayweed. It would be unusual for someone to be traveling so early on a country lane, but it was possible.

A breathless anticipation laid hold of Angela and she stood very still watching the road, blending into the trees and bushes like a wood nymph. A wild impulse to run, to escape from unseen danger raced through her, but her feet were rooted to the ground. It was like being chased in a dream by some unknown terror and being unable to flee.

A huge black stallion materialized out of the fog right before Angela's startled eyes. The powerful muscles rippled on the magnificent beast, as smooth and glossy as satin, and the horse and rider stopped in front of her.

"You—girl!" She jumped as his arrogant voice assailed her ears. "I've lost my way in this damnable fog."

Another movement caught her attention as a pure white stallion solidified out of the mist. He was the most beautiful thing she had ever seen. Without even thinking she moved to his head, putting out a hand to touch the soft nose. He nudged her, gently breathing in her scent, and Angela wished she had a bit of sugar or an apple to give him.

"I don't have all day," the man said impatiently, and she looked up at the figure towering over her.

He was dressed in unrelieved black, except for the white shirt revealed beneath the unbuttoned greatcoat, but it was his eyes that held her. There was a recklessness in those narrowed brown-velvet eyes. They gleamed with flecks of light as if they had been blasted with gold dust and their boldness struck an answering chord in her.

"I'm looking for a cottage—Windy Arbor. I have business there with the Carlyles. Do you know where it is?"

Angela scrutinized him, wondering what he wanted. Perhaps he had some business with her father, maybe he was a poet. No, he looked like a man of action, not one that spent long days and nights hunched over a desk. His skin was brown as if he passed most of his time outdoors, and his hair was sunburnished bronze. He had a strong face with a straight nose and square chin deeply indented with a cleft, excessively masculine and hard.

He dismounted and still she had to look up. The top of her head didn't even reach to his shoulders. Warily, Angela backed up disturbed by his closeness, uneasily thinking that just beneath the civilized veneer was a savage animal waiting to leap out. She had never met anyone like him before.

She spoke, breaking the tension that had built like a tangible force between them. "I know Windy Arbor—I will take you there if you wish."

"Is it far?" His straight brows drew together in a scowl, contemplating a distasteful duty he longed to be done with.

"A few miles."

"Do you ride?" At her nod he smiled for the first time and strong white teeth were revealed, changing him —he was no longer frightening. The lopsided smile made him look young, boyish and a warm melting feeling went right through Angela.

Then before she had recovered from the devastating effects he had caused, she found herself being helped onto the white horse. His fingers lingered for a moment at her waist as she settled onto the sidesaddle and she wondered who the stallion belonged to. But the thought disappeared at the feel of the wonderful animal beneath her. With a surge Angela vanished into the mist, laughing in delight that for even a few minutes she could lose herself in the ecstasy of riding.

The horse was a wonder and she had only to touch him to urge him into a gallop. He responded to her thoughts and she forgot the man on his black horse, forgot she was supposed to show him the way to her house. Leaving the road Angela easily crested a hill, feeling her way through the fog with instinct and an intimate knowledge of every tree and stone in the area. This was paradise. The mindless delight of being at one with nature, feeling herself an extension of her mount. She was a child again, free and wild, flying over the grass heedless of anything but her own enjoyment.

"Damn! Where is that little baggage?"

His only clue was a trail of laughter and the soft thuds of hooves against wet grass. Now that he thought of it she looked like a gypsy, and everyone knew they were horse thieves. It would be just his luck to have chosen a gypsy wench as his guide. He would never find that horse again and it had cost a small fortune.

He went after her intent on catching up, but he was at a distinct disadvantage. She obviously knew the area well, and with the fog as cover, could be anywhere. Her laughter floated back to him again, taunting, making him angrier by the second.

The mist thinned at the top of the hill and he saw her retreating outline. He would catch her yet and make her pay for her insolence! Playing a game of hide and seek with an elusive apparition, when he had pressing business, did nothing to improve his mood. It grew darker by the minute as he thought of her impudence.

He had to slow as he entered among the trees. The mist thickened again pressing white and heavy against his eyes, rendering everything invisible. There were no telltale sounds now, only birds chirping, the gurgle of a stream, and the rustle of dry brittle leaves falling from the trees. He stopped, straining to hear something, and only heard his own heavy breathing and the movement of his horse.

The black stallion was winded after the wild chase and he headed toward the rushing water guided by his ears. She couldn't be far away. After watering his horse he would begin searching again. He would find her if he had to cover every inch of the woods and surrounding countryside himself.

"Oh!" Her voice sounded as startled as he felt.

She seemed to float on the curling tendrils of mist and

then he saw the white horse drinking from the stream, with her sitting him easily as if she had been born in the saddle.

"I'm sorry—I forgot all about you."

"This sure as hell isn't Windy Arbor," he snapped, hitting his riding whip against a highly polished boot. She made no move to flee and he wondered why. "I could have you arrested for stealing my horse!"

"But I didn't," she protested vehemently.

Looking at her closely he saw open honesty in her unusual eyes. The hood had fallen back, revealing a thick mass of midnight-black curls, and her creamy complexion reddened beneath his careful examination. There was a look of innocent vulnerability on her delicate features and just a hint of rebelliousness.

She was as fragile and exquisite as a porcelain figurine, with a touch of exotic radiance. But he sensed an inner strength of character, an iron will that glowed in her green-blue eyes. He felt himself drawn to this child-woman in an unfamiliar way that disturbed him, and his eyes quickly assessed her, finding nothing lacking.

Angela was confused by the intense gaze, his accusation, and the unreadable expression on his face. Then he smiled again and the sun seemed to burst from behind storm clouds.

"We will let the horses rest and then you will show me the way." It was a command rather than a question.

With a lithe movement he sprang from his steed and went to her, holding out his arms to help her down. She put her hands on his broad shoulders and he lifted her as if she weighed less than the enclosing mist. Slowly he lowered her and she was helpless to keep the length of her body from touching his.

Angela gasped. He had done it deliberately and now his arm was around her waist allowing no escape. The warmth of his hand through her clothes was as disconcerting as the glowing sparks dancing in his eyes, igniting something in her. Trying to push him away, she found him as hard and immovable as a boulder.

"Let me go this instant!"

"Not quite yet," he drawled, a sardonic smile lifting one corner of his mouth.

She raised her hand to slap him but he caught it easily and then with no warning pressed a hot kiss on her soft palm. Angela's flesh burned, tingling with unknown sensations that ran up her arm and beyond. He watched her flustered reaction, his eyes holding hers as surely as his hands clasped her. And she found herself thinking, if a kiss on the hand can do this, what would happen if his lips touched hers?

As if reading her mind he released her hand and she snatched it away, but his fingers slid into her hair holding her head still as his mouth lowered toward her. Angela's heart hammered frantically; there was no escape. And as his lips grazed hers, her heart exploded, sending flames licking through her whole body.

So this was what it was like to be kissed by a man. Not just an isolated pressure of lips, but a total involvement of body and emotions. As his tongue invaded her mouth gently exploring, teasing, Angela's mind whirled. She had never imagined this in her wildest fantasies and her arms involuntarily went around his neck.

It was wrong—wrong! But her blood surged wildly through her veins and a half moan caught in her throat at the tightness of her breasts and the shaking of her legs. What was happening to her? Angela had never felt such sublime sensations and the hunger in her made her ashamed, yet invigorated.

She was frightened of him; the demands his body made on hers were new and strange—and she didn't even know his name! This should only be done with a husband and the thought of the duke kissing her made her stiffen with revulsion.

He raised his head and said, "You are sweet—so sweet—"

"And you are no gentleman! You shouldn't have done that. Please, will you let me go now?" She felt she would die if he did.

"And I don't think you are a lady. You liked it." His

voice was mocking, but his eyes were soft and his lips hovered so close. "I want you!"

He kissed her cheek and his fingers sought the warmth of her firm, round breast. She drew a sharp breath trying to drag his hand away, trying to stop her nipple from swelling hard against his hand.

"Stop! Don't! I'm. . .betrothed. We are to be married next month. Please—I've never. . ." There was panic now, so real it vibrated through her and he released her.

Without the support of his arm she sunk down onto the carpet of bright leaves and burst into tears, covering her crimson face with both hands. What was she doing here in the woods kissing a perfect stranger, letting him touch her and wanting more? Angela felt as if every feeling had been drained from her. She jumped as he touched her shoulder, pushing a handkerchief into one hand.

"If I had known, I wouldn't have. . .Damn! I thought you were some little gypsy." He was at a loss to deal with tears or virgins; both were beyond his knowledge, and he felt extremely uncomfortable.

Angela wiped her eyes and looked at him guardedly. There was regret on his handsome face, but whether it was because she had stopped him or that he was truly sorry she couldn't tell. It didn't matter. Soon she would be gone and she would never see him again. There would only be a memory of their meeting, her first kiss, a tempting interlude—there could never be more.

"I. . .I'm all right now. Shall we go? I promise I won't steal your horse and I will take you to my father."

"What?"

"To Windy Arbor—my father's house," she told him getting up and dusting herself off. "You did want to see him, didn't you?"

"No, I came to see a young lady." He hesitated, positive he was in for a nasty shock. "Your older sister."

"I have no sister. There's only me—Angela Carlyle."

Derisive laughter broke from him and he stared at her disdainfully, eyes hardening, all tenderness wiped from his face and manner. She was his nemesis, the woman who was his sworn enemy! Why did it have to be her? He wished it was anyone but her—Angela Carlyle—his future stepmother. He laughed even harder. He couldn't afford to feel any pity, not with his inheritance at stake.

Sweeping her a mocking bow he said bitterly, "Permit me to introduce myself. Scott Campbell Harrington, Viscount of Winsley, Earl of Seafield—at your service!"

Angela's deep rose-colored mouth opened in a silent *O* of surprise. This couldn't be her cousin of the shared bad blood. He couldn't possibly be the duke's son, her future stepson. The implications were mind-boggling! She had pictured a younger replica of Percival Harrington, not this dashing, lean-muscled brigand who had stolen a kiss as if it was his property to begin with.

"Shut up! Don't you dare laugh at me—you. . . you. . .beast!" Angela shouted, working herself into a rage. "You are abominable! I hate you!"

"The feeling is mutual," Scott scoffed, the chiseled lips that only minutes ago had been kissing her, curled with disgust.

Angela brushed past him and he caught her arm. "Just where do you think you're going?"

"Home! And get your hands off me!"

"You didn't mind a while ago," Scott reminded her moodily, dragging her over to the stream where the horses cropped the grass. "Here!" He placed the reins of the white stallion in her hand, closing her fingers around them. "Your wedding gift—from me. His name is Pegasus."

Angela opened her mouth to say something, she didn't know what, but he broke in abruptly. "Don't say anything. The next time we meet will be on your wedding day. Forget what happened here today because I will." He ended on a strange, harsh note.

As he mounted his horse, Angela thought she saw a

pained expression flit across his face but she must have been wrong. Just before he left, Scott looked at her long and hard as if memorizing everything about her. She stared back, unwilling to shrink from his gaze; her pride wouldn't allow it.

"Enjoy your Trojan Horse," he murmured softly. Then he wheeled his mount and galloped off at a furious pace, not once looking back. The mist quickly enveloped him.

What had he meant by that? Pegasus was the winged horse, created from Medusa's blood, not the Trojan Horse. That was the huge wooden horse the Greeks secreted themselves inside in order to conquer Troy. He must have been a poor student in the classics, or else there was a hidden meaning to his words.

Angela looked at the spot where he had disappeared. "Beware of Greeks bearing gifts," she whispered, upset by all the events of the morning. "And Englishmen with wild Scottish blood!"

Chapter Two

The coach jolted over the rutted road giving the passengers inside a rough ride. It was a new, luxurious vehicle and well sprung, but the roads were atrocious. It was cold inside as well as out and Angela covered her dozing mother with another blanket, though how she could sleep was beyond comprehension.

Nigel was trying to read and he glanced up, brushing his sandy-brown hair from his eyes and gave her an encouraging smile. Angela looked out the window burying her hands in her fur muff, wishing she were riding Pegasus. No matter that Scott Harrington had given her the animal, she loved the spirited stallion, and the two of them were fast friends. She spoiled him with apples and carrots, and he responded by doing anything within his power. At least one good thing had come out of that distasteful encounter.

But she had to admit, only to herself, that she had found that kiss thrilling. Just thinking about it made excitement bubble in her. *Don't* think of it, she cautioned. He had turned hateful after finding out who she was, and she couldn't think of why. She was the same person she had been before he kissed her, but then he hadn't known she was going to marry his father. It must have been the shock of finding out that had turned him nasty.

When she saw Scott she would thank him for the gift and see if they could start over again. After all, they would be part of the same family. The thought of him as her stepson made Angela giggle. He must be at least ten years older than she was and his father was going to disinherit him. Somehow she didn't like being a party to that, even though it would be her own that would benefit. It seemed like a betrayal.

The countryside was flat and uninteresting, lowlands and marshes dotted with windmills. It looked like a foreign country. The scenery they had passed through in the morning had been eerie, full of creaks and small islands, so desolate they had seen no fellow humans. Now they were in Essex and Angela swallowed hard trying to keep down the lump in her throat and the homesickness that threatened to engulf her.

She longed already for the lush, green hills and colorful orchards and woods of home. No, she corrected herself, not her home anymore. This strange treeless region was her new home and she must get used to the idea.

The land began undulating in very gentle hills, and they turned into a long avenuc between massive stone gateposts. Leafless beech trees lined the road and as they progressed she saw that lavish woods had been planted on the estate. Angela's spirits rose slightly. It wasn't so bad after all. She craned her neck trying to get a glimpse of the castle but it was a long way from the main gates.

Then they went around a curve and there it was straight ahead, dazzling in the sunlight. Angela's mouth opened in astonishment at the splendor of the sight that greeted her. The classical mansion was of white stone, the main part four floors high. On each side long, low colonnades curved forward each ending in a one-story wing topped with a cupola and facing the avenue. It looked like a graceful swan, wings outstretched against the emerald lawns.

The duke met them at the door, imperiously issuing orders to the servants and kissing Angela's hand. She hadn't seen him since the day they had made their bargain over a month ago. Now, knowing what she did about kissing she felt like backing out. Would he kiss the way his son had? The thought was sickening.

The interior was more breathtaking than Angela's wildest dreams. She stepped onto large squares of black and white marble in the great hall. The ceiling was intricately plastered and painted in pale pink, lavender, blue, and green, highlighted with gold. Family portraits alternated with magnificent tapestries and mirrors along the walls, and a gigantic crystal chandelier sparkled in the late afternoon sun, reflecting thousands of tiny rainbows around the room.

They were escorted up the great oval staircase by the majordomo and shown to their rooms to freshen up after the long journey.

Molly had agreed to stay on after the wedding as Angela's maid and she now bustled around the room telling the servants where to put the trunks and bags. She was in her glory as Angela sat tensely on a small French chair waiting until they were alone.

"This is the most beautiful place in the world!" Molly exclaimed, eagerly exploring the wonders of the dressing room and the cubbyhole that would be hers. "Oh," she squealed in delight, "there's even a room just for the bathing, with a little stove to heat water on. I would gladly marry an ugly, old man if I could live in such style!"

"You should be glad you don't have to," said Angela crossly. "I would rather be at home. It's so warm and cozy, and this is so grand and cold!"

"Now, now," Molly scolded. "You are just overtired from the long trip. I'm going to start heating water for a nice bath and then you can have a nap before dinner."

Angela kicked off her shoes and settled back on a chaise, observing the exquisite room. The furniture was all French, curving white and gold. The carpet was Aubusson in delicate shades of blue, apricot, green, and cream. Painted Chinese silk covered the walls in a tracery of palest apricot and green, and the bed hangings, coverlet, and draperies were the same apricot silk lined with cream. Two large armoires stood on either side of the bed, and a desk and dressing table were across the room by the large French doors that opened onto a balcony. Below were the terraced gardens.

There must be a hothouse, Angela pondered, noting the large vases of flowers on the ornately carved mantel. A newly lighted fire crackled merrily on the hearth, smelling of applewood. It was too perfect, and she wondered how she would ever manage to keep herself busy in a place run by a staff of highly trained servants. Being a duchess might prove to be very boring.

The few days before the wedding passed in a whirl of parties, hunting, and entertainment. The mansion was filling with guests, up from London, eager to see the spectacle of the duke's fifth marriage. Some of the gossip and comments that Angela overheard set her seething. She longed to slap the malicious smiles right off the faces of those elegant ladies, but instead she squared her shoulders, determined not to bring herself down to their level. She remained cold and reserved on the outside even thought she was fuming just under the surface.

The duke was enjoying himself immensely, glorying in being the center of attention. He delighted in showing Angela all over the estate, from the woods that had been planted and carefully nurtured for one hundred and twenty-three years, to the boundary of the cliffs dropping into the ocean. He insisted she call him Percy and laughed every time she did.

One cold, crisp morning as they rode through the trees and around a lake, Angela tentatively asked the duke about his son.

"The blackguard is off again on one of his mysterious trips," Percy explained. "Said he would be back for the wedding, but I don't give a damn whether he's there or not! Scott is a troublemaker and the less I see of him the better. Believe me, there's no love lost between us."

"Does he live here at Brightling Castle?" she inquired, leaning forward to pat Pegasus's neck.

"Not in the castle," the duke wheezed, tiring from the unaccustomed exercise. "Neither one of us could stand that. We would be at each other's throats constantly! He has the dower house. I don't think you have seen it yet. It's near the woods about a mile from the castle, quite close to the ruins of the old castle. No one goes near it because they think the ruins are haunted."

After Percy returned to the mansion, exhausted from his ride, Angela set out again on her own. The dower house drew her like a magnet and she was powerless to keep herself from at least riding by. She found it on the edge of the woods surrounded by large denuded oak trees. It was a small two-story Tudor house, much older than the present castle. The ruins Percy had told her about stood impressively a quarter of a mile away. They looked gray and forbidding even in the bright sunlight.

Her attention drifted back to the dower house. It looked deserted, but was it? What if Scott Harrington was looking out a window at her, shaking with that mocking laughter? She mustn't just sit there and stare. Instead she rode slowly around the house scrutinizing the windows, with the draperies carefully concealing the interior from her eyes. There was something curious about the place and something peculiar about the man who lived there.

A shiver of apprehension went through her and Pegasus responded instantly to her demands. They shot through the trees away from the house and ruins. It didn't matter where she went or how fast, her problems kept pace, not leaving her alone for a moment. The closer the wedding day, the more she dreaded being married to the duke. It made her depressed and moody but there was nothing she could do to stop it.

The cliffs approached so fast it scared her but Pegasus knew what he was doing. He found an almost invisible path zigzagging down to the beach. The tide was out and the wide expanse of wet, golden sand was made for an invigorating ride. She raced along the shore and the horse was as frisky as a colt, spattering sand and water in every direction. They played tag with the waves until both horse and rider were tired.

The fresh sea air was intoxicating, the rhythmical pounding of the waves soothing to Angela's frazzled nerves. By the time she got back she was cool and calm, and disgracefully drenched with salt water. It didn't matter. She could do anything she wanted now, anything but back out of the marriage.

The wedding day dawned clear and crisply cold. Already the household was stirring in preparation for the big event scheduled for two o'clock. Angela soaked in a hot tub with her head resting on a folded towel and her eyes closed. But her long curling lashes moved restlessly against pale cheeks, at odds with her still body.

In a few hours she would belong completely to a licentious old man—Angela who had always been totally her own person, never owned by anyone. Percy would have every right over her, and she could do nothing but submit to the vile act expected of her. All her life she had known the ways of animals and all living things and it seemed right and natural, but not this—never this.

She had hardly slept all night with the horrible pictures dancing in her darkened room. The duke kissing her, touching her naked flesh—the thought of doing that with him was inconceivable! Angela's nerves were as brittle as glass and she felt like running away, like screaming but instead she flung a bottle of bath oil at the tiled wall. There was small satisfaction, but some release as she watched it shatter into tiny fragments.

Collapsing after her sudden outburst of temper, Angela forced herself to lie very still, breathing deeply. Slowly she forced the jittery feeling back, willing herself to be numb, indifferent. That could be her only defense. No matter how agitated she felt on the inside, she must be cool and placid, unmoved—not only in Percy's bed but in her new role as the Duchess of Brightling.

With infinite care she formed a protective shell around her vulnerable emotions. A suit of armor would have suited her admirably. By the time her bath was over Angela felt like a butterfly safely shut away in a carefully woven cocoon of her own making.

Angela let herself be dressed by Molly and Clarissa, responding woodenly to their ministrations. They exclaimed over the richness of her gown and jewels trying to draw her into the conversation but she remained silent. When they had finished her mother drew her over to the pier glass to inspect their efforts.

Angela stood as stiffly as a well-dressed doll in a creamy confection of irridescent silk. The bodice was low and square cut, exposing the swell of her breasts, embroidered with seed pearls and crystals that twinkled with every breath. The embroidery also covered the long sleeves and edged the hem and train. The Empire waist was fashionably high, falling in soft folds to her white satin slippers. Handmade lace as delicate as a cobweb veiled her, topped with a diamond tiara.

"You are the most beautiful bride in the world," sighed Clarissa, echoing the words of countless other mothers throughout the ages. With care she adjusted her daughter's three-strand pearl choker and smoothed her hair. The loose raven curls cascaded down Angela's back in a startling contrast to her white gown.

On the short drive to the church Clarissa thought in vain of words to comfort the silent girl, but in the end she too sat quietly. Nothing she could do or say could stem events from rushing forward to completion. Worried, she observed the feverish cheeks and brilliant eyes with the faintest of shadows from too little sleep. Her baby getting married! Why it seemed like only yesterday she had been rocking her to sleep in her arms and tonight she would be in the arms of an old man. It was obscene!

The coach pulled up to the church door and stopped. Clarissa gave Angela one last kiss and an encouraging smile. Then she was on her father's arm being led into the overflowing church and down the aisle to the man that would be her husband before the day was over.

She was shocked into awareness that the ceremony was over only when Percy lifted her veil. Crushing her in a bear hug he planted a long slobbering kiss on her unwillings lips, and she shuddered trying to escape again into her own tranquil world. Percy's mouth gagged her and wildly Angela wished she hadn't stopped Scott when he had said he wanted her. To be loved by a young virile man, at least once, would have been worth any embarrassment and pain.

They made a slow progress back to the castle where everything was in readiness for the guests. The feasting, dancing, and celebrating continued through the afternoon and on into the night without letting up. Angela felt like a tiny boat tossed about on a vast, stormy sea. She passed from person to person, hand to hand and was kissed, petted, cooed over, and danced with until she was ready to drop with exhaustion. Unable to eat a bite of the sumptuous food she only had a few sips of champagne. Finally after an endless day she was led upstairs to be prepared as a virgin sacrifice upon the matrimonial altar.

She was bathed, perfumed, brushed, and dressed for bed, and then installed in the large master bedroom to await the duke's pleasure.

Angela couldn't stop shaking as she lay in the huge, velvet-hung bed. Now that she was alone, the feelings held in check all day broke through the facade she had erected. She was sick. If only it was over, if only she could drop dead right now! She prayed it would be over quickly.

A loud knock sounded on the door and she sat up pulling the covers up around her neck. Not that they would be any protection from what was to come. The duke limped into the room wearing a long red velvet dressing gown and a ridiculous turbanlike nightcap on his bald head.

"Well, my little bride, shall we make us a fine lusty son tonight?" He leered at her as he tottered around the room blowing out the candles. Removing his dressing gown he fell heavily onto the far side of the bed.

Angela lay frozen, a cold sweat breaking out all over her stiff body. She kept her eyes tightly closed, fearing what she might see in the flickering firelight. At any moment he would touch her and she knew she would fight him with every ounce of strength that was in her.

Minutes ticked by and nothing happened. Then a

loud snore accosted her ears and she sat up abruptly, looking toward the mountainous bulk beneath the covers. He was asleep! Probably Percy had drunk too much and now he was out like a light. Thank goodness! Falling limply back onto the yielding pillows Angela let out a long, pent-up sigh of relief. This was only a reprieve, but most welcome, and little by little the tension drained from her body and she felt herself drifting toward sleep.

Turning over, Angela snuggled deeper into the bed, the snores of her husband comforting as a lullaby. For as long as he slept she was safe. With her last sleepy thought she wondered where Scott had been. He had said he would see her next on her wedding day, but had never shown up at the church or reception. Irresponsible, Percy had called him, and she had to agree, adding liar to his list of deficiencies.

She awoke from a sound sleep with her heart racing. Something had disturbed her; a faint squeaking noise accompanied the steady snores from Percy. Opening sleep-heavy eyes she saw that it was very late, for the fire had burned down low. Only a faint glow illuminated the room which was deeply shadowed.

Something moved, a shadow in the far corner of the room. No, it was just her imagination. Curling tighter into the covers Angela let her eyes close again. This might be the only peaceful night she would have for some time.

Something touched her hair and she sat bolt upright stifling a scream. The tall dark shadow of a man bent over her, obscuring the light from the fireplace. Panic and terror raced each other through her veins to her heart, arriving simultaneously. She opened her mouth to scream when he spoke.

"Don't be afraid, Angela. I mean you no harm—if you cooperate!" The voice that she had heard on only one occasion fell softly on her ears.

"What are you doing here? This—this is unheard of!"

"I told you, I would see you on your wedding day.

Did you forget, or did you think I had? I try and keep my promises." He sat down on the edge of the bed looking deeply into her amazed eyes that shone like aquamarines in the dark.

"Is something wrong? Did you want your father for something?" Her confusion was total.

"No," Scott drawled, boldly reaching toward her. "I want you!"

Angela scrambled toward the center of the bed, away from his seeking hands, shaking her head to clear it of the vestiges of sleep. Black hair, glinting blue in the dying light, tumbled over her shoulders like a dark cape.

"I don't understand," she whispered, not at all sure she had heard him right. "Shall I wake Percy?"

His smile flashed white in the darkness. "I doubt if a cannon going off under his nose would wake him now. You see—I had him drugged."

An alarm sounded in Angela's head and she leaped from the bed and ran across the room tugging frantically on the bell pull.

"You'd better go now, before the servants get here and I have you thrown out!" she yelled, running to the door.

What was he doing, lighting the candles as if he had all the time in the world? Then Scott turned, walking toward her with a maddening smile on his face. In a frenzy she tried to open the door and escape but it was locked and the key was nowhere to be found.

Angela turned, her back to the door, as he unhurriedly came forward, like a wild animal stalking its prey. His eyes were warm, glowing as he surveyed the exquisite body, her perfect breasts revealed to him by the thin material of her nightgown. She pressed herself against the wood, hands flat against the immovable door.

She opened her mouth to scream but his lips came down hard on hers, his tongue invading the sweetness of her mouth in a long brutal kiss. With her heart pounding like crazy in her throat and her body crushed against his, Angela could hardly breathe. She struggled, hitting him with her fists, kicking, all to no avail. Only when she went limp in Scott's embrace did he let her go.

"I—I don't understand what you are doing," she stammered. "Why?"

Scott's hand cupped the softness of her breast. His fingers moved warm and caressing over the delicate peak feeling it pucker, feeling her shiver with unsuppressible emotion. That was good, she wasn't fighting him—too much. Her breath came faster through parted lips and he could feel the beating of her heart.

Angela raised her hand and slapped him across the face with all her strength. He took a step back in surprise, eyes darkening with anger. A small handprint stood out red on his now unsmiling face.

"Don't fight me, Angela," Scott warned. "There is a long night still ahead of us and it will go better for you if you submit to me. I don't want to hurt you—unless you make me."

"Why do you want to dishonor me? I am your father's wife. If you wanted to—rape me you could have done it weeks ago, when we first met."

"There is a method to my madness," was all he would say as he reached for her again.

"Never!" she screamed as Scott's fingers closed over her shoulders, digging into her shrinking flesh. "Never will I submit to you. Would you take your father's wife right in the bed he is sleeping in? What kind of animal are you? You're despicable and I hate the thought of you touching me. Monster! Pervert!"

He shook her until she couldn't see through her flying hair. "And how do you think I became a monster? I wasn't born one, Angela. Who do you think turned me into what I am today? That old bastard snoring away in bed!" Scott's voice was a low, dangerous growl, so close to her ear that his breath seared her. "I don't give a damn what you think, or what he thinks about me."

Catching her up into his arms Scott strode toward the bed. "And to answer your questions—yes! I am going to take you in my father's bed—with him sleeping right next to us. Everything will go according to my plan!"

Throwing Angela onto the bed he grasped the top of her nightgown and giving a mighty yank, ripped it right down to the hem. She came at him like a tigress fighting for survival. Her nails curved into claws scratching the back of his outflung hand, just missing his startled eyes. Quickly Scott seized her arms twisting them cruelly behind her, dragging her body up against his.

Angela screamed at the top of her lungs in pain and fear, trying to twist from his grasp. His lips ground into hers, deliberately hurtful, burning into hers like a brand—unending, it seemed to go on forever. Shocked at the savagery of his attack she desperately sunk her sharp teeth into Scott's bottom lip, tasting his blood in her mouth.

Grunting with pain he flung Angela from him, catching her across the face with his open palm. Her head snapped to one side as she fell stunned to the bed. Scott dabbed at his mangled lip with the ruffle on the cuff of his shirt, gazing with passion-narrowed eyes at the still, unclad form.

Crossing to the fireplace he sat down on a chair leisurely removing his boots, all the while never taking his eyes from the tumbled body. He might as well take his time now and enjoy this girl he had wanted from the first. Desire coursed through him, growing with each passing moment. Perhaps it would be more interesting this way than with a willing victim. Never before had Scott raped a woman, never had he taken a virgin.

Yes, he pondered, this would better appease the burning vengeance he felt toward his father and the anger he felt at Angela's rejection of his advances. He would show her who was the master and punish her for daring to become the Duchess of Brightling.

Quietly Angela struggled through a painful haze and came to her full senses. Peering through her lashes, she saw Scott standing before the fireplace stripping off his shirt with purposeful movements. This was absolutely incredible! The whole situation was preposterous, but when he started to remove his breeches that motivated her to action.

Leaving the bed she flew to the door screaming for help and pounding with her fists against the thick wood. Scott watched with amusement at her futile efforts.

"Sorry to disappoint you, love," he laughed, "but even if anyone hears you they're not about to interfere with the duke's wedding night. I'm sure many a little virgin bride has screamed her head off in this room. And it's no use trying the bell again—I disconnected it."

She stood frozen, her hand still clutching the bell pull. Hostile green-blue eyes stared at him from a bruised face. Her coal-black hair fell in wild disarray over high, heaving, pink-tipped breasts, past her tiny waist and flat stomach to her gently curving hips.

Realizing her nakedness for the first time Angela tried to cover herself. Then she started as Scott removed his breeches revealing his vigorous male body, the rippling muscles thrown into relief by the firelight. She stared openmouthed at her first glimpse of a naked man. He looked like one of those bronze statues she had seen in Italy—but he was alive. Blushes stained her cheeks at his unconcealed desire for her and she lowered her eyes, looking at the floor.

She trembled with fright and something else she couldn't define. Just this morning Angela had wished she had let him make love to her and now he was proposing to rape her. One was an act of giving, the other a crime of violence—there could be no comparison. She would fight him for her honor if she had to die doing it.

At his approach she slid along the wall to the window. Flinging it open she leaned out seeking escape, swaying as she looked down two stories to the paved walkway. Swiftly a steel arm went around her waist pulling her back in.

"You little fool!" Scott breathed in her ear. "Were you going to jump? If I hadn't grabbed you in time you would be lying dead on those paving stones. But I have something better in mind for you!"

"No!" she yelled, trying to free herself from his clutches. "I would rather be dead than violated by you!

I will tell your father everything as soon as he wakes up," she threatened. "He will have you killed!"

Burying his face in her fragrant hair Scott breathed in the spicy-sweet scent of wildflowers, feeling its silky softness against his cheek. "You won't tell anyone what happens tonight, Angel," he whispered huskily, running his free hand exploringly over the curves of her body. "My father is not the man to accept damaged goods, especially in a wife. He will get an annulment so fast it will make your pretty head spin!

"Then where will you be? No money for doctors to save your mother's life, no trip to Italy, and perhaps my seed growing in your belly. What would your family and friends think of that? Even if you didn't have a child your reputation would be ruined, no man would ever marry you. I might make you my mistress—if you please me—or maybe you would rather become a whore!"

He kissed the graceful line of her long neck and shoulder, pressing himself against her back. Teasingly his fingers moved lower over her taut belly, stroking her intimately, relishing the thought of the greater joy to come.

She was cold and hot, trembling limply with an inner turmoil. His probing fingertips skillfully explored her, awakening a mysterious yearning that was half pain, half rapture. Coming back to life she fought the feeling and fought him.

"If you say nothing," Scott continued, "then no one will know. It will be our secret—yours and mine. My father will awaken from his erotic dreams with a headache, remembering nothing of his wedding night. Think of his delight when he finds his deflowered bride beside him and imagines the great feat he performed at his age.

"You see—everything will work out nicely. Then if there is a baby, he will think it is his and nobody will be the wiser."

Scott lifted her into the air and deposited her back on the bed. He held her hands over her head with one of his and rolled his body over hers. Angela twisted under him trying to elude him. Pulling one hand free she raked him all the way down his back.

"Bitch!" he swore reaching for the torn nightgown. Binding her wrists with strips of the material Scott tied them to the headboard.

He tried to kiss her but Angela turned her head from side to side, thrashing, maddened with the fear of his hard demanding body on hers. Grabbing her stubborn chin he intentionally took his time kissing her face and lips, slowly caressing her tender mouth with his tongue. His hands were all over her squirming body, touching, petting, trying to arouse her to the same fevered pitch he felt.

Scott's warm, naked skin felt like fire against hers but she lay stiffly under his burning kisses, arching in shock as his hot mouth seared her breasts.

"Stop it!" she moaned, writhing to escape the inevitable. "I hate you!"

"It had to happen sometime, love," he said, unable to control his urgent need for her any longer. "Wouldn't you rather have me than my father?"

"No! No!"

His hands slid under her hips, fingers cupping her firm round buttocks, lifting her up off the mattress. With a vigorous lunge, Scott ripped past the fragile barrier to her body, hearing her screams echo loudly in his ears.

There was pain, sharp and hard as if a dagger had been plunged into her cringing flesh. Tears sprang to her eyes, squeezing out of tightly closed eyelids, wetting her hair and pillow. She was hurt, bleeding, shuddering under his violent attack and it had only just begun.

He moved, tearing her apart, rending her like a rutting animal. Never had she felt such agony or humiliation, never endured such excruciating suffering. It went on and on, never ending and she had had no control over her own body.

Scott was possessing her totally, making her move to his quickening demands. His hands lifted her hips against his and she cried out again at his deliberate torture, the fury of his attack. Angela moaned as he drove faster, harder revenging himself on his father and on her. Then he shuddered, heaving in a series of convulsions that seared into her like a hot iron.

He collapsed on her, still at last, his chest moving heavily, crushing her breasts with each panting breath. Angela sobbed uncontrollably, her whole body bruised, her tender flesh wounded. When he finally moved off her, she saw her blood on him and his eyes widened as he looked at her. Quickly he went to the table and poured cold water on a towel. She gasped as he pressed it tightly between her legs.

"Don't squirm," he ordered, beginning to untie her hands. But when she was free she sat up and saw the blood on her thighs and a spreading stain on the sheet.

He pushed her down and got another towel and she put her arm over her eyes feeling faint. "Something's wrong," he muttered to himself wiping her off, listening to her soft hiccuping sobs. There shouldn't be so much blood, he had really hurt her, more than he had thought. Maybe she was still too much of a child, too small for anything but the tenderest, most considerate lovemaking.

An hour later, much shaken, Scott had everything under control. Pulling the covers over her pale, unmoving form, he brushed the hair out of her face, softly kissing her velvet cheek.

"I'm sorry," he whispered. But Angela's eyes were closed and she gave no indication she had heard him. With nothing else to do and feeling like a brute, Scott gathered his clothes and departed the same way he had come.

Chapter Three

Angela was jerked out of a deep sleep as the covers were flung off her. Opening red, swollen eyes she found Percy grinning down at her, his gaze taking in the rumpled bloodstained sheets and his battered bride.

"Good morning, sweetheart," he chuckled at the evidence of his prowess. "Did you sleep well?"

The memory of the dark night came crashing down on her with the intensity of an avalanche. The last thing she remembered was Scott pressing cold cloths to her protesting body and then she must have fainted. The things he he done to her were too horrible to remember, but past forgetting. He had made her a woman and made her his in a sadistic mating that was indelibly seared into her mind and body.

"You're a bit prickly this morning," observed the duke, "but don't worry—the first time is always the worst. It will be much better from now on. I don't feel very well either," he continued, belching. "I must have had too much to drink. I've got a big head and I'll be blasted if I can remember anything about last night!"

Stiffly she got out of bed and wrapped her nakedness in a blue velvet robe. She tried not to think of last night but she couldn't help it when her body hurt all over and there was a terrible ache between her legs reaching all the way up into her abdomen.

With a moan she pressed her hand against her belly, wondering if she would ever be the same again. He had torn her and used her for his own gratification without a thought to her feelings. Never could she forgive the indignity of that act of violence. No woman could ever forget the man that took her virginity; no woman alive could forget the panic and terror of being abused and raped. The fact that these two things had been done simultaneously by one man only made it worse.

A hate as deep and cold as an advancing glacier sheathed Angela's heart as she made her way to her own bedroom. And within those sheets of ice was the throbbing volcanic fury of a woman wronged. Scott Harrington should be made to suffer for what he had done to her and there was no one who could punish him but herself. She would make his blood flow as hot and scarlet as her own.

Not allowing herself the luxury of tears she summoned Molly and ordered a hot bath. Stilling the maid's alarm over her condition with an icy look, Angela dismissed her and sank into the scalding tub. She scrubbed frantically at her skin, washing herself over and over, trying to rid herself of the way she felt. But though she could wash away all evidence of Scott's body from hers she still felt dirty inside.

Why had he done it? Not just because he wanted her, that was too simple. He had gone to great lengths to arrange her wedding night to his satisfaction, according to a predetermined plan. Scott must have schemed for weeks to bring about the desired results. He had drugged the duke, silenced the bell pull, and locked her in a chamber of torture; coldbloodedly he had played with her, trying to seduce her and then raping her.

Angela drew a sharp breath, knowing positively that the stratagem was plotted before they had ever met. Any woman who had married Percy would have fallen prey to Scott's intrigues. It was just her misfortune to have been the duke's bride.

She couldn't let it happen again. Last night's actions had been totally unexpected and she had not been able to defend herself. Now she was forewarned and if she had to sleep with a pistol under her pillow in order to feel safe, then she would. Let him even look at her again and she would kill him with pleasure.

The only people she had seen since waking were her parents. She dug her nails into her palm thinking of their reactions to her bruished cheek and red swollen lips. Clarissa had cried and her usually calm, gentle father had sworn, wanting to beat Percy within an inch of his life. She managed to settle them both down, thankful for the clothes which hid the worst of her bruises. There were black and blue marks everywhere: on her arms, shoulders, breasts and thighs, even on her buttocks where Scott's fingers had dug into her flesh forcing a reciprocation.

She hated to admit it but he was right. There was no way she could ever tell Percy or her parents about what had really happened last night. It would be her secret—and his. And if she wanted revenge, she would have to do it herself.

Why was she cowering in her room when she had done nothing wrong? Angela's chin tilted upward, set with determination. She wouldn't hide from him! The sooner they met again, the better. They would have it out once and for all, and she would never let Scott intimidate her again.

After some involved preparations to make sure she would be safe no matter where she went, Angela went for her ride. She laughed out loud feeling the cold wind against her face, biting through her layers of clothes. It was worth the effort to be outside and free of the confines of the house and the knowing smirks on the faces of their guests.

Ignoring the jolting pain that went through her, she galloped full tilt toward the cliffs bordering the sea. Only at the last minute did she pull up, stopping inches from the edge, just in time to prevent herself and Pegasus from hurtling to the sands below.

In the west the huge, pink fireball of the sun was caught in the clutches of tree branches. They were starkly silhouetted against the fading blue of the sky, jagged lines drawn with India ink. Below, the shore was purple-shadowed and soon would be in darkness.

There was time for a quick gallop, no more, and Pegasus needed no urging to find the cliff path and nimbly make his descent.

It was freezing below and a stiff wind hurled spray against the base of the cliffs. Angela shivered, but not from the cold, and then she whirled around to see a figure half-hidden by the shadows. Scott emerged astride his black stallion with a smile upon his darkly handsome face, all the more dangerous when he flashed that boyish grin.

"Well, Angel, I see you have recovered. Are you ready for your second lesson in love?"

She stiffened. How could he call it loving? He was as bold as brass and twice as impudent, with not a sign of regret over having hurt her. Love indeed!

"I was hoping to meet you today," bluffed Angela giving him an enchanting smile. Today she was a child no longer, she could dare anything and succeed.

"So you are ready," Scott countered with a devilish gleam in his eye. "Perhaps I should have stayed longer last night. I had no idea you would change your mind!"

"Isn't that a woman's prerogative?" she purred. "I had in mind teaching you the second lesson, though. You don't mind do you?"

He moved closer, suspicion on his face. "Depends on what you have in mind."

"First—I want to know what your motives are. Why did you. . .rape me?" Her aqua eyes glinted dangerously, carefully assessing the distance between them.

"I just couldn't resist you, love. You were so sweet and eager the first day we met. I was sure you would rather have me as a lover than my father."

"Liar!" she flung at him, noting the amused half smile and raised eyebrow. "It had something to do with your father. You want revenge on him in the worst way, but how can what you did affect him? He knows nothing about it and never will. It is me you hurt!"

"But not without provocation! You fought like a wildcat!" He fingered his torn lip. "I did enjoy making a cuckold of my father but that's not the main reason."

"I thought not! You planned everything very carefully—and I don't like being on the receiving end of your plots!"

Even in the semidarkness, Scott could see the delicate flare of her nostrils and feel the rage emanating from her. He moved slightly farther away as if distance would quell her temper.

"Why?" Angela screamed. "Why? Or do you plan to keep it a secret?"

"My father is going to disinherit me when you bear his son." Her anger was firing his and when he spoke of his father the past rose like it was happening all over again. "You will never have his child—you will have mine."

"Never!"

"You will give me a son, my sweet little stepmother, and my father will think it is his. His plot will have failed, because indirectly I still get everything!"

It was so simple! Why hadn't she thought of it? He meant to use her for his own ends, and if she wasn't carrying his child now he would try again.

"I will not have your child!" Angela spat at him. "You conceited boor! Do you think I would submit meekly to another rape? You will never touch me again—I won't permit it!"

"Well, Duchess, I admire your courage but I can take you any time I want—here if I was so inclined." His voice was taunting her beyond anger. "There is nothing you can do about it. You didn't defend yourself very well before—I got what I wanted!"

With a smooth, precise movement Angela pulled something from her pocket, and he found himself looking down the barrel of a small but potentially deadly pistol.

"Put that down before you hurt yourself!" Scott didn't dare move; her finger was on the trigger.

"Or someone else," she laughed, enjoying the feeling of her total power over him.

"Now, Angel," he coaxed, "be a good girl and put it away. I promise I will go without touching you again. After all—you wouldn't want a dead lover on your hands. Think of all the explaining you would have to do!"

"Lover!" she yelled enraged, the smile wiped from her face. "You are not my lover! I hate you! I hate you!"

Her finger tightened on the trigger and Scott jerked, almost falling from the saddle. Blood, a scarlet welling of it, pumped between his clutching fingers and there was pain and surprise in his brown eyes. The shot echoed up the face of the cliffs and Angela watched him, a strange, satisfied smile on her face.

"I should have killed you," she said with mild understatement, "but I hope you have learned your lesson well. I will not be trifled with, and if you ever even think about touching me again, I'll put a hole right between your eyes."

Wheeling her horse she made for the path in the fading light. Not once did she look back even as he called out to her, his voice harsh with pain.

"Damn it, bitch—Angel! You are some woman—and you are mine!"

He was laughing at the joke she had played on him and the sound followed her up the cliff and beyond. As the day died and Angela galloped away she could still hear it in her ears—long after she was too far away.

And he haunted her dreams that night.

Nigel and Clarissa left a few days later and Angela felt abandoned. She tried to persuade the duke to teach her about running the estate but he just laughed. The estate managed itself and he had a competent staff. Why would he want a mere girl messing up all his years of careful planning? He did concede that she could do whatever she wanted about the castle and she set out to discover how it ran.

Inspecting the castle from attics to kitchens she poked her pert nose into everything, annoying many of the servants even though they were invariably polite but distant. Much to her disappointment she found that everything was managed perfectly by the housekeeper and run like a well-oiled machine. She wasn't needed anywhere to do anything. Her only purpose, she reminded herself, was to provide Percy with an heir, and she couldn't do that with him dropping off to sleep as soon as his head touched the pillow. Briefly Angela wondered if Scott was still having him drugged. Whatever the reason she was relieved that he made no physical demands on her.

The duke and Angela rarely saw each other except at meals and bedtime, and she felt at loose ends with nothing to do and the weather so foul she couldn't leave the house for days on end. Consequently she spent much of her time in the library reading or in the round sitting room, doing her needlework, looking out the tall elegant windows at the rain and gales playing havoc with the gardens. Sometimes she just wandered from room to room touching the priceless objects of art, losing herself in the sheer beauty of her home.

One set of rooms caught her fancy. They were on the third floor and took up a whole wing of the house. Dusty and full of old-fashioned furniture, they showed promise. The bedroom had two fireplaces and would be warm in the winter and the huge expanse of windows made it like being outdoors. It was possible to see the sunrise and sunset from those rooms and Angela knew she wanted them for herself.

Going to confront Percy with her idea, she found him in a temper, stomping around the morning room sweeping everything from his path with his cane.

"Percy, do sit down," she urged. "Your face is purple and if you don't calm down you will have an attack of apoplexy. Now," continued Angela after settling him in a comfortable chair, "what is the matter?"

"That scamp has gone and got himself shot! I knew it! I told you he would!" he shouted, emphasizing each word by banging his cane on the floor.

"I take it that you mean your son?" Angela forced herself to keep a straight face.

"Who else? The ruffian! He has no right to get himself killed before I have another son to take his place! Then he can do it with my blessing. I'll bet the dragoons shot him!"

"Was he seriously injured?"

"Shot in the shoulder at close range. The ball went through and didn't shatter any bones, but still he almost bled to death before he had it looked after. The fool!

"And I had to hear about it from a neighbor! Well I stormed over there today and he was in bed. Must have been feverish because when I wanted to know how it happened he laughed like the devil. Said it was an affair of honor and he deserved what he got."

He did indeed, thought Angela, it was too bad he hadn't bled to death. "Since he's mending I don't think you should get yourself so worked up about it. After all you have your own health to consider and you shouldn't jeopardize it over such a trifling matter." She gave him a cheerful smile.

"Yes, you're right, my dear. You are very good for me—make me feel young again." His eyes gleamed mischievously. "Let's go upstairs and have another go at it!"

Frowning, she wondered what he was talking about. When it finally dawned on her Angela paled, but dutifully responded, "Of course, Percy—whatever you want." Could it be any worse than the first time?

They went up the stairs together and he locked the door. She felt trapped and her heart beat like a cornered doe. He was her husband and she had made a bargain.

"Come, come, my dear—don't just stand there, take your dress off. I want to see all of your lovely figure."

Blindly, Angela obeyed, turning her back on him. Numb with fear, her fingers wouldn't work and most of the buttons got pulled off and rolled across the floor. When she was standing in only her chemise she felt his cold, clammy hands on her shoulders, his sagging belly pressed against her back as he placed wet, smacking kisses on her neck. She shivered, freezing as he lifted the chemise, pulling it roughly over her head.

"Lie down, sweet," Percy croaked softly, turning her around and pushing her onto the bed when she didn't move.

He stood there for a moment gloating over the beautiful young girl that only he possessed. Her eyes took in the large man, his pasty white skin hanging in folds and wrinkles and covered with silvery hair. The only part of him that wasn't wrinkled was the pendulous belly.

Closing her eyes she saw firelight playing over a tall, well-muscled man, turning him to bronze. They were father and son but there could be no comparison.

The duke fell onto the bed next to Angela, pawing her, exploring every curve and hollow of her cringing flesh. His mouth fastened on hers like a leech, sucking and then thrusting his tongue in and out.

I'm going to be sick, Angela groaned to herself, shuddering in revulsion as he forced her to touch him. Grunting like a pig he closed her fingers around his withered flesh and she felt wild sobs forming in her throat. It was worse than before—much worse!

"Quick!" he whispered urgently. "Open your legs!"

Instead she locked them together and they grappled together on the bed until he fell heavily on her, knocking the breath from her. Frantically, Percy tried to pry her thighs apart and she felt a throbbing against her stomach as his seed spilled warm and sticky on her belly. He snorted and heaved and then lay still, wheezing, unaware of his bulk pressing the breath out of her. She pushed at him and he finally moved, falling by her side.

"Sorry to disappoint you, sweetheart. Guess we've been trying a little too hard lately to make a son. I'm not young anymore you know."

Angela escaped, running to the bathroom. She was violently sick in the basin and then fell on the floor in a shaking and crying heap. It had been vile, obscene in a manner that even her ravishment had not attained.

Her wish granted, Angela ran with delight to her new rooms. Paper in hand she made notes on the changes she wanted. First, all the furniture must be removed before the place could be cleaned and painted. While that was being done, she would choose materials for the bed and draperies, and new furniture.

The rooms had belonged to the duke's sister, Lady Blanche Harrington, who had died fifteen years ago. They had been left almost untouched until now, except for an occasional cleaning.

Today Angela was elated about everything. First her husband agreeing to her request and then the signs that she was not carrying Scott's child inside her. She smiled. His plan had been foiled and he wouldn't get near her again. The small pistol was always within reach and she had proved she knew how to use it.

Kneeling down she opened the dust-covered chest at the foot of the bed, removing clothes and what were evidently keepsakes that the dead woman had carefully kept. A broken fan, pressed flowers, a packet of yellowing letters, a scarlet shoe with a missing heel, a stuffed toy dog cut to ribbons—bits and pieces of a spinster's life.

The rest of the room was devoid of personal items, the closets bare and the drawers empty. Angela tried again to open one of the desk drawers but it wouldn't budge. It had no lock so it must be stuck. Removing all the other drawers she poked her head through the large bottom opening. There seemed to be some papers stuck at the back of the drawer.

Jiggling the drawer she pulled hard on the papers. The drawer opened with a jerk and Angela bumped her head. Reaching back into the interior she found a small blue leather book—a diary. Opening it she saw faded cramped handwriting filling every page and she squinted trying to make out the dates.

Putting the drawers back she hurried to her room intending to read it through. Maybe she could find out a few new things about the odd family she had married into. Angela read all afternoon and into the evening, covering about two years in the life of Lady Blanche. What a tyrant Percy had been, inflicting his iron will on everyone with no thought to the consequence.

Lady Blanche had loved her nephew above all others but had been too weak and often too ill to protect him from the wrath of his father. The brutalities heaped upon Scott as a boy were almost too disgusting to believe. No wonder he hated the duke and wanted vengeance.

When she had called Scott a monster he had said his father turned him into what he was today. Finishing the diary, Angela believed it. She cried over the incredible cruelties dealt to such a young child. He had been unloved, unwanted, and rejected at every turn and she couldn't help but feel sorry for him, thinking of her own gentle upbringing. When she fell asleep that night it was with an understanding of some of the complexities of his personality.

In the morning Angela bundled the diary together with the souvenirs and carefully wrapped them, tying it with string. No one in this house would want them, unless Scott would.

Snow fluttered gently to the ground, clinging to the trees, turning a dull brown world into a sugarcoated fairyland. Blinking rapidly to free her long lashes of the flakes, Angela rode slowly toward the dower house. She had turned back several times, undecided—but now she clutched the package tightly and continued on. She would simply hand it to whomever opened the door, tell them to give it to Scott and be on her way.

She knocked on the door, waited, then knocked again. It swung open and she was totally unprepared to see him standing there. Scott's shirt was open to the waist, white against sun-browned skin, his left arm was in a sling and his wavy hair was all tousled. Without saying a word Angela thrust the bundle at him and turned to go but he caught her wrist and pulled her inside. The door closed firmly behind her.

"I'd forgotten how beautiful your eyes are," said the smooth husky voice falling softly on her ears. "They're the color of a tropical lagoon—green and blue all mixed together."

Cautiously she looked up at him wondering what he was up to with his glib compliments. Was he trying a new line? Nothing he could say would win him anything from her, he should know that.

Scott took her cloak and ushered her into a small booklined room, rather disorderly and masculine looking. She stood with her back to the fireplace as he sprawled in a big leather chair. Lazily his sparkling eyes stripped her of her green velvet riding habit.

Clearing her throat nervously, Angela said, "I found some things when I was cleaning out Lady Blanche's rooms and I thought you might want them."

"How thoughtful of you, Angel. Why—"

"Don't call me that! My name is Angela," she burst out. The very way he said it, like a caress, made her think of things she only wanted to forget.

"Of course, love," Scott drawled, enjoying her reaction to that endearment. "Sit down—we have things to talk about. Don't be so jumpy—I'm not going to attack you. You're not hiding a pistol on that pretty little body are you? I don't feel like being assaulted again either."

What was she doing in Scott's house talking to him as if they could ever be anything but enemies? He was so unpredictable—one minute spouting compliments and the next, who knew what would happen? She desperately wanted to go but instead sat stiffly on the edge of a chair ready to bolt at his least movement in her direction.

"Now, I don't want to upset you, but we do have some business to discuss." He gave her that boyish smile that crinkled the corners of his eyes, and she almost forgot how dangerous he could be. "One way or another you must give me a son."

She sprang to her feet but he was too quick. With a pantherish movement Scott slid from his chair slamming her back down—holding her there with his hand on her shoulder.

"You won't leave until we have settled this," he commanded bluntly. She caught her trembling lower lip between her teeth as he continued. "You have two choices—first we can become lovers—"

"No—never!"

"Hear me out." He sat on the small stool at her feet, his eyes piercing hers, holding them captive. "If you agree, I promise I will never hurt you again. I will be a gentle and considerate lover—you may even come to enjoy it." Angela gave a muffled sound of protest. "The other alternative, if you fight me, I'll have to take you against your will—by force. I don't want to but I will."

He released his grip on her, one eyebrow lifting questioningly. "Which will it be?"

Angela's voice was low, and he had to lean forward to catch the words. "No, to both of your—propositions. I warned you before and will say it once more—if you ever lay a hand on me again I will blow your brains out! I'll sleep with a pistol under my pillow if I have to, and I think I have already proved that I would just as soon shoot you as look at you!"

She stormed out of the house and Scott made no effort to stop her. Tears of rage blinded Angela as she galloped off not noticing or caring where she went. And she had felt sorry for him! He didn't need or want another person's sympathy, and she swore out loud using all the new words she had picked up in the past few weeks. She was gaining quite a vocabulary from the Harringtons.

Angela rode on, unaware of her surroundings until her horse started slowing down and she was jerked back to reality. A man was riding beside her, his gloved hand on her reins. They stopped and she stared around in confusion, the man and the landscape unfamiliar.

"Are you all right?" he asked, his sapphire eyes devouring the most ravishing creature he had ever seen. "You were going so fast—I thought your horse must be a runaway."

Laughter bubbled up out of her throat and she couldn't stop it—the first real, unrestrained laughter since her wedding. Angela gasped for breath, clinging weakly to the pommel, unable to speak. He must think her a complete idiot for he had an amused smile on his face and a look of amazement in his eyes.

Dashing the tears from her eyes with the back of her hand, Angela thought he looked like a Greek god. Why hadn't she met someone like him rather than Percy? With his golden curls and classical profile he was the hero of every novel she had read. Panting, she started to gain control of herself, accepting the handkerchief he held out to her, wiping her streaming eyes and blowing her small cold-reddened nose.

"Thank you," she managed at last. "I'm all right now. You must think I'm demented but—I really can't explain—"

"You must be upset from that wild ride. I don't live far from here, why don't you take tea with my sister and me and calm down before going home." He stopped as it dawned on him how unconventional he sounded. "I beg your pardon. Let me introduce myself. I am Keith Montgomery, Earl of Osgood."

"I'm pleased to meet you," she was still smiling, "I am Angela Harrington—"

"You must be related to the Duke of Brightling then. We're his closest neighbors. Will you be visiting for long?"

"Oh, yes—you see, I'm his wife," she stated baldly, noting the incredulous expression that crossed his face—then disappointment.

"But—I didn't even know he had remarried."

"We have been married less than a month."

"Then that accounts for my not knowing. We have been in London until last week." Keith paused. "I wish I had met you before your marriage."

Could she have heard right? He was echoing her unspoken thoughts and there was a mutual attraction between them, cutting through convention. After being in Scott's presence, Keith was like a breath of fresh air, with nothing more complicated about him than the way he tied his cravat. Open admiration and honesty were in his eyes and his face was smooth and uncomplicated, not like the inscrutable brown one she had just left. She could still see those dancing sherry-brown eyes daring her to choose the lesser of two evils.

Keith Montgomery and his sister Jane lived in a mellow, old Elizabethan house called Bentwood, about five miles from Brightling Castle. The faded pink brick gem, nestled between two hills, looked so comfortable and homey that Angela longed for Windy Arbor. A light frosting of snow glinted on the roof, and smoke poured from the chimney pots. Angela knew already what the interior would look like—as welcoming and cheerful as the man riding beside her.

Jane greeted Angela warmly and took her to her room to freshen up and repair her wind-blown hair. She was a smaller duplicate of her brother, tall and slender, with the same blond hair, blue eyes and symmetrical features: a cool English beauty that glowed with vitality and talked incessantly. By the time they joined Keith, Angela had learned that both their parents were dead, Jane was twenty-two and Keith a year older, and they had spent the past year in Switzerland.

The affection between brother and sister was tangible and Keith looked with fond amusement at Jane as she chatted on and on. Neither of them could get a word in until she slowed down and said she wanted to hear all the latest gossip. Keith surprised Angela by winking at her and she couldn't help laughing. Her dimples flashed because of his lack of restraint and an instant friendship was born between the three. They were both so guileless and straightforward that Angela was completely disarmed. How could anyone not like the Montgomerys? Their charm was infectious, their warmth a soothing balm.

"You are only fifteen?" Jane chortled with laughter. "That must have set the whole town on its ear! I wish I had been at your wedding just to see the looks on their faces. But really—how can you stand being married to the duke? Such a grumpy old man, and he was a horror when we were children. I can still remember some of the stories about him and what went on at the castle. Oh—but I do go on. Just ignore me!"

"That is an impossibility," laughed Keith with a mocking, long-suffering glance at Angela. "And to think I have to live with her! Is it any wonder I went for a ride today to get away?"

"And it's a good thing you did or we would never have met Angela—and think what a loss that would have been, Keith." Jane shot him a roguish look. "I do believe you have made a conquest, Angela. I've never seen my brother so bewitched before and he has had all of the prettiest girls in London throwing themselves at him for the past month!"

"Jane!" He was blushing at the truth of her observation, and when his eyes met Angela's she too colored, and there was a queer fluttering in the region of her heart.

She would have to be very careful, it would be entirely too easy to fall in love with a man like Keith Montgomery—and Angela thought that perhaps it was already too late. She didn't ever want to leave and go back to cold, elegant Brightling Castle, where she must dodge the duke and carry a pistol to protect her honor from his son. Here she could relax and be herself—but never completely herself—for no one could ever know her secrets; and the fact that she shared them with her worst enemy, Scott Harrington, only made things worse.

As if her thoughts had been read she heard Jane say the hated name, bringing her back to reality. "I'm sorry, what did you say?"

"I heard that Scott was shot. Is he all right? What happened?" Jane was sitting on the edge of her chair, all concern, her smile gone.

"He's back to normal," Angela retorted, thinking of his nefarious proposal. Lovers indeed!

"But do you know what happened?"

"I heard it was an—affair of honor," Angela responded ambiguously. More like an affair of dishonor!

"A duel? Oh no! I wonder if the other man was killed. Scott has always been one for getting into trouble," Jane reminisced. "He used to propose the most outlandish pranks when we were children. It's a wonder he's alive today! Although we hardly ever see him anymore. Do you see much of him?"

"As little as possible." Angela's tone was cool. "My husband doesn't get along well with him."

Jane lowered her voice to a secretive hush and asked, "But don't you think he is one of the most striking men you have ever met? Not only the way he looks, but the way he acts is so—bold and. . .wicked." She smiled and shivered slightly. "When he looks at me I get the most delicious feeling—" Angela stood up suddenly. "Oh—but I'm digressing again—"

"I really must go," said Angela agitated with the turn the conversation had taken. Was Jane in love with Scott? It would be her misfortune if she was, for he loved no one but himself. "You see no one knows where I am and I have been gone so long."

"May I escort you home?" Keith asked, silent pleading in his eyes.

"No—no! With your directions I am sure I'll find my way back just fine. Besides, I would rather be alone."

They said their good-byes, with the Montgomerys insisting she visit them often, and brother and sister stood watching her gallop off in a flurry of snow.

"I do like her," Jane stated, "but she's not at all like us. She's so quiet and rather mysterious—don't you think?"

"That's because she couldn't get a word in with all your talk. Have I told you lately what a chatterbox you are?"

"Silly—you tell me ten times a day. Still, she did leave rather suddenly. Do you think I said something wrong?"

Keith stared off into the distance. "I couldn't hear what you were whispering about—but knowing you, you probably did."

"I was just telling her about Scott."

"Maybe she doesn't like him either." There was a frown of concentration on Keith's face. "And another thing where do you get off telling her what you did—"

"But I could tell the minute I saw you together that it was love at first sight! You can't hide it from me—we're too close," Jane laughed teasingly. "But it's too bad she's married. My brother in love with a married woman! Maybe you could become lovers. She certainly can't be in love with the duke—ugh!"

"Jane!"

"But he can't live forever—can he? And here you'll be, right next door—waiting. I guess we won't be going on any trips for a few years. I must say, you have good taste—she's exquisite—foreign looking, rather exotic. Are you going to make an assignation with her?"

"Jane, you are too much! We have just met and you have us as lovers!"

"Well—wouldn't you like to be?"

"No," Keith replied very seriously. "I want more from her than that."

"More! What more could you want?"

"Some day Angela is going to be my wife!"

Chapter Four

Dreams—such nightmares she had endured—her wedding night happening all over again.

Scott's mocking smile burned behind Angela's closed eyelids and she pressed her fingers against her throbbing temples. She couldn't even wake up; lead weights held her eyes shut and her body was heavy and useless. Struggling against a terrible lethargy, she sat halfway up and the covers slipped down, making her shiver as the cool morning air touched her naked skin.

That forced her eyes open and she looked in confusion at the blur that was her room. Slowly her eyes focused and on the carpet were torn shreds of white lawn and lace, the remnants of her nightgown.Then she became aware of the ache between her thighs that she had felt only once before.

"No! No!" Angela's protests were just a hoarse whisper and she fell limply against the pillows, too weak to even stem the flow of tears.

He had drugged her! Her head pounded and she remembered the headaches Percy woke with each morning —and now Scott had done the same thing to her. Blushes stained Angela's wet cheeks as she thought of him having free access to her body, plundering its hidden treasures, while she lay unconscious beneath him.

The depths to which he would stoop to possess and humiliate her were incredible. And he had the audacity to suggest they become lovers! He was utterly depraved and she, it seemed, was at his mercy.

Slipping her hand beneath the pillows Angela found her pistol gone. She would starve before she let herself be drugged again, that or prepare her own food so that

Scott could not render her helpless a third time. No—she had made him a promise and she would keep it.

The morning passed with Angela lying quietly in bed with cold cloths on her forehead and over her eyes. With detached calculation she planned her next move; it was her turn to attack. Scott had won the first battle, she the second—he had undermined her defenses and now she would put an end to the contest.

Hatred filled her like a sickness, quickening her pulse until she could think of nothing but the satisfaction she would feel as she pulled the trigger. Angela had never thought of killing before, but Scott called out to the warrior blood in her and it answered, the fierceness of her lineage springing to her aid.

He deserved to die for what he had done to her. In a court of law he would be found guilty and hung. But no one must ever know, no public knowledge besmirch her for something she could not help. She would be the judge and jury—and the executioner.

When the effects of the drug had worn off, Angela choked down some lunch and hot black coffee. She would need a clear head and all her strength to accomplish the task she had set herself. Percy had been right all along—his son was a barbarian masquerading as a viscount and nothing good would come about by the lengthening of his life.

The gun room was deserted, as Angela had known it would be. She took her time selecting two dueling pistols, weighing them carefully in her hand, examining every minute detail. When she found the ones she wanted she cleaned them and primed them, thankful that her brother had taught her how to use firearms.

Snow was heavy on the ground and the holly was the only color in the woods. Blood-red berries against pristine white fired Angela's imagination and she could see blood soaking a white shirt, pooling on the carpet of that booklined room. With that picture before her eyes the ride to the dower house took only seconds.

He was home, she knew he was, recovering from the rigors of the night. That only increased her cold fury and Angela burst into the house without knocking, the pistols concealed beneath her flowing cloak. A middle-aged servant was startled by her unannounced presence, her blazing eyes and disheveled appearance. He scurried out of her path as she brushed past him into the small room.

Scott looked up as if he had been expecting her, a lazy smile tugging at his lips as he got slowly to his feet. He didn't even flinch when both pistols were pointed unwaveringly at his head.

"Would you care for tea?" he asked politely, ignoring his dangerous position and the anger assaulting him from Angela's flaming eyes.

"How dare you—drug me—use me! I hate you, Scott Harrington! I have come to fulfill my promise—a neat hole right between your insolent brown eyes."

"Wouldn't you like to know how many times I took you first?" he jeered. "All the details of last night?"

"Shut up!" Angela moved the pistols lower. "I've heard that a man dies a slow agonizing death if he's shot in the stomach. " She was icy calm now. "Or. . ." One pistol went even lower, pointing at his groin.

Two shots sounded simultaneously—one plowing into the ceiling, showering bits of plaster into the room, the other shattering a window. Angela grappled with the servant who had crept up behind her, and was quickly disarmed. He released her to the tender mercies of Scott.

Without saying one word Scott grabbed Angela and flung her over his shoulder, jolting the breath out of her. With slow purposeful steps he marched up the stairs and into his bedroom. Setting her on her feet he slapped her twice across the face and with her head still reeling from the blows he sat down and pulled her over his knees.

She kicked and screamed as he flipped up her skirts, then jerked in pain and surprise as a leather strap made stinging contact with her naked bottom. He was spanking her like a bad child, but with all the anger and vigor in him. Tears spurted from her eyes—impossible to hold back—and the blows were coming faster, harder so that another landed before she could draw another breath to scream.

Scott beat her until his arm was tired—her cries dying to whimpers and her body limp, the flesh criss-crossed with ugly red welts and blue bruises.

He laid her on the bed swiftly removing her clothes and Angela watched through glazed, half-closed eyes as he stripped himself. Hard lips closed over hers, cutting off the moans of pain that came unbidden to her lips as his weight pressed her into the bed. She lay vanquished under his attack, allowing him to have his way with her, helpless to stop him.

When it was over Angela turned onto her stomach, hiding her ashen face in a pillow. He touched her with light fingers, gently stroking her silky hair and the long slender line of her neck.

"Look at me," Scott ordered brusquely and she turned her head, dazed green-blue eyes staring reproachfully into his. "Don't ever try anything like that again —because the next time you point a pistol at me I'll take a buggy whip to you—and I won't leave an inch of skin on your back."

"Is that what your father used on you? Like father, like son!"

The crescent-shaped scar she had made on his bottom lip stood out white against the dark skin. "I can see I didn't beat all the spirit out of you—good! I like my horses and my women untamed—but obedient. You should probably be beaten regularly, just to keep you in your place."

"I want to go home!" She was crying again. "I want my mother!"

"Damn! Listen to me, you spoiled brat! I won't drug you again—unless you make it necessary by your disobedience. But you can expect a visit from me every night—until you get pregant. And you had better pray you have a boy. . .otherwise we will just have to try again."

"I hate you!"

"Yes, I know," Scott replied unconcerned, turning her over, sliding into her still moist body once more —losing himself in the primitive urge to reproduce.

Long, dark winter nights enveloped the estate, pressing against the windows as if trying to enter and devour the brightly lit rooms. Angela dreaded their approach and the swirling undercurrents tugging at her, threatening to drag her down. And they did—every night the nightmare began, then ended—only to be repeated again the next night. He too believed in keeping promises.

The estate and castle were riddled with a maze of forgotten underground passages that Scott had discovered as a boy. He had explored them, learning every twist and turn, never dreaming of the part they would play in his future, secret life.

He came to her every night through a panel in the closet and when she felt well enough to start fighting him again he carried her through the cold, narrow tunnels to his house. "No one will be able to hear your cries of passion here," he would tell Angela, a sarcastic smile lifting the corner of his mouth.

Most of Angela's nights were spent in his bed, locked in useless combat for he was always the victor. In the end she lay sprawled under him unresisting, unmoving until he rolled away from her, swearing. She was the loser in the eternal battle of the sexes, her delicate body no match for Scott's brute strength. But when it was over she had the strange feeling that he derived little pleasure from their contact. And that pleased her, for he always inflicted extreme discomfort on her, sometimes deliberately hurting her—though it was never as bad as the first time.

On dark, moonless nights and on stormy ones he came very late, smelling of the ocean, lines of fatigue etched on his face. Snatching her sleepy and protesting from her warm bed Scott would take her in front of the dying fire, without a kiss or caress. Silently he would lift up her nightgown, unbutton his breeches and use her casually, unemotionally—like a whore. Five minutes later he would be gone, like a phantom-lover melting into shadows. Somehow those were the worst times—the way he took her like an object to appease his lust, with no feeling, not bothering to undress, not uttering one word.

After one of those nights, Angela rode over to the Montgomerys' where she spent much of her time. She and Jane had become close friends. With Keith, there was something more than friendship, although neither one of them had admitted it with spoken words. But a quick glance revealed it, and when they were together it was obvious.

Keith could sense her unspoken feelings, and the fact that she was troubled. But he was always the gentleman, never questioning Angela's dark moods, and he treated her with a kindness and gentle consideration that was a far cry from her violent clashes with Scott. There was peace where he was and more than anything Angela needed solace and quiet companionship, free of deceit.

"Is your husband any better?" asked Jane, pouring tea into fragile, paper-thin china cups. She passed them to Angela and Keith, intent on her duties as hostess but with her ear always inclined for the latest gossip.

"No," responded Angela, sipping the hot delicious brew, trying not to spill it. The cup rattled against the saucer. She was as nervous as a cat today. "He still wakes up with those terrible headaches. The doctors can't find anything wrong with him."

"It must be old age." Keith couldn't keep the hopeful note from his voice.

"I suppose so," she said, knowing all along what it was and feeling like a hypocrite. But she couldn't just burst out with the truth that her lover was having Percy drugged so that they could carry on their clandestine affair right under his nose.

Keith was looking at her as if he knew and she blushed, hurriedly putting down the cup lest she upset it. His eyes lingered on her face, the shadowed eyes and swollen lips, the quick nervous gestures. Was that sparkle escaping from her eyes tears, hastily concealed and never allowed to flow? Jane had seen her mystery on the first day, and now that Keith knew Angela he too was intensely aware of it. If only she would confide in him, but he couldn't press her. When the time was right she would tell him her problems of her own free will. He would willingly die for her love.

"It's been a dead bore around here lately," observed Jane, not missing a nuance trembling in the air. "We really must plan a party, don't you think, Angela? Liven things up."

Things were too lively already. If only they knew! But she responded favorably to the suggestion, clutching at any diversion to keep her mind off tonight.

Keith reluctantly went back to his accounts, leaving Jane and Angela looking over color swatches for Angela's new room. She had thrown herself into the shopping and remodeling with a frenzy, at times almost blotting out the thoughts of the double life she was leading. But then the shadows would lengthen with the approaching twilight and it would be time to go home and wait as darkness closed in—dreading the consequences of another night as an unwilling captive of desire and revenge.

The sky was a somber gray as Keith escorted Angela back home. She was very quiet, wishing it was summer because then the sun would stay until nine or ten and the nights were blessedly short. How much longer could this go on? And a husky voice answered immediately, "Until you are with child."

She shivered, pulling her hood closer around her face. It would be almost a relief to bear Scott's son—at least then their midnight escapades would come to an end. Would he believe her if she lied—if she told him she was pregnant? It was worth a try. But then she caught her breath in horror. When he found it wasn't so, what would happen? Would he flay the skin from her with a whip as he had threatened? She couldn't chance it.

"Oh, look!" Angela pointed to the melting snow beneath the stark trees.

A colony of snowdrops had sprung up overnight, nodding icicle-like flowers on stiff green stalks. They poked through the glittering, receding snow, a refreshing glimpse of life in the midst of winter.

With delight drowning her speculations Angela pulled up and slipped from Pegasus's back. Like a child on a journey of discovery she ran to the clustered flowers, dropping to her knees heedless of the damp. It was in moments like this that her life was worth living, and she stripped off her gloves and picked a small bouquet.

When Keith knelt beside her, his blue eyes merry because she was happy again, she had her nose buried in the sweet smelling snowdrops. "They smell just like honey." Angela extended them for Keith to savor and he sniffed, his fingers touching her hand.

"But you are much more beautiful."

She was so close that he could feel her warm breath against his cheek and she smiled shyly, her dimples deepening, but her aqua eyes were sad. Keith picked some more of the flowers to make a larger nosegay and wrapped the stems tightly in his handkerchief.

"Thank you."

She swayed slightly toward him and Keith's hand touched her arm. With gentle fingers he traced the mauve shadow beneath one eye, looking at her questioningly, trailing fingertips over her cheek.

"I. . .haven't been sleeping very well lately," she explained lamely.

"I knew something had been bothering you." Keith's voice was soft and low, concern evident in his sapphire eyes. "You're not happy. I don't want to pry, but if I can help you in any way I would do anything in the world for you!"

"Keith, how I wish I could tell you, talk to you, but. . .I can't! Could you ever understand? I can't even tell my own parents. . .it's too unbelievable—too horrible."

A tear escaped before she could stop it and he caught it on the tip of one finger as if it was a jewel of rare beauty. He touched her hair and her trembling lips and a turmoil began deep within him.

"I know I have no right. . .but Angela—I love you! Ever since the first day we met—I can't think of anyone but you. You haunt me day and night and torment me with your closeness."

Keith couldn't stop his lips from touching hers, so soft and sweet. They parted with a dulcet sigh and her arms circled his neck, fingers tugging gently in his golden hair. Her tongue was an arrow straight from Cupid's bow, touching his, piercing his heart with exquisite pain.

Angela responded to the gentle pressure of his lips, knowing that this was a lover's kiss, not the demanding hardness she had experienced with Scott. A melting softness went through her, a glow of happiness, warming her blood, and she pressed her slight body against the leanness of his.

With Keith the disgusting act of procreation might even be pleasurable. He would never hurt her or use her —he loved her! To him she was a living, breathing person in her own right, with thoughts and desires and feelings to be taken into consideration.

His hand at the small of her back held her firmly but not too tightly, and his mouth was cherishing hers, growing hot with desire but not alarmingly so. Angela leaned against him to support her shaking body, heedless of the snow soaking her skirt, feeling her breasts tauten with a quivering receptivity. And then, as if her body had sent a silent message, his hand covered her breast, moving ever so sensitively, until she wanted to fall back in the snow dragging Keith with her.

Mocking laughter rang out, shattering the silence, breaking them guiltily apart. He looked like the devil himself astride the huge black stallion, looking down at them with dangerous, glinting brown eyes.

"Well—it looks like you could use a chaperon, Stepmother!' Scott remarked caustically.

Keith helped her to her feet holding her hand in his, and Angela gripped him tightly, knowing that look in Scott's eyes, dreading what must come.

"She's perfectly safe here with me," Keith flung at him. "After all, I'm a gentleman!"

"Meaning that I'm not?" Scott continued laughing with a rash undertone. "You're right! But no gentleman would maul a married lady in the woods, no matter how delectable her breasts are."

Angela hid herself in back of Keith wanting to melt from sight as quickly as warm snow. So he had seen even that! How long had he watched while they had been unaware? He had spoiled everything making it seem cheap and tawdry.

"My seconds will call on you in the morning!" Keith held himself back with rigid control.

"Seconds! Don't be a fool—you were the one at fault. If I told my father, he would have you caned by his servants like the puppy you are. Besides," Scott shot Angela a threatening look, "I will be very busy in the morning—very busy indeed!"

Now what was he planning? Whatever it was boded no good for Angela and she peeped at him with apprehension from behind Keith. He looked as if he wanted to strangle her or at the very least beat her again, and she held herself inflexibly for fear she would collapse in fright.

"Now Angela—get on your horse and I will see you home!" Scott's voice held the command of a ranking general.

"No!" She was scared but refused to let him see it.

"What about your. . .appointment tonight? You want everything to go well don't you?" He was threatening her now and it worked.

"I. . .I had. . .forgotten. Yes—of course." Angela turned to Keith. "Thank you for bringing me this far, and for the flowers. I'll go with Scott now."

"I'll go with you," Keith said suspiciously. There was an unvoiced communication between Angela and Scott, and he didn't like it.

"No, please!" she entreated, hastily mounting Pegasus. "I will be fine."

As soon as they were out of sight Scott stopped both

horses. He was so close his thigh touched Angela's and he grasped her wrist in an iron grip, pulling her toward him.

"You little bitch!" he swore furiously. "What the hell do you think you're up to, fooling around with Montgomery? Don't I keep you busy enough or do you want more? I should have stayed longer last night, worn you out!"

"You . . . dirty minded . . . abominable—brute!" Angela shouted, wincing as the pressure on her wrist increased. "Let go—you're hurting me."

Instead he plucked the flowers she was still clutching and threw them on the ground. "I'm warning you, Angela—keep away from Keith Montgomery. I want it to be my child you have, and will go to any lengths to be positive it is!"

Angela's protest was cut off as his mouth possessed hers with practiced brutality. His tongue thrust down her throat, choking her, and he held her until the struggles ceased and she leaned weakly against him. When she was released Angela raised her quirt, striking at Scott's arrogant face but he caught it deftly and threw it down.

"Damn! I promised you a good beating and I think you need one—tonight!"

He saw the quick dilation of her eyes, the flare of her delicate nostrils and knew she was afraid. But Angela tilted her chin defiantly at him and scowled. "Don't you dare try and intimidate me, Scott Harrington! If you touch me, you will be dead in the morning!"

"It seems I've heard that before, love—but it always comes to naught." Scott forced himself not to smile.

Angela looked back once, as they made their way home. The delicate virgin-white snowdrops were trampled into the mud—like her, just like her!

It was early that night. He usually didn't come till midnight or later, but now he was confronting her and it was only ten.

"Put on your cloak, Angel, we are going to my house."

"I will not! I'm not going!" She pulled back, terrified by the roguish look of him. He was up to something different tonight, she could tell by those eyes—they glinted with wicked merriment. He wouldn't dare beat her again. Yes he would!

Rummaging through the closet Scott found a cloak and throwing it around Angela's shoulders he twisted her arm tightly behind her back, forcing her through the small opening. The panel clicked shut behind them and he picked up the lantern he had left in the passageway.

It was damply cold and the walls dripped with water and slime beneath the house. He rushed her through the labyrinth, turning this way and that, and her lungs were bursting for a breath of fresh sweet air. It was stagnant and dead under the ground, like being entombed alive, and there were sounds of rats and dusty trailing cobwebs.

It was almost a relief when Scott shoved her out, fifteen minutes later, into his upstairs hallway. Their final destination she knew well, the bedroom—more particularly the great bed hung with burgundy velvet. She wondered what refined tortures he would inflict on her now.

Pushing her roughly into the room Scott locked the door. Angela's eyes widened, staring as he picked up a whip from the table. Her lips formed a silent no.

"It's time for another lesson, my love." He spoke coolly, with bored detachment. Angela pressed both hands tightly to her mouth to keep from screaming.

"Take your clothes off! For once I'm not going to undress you—you will do it for me."

Frozen into immobility she just stared, until the lash curled toward her, slicing neatly through her skirt and petticoat. Then Angela jumped, startled into action—her fingers tearing at the hooks on her dress, stripping the clothes off, letting them drop to the floor.

She shook her hair around her nakedness, crossing her arms over her breasts. Never would she overcome her shyness, especially when his eyes devoured her like they were doing now. He had no right to do the things he did, no right to look upon her bare flesh or touch her, or kiss her—or lay with her. And now what? She couldn't tear her eyes from the whip.

"Come here," Scott's voice was stern, contradicting the look in his eyes—as if he was secretly amused, aware of some private joke that she knew nothing about. Angela hesitated and he yelled, "Now!"

She went with trepidation and he brushed the hair back from her shoulders, loosening her concealing arms and hands. Ashamed, Angela looked down at the floor, standing very still, her arms at her sides, so that she looked like a perfectly formed statue of a goddess. She could have been carved of marble but for the tremors that rippled over her skin and her breasts, throbbing visibly from the frenzied commotion of her heart.

He was dallying with her, drawing out the torment until her frazzled nerves screamed—and he hadn't even touched her yet. When he did she would die, her heart would burst with terror and she would fall at his feet. Then she wouldn't feel the whip or her shame anymore. It would be a relief!

"You are getting better at following instructions, my sweet stepmother," Scott observed. "Now you may undress me—and start with my shirt."

Slowly, because her fingers were shaking, Angela unbuttoned his shirt and Scott shrugged out of it revealing his bronzed, lean-muscled torso. Then his arms went around her clutching the whip so that the wooden handle pressed into the small of her back, making her move closer until she was standing between his spread legs, his loins tight against her belly. The lash dangled the length of her leg, caressing her from hip to ankle and she shivered, closing her eyes, wondering why she was still alive.

"Touch me, Angel—I want to feel your hands on me in something other than a blow."

She put her hands flat against his chest, moving the soft palms down through the light fur, over the hardened nubs of his nipples, holding their bodies apart so that the crests of her breasts just grazed his skin. His desire was tangible now, hard against her softness—and the heat from his loins and where her breasts touched him radiated to Angela's body, burning, searing, as if he would consume her flesh in flames.

"Better and better—but I'm afraid I've sadly neglected your education in the. . .erotic arts," he murmured softly, all the more fear-inspiring because she knew there was nothing kind about him. "You have made a good beginning—shall we commence with the next lesson?"

She needed to be gentled, this wild, startled little creature, that could be held in his arms but never captured completely. Angela was elusive prey, slipping through his fingers like the wind, unable to be held even when he was possessing her totally.

Scott had only meant to intimidate her, not frighten her out of her wits and the whip dropped to the floor, forgotten. "I wasn't going to beat you." His voice was husky with desire. "I could never mar your lovely body—your skin is just like silk and your hair is as soft as thistledown. I just wanted. . ."

His lips brushed hers in a closed-mouth kiss, as light as the touch of a butterfly's wing. They moved slowly with infinite tenderness over her cheeks, brow, eyes, and back to the corner of her mouth. Then Scott let the tip of his tongue trace her closed, trembling lips, their sensual curve made only for kissing, until they opened of their own volition like a flower blossoming beneath the warmth of the sun.

Their breath mingled as the tender kiss deepened, and tentatively Angela touched her tongue to his, kissing Scott back for the first time since the day they had met. She shook in his strong arms with shock and reaction, her raw nerve endings exquisitely sensitive. First he had been so harsh and now he was kissing her like a lover—like he had never done before. Scott was an enigma, swinging from one extreme to the other, puzzling, inscrutable.

But how could she think when his hands were fondling her, moving lightly, stopping to explore and press, making her tingle all over? Powerless to stop the betrayal of her body, Angela strained against him, her breasts molding to his chest. Her hands slid up, pausing at the scar on one shoulder, encircling his bowed neck. Scott's thick hair between her fingers was like raw silk, and a sobbing moan rose in her throat at the ache he was kindling within her.

Scott hadn't expected her to respond with such sweet abandon to his advances. He picked her up and put her on the bed, flinging the rest of the clothes from his body. Then he joined Angela, his skin hot with a burning fever of passion—wanting her now. But he delayed deliberately, forcing himself to postpone the final joy until her desire matched his.

Riotously his hands ran over the luscious curves and hollows of her quivering form. With his mouth Scott teased her small shell-pink nipples, flicking his tongue over each in turn, nibbling gently with his lips until they rose up hard and pointed. Angela cried out, her nails digging into his shoulders as his head moved lower, his hair a tickling trail as he pressed kisses into her taut belly, exploring her dimpled navel.

Scott was a flame, devouring her, igniting her body with forbidden realities that burst like many-hued fireworks, illuminating the darkness of her mind. Everything was color and sensation, noise and tumult. And much to her surprise Angela found her hands exploring his hard man's body: feeling the play of muscles beneath his skin; touching him, hearing him gasp; closing her fingers around him, cupping him, feeling the pulsations throb through him, his breath quick and hard, panting as she pulled him gently toward her.

But he paused gazing deeply into her feverish aqua eyes, wanting her more at that moment than he had ever wanted any woman. "Do you want me, Angel? Shall I make love to you—or stop? Tonight the choice is yours—tell me what you want." His fingers stroked up her slender thighs, hard from riding, satin smooth, and they parted for his touch.

The choice was hers this one time, and Angela felt she

was on the brink of some great discovery. There could be no denying it if they proceeded, and it was impossible to turn back. There was a disconcerting need in her, totally alien to anything she had ever felt before, and she had a terrible feeling that only Scott could fulfill it. Even if he hurt her, she needed that hurt.

He waited, his eyes golden, melting her resistance, driving her past the point of no return.

"Yes—yes! Take me now!" she cried, her voice low and sultry.

"Why, Angel? Why, love?"

"Please," she pleaded. "I need you—I'm on fire for you!"

She guided Scott to her, arching up to meet her fate, shuddering in ecstasy as they melted, one into the other. There was no pain, just a building pressure, an undeniable urge for—she didn't know what.

United, they moved in cadence and Scott kissed her with a fierce demand that no longer frightened her. It made her soar to dizzying heights that she hadn't known existed. He was a fire, consuming her, blazing, wiping everything from Angela's mind but assuagement. Time was suspended—there was no reality, no world beyond this silent homage to love.

Her writhing body convulsed in a red-hot blaze as the conflagration caught them both up, bursting, exploding with a deathlike intensity that left her shaken to the very core.

Slowly reality returned, the flames subsiding, dying down to a warm glow. Angela lay limply, their bodies still joined, slippery with sweat. So that's what it felt like to love.

"I didn't know," she murmured against his shoulder, and Scott lifted his head from beside hers, his eyes soft with wonder.

"It's like dying a little—isn't it?" he whispered, kissing her gently. "The French have coined exactly the right phrase to explain it. *La petite morte*—the little death."

Never had Scott felt such pleasure with anyone

before. It had been worth every effort to draw Angela out of her shell, worth every delaying tactic he had employed to control himself so that she could attain her fulfillment. And her excitement had only fueled his, to the mutual satisfaction of them both.

"Angel—love!" He almost told her how he felt but paused, sensing her withdrawal, noticing the guarded look returning to her face.

It was impossible—she could never have acted so wantonly with him! Scott had stripped away her last vestige of self-respect by forcing a response from her body. Her own flesh had turned traitor, rebelling against every code of morality she had been taught. No—Angela could never call it loving. It was lust pure and simple.

"I hate you!" Angela told him, imagining she saw a hurt look flicker quickly across his face. "More than ever now!" That couldn't have been pain in his dark eyes, he wasn't human—he couldn't feel and react like a normal person.

Scott's gaze was hard again as he rolled away from her, feeling as if he had lost something very precious—if indeed he had ever possessed it. Women! Who could understand them? Blowing hot and cold—and just when you thought you understood them, they changed in midstream.

But he still wanted Angela and kept her beside him all night, making love to her, delighting in the power he now had to make her body respond and cling to him, even as she cried out her hatred.

And Angela could not understand the turmoil within herself—she wanted to resist but found she couldn't. The sensuous fire Scott had lighted was unquenchable—his least kiss or tough igniting it again, rendering her mindless, helpless.

Chapter Five

What a fool he had been last night, risking everything on the turn of a card. But Scott had felt so lucky, and when he had won, he sighed with relief, gathered his winnings and left. He shuddered at the thought of what would have happened if he had lost; all his savings and plans tossed away. As it was he had doubled his money and more—the plantation in Jamaica was an unexpected dividend.

Now he was anxious to be off across the sea to inspect his newly acquired property and if this night's plans went off without a hitch, he would have just enough for a ship and cargo—years sooner than he had expected.

Scott's blood raced at the thought of tonight. He actually enjoyed the danger, not caring what happened to himself. England was far too tame a place, it stifled him and he longed to embark on new adventures with the wind in his hair and the deck of his own ship moving beneath his feet.

Frowning, he thought of his men. Most of them had wives and families and he didn't like the odds of one of them being killed or captured. But they had known the risks of smuggling from the start, and the consequences if they were caught: imprisonment and hanging—not a way any of them would choose to depart this world. It made them all the more cautious, however, and over the past three years only two had been wounded, one captured and hung.

Everything was arranged in readiness for tonight, and now he had to get some sleep. He yawned and sipped at a brandy, smiling because it was illicit and he had smuggled it in from France himself. His grin broadened as he recalled his busy night—up half the night gambling and the rest spent with Angela. Smuggling was not his only transgression.

Angela—she haunted his dreams and even his waking moments. She was so beautiful, half child and half woman—until he had finally awakened the slumbering passions in her. Scott had never meant to get emotionally involved, but it had happened so subtly. In the beginning it hadn't mattered what she thought of him or whether she responded. His only objective had been to impregnate her as quickly as possible and get on with his own life.

What a task he had set himself! It was impossible not to get entangled mentally as well as physically with her. He should have known it the first day he set eyes on her. She was as bold and daring as he was, with an explosive temper and a streak of sensuality that could match him at every turn. There was never a dull moment with Angela around, and with her the unexpected became commonplace.

The day Scott had found her with Keith he had felt something close to jealousy. The thought of her betraying him infuriated him. First he had wanted to hurt her, then all he wanted was the same response she had given Keith—to make Angela want him as much as he wanted her. The total abandon with which she had given herself to him was a shock after the icy coldness and passivity of the weeks before.

Since that night their relationship took a new turn. She hated him, but at the same time wanted him, fighting the craving in herself, striking out at him until she could no longer resist. Caught up in her own renegade feelings she would give in and Scott reveled in his hold over her then—the only time he could be sure of her feelings and get the mastery over her.

The picture of Angela was vivid behind his closed eyelids: the long blue-black curls spread over white pillows, her small perfect body sprawled under him, those bewitching green-blue eyes, darkening with passion like cloud shadows crossing a tropical ocean. And her kisses, they could drive a man wild, provocative and at the same time innocent. He craved them as much as her body.

"Damn! She hasn't been out of my bed for two hours and I want her again!" His voice was loud in the silence of dawn.

Scott pushed the thoughts of her from his mind. Women always meant trouble and he would never let himself fall in love. An affair was bad enough and from his past experience he knew they were two-faced and devious, never to be trusted. The only place a woman belonged in his life was in bed and that's where he was going now, but alone.

Slamming down his glass, Scott sprang to his feet and went upstairs to his room. Dropping his clothes carelessly on the floor, he fell exhausted on the rumpled bed. Thoughts of Angela returned, refusing to be kept at bay. Her scent still lingered spicy-sweet in the bed clothes.

Closing his eyes, Scott concentrated on his forthcoming voyage, and as he drifted off to sleep he could feel the hot tropical sun kissing his face, smell the languid sea breezes and the fragrance of distant islands. But the ocean was a disturbing color, a pale sparkling aquamarine and she troubled him even in his sleep.

Angus eased Scott into a forest-green velvet coat, smoothing it over his broad shoulders. Scott was elegantly attired tonight from the pale gold brocade waistcoat to skintight fawn-colored breeches and Hessians polished to a mirror shine, all in honor of the dinner party he was attending at the Montgomerys'. At first he had hesitated to accepted the invitation, but it would give him a good alibi should any questions be asked about his whereabouts that night.

"Is everything going according to plan?" questioned Scott, throwing a greatcoat around his shoulders.

"Aye, nothin' has changed since mornin' and all the lads are eager to be off. 'Tis gonna be a foine dark night!"

Angus had been with Scott for the past ten years,

since Scott's grandfather died at the ripe old age of eighty-three in the medieval castle in the Scottish Highlands. The only heir he had left was his daughter's son, and on his deathbed he had extracted a promise from Angus that he would look after Scott even if it meant living in England.

Old hatreds die hard, and even though Angus had been born many years after the Scottish defeat at Culloden in 1746, his intense dislike of everything English still persisted. He had kept his promise however and as the years passed transferred his love and devotion from the old laird of Seafield to the new one. Even though Scott was half-English, Angus knew that the other half of his heritage was the stronger. His wild, adventurous spirit reminded Angus of the old man, as did many of his other traits.

There were no secrets between the two and Scott always treated the short, stocky servant as his equal, formal only when in the company of others. There had only been one disagreement between them, and that a recent one, about Scott's planned revenge against his father using Angela. On the day she had almost murdered him but for Angus's help in disarming her, they had had a furious argument. Angus asserted that no one, not even a Scott, should beat and rape a lady—and his stepmother to boot! Afterwards he kept his own counsel, not voicing his opinion on that touchy subject. But that didn't change his mind about the affair—the duchess spelled trouble and more of that Scott didn't need.

Scott rode through the night, pinpricks of stars the only illumination, and they would soon be gone with the rapid cloud cover moving in from the east. A stiff, rushing breeze blew in from the ocean, a night tailor-made for brigands. There was the smell of rain in the air and frost on the ground and spring was just around the corner.

Bentwood was an oasis of light and gaiety after the dark woods and Scott threw the reins of his horse to the waiting groom. From the look of things he was late, but then he didn't much care for gatherings of this type. He had accepted mainly for Jane's sake, having no use for her brother and his obvious infatuation with Angela.

Jane greeted him at the door, a vision of loveliness in yellow with pearls clasped around her neck and arms and dangling from her ears. With a wicked twinkle in his eyes Scott kissed her hand, far longer than was proper, and she was prettily flushed when he raised his dark head, smiling into her sparkling eyes.

"You are just like a sunbeam, lighting up this cold, dark night, Jane," he said smoothly.

"Why thank you, sir! Now come along and meet the rest of our guests. You are very late," she scolded fondly, taking his arm and steering him toward the hum of conversation. "I was saying to Angela just the other day what a thoroughly disreputable character you are." His arm tensed beneath her fingers and she looked at him curiously.

"And did she agree?" Scott's smile belied the rigid inflexibility of his face, not reaching to his eyes.

"Most emphatically!" Jane teased, wondering at the sudden undercurrent at the mention of Angela's name. "In fact she added a few observations of her own about your character, or lack of it, which I won't repeat. I don't think she likes you at all, Scott—and that's unusual. Most ladies find your charm irresistible, to say the least."

"Perhaps she knows the darker side of my nature."

"Nonsense!" laughed Jane. "If anyone did it would be me. After all we have known each other forever. Maybe she doesn't like having a stepson that's ten years older than she is. In some ways Angela can be such a child and in others—"

"I know—believe me I know!"

And Jane believed that he did know much more about Angela than she and Keith would learn in a lifetime—and they had just known each other for a few short months. They mystery was becoming intriguing, and she had a feeling that there was some intangible bond between the two, something other than their relationship by marriage.

But of course! They were distant cousins and that drop of shared blood made them antagonists. The Scottish had unpredictable ways, a savagery just beneath the surface and she had sensed it in both of them. They were so much alike they clashed continually, like rapiers in a never ending duel.

His father and Angela were there, he should have known. She looked up at his entrance with an amused smile and one dark eyebrow uplifted questioningly—or was it a taunt? The woman on his arm paled to insignificance before Angela's dark beauty, and the message that emanated from her green-blue eyes struck him like a slap—or a caress. With her it was hard to differentiate between the two. Whatever that look was, it was a challenge and Scott longed to find out which mood she was in—later.

So he gave her that purposely boyish smile that he knew irked her and let his eyes say the rest as they quickly assessed her. She was a masterpiece of artlessness, her hair in the Grecian style, threaded with a silver ribbon, with one long ebony curl finding a soft resting place against her bosom. The dress of rose silk and silver lace was a creation for enticement. Damn! It was so low cut that if she did more than breathe her divine breasts would almost certainly be fully exposed, and Scott wondered whose benefit that was for.

Keith seemed to appreciate the effect, in fact his eyes were glued to where a huge blue-fired diamond resided against a shadowed hollow of gleaming skin—but he wasn't admiring the gem, rather the two jewels that cradled it. Scott greeted him curtly, still put out over the flirtation and the moonstruck glances he shot at Angela with every other blink of his eyes. An unwarranted irritation laid hold of Scott and gripped him for the rest of the evening. It was a green-eyed monster sitting on his shoulders, goading him mercilessly.

He barely spoke to his father, noticing the yellowed, unhealthy skin and pinched look around his eyes and mouth. "Why, Father, you look tired," Scott said haughtily. "Is your lively young wife taxing your strength?"

"Not in the least," the duke huffed, taking Angela's arm possessively, as she shot Scott a venomous look. "No one could have a better wife!"

Like hell! thought Scott. Angela was enough to exhaust an army bent on rape and he was the one that had aroused her, stirred the embers of her passion into a blaze that could make any man's blood boil—but he alone was her man.

Vicar Grindell and his wife were present with their plump, mousy daughter Maude, and the Baron and Baroness of Rowney, a lively couple in their mid-thirties, completed the small dinner party.

On the surface everything went smoothly. At dinner Angela engaged Baron Rowney in a heated discussion on politics, ignoring Scott. Keith was in misery at the other end of the table trying to entertain the shy Maude and her self-righteous parents, wishing he were near Angela and keeping a careful eye on Scott's flirtation with Jane and her obvious encouragement of him.

Scott relaxed a little, letting his guard down. With Jane this was possible because she put him at ease with her undemanding banter and light-hearted charm. She had changed from a skinny, freckle-faced little girl into an elegant lady. But the girl lurked just beneath her sophisticated veneer, and to his delight and at his instigation she broke through occasionally.

He would never forget the day they had gone fishing on the lake. In her excitement over catching her first fish Jane had stood up, lost her balance and fallen in. She had been madder than a wet hen when he had fished her out, accusing him of pushing her in deliberately, and his hilarity did nothing to endear him to her that day. He smiled at the faded picture and Jane responded, forgetting what she had been talking about.

Jane had loved him all her live yet they had never been anything but friends. Consequently she was alert to his slightest change in mood, and in spite of the fact that she chatted and supervised the serving of dinner nothing escaped her attention when it came to Scott.

The suspicion she had earlier about Scott and Angela became manifest. The air fairly crackled between them each time their eyes met and such passion could mean only one of two things: they either hated with the puissance of mortal enemies or they loved with such compulsion it could not be denied. But which was it—and did they both feel the same or did one hate and the other love? Jane could not tell and her perception of their plight made her uneasy. Where such supercharged emotions existed there was sure to be an explosion.

Did she dare ask Angela? No, she couldn't chance being the catalyst in such a critical state of affairs. Maybe by other means and by quietly observing she could discover their secret—for Jane was positive their feelings were not unknown to each other.

As the ladies got up to leave after dinner Jane drew Angela aside, her blue eyes still on Scott. "I have known him since I was born, yet there are so many things about Scott that are mysteries to me. Sometimes he gets such a wild look in his eyes—just like a pirate! Wouldn't you love to be carried off by someone like that? And. . . and. . ."

"And what?" snapped Angela crossly. "You've been reading too many novels! Do you think a buccaneer would make a gentle lover? Well you are mistaken—you wouldn't like it one bit!"

"Don't get so upset, Angela," Jane soothed. "I was only daydreaming out loud. Why from the way you talk, you would think it had happened to you!"

The cool composure was back almost as soon as the words left Angela's mouth, revealing slightly too much of the volatile temper usually kept in check, except around Scott.

"Don't be silly," Angela teased, smiling, trying to mollify her friend. "Why I've never in my life even made the acquaintance of a pirate, much less been carried off by one!" She dismissed the whole conversation with a wave of her hand as they went upstairs to freshen up.

A lantern flickered, casting long shadows on the damp stone walls, illuminating the faces of two dozen men and turning them into crude caricatures of reality. It was two o'clock in the morning and Scott and all his men were assembled in a secret room beneath the ruins of the old castle. The locals believed the place haunted and steered clear, an attitude he did nothing to discourage. The dungeons made a perfect hiding place for the contraband that arrived regularly from France.

As was the common practice, most of his men had borrowed the horses of local townspeople and farmers so their own wouldn't be recognized. In the morning a tired horse and a gift of tea or brandy would be left in many barns and stables across the countryside. The people were blind and deaf to the ancient and very common practice of smuggling, and if they heard unusual sounds on dark nights they just turned over and burrowed deeper into their warm beds.

Woe to the man or woman who turned informer in those parts! Most wouldn't because relatives and friends were involved in the lucrative business, but on occasion it had been known to happen. If they were found out it spelled instant ostracism from the whole community, forcing them to leave—or they could stay and risk a ball in the back or a knife swiftly drawn from ear to ear.

A feeling of uneasiness communicated itself from Scott to Angus. "Careful, lad!" the servant whispered as he and his men left, disappearing into the night. Angus sat down on a cask of cognac, starting his long vigil.

On they rode at a moderate pace, sure of their surroundings and their destination, sure of the outcome of this foray. It had been repeated an endless number of times: a quick ride to the cliffs, down the steep path to the wet crunching sand, a signal flashed over a pitch-black sea and one returned. The nocturnal enterprise had started, warming their blood in the raw sea air, an adventure *extraordinaire,* the ultimate challenge.

The cliffs were tall quiet sentinels, cover for the band

of outlaws and they stood close to the base enshrouded in the gloom. Tension mounted as they waited in the hush, the sucking waves pounding and receding before them. Scott shivered in the blast of wet air, apprehension laying hold of him with rough hands.

It was too late to abort the venture now, the boats were beaching and every man rushed forward, plunging into the surf to wrestle them to shore. Scott supervised the unloading of the precious cargo: small casks of brandy and wine, oilskin bags full of tea and delicate laces and materials that the ladies of London would pay dearly for. He strode back and forth the length of the frenzied activity, giving an order here, a helping hand there; all the time with an eagle eye to the clifftop and the margins of the beach.

Within the hour the transaction was completed and the boats vanished like specters, to be seen no more. This was his last job, the fruition of over three years of duplicity and surreptitious scheming. There should be relief but Scott felt only dread. With care he examined the burdened horses, tightening the ropes on his own stallion, Styx.

They began the climb, painstakingly retracing the steep trail and then all hell broke loose. Flashes and shots rent the fabric of night. Plunging, screaming horses panicked and there were sickening moans of wounded, dying men, the whiz of balls flying as thick as mayflies in the spring.

"It's an ambush! Every man for himself!" came the shout over the noise of exploding pistols.

The acrid smell of gunpowder was in the air. They were surrounded by dragoons, every avenue of escape cut off. With a quick appraising look Scott headed for a small opening in the ranks and miraculously got through. The whine and breeze of a pistol ball winged past his ear and he bent low lying on his mount's neck, pulling a dagger from his boot top. With no wasted movements and at a full gallop he sliced through the ropes holding the heavy cargo to his saddle. It fell free bouncing and rolling down the hill.

Briefly he turned to witness the massacre of his men and saw two soldiers pursuing him. One of the horsemen went down stumbling over a cask in the darkness, and Scott urged Styx forward, the black stallion blending into the shadows of a copse. Pausing in the scanty cover he took aim and fired, waiting only to see that his target was hit.

They had been betrayed! One of his men was a traitor, one of his loyal trustworthy cohorts; for only they and Angus had known of tonight's work. Or there was the remote possibility that one of them had slipped, inadvertently alerting an outsider to their plans. It was too late to think of it now—the damage was already done.

Escape! Ride! Dodge through the quiet, peaceful countryside fraught with danger, laced with dragoons. Scott headed away from the dower house, in the opposite direction of the ruins. It would be folly to ride into another trap, inconceivable to lead them to Angus. He galloped madly with disaster on his heels.

Bentwood! He slowed, dismounting near the stables, giving the horse a sharp slap on the rump with his riding whip. Startled, Styx tore off for parts unknown.

Running to the back of the house, Scott quickly ascended a tree that he had climbed many times as a boy. Frantically he tapped on the window, soaked with sweat in the chill wind. A pale face surrounded by a halo of golden hair peered through the diamond panes and then flung the window wide.

"Scott!" Jane reached to help him as he climbed through the casement and he slipped into the room like a shadow. "Are you hurt?" Her hands touched his white, drawn face, running down his heaving chest and over his arms.

"I'm all right," he managed to gasp between breaths. "Quick—the priest's hole—hide me there!"

With shaking fingers she lit a candle and he followed her speedily through the doorway and down the hall. She held the candle high, a point of yellow illuminating their way in the blackness. He could see the outline of her body through her nightgown, and the padding of her bare feet seemed loud until the commotion began below.

A thunder of hooves, shouts, and pounding on the door. Jane stopped and he collided with her, grasping her hand tightly in his. Shaking her head, she motioned to him whispering, "There's no time! Back to my room!"

"But—"

"Hurry! Keith—the servants!" She half dragged him back and pushed him inside, closing the door behind her.

He smiled. The usually loquacious Jane could be counted on to keep silent when trouble was afoot. She had only asked him one question so far.

"Dragoons? Smuggling?" They were more statements than questions.

"Yes!" Scott went back to the window swinging his leg over but she flew across the room grabbing his arm.

"You stupid fool! If they are at the door then they're surrounding the house. Get back in here, and take off your clothes!"

"No, Jane—I'll take my chances outside. I can't involve you in this!"

"Shut up!" she ordered. "There's no time to hide you—no time to argue. Just do as I say."

"But your reputation—"

"Can go hang," she said, finishing his sentence. "And if you go out that window it will be you they hang! Do you think I could bear that, loving you the way I do?"

He stopped, gold-starred eyes shocked and boring into the luminous, tear-filled blue of hers. She was already unbuttoning his coat but Scott pushed her away. "Now I have no choice—I must go."

Jane slapped him across the face with all her strength, which was considerable in spite of her willowy delicacy. While he was still stunned she dragged him back in and slammed the window shut, tugging his coat off and ripping at his shirt.

"Hurry! Help me—please!" she pleaded. "I can hear the servants below. It's only a matter of minutes."

Scott was caught between the soldiers and the deep blue of Jane's eyes. She was right, but it would be so wrong to sacrifice her to save himself. The slender hands stopped working on his clothes and instead she bent down and caught the hem of her nightgown pulling it up over her head, letting it drop on the carpet.

"Now," she whispered, her full pointed breasts puckering in the cold of the room, "take off your breeches and boots and come to bed."

He did as he was told joining her beneath the covers less than a minute later. This couldn't be happening—he naked in bed with little Jane. But she wasn't little anymore and her freckles were gone. Now she had breasts touching his chest and long slender flanks smooth against him.

"I can hear them coming up the stairs," she observed looking toward the door.

"Well. . ." Scott whispered hesitantly, "I guess we had better make it look good." He leaned over her for a moment, then said in a husky voice, "I thought of you as a friend—almost a sister. . ."

Her arms went around his neck pulling him down until their mouths met and clung, hers parting under the invasion of his lips and tongue. The hands at her shoulders were gently caressing and Scott trailed one down over the slope of her breast, cupping the soft flesh. She was hot, trembling with unleashed desire. This was the fulfillment of her wildest dreams, but why did the dragoons have to be just down the hall inching their way to her bedroom? Yet if it wasn't for them he wouldn't be here—she wouldn't be naked, in bed with her one true love.

"Oh, Scott—oh!"

His skin slid scorchingly against hers as he pressed Jane into the bed, his body covering her. He was a vigorous male animal and couldn't help responding to the woman's body beneath him, and she writhed with the pleasure of it.

If only they could have a few more minutes alone—he wanted her, she knew he did. And she wanted the consummation of her love, even if he didn't love her—in spite of it! Then she would always have the moment to cherish in the secret recesses of her heart.

But it was not to be. There were footsteps outside the door, soldiers' boots clattering against polished wood floors. A quick knock and the door was flung open before they could do more than look up. Jane stared at the faces: the surprise on the servants', the smirks on the dragoons', the total shock on Keith's.

"Jane—Jane! How could you?" Was that her brother's voice? It sounded strangely unlike him.

She clung to Scott as the dragoons pulled him from her bed, tearing him from her embrace. The crowd at the door grew—a strange mixture of nightclothes, uniforms, and hastily flung on clothes—gaping at the sight of the viscount as naked as the day he was born—as big as life and twice as magnificent. And Lady Jane huddled on the bed, covers pulled up to her neck with bright red spots of color high on her cheeks.

"What is the meaning of this intrusion, Captain?" she asked haughtily.

"Your. . .lover, Lord Harrington, is under arrest for smuggling," explained Captain Latham in a hard clipped voice.

"What is your evidence?" drawled Scott, still naked and held by two soldiers, making no effort to escape.

"We can't very well talk here, with you and the. . . lady, unclothed and all these servants looking on! Clear the room!" barked the captain. "You two—get dressed and don't try to escape. The house is surrounded."

The door slammed shut leaving them alone. Jane sprang from the bed hurling herself into Scott's arms, pressing her face against his shoulder. "They can't take you—I won't let them! They have no proof!"

"Hush, Jane! Hush. Everything will work out." Scott loosened her arms from his neck and smiled at her with marvel in his eyes. "Have I ever told you that you are wonderful? Oh, Jane—Jane what a moment to discover—"

"What?" She trembled with anticipation.

He hesitated, touching her bright hair, taking her face between both of his hands. "I only wish—they had taken longer to find us . . . much longer!

"Do you really mean that? I wish they had never come!" Jane smiled through the tears rolling down her cheeks and Scott bent down and kissed them gently away; kissed her forehead, the tip of her nose, and finally her waiting mouth.

A sharp knock brought them up short. "Get dressed, Jane," Scott whispered pushing her away. "I'm afraid the night is far from over. . .for me. For my men it has ended and most of them will never see the dawn."

They dressed, unspeaking, Scott hooking up the back of her dress. He had run when he should have stayed, lived when he should have died. Now he was caught and instead of a clean, quick death there would be prison, a trial, and the slow strangulation they called hanging.

"Scott," Jane said putting her hand on his arm. "Don't regret what you did—be glad you are alive. Could you have saved anyone if you had stayed?"

"I don't think so, but I could have tried!"

"Perhaps you will be of more use to your men alive and free. There are sure to be survivors. Isn't there any way to help them?"

Jane knew she had said exactly the right thing. The defeated look was gone and there was dawning hope on Scott's face, the light of battle in his eyes. Together they went downstairs, escorted into the library by four dragoons.

"Well," said Scott coolly, striding into the room, "I asked for your evidence—have you come up with any yet?"

Keith glared at him pulling Jane away from his side, averting his gaze from her eyes. She had shamed him in front of servants and soldiers, and tomorrow everyone would know that she had been found in bed with her lover. There was a blot on their good name put there by no less a person than Scott Harrington. All the hostility of the past months had crystalized at the moment the door to Jane's room had been flung open revealing the perfidious act.

Captain Latham strutted over to Scott with a pleased look on his face. His thin lips twitched with anticipation at the thought of finally breaking up the smuggling ring that had been his scourge since he was assigned the task. In a few moments the viscount would be in his custody, that haughty aristocrat looking down his nose as if he was dirt beneath his feet. How he hated the supercilious gentry with their arrogant ways and exalted eccentricities. It would be the supreme pleasure to cut one down to size—and such a one!

"The evidence. . .my lord," Captain Latham mocked insultingly, "is indisputable. We found your horse not far from here all lathered with ropes hanging from the saddle that held the loot!"

"Damn!" Scott exclaimed in surprised. "Do you mean to tell me that while I was. . .occupied, those rogues borrowed my horse? Of all the gall!"

"Don't play the innocent victim with me, Lord Harrington! We were informed that you might be the leader of the band we have been hounding." The captain paused, then continued, "You broke through our ranks and killed one of my men as you fled, stopping here only long enough to get into Lady Montgomery's bed to throw us off the trail. Very clever, but your little ruse didn't work. You have much to answer for, including murder, and I will see you brought to justice. You are under arrest! Take him!"

"But, Captain," protested Scott, "if that's all your evidence it will never hold up in court. Any fool knows that smugglers often borrow the horses of the locals for a night's work. I left mine tied in back of the stables when I came here. It would have been very easy for one of them to slip off with it."

"Besides," Jane went to Scott's side and slipped her hand into his, squeezing it, "he has been with me since midnight—and before that he spent the whole evening here at our dinner party. You may confirm that with the vicar. So you can't arrest Scott. He had nothing to do with any smugglers."

"I can—and I will!" Captain Latham said, slashing angrily at his boot with his quirt. They were making him out to be a fool—and nobody did that to him.

Jane started laughing and they all looked at her as if she were out of her mind. "You must excuse me, but this is too, too amusing! Will you be stopping at the rectory to drag the vicar off to jail? Why only last month two of his horses were used by the smugglers, so he must be doubly guilty—though he did try to exonerate himself with a very long, dull sermon on the subject the next Sunday.

"Oh! And Mrs. Bewly's horse was borrowed also, but when you arrest her speak up because she is hard of hearing—after all she is ninety-three. But then I suppose smuggling must keep her feeling young!"

As Jane continued, naming a number of other unlikely candidates, Captain Latham's face got redder and redder, and even Keith couldn't suppress the smile threatening at the corners of his mouth.

Scott finally interrupted. "I'm ready to go now, seeing that I will be in such good company."

"Stop it—both of you!" the captain burst out. "No one makes an ass out of me!"

"Then if you don't want everyone from here to London to know what an idiot you really are," Scott said scornfully, "you and your men had better get out —now!"

"Please, just see yourselves out, Captain," smiled Jane pleasantly. "I'm sure you remember the way."

They were laughing at him—all of them! And there were even smiles on the faces of his own men. Well, he wouldn't stand for it, to be humiliated and taken down a peg in front of them. Tomorrow the whole town would be buzzing about his blunder, joking behind his back, sneering at his ineptitude.

Captain Latham looked straight at Scott unleashing a look of distilled hate from his cold eyes. "Believe me," he stated with a snarl, "I'll get even with you for tonight

—if it takes me the rest of my life." Then he was gone storming out and slamming the door.

"We did it, we did it!" Jane flung herself at Scott and he whirled her around.

"You did it, Jane," said Scott.

"You sure as hell did!" Keith grabbed her away from him and struck Scott full across the face. "My seconds will call on you tomorrow!"

"No, Keith, no!" Jane opened her mouth to tell him that nothing had happened, and closed it again. If she said that, he would know Scott really was the leader of the smugglers and would go straight to Captain Latham.

"Go to your room, Jane—now!"

"Don't you dare speak to her that way!" Scott said protectively.

This whole mess was his fault. He had been uneasy from the start of tonight's venture and should have put a stop to it then. Most of Scott's men were dead or in jail, and now he had ruined Jane completely to save his own neck. Well nothing could raise the dead, but he could remedy this situation and right the wrong he had selfishly inflicted on the only true friend he seemed to have.

"I will not accept your challenge, Keith. Call me a coward if you want, but I refuse to kill you, for Jane's sake." Plunging recklessly on he said, "Jane and I are going to be married as soon as possible. That should be a quick stop to the gossip, and in a few years no one will even remember the incident."

"Is this true, Jane? You're going to marry—him?"

She looked between them in confusion, her heart erratically beating a tattoo. This was her chance to grab happiness and love—and Scott. Then why did she hesitate? She had wanted him forever, dreamed of being his wife and bearing his children, and she would be a good wife, the best. But he didn't love her, not in the right way. Could a marriage be built on one-sided love? Could he ever come to love her?

His sherry-brown eyes pleaded with Jane to say yes.

Keith was waiting for her to confirm the truth of his words and she stood there torn. Did she love Scott enough to turn him down—or did she love him so much that she couldn't say no?

"Of course it's true," Scott answered for her, drawing her arm through his. "You once told me that I wasn't a gentleman—but I do have enough honor not to ruin a lady and leave her in the lurch. Jane will be my wife, and you, my brother-in-law, before the spring is here. Now, since I cannot possibly ruin your sister's reputation any more than I already have, I would like to speak with her alone."

Convinced, Keith left the room and they were alone at last with a terrible decision unmade.

"Say yes, Jane—one little word—"

"How can I?" She pulled away from him going to stand by the fireplace. The leaping flames held her eyes and she could not look at Scott. "You were very gallant, but you don't love me." Her heart was breaking.

"I do love you." His breath was soft against her hair and he put his hands on her shoulders. "No—don't protest. I know what I said earlier about loving you as a friend or sister. But that was before I touched you, kissed you, and lay by your side. Can anything be the same again? We could never go back to the same relationship we had even an hour ago. Circumstances catapulted both of us forward in time, threw us into each other's arms and in doing so taught me a much needed lesson.

"Perhaps I don't love you with the intensity you require but give me time, sweetheart—let me get used to loving you. If one hour can make such a change, think what one day, one week, one year will do. Marry me, Jane, and you will never regret it! I promise to make you happy! Let me devote my life to you—for without you I would have no life to offer.

"Say yes—please! Nothing stands in our way. The future is ours to do with what we will, but let's do it together."

Jane turned, gazing deeply into his sincere impassioned eyes, and he waited beneath her scrutiny. "Answer me only one question, Scott, and I will give you your answer. Do you hate Angela?"

He didn't move, but the reaction of his eyes, the quick dilation of the pupils could not be concealed. She couldn't ask him if he loved Angela, so she had asked the opposite. His answer would tell her one way or the other, because he either loved her or hated her, there could be no in-between.

"Has she been talking to you, Jane. . .confiding in you?" Scott's soft voice told her nothing.

"No. Angela is a very secretive person."

"Then why—"

"Just answer me," Jane insisted. "Do you hate her? Yes or no—it's simple."

"No—I have no reason to hate Angela. Does that answer the question to your satisfaction? You will have no disapproving husband insisting you break off certain relationships."

"And Angela—how does she feel about you?" He had misunderstood completely.

"She can't stand the sight of me!" He laughed thinking of her vehement protests dying away to abject surrender. "But what do you want, a husband or a friend?"

"I want you, Scott," Jane answered. "You—you! only you!"

A knife twisted in her breast as he held her and kissed her, because he was in love with her best friend. But somehow, now that it was out in the open, it didn't matter. Angela hated him and was married to his father and nothing could ever come of the relationship while she was free and loved Scott with every last ounce of strength. She would love him and make him forget the woman that was his stepmother, forget the few short months he had known her. Jane would drown him in her love and let the years do the rest.

"Yes, Scott—yes! But let's go away—somewhere far away."

"To Scotland—Jamaica?"

"Yes, anywhere with you. Jamaica—the farther the better. Oh, how I love you!"

The ardor of her kisses inflamed him—at least he would have no cold wife performing a distasteful duty in his bed. Then why when he closed his eyes did he see Angela's face, feel sable hair twining around his neck and body, binding him so close he couldn't breath?

"Scott—love me. Take me now," Jane murmured and he roughly broke the embrace. "Please, my dearest love. Lock the door, no one will dare disturb us now. I need you so much—I ache for you."

"Jane, be sensible—we will be married soon enough." Scott paused remembering the way he had hurt Angela. "Besides, it's not always pleasant the first time for a woman. I don't want to hurt you, or disappoint you."

"You never could! Please—please, I need you now!"

And so he became the reluctant lover, making love to Jane slowly and with infinite care on the sheepskin rug in front of the fireplace.

Together they forgot the disastrous events of the night, concerned only with pleasing each other. At their confluence Jane's eyes opened wide but she didn't cry out against the pain, rather accepted it and Scott, offering herself with reservation. Then the pain was gone and she clung to him fiercely, amazed by the wonder of it and the delirious heights he was taking her to. They reached the final tempest together, buffeted from within and without by the breathless gale of desire that shook them both.

A gentle breeze wafted them back to earth and reality—and there were tears on her face from the indescribable joy of the miracle that had happened.

Scott kissed her. "Are you all right, my dear?"

"Yes," Jane whispered hiding her smile against his shoulder. "I never knew that anything could be so perfect."

"It will get better and better, every time we do it."

"Then you will kill me with delight!"

He smiled, stroking the soft bright hair, lovingly

touching her breasts and the curve of her hips. Jane had driven Angela from his mind with her sweet, generous giving. She had wiped away some of the sorrow and regret of this long night—for with such an ending, the next day must surely dawn with hope.

"Look," Jane whispered against his cheek, her eyes reflecting the light from the window.

And they lay entwined watching the sky flame with color as the sun chased the shadows from the night and edged the clouds with gold.

There could be no doubt about it. First Angela cried, then she swore out loud, using every word she had picked up from Scott.

Stripping off all her clothes she examined herself carefully in front of the pier glass. Her hand rested on her still flat abdomen where the seed of her arch-enemy grew inside her. Other than slightly fuller breasts there was no visible evidence of her condition.

At first she had tried to ignore the signs—or lack of them—putting it down to the upheaval in her life and all the upsetting things that had happened since her wedding. Now it was impossible. Angela was pregnant and there was nothing she could do about it. The furious rides on Pegasus had done nothing to dislodge the unwanted invader.

Wait till Scott found out! She could just see the conceited smile on his face, the pride that he had finally accomplished his goal. Now what would happen? His revenge would be complete—would he leave her alone and stop making outrageous demands on her?

Angela shivered. He had awakened some primitive urge in her that she hadn't known existed, and only his hard man's body could slake the need in hers. She hated him, yet she wanted him, and all the while her mind urged her to common sense, her treacherous flesh longed for what he could do to it.

What a restless night she had spent waiting for Scott who had never come. She had hardly slept with the turbulent seesawing of emotions and the wind rattling the windows of her room. It had been a dark moonless night and she had come to expect him late on those particular nights, late and smelling of the sea. What was he up to—smuggling? It wasn't unheard of in those parts.

"Damn him! I wish he were dead!"

"Who?" Molly appeared with the breakfast tray to find her mistress red-eyed and naked, talking angrily to herself.

"Shut up and hand me my robe! I'm famished!" Angela snapped, contrite when she saw the hurt expression on Molly's plain face. "I'm sorry. I'm in a foul mood today and probably will be for the next several months!"

"You're not. . .you are with child?" Angela nodded and Molly hugged her and danced around the room with joy. "Lady Angela, that's wonderful news! A baby! Does the duke know? Oh, just wait till your mother finds out!"

"Molly, you're not to breathe a word of it to anyone —not yet. I'll tell at the right time." She must tell Scott immediately.

As Angela ate, Molly sat watching her. "I almost forgot with the excitement of your news. Everyone is talking about what happened last night. The dragoons killed a bunch of smugglers and the rest are in jail!"

Angela felt the color leave her face and put down her suddenly heavy fork. He was dead—Scott Harrington, the father of her child, was dead! Nothing else would have kept him from her bed last night and she didn't know if she was sad or happy—only dreadfully empty inside.

"And you will never believe what happened after that!"

"What?" whispered Angela, her full attention on her maid.

"Well, the dragoons chased down one of the smugglers—the leader, some said, and they found the viscount's black stallion near Bentwood." Molly paused for dramatic effect. "They found him in Lady Montgomery's bed making love to her. Caught right in the act, they were—everyone saw it, her brother, the dragoons, and servants! The soldiers dragged him mother naked from her bed." Molly rolled her eyes. "You should have heard the description I heard—but I could never repeat that!

"Captain Latham arrested him for murder and smuggling, then he and Lady Montgomery and her brother and the captain went down to the library. No one knows what happened behind closed doors but they left without the viscount and there's talk in town that the captain's an incompetent fool for letting that one slip through his fingers."

Molly's brown eyes were round with the wonder of it all. "There's some," she whispered, "that says Lord Montgomery called the viscount out, and others say there's a wedding in the air!"

Breakfast was forgotten as Angela ordered Molly to prepare her bath and lay out her riding habit.

So, Scott had succeeded in ruining Jane's life now too. Was there nothing the man wouldn't stoop to? Lovers! Had they really been engaged thus when found, or had it been a sham? Caught right in the act, Molly had said. What beasts men were! But not all men—poor Keith, poor Jane. The scandal of it all!

She had to get out of the house, see Jane and find out the truth—separate fact from fabrication. They couldn't be lovers, couldn't be engaged! When Angela was halfway to Bentwood she stopped. It wasn't even eight yet and they would all be abed, especially if they had been up half the night. So she gave Pegasus his head, letting him wander at will to kill time before confronting Jane.

And what if they were getting married—could she warn Jane, tell her of the child growing within her, the creation of a lust so overwhelming nothing could belie its existence? No, it was impossible, but somehow she would warn her. She must find the right words, the correct argument to sway her mind. Marriage with Scott would be Jane's tragedy.

Pegasus started galloping, the game they always

played as they approached the cliffs. The grass was slippery and green beneath his hooves, and early wildflowers dotted its expanse. Spring was almost upon them, and with it would come Angela's freedom from passion's enslavement. The winged horse flew, skimming the surface of the earth, a white flash against an azure sky, leaving far behind the dark, shadowed winter nights.

They stopped at the very edge of the precipice and she laughed, invigorated from her wild ride. But she was not alone.

"What are you trying to do, kill yourself?" Scott's face was drawn with exhaustion and he scowled darkly and dragged her off the horse.

"What difference does it make? You care nothing for me. I'm sure the news of my demise wouldn't affect you in the least!" In spite of her cool tone, Angela's eyes were angry and she continued, purposely baiting him, "In fact I know that you don't care for anyone but yourself. What gives you the right to go around wrecking people's lives—first mine and now Jane's?"

"I see the gossip has already spread. The king probably heard it first thing this morning in London!" Scott's voice was sarcastic and he was tired and angry.

He had come to inspect the battlefield on which nine of his men had died in the chill of a fateful night. Splotches of brown dried blood marred the landscape, calling out to him for vengeance. Fourteen others were in the local jail, some wounded, some not but all doomed to the hangman's tender ministrations.

Scott's spirits were at their lowest ebb and Angela's taunting snapped something inside him. Why was it that she always made him furious, brought out the worst in him? He shook his head to clear it, and she laughed at him scornfully. Without warning and not knowing why, he grabbed her and kissed the smile off her face.

Upset at the turn the day was already taking Angela lashed out at him with the first words that popped into her head. "Was this where it happened—where your men were killed and taken? I wish they had killed you too! Why didn't they—deserter? You coward—hiding behind a woman's skirts—or should I say hiding in her bed!"

The moment the statement was out she knew she had gone too far. Scott hadn't looked like that even when she had tried to kill him. Fear took hold of Angela as suddenly as his arms, sweeping her up as if she was a feather, carrying her kicking and screaming toward the cliff path.

He was going to hurl her from the top, and she clung tightly to his neck so he couldn't throw her over without jumping himself. But Scott didn't stop there, he carried her slipping and sliding down the path to the golden sands below—and beyond.

The foam swirled around his boots, turquoise waves surged against his knees as he waded into the ocean with a red haze coloring his world. The slut—the sharp-tongued, lying bitch! He should have done this long ago, silenced her full pink lips that only spewed forth hatred.

She was petrified, frozen by the murderous rage darkening Scott's eyes and by the icy sea dragging at her heavy skirts. The bottom went out from under her feet and only the hands at the waist kept her afloat. He was going to drown her! Angela intensified her struggles clutching at his coat, shivering as the cold water crept up her neck.

"Damn you to hell, bitch!" His words came from between clenched teeth as cold and deadly as the current sucking at her.

"You can't," she cried sputtering as the water invaded her mouth. "I'm going to have your ba. . . ."

The waves closed over her head, salt water stinging her eyes and nose and his hands released her as she tried to claw her way to the surface. Angela's lungs were bursting and she gasped for breath, only to have the frigid water invade her insides, tearing and hurting as it gushed down her throat.

She could see him from the neck down wavering through the blue-green liquid and she stretched her arms out to him in a silent plea. He was so close yet so far away and black dots danced before her heavy-lidded eyes. Suddenly the pain and panic gave way to a soothing lethargy and she went limp, letting the waves rock her in a relaxed embrace. Cool fingers caressed her fevered brow and the sea whispered a lullaby, luring her to sleep. With a last effort to resist, Angela wordlessly called his name, then closed her eyes and let the waiting darkness claim her.

Baby? His baby! The words he had barely heard penetrated Scott's enraged mind, jerking aside the crimson veil of anger, jolting him back to reality. He groped for her beneath the waves but she was gone. Angela and his child were gone!

Taking a great gulp of air, Scott dove into the water searching with a frenzy. He saw her a few yards off floating face down near the bottom; black hair reaching for the sun like seaweed. Grabbing the wet tresses, he hauled her up, held her face out of the water and struck out for shore.

As he dragged her up the beach she was so still, and he placed her on the sand pulling the wet clinging hair from her face. Her eyes were closed and her face was as pale as. . .death! Angela wasn't breathing—he had killed her!

Wild consternation shook Scott as he pressed down on her ribs several times trying to force the water from her lungs. There was no response. He put his mouth over hers and breathed his breath into her, stopping only when he heard her choke. Turning Angela quickly on her side he held her as she violently expelled the salt water, choking and gasping for air. Her small frozen body heaved with violent convulsions and when she was still again, her spiky, black lashes fluttered slowly open.

Uncomprehendingly she looked up at him, sand streaked over one pale cheek. "Hurts," she croaked faintly and her aqua eyes shut once more.

Gathering Angela into his arms, he rocked her back and forth like a child. "Thank goodness you're alive! I must have been insane! Mad!" Scott buried his face in her hair and since they were both drenched he never even noticed the hot tears that slid down his face and lost themselves in the dusky wetness.

How long they stayed like that he didn't know, but when he felt her start to shiver his senses returned, and he picked her up and carried her back up the cliff to the waiting horses. With Angela cradled carefully in front of him on Styx he took her to his house.

"Wha' ha' ye doon to her now?" Angus asked in amazement as Scott strode into the house with his streaming burden.

"For heaven's sake!" snapped Scott, making for the stairs, "don't ask questions now! Turn down my bed and light the fire. Then get some brandy, and be quick about it!"

Angela was only half-conscious as he stripped the clinging green velvet from her. Angus bustled around the room with averted eyes as he rubbed her dry with a towel and tried to chafe some warmth back into her cold limbs. They piled extra blankets on the bed and between the two of them managed to get a few drops of brandy down her throat.

"Now I'm thinking, lad, tha' ye ha' best get oot of those wet clothes and tell me wha' happened." Angus's stern voice brooked no reproach.

The eyes Scott turned toward him were filled with misery. "I almost killed her with these two hands of mine! She made me so angry—I must be out of my mind!"

"Now, lad, ye'r oot of yer head wi' grief and sleeplessness, and numb fra everything tha' has happened." Angus helped Scott out of his clothes as he talked. "Sleep now an' everything will be foine. See! Some color is back in the lassie's face already."

"But you don't understand—I almost murdered Angela and my unborn child with her!"

Angus stopped short at that revelation but said nothing as he poured another drink and handed it to Scott. He tossed it off in one gulp and got into bed, gathering the still form in his arms.

He placed his hand on her belly where their child was growing and hoped he hadn't injured either of them. A sense of wonder filled him at the new life they had started, and a feeling of joy spread through Scott's veins warming him.

"Oh, my love—I'm so sorry," he whispered. "I never would have touched you if I had known. Angel—Angel—please be all right!"

But she was asleep and her quiet breathing seemed like a miracle. He held her tightly, warming her with his body, touching the fragile hollow of her throat with his lips, where her pulse fluttered reassuringly.

Disoriented, Angela opened her eyes. She was warm and drowsy and there was no doubt in her mind as to where she was, but she couldn't seem to remember how she had come to be there. Frowning, she tried to think, but somehow the effort was too much. It was better just to feel: the beam of sunlight from the slightly parted draperies falling warmly on her skin, the heavy weight of Scott's leg thrown over her thighs, his hand on her breast and the warmth of his breath stirring her hair.

Turning her head she studied his face so different in repose, without that guarded harshness he usually displayed. He looked like a boy with his tousled brown hair and parted lips—far too handsome for his own good, or hers. Angela hadn't observed him like this before, caught unaware, for when they were together it was night and they usually didn't sleep. What was she doing there in the daytime? Suddenly it wasn't important—it was enough that they were both together and not fighting for once.

Glinting lashes stirred against his brown cheeks, far too long to belong to a man, and Angela couldn't resist touching him. Her fingers lightly played through the bronze strands of his hair, touched the cleft in his stubborn chin. For this one suspended moment in time she felt no antagonism and she couldn't help touching her mouth to his, tracing the chiseled outline of his lips with the hot tip of her tongue.

Scott's eyes opened and she smiled at him, seeing her

reflection in their depths, sighing as he kissed her gently as if they had all the time in the world. He too seemed to be in a daze and they made love slowly, silently, lazily drawing out each kiss and caress.

The slanting sunlight turned their entwined bodies to gold, and as he moved to put her beneath him Angela pushed him away, postponing their joining, both of them lost in a feeling of unreality. She said things with her body that he knew would never pass her lips, yet Scott longed to hear her whisper just one endearment—even if she didn't mean it.

His heart was bursting with unknowable feelings as she slid over him, kneeling, teasing, placing him at the fevered threshold, then withdrawing. With a groan of unendurable frustration Scott grasped her hips, laughing at her surprise when she found herself sitting instead of kneeling, feeling her arch in pleasured shock at the swift impalement.

"Angel—love!" He fondled her breasts and belly, cupping her buttocks and let her set the pace, slow at first then faster.

"Scott! What are you doing?" His fingers were doing delightfully indecent things to her moist flesh and she couldn't stop him or herself. She gasped for air and expelled it in soft moans.

For a second Angela paused, transfixed—head thrown back, eyes closed and nostrils flaring—then she collapsed on him in systaltic rapture, sooty hair lashing them both with the frenzy of her movements.

She lay inert and trembling with her face against Scott's neck and a mantle of silken curls covering them both. He clasped Angela tightly, feeling her breasts soft against his chest and the agitated beating of her heart. For the first time she had given herself willingly from start to finish, with no coercion or seducement. She had initiated the diversion and seen it through to its fervent end. He knew what she had felt but he wondered what she was thinking now. Scott smiled, stroking her hair, remembering her outraged protests—what an innocent she still was, what a delight! She was a fragile, exquisite zephyr fanning the flames of his desire, dancing always just beyond his reach.

Angela held her breath unsure of what had just happened. It occurred again, a soft flutter deep inside her—her child moving for the first time. A wave of warm love and possessiveness surged through her, making her forget that she hadn't wanted it. It was part of her, depending on her for its very existence—her baby, their child!

There was a warmth of wet tears against his skin and he had felt her tense and wait. "Angel, what's wrong?" Scott turned her face so that she saw the concern in his eyes.

"I felt. . ." She hid her face again, then continued softly, ". . .our child!"

He laughed with joy, startling Angela and she looked at his smiling face to find golden specks dancing in his eyes.

"Our baby, our son!" His mouth found hers and he kissed her deeply, tenderly. Then he put her gently by his side, pressing his ear and cheek against her belly.

Amused, she stroked his hair away from his forehead, their eyes meeting in wonderment. "You're not going to feel anything yet."

"Shh! My son is talking to me!" Scott kissed the silken skin beneath his cheek as a shaky bond of the common love for their child was tentatively formed between them, binding them forever in some inexplicable way.

She had to go. It was almost dark and they had lingered far too long. Dressed in her now dry riding habit Angela stood before the mirror trying to arrange her hair. Her throat felt raw and sore and she swallowed hard, wondering if she was getting sick.

Scott came up behind her, resting his hands on her shoulders. Stooping he kissed the nape of her neck and their eyes met in the mirror, his dark and serious, hers mysteriously misted by obscurity.

"My sweet little Duchess, you haven't told me once today that you hate me—but when you remember what

I did to you this morning you will hate me more than ever." There was an odd breathless catch in his voice that Angela couldn't comprehend and he looked so sad.

"I don't want to remember!" she said, still caught up in the illusion of their afternoon flight of fancy. It was wonderful to feel such languorous forgetfulness like the ancient lotus eaters.

"But you will," whispered Scott unhappily. "Tomorrow, you will ride to the cliffs and look out over the ocean and you'll remember. But when you do, love, remember this too—I'm sorry! I was in a blind rage and didn't realize what I was doing. I hope you can forgive me, Angel. . ."

His voice trailed off as if he had meant to say more and Angela looked at his reflection in the mirror for a long time. Scott had never apologized to her for anything and he had never been so tender and understanding. She was puzzled at his strange behavior—but then hers, on this long chimerical afternoon, had been no less unusual.

Chapter Six

The plush, emerald-green carpet was like velvet beneath Angela's bare feet as she walked back and forth dressed only in her nightgown. Her new rooms were a pleasure to behold furnished all in Chinese Chippendale, but disquietude broke the calm surface of her emotions. Her night had been peaceful and serene with no interruptions, for Scott hadn't come. Why should he when they had loved the whole afternoon away?

But still she had wanted him, more than ever since their interlude, and that disturbed her. He was selfish, arrogant, and didn't care about her at all, yet sometimes he looked at her with such affection in his irresistible brown eyes that she felt her hatred thaw and begin to dissolve like spring snow. Her own vacillation threw her into a quandary. Exactly what did she feel for Scott Harrington?

Hate was the only safe alternative and Angela rang for Molly determined to go to the cliffs and remember. He had said she would hate him even more when she recalled an incident from yesterday morning. Good! She needed that.

While she waited for breakfast Angela reclined on the chaise, letting her gaze wander vacantly from the walls covered with yellow, green, and white hand-painted silk to the sunny yellow bed-coverings and draperies. She had changed the whole aspect of the once dusty apartment into a scene of springtime tranquility. White, fluffy clouds floated dreamily by on the sky-blue ceiling.

A secret smile curved her mouth as the baby moved inside her. It was a girl—she knew it was, despite Scott's assurances that it would be a boy. That's what the problem was! Her mutability was all because of the changes in her body. Nature itself was conspiring to make her feel something for the father of her child, a softening in attitude, a need for a husband's support and understanding during the ensuing months.

And in actuality Scott was her husband in everything but fact, their child a bond between them. Now that she understood the reason for her own inconsistent behavior Angela relaxed. There was no need to worry, she disliked Scott as much as ever, and now that he knew she was pregnant there would be no reason for him to sneak into her rooms anymore. His goal was accomplished, she need never see him again.

With buoyant spirits she had breakfast, eating hungrily, not at all disturbed by even a touch of morning sickness. First she would go to the beach, then do her duty and forewarn Jane to have nothing to do with Scott. It would be hard but she must convince her, for her own good.

This time Angela didn't let Pegasus play his usual game of dashing at the cliffs. The safety of her baby was her responsibility, and she felt a warm complacency as maternal feelings stirred within her. Instead she stopped far short and slipped from his back, approaching on foot.

The sky was a leaden gray, threatening rain and she looked down on a choppy slate-colored sea. Spreading her cloak over the bright grass Angela sat down and picked a tiny nosegay of wildflowers. Twisting their stems together she sniffed the scent, remembering the trampled snowdrops.

She shivered as she looked down at the ominous waves foaming against the sand and caught her breath in a feeling of panic. Scott had almost drowned her yesterday! Angela could feel the water closing over her head, choking her, and she gulped down huge breaths of air at the horrible feeling. But strangely she didn't hate him even more for that. Most of it had been her fault anyway for goading him into anger after the disastrous night.

The wild blood made both of their temperaments mercurial—why, she would have killed him with pleasure if Angus hadn't stopped her. But Scott had evidently stopped himself, otherwise she wouldn't be sitting there. A great sadness overcame Angela—their afternoon together had been so beautiful and imponderable, she had never wanted it to end, but now it was just a memory. Tears spilled out making a sparkling river down her cheeks and she couldn't seem to stop, just sat there looking at the ocean, crying with the flowers crushed between tightly clenched hands.

When she gained control of herself Angela resolutely mounted Pegasus and made her progress to Bentwood. Scott was there ahead of her, his black stallion tethered outside the house. She almost turned away, not wanting a confrontation with him at the moment, then changed her mind. He had to be with Jane, so she would visit Keith until he left.

As she followed a maid to Keith's study Angela glanced through the slightly open door of the sitting room. They were wrapped in each other's arms, a dark head bent over a bright one, lips joined in a lover's kiss. Her step faltered and her heart skipped a beat. So it was true, they were lovers!

The blood rose and pounded in her head so that when she entered the study Angela didn't even see Keith rise and greet her. Lovers! And only yesterday he had been with her. Had they spent the night together—is that why Scott hadn't come? For some reason the thought of his making love to Jane infuriated her beyond all comprehension.

"Angela, are you all right?" Keith took her arm afraid she was going to faint. The furious color in her cheeks had drained away to an unusual paleness and now the flush was returning.

With absolutely no warning she burst into tears, flinging herself into his arms to be cosseted and rocked by a bewildered Keith. When the storm gave no sign of abating he drew her over to the sofa, surprised that he was daring enough to cuddle her on his lap. She lay against his chest, tears soaking into his shoulder and both arms wrapped tightly around his neck as if she were afraid he would escape her. But he could do nothing except stroke her hair and heaving shoulders, whisper comforting words that she didn't hear.

What was the matter? The usually cool, calm Angela was gone, replaced by a lost little girl that he felt needed her mother more than him. What upheaval had brought about such an outburst of emotion? Someone must have hurt her deeply to so affect her and he wasn't above feeling pleased that she had turned to him in her time of need.

Angela cried for a long time with an unparalleled violence, and when she finally stopped, tremors still shook her as she lay spent against her bulwark. She felt better just being near Keith, and her need to be wanted after her rejection by Scott was overwhelming.

"What's wrong, Angela? Please tell me so I can help." The sincere love and friendship in Keith's voice and his total acceptance of her mood deserved an explanation.

"Tell me," she whispered, "how you feel about me." And she pressed a hot wet cheek against his cheek.

"You know how I feel, sweetheart. I love you," he reassured her. "There could never be anyone for me but you. I loved you from the moment I saw you and will love you till the day I die."

"Oh, Keith, love me!"

"I do, darling—more than you will ever know."

"No," Angela looked at him with reddened eyes, her face so close he could feel her breath against his lips. "Make love to me, Keith, I need to be wanted, to feel safe again. . ."

She felt his heart leap against her breasts and his loins tighten against her thighs as she closed her eyes for his kiss. But he only grazed her cheek, and her aqua eyes flew open to see his golden head shaking.

"You need a friend right now, not a lover. I won't make love to you just so you can momentarily forget what's bothering you. What happened?"

She hesitated, knowing she must tell him something but unable to blurt out that she was angry because she had just seen her lover kissing her best friend. The delicate balance of her temper was all askew because of her pregnancy, her emotions extremely sensitive because of Scott's betrayal.

"I. . .will you love me if I tell you?"

Keith waited, without answering.

"I'm with child," Angela said finally, feeling his body stiffen.

"But—but, you're only a child yourself!" The thought of the duke laying with her made him sick—that gross old man owning and reveling in such youthful beauty was a rude obscenity.

Angela saw it all in his sapphire eyes, and she placed his hand against her still flat belly. "I don't show yet, Keith—I am still pleasing to look at. Will you—"

"No!" Her lower lip was trembling again but how could he explain that he wanted more than just her body when that's all she understood. He wanted her love, her body and her soul, and all Angela wanted was comfort.

Keith couldn't take advantage of her like that and his mind cringed from the signs of brutality he had tried to ignore during the past months: her swollen lips, shadowed eyes, and the occasional bruise on her creamy skin. The duke was a monster to use her so roughly, but she was his wife and he could maul her if he wanted to. When Keith made love to her for the first time it would be with gentle reverence, not a hurried tumble on the sofa of his study. He would make the experience a beautiful one and show her that there was another side to lovemaking.

But Angela had other things in mind and her fingers loosened his cravat before he could stop her, unbuttoned the top of his shirt before his hands closed over hers.

"Not like this, Angela. You're upset and don't know what you're doing. Heaven knows I want you, but—"

Her lips cut off his words moving invitingly forward

and he couldn't keep from embracing her, from weakening for just a short moment to taste her rarely proffered delights.

"How many?" asked Jane, watching Scott pace distractedly across the room and back again.

"Fourteen are in the jail, nine dead." He stopped and looked directly at her. "I'm the only one that escaped, Jane—I'm the one that must help them."

"How? You are only one man—what can you do alone?"

"But I won't be alone—I'll get help, and I need yours." Scott saw the hastily concealed surprise on her face. "Will you help, Jane? I have the whole plan worked out in my mind—now we just have to put words into action."

Jane could still feel his kiss on her lips and the glow from a long stolen night. What heights they had attained together, each more lofty than the last, and tonight they had another tryst planned. She could deny him nothing.

"I will do anything you want," Jane said too eagerly. "You know that I always will!"

Scott smiled appreciatively; she was so unlike the recalcitrant Angela, so eager to please. But he was thinking of her again, that black-haired sorceress who had cast her spell over him, whose presence could be felt even though she was miles away. The smile abruptly disappeared and he eagerly launched his plan, words dispelling thoughts of a golden afternoon when all his dreams had materialized in the green-blue of wide, eloquent eyes.

"I can't let my men rot in jail only to end up dancing at the end of a short rope. They have always been true and loyal conspirators—they have wives and children and homes. I'm going to get them out—or die trying!"

"No!"

"Don't worry, nothing will go wrong. The timing is perfect. The trial is set for May tenth—that gives me less than two months to see to all the details. First I need a ship and crew."

"Whatever for?" inquired Jane, sitting nervously on the edge of a chair and twining her fingers together.

"It will be impossible for the men to remain as fugitives in England. They would be hunted down and recaptured in no time. We are going to sail to Jamaica—you and me and my men—their wives and families too if they want. They will have new identities and new lives."

"And we will have a new life too," interjected Jane. "But how will you get them out of jail?"

"That's where you come in, sweetheart. Every day you will visit my men. Take a big basket of food and medicines, lull the guards into accepting your presence without question. I know you can do it—put on your good Samaritan act, the lady of the manor visiting poor unfortunates, making their last days on earth tolerable.

"In order that no suspicion be attached to your concern over a group of smugglers we must keep our marriage plans secret. It would spoil everything if they found out you were betrothed to the suspected leader. You don't mind do you, Jane? We'll be married on board the ship. I know most women want a large, fussy wedding. . ."

"All I want is you, Scott! I'll do what you say, starting today. This is so exciting—the start of a great adventure!"

"I'm afraid life with me will always be a risk," Scott grinned, taking one of her hands and pressing a kiss on her slender fingers.

"I don't care," stated Jane emphatically. Then with more practical things in view she asked, "Where will you get the ship?"

"I'm leaving for London tomorrow and if I can't find one there I'll have to travel on to Plymouth. Can I borrow three hundred pounds, Jane? I would have had enough if the last haul hadn't been confiscated."

"I'll get a bank draft this afternoon. Do you think you can make all the arrangements in time?"

"I have to!" Scott knelt beside her chair, looking straight into her eyes. "What would I do without you,

Jane? Already you are essential to me. It's only a loan—I promise to pay back every penny."

"Whatever you want, dearest—it doesn't matter to me. Everything I have is yours."

"Literally," he murmured with a wicked sparkle in his eyes.

Jane smiled and nodded her agreement, running her fingers through his thick, glinting hair. "I miss you already."

"We still have tonight!"

And it was almost dawn by the time Scott found himself in the passageway between the dower house and Brightling Castle. It was folly but he couldn't help himself, couldn't stop the force that drew him on through the dark tunnels deep beneath the earth. Angela's allure was palpable, and even after he had made up his mind not to see her again she bedeviled him so, that he had to see her one last time.

She stirred as he entered her room, flinging one arm over her head and moving restively beneath the covers. As he undressed he watched Angela, aware of his presence even in sleep. She was a Circe, totally irresistible in her sensual innocence, the most entrancing woman he had ever seen or touched or bedded.

Joining her, Scott kissed her parted lips and loosened her nightgown, slipping it down Angela's soft, warm body. Her eyes flickered open, confused with sleep and his presence, but he had already begun his arousal of her and she forgot, in her drowsy state, that she was angry with him.

"Scott?" His gold-fired eyes wiped out every memory of her fruitless seduction of Keith. This man took what he wanted and he wanted her.

"And who else would it be, love?" Scott flashed that melting smile that annoyed her because it left her defenseless. He kissed her breasts and laughed as her fingers clutched his head closer.

"I thought I was dreaming."

"This is no dream," he said huskily with a quick sure movement that she met with an ardent response. "This is reality!"

"Oh, yes!" Angela sighed as he took her gently.

As the misty oblivion closed quickly in on her, she heard him groan, "There's no place I'd rather be than inside you. Angel—love!"

The interior of the pub was dim and smoky, almost deserted, and Scott lounged near the window sipping a drink, gazing with bored detachment through the dirty panes. The sun struggled to enter the room, casting a warm spotlight on the red tulips in the window box outside. A fly buzzed annoyingly close and he swished it away, waiting.

Scott had returned to an early spring and the perfect execution of the first part of his strategy. Everything was going well. A trim ship was now his and being readied for the long voyage. The cargo would be ready on schedule and a crew was signed up.

He smiled to himself, well contented with the progress, seeing gilt letters dancing before his eyes. He had named his ship the *Dark Lady*, a reminder of Angela. She troubled him but this time he wouldn't weaken and go to her. His life was taking a different course, the tide sweeping them apart, and his only regret was that he wouldn't be present to see his son when he was born in the fall. But when he returned, if he returned, perhaps he would allow himself the luxury of telling his father just who the child belonged to.

That would be the perfect final revenge, shattering the duke's hopes and plans, because by that time his father would have acknowledged the boy as his own. It would be impossible for the duke to disown the child, unless he wanted to dishonor his name, which Scott knew he would never do.

His attention was diverted by the event he had been waiting for. Jane dressed in cinnamon velvet stepped from a carriage near the jail, accepting the big basket a servant handed to her. Scott had forgotten how her hair shone like newly minted gold in the sunlight. She carried the heavy burden with a regal bearing, a lady condescending to visit the needy.

She spoke to the soldier outside the door briefly, laughing familiarly at something he said. The redcoated dragoon opened the door for her, his eyes covertly watching her progress until she vanished inside and he resumed his post. So, she had charmed the soldiers as he knew she would, fulfilling her part of the agreement during the five weeks he had been gone. Jane didn't even know he was back yet but he would let his presence be felt tonight when he slipped into her window.

A half hour later Jane had finished her mission and entered the carriage with an empty basket. The soldiers always searched it, but took her daily visit as a matter of routine and even looked forward to it. The smugglers had been suspicious of her at first but had grudgingly accepted the charity, unaware of her connection with Scott. They were still in the dark as to the jailbreak and would only be told the day before the carefully planned event.

She leaned back against the seat, glad the task was over. In a few more weeks they would be free and she would be a married woman. It was amazing how much she missed Scott in spite of his frequent letters, and Jane wished he were back right now. Unbidden, passionate thoughts filled her head and she blushed at their unbridled intensity. After loving Scott she could never be the same again—and didn't want to be.

When the tap came on her window in the dead of night, Jane rushed to open it. Scott bounded into the room with vitality and swept her up in an embrace that knocked the breath from her body and sent her head whirling dangerously.

"Scott, Scott!" Jane cried before his demanding lips stifled her welcome and made her forget he had ever been gone.

Her nightgown ripped easily beneath his fingers and she gasped at the unaccustomed roughness and urgency of his caresses. Before, Scott had treated her with a gentle reverence, but now his emotions were totally unleashed, exigent beyond her limited experience. So this was his other side, the dark emotions he had only hinted at before. He was like a different, frightening person, requisitioning her body for his own frenzied needs with hardly a thought to hers.

Fear and resentment fought within Jane against the love she felt, the latter overruling the others. She wanted Scott in all his moods and had to learn to accept his capricious ways just as she absorbed his hot flesh, crying out against the pain of his forced entry. The involuntary sound jolted him back to reality, and though he couldn't stop the onrushing tide of desire he took Jane along with him to that place of momentary unreality that was all too fleeting an experience.

"I'm sorry, sweetheart," Scott said when they were spent, brushing a kiss against her mouth. "I wanted you so badly that I couldn't stop myself. I didn't mean to hurt you, Jane. Can you forgive me?"

"When it ends like that, how can I not forgive you?" Jane pondered, sensing a curious restlessness in him in spite of the violent release.

Scott seemed far away, hovering just beyond her reach and comprehension, and she felt that in a way she had failed him in spite of her reciprocation. She could read nothing in his closed eyes or the tense lines of his face, and the muscles of his shoulder were taut beneath her cheek, belying the slaking of his lust that had left Jane weak with languor.

If only she would go away, but those bewitching aqua eyes lingered on the fringes of his mind taunting him as he lay in Jane's arms. If only the apparition with hair like the long, dark wisps of the encroaching night would leave him in peace for a moment. Scott had even forced himself not to cry out her name at the moment of completion and now her presence was summoning him, beckoning him on.

Deliberately he opened his eyes and let them fill with the lovely vision of Jane's flushed face and outflung blond hair. With desperation he began talking, telling her about his trip and plans, and if she thought it strange she gave no indication, only listened with a bemused smile on her lips and her eyes hungrily devouring his face.

"Everything is set, Jane—awaiting the day of the fair. An old friend of mine, Captain Edward Darnell, signed on for a share in the profits. He has his instructions and will anchor offshore on May first to wait for my signal.

"Tomorrow I'll start visiting the families of my men—feel them out to see if they will be willing to make the voyage and make a new start in life. It's going to work, Jane—it has to!"

"Of course it will, dearest," she agreed, stroking the bunched muscles of his back as he leaned over her. "You can do anything you set your mind to—of that I have no doubt."

But Scott had his own misgivings, not about the jail-break, but about how long he could keep himself away from Angela.

In the next few weeks he busied himself with his plans, happy to find that every wife but one would accompany her husband on the tentative journey. Only Matthew Grey's wife, Sally, had declined the offer and Scott had found out later that the two had been having marital difficulties and she was suspected of having a lover. But he extracted a promise from the young woman that she wouldn't breathe a word of what they had discussed together and had to leave it at that.

The other families had jumped at the chance to start new lives with their freed men, far from the injustices they had felt being part of the lower class. It was like a glimpse of paradise in spite of having to uproot themselves and face unknown dangers in a foreign country. They would have to be ready at a moment's notice, taking only what they could carry, Scott had explained, cautioning everyone to continue in the same daily routine so as not to arouse the suspicions of their neighbors. Fearful of a slip, he didn't name a day or time, cognizant of the fact that any knowledge on the part of the dragoons would result in a worse catastrophe than the ambush. The children were to be left in complete ignorance, aware that they were leaving only when Scott came for them.

Scott resumed his midnight rendezvous with Jane, meeting her almost every night of the week in back of the Bentwood stables and riding to his house. There they could love without restraint and the fear of discovery, and she made his evasion of Angela almost bearable. She was such a sweet and gentle lover, wanting to please him in everything but falling short of his expectations.

With Jane he couldn't quite let himself go and abandon himself to the total enjoyment of carnal gratification as he could with Angela. She was too sensitive and easily shocked, and some of the things Scott had tried had met with firm disapproval and she stopped him before he had really started. On the other hand, Angela usually gave in easily in spite of her reservations, the sensuality of her nature overruling any inhibitions, as long as what he did gave her pleasure.

They were as different as night and day and though his body urged him to seek out Angela, his mind argued against it. It would be better to break it off now without further entanglement, get it over with once and for all. And in some ways Jane diminished his physical need for Angela, but with Angela he could do anything he pleased. What did it matter if she protested or if he hurt her? She hated him anyway and he didn't have to impress her—and in the end her body always responded, giving him the intense extreme ecstasy that he had never felt with any other woman.

She had taught Scott an important lesson: that a man and woman complement each other and his pleasure is only as great as the heights he stirs her to.

"The bastard! Damn him to hell! I wish he was dead!" Angela swore, seething with anger. She had just found out from Jane that Scott had been back for over two weeks and he had made no attempt to see her.

It was all his fault, the way she felt; hot and tense, wound as tightly as a spring. After all, Scott was the one that had made her aware of the passionate fires smoldering deep within her body. Angela had tried to suppress those urges for almost two months and it was a losing battle that left her short-tempered and furious, bursting into tears at the least provocation.

If only she could sleep, but between the desire stirring in her and the ever increasing movements of the baby she was wakeful, knowing what the problem was but having no solution. Keith could have stilled the yearning but declined to, for mysterious reasons of his own. The only other alternative was Scott and he was avoiding her as if she had the plague.

After dinner she began reading a long, dull book hoping it would put her to sleep. Then Angela rang for a glass of warm milk, but the effort was useless. In the early hours of morning she was wide awake, moving restlessly on the bed. Her body screamed for a man, any man and coming to a sudden decision she threw back the covers and got up, stopping only long enough for a candle and her slippers.

The panel opened at the touch of her fingers and Angela entered the secret passageway oblivious to the cold air biting through the thin lace nightgown. The way was indelibly impressed on her mind and she skimmed surely through the maze of tunnels, turning at all the right places. How many times had she been dragged along as an unwilling victim? Well tonight it was her turn to victimize Scott.

"He's taken me often enough just to appease his own desire!" Her words echoed within the vaulted stone confines. "Well tonight I'm going to use him—after all, turnabout is fair play, especially when dealing with someone like him!"

Another panel opened into the hallway of the dower house and Angela hastily put the candlestick down on a convenient table, shaking with anticipation as she approached his bedroom door. It opened silently, and she smiled at the thought of his shock at finding her there.

She could hear his breathing in the silent room and

the rustle of bedclothes as she let her eyes grow accustomed to the dimness of the room. But Angela was the one in for a shock.

"No!" she cried, startled to her toes by the sight that met her eyes. For there on the bed were two entwined bodies—he was making love to another woman! This was the ultimate outrage in her protean state.

Scott's head went up, his velvet-brown eyes focusing incredulously on the embodiment of his fantasies. She wavered in the doorway, the candlelight behind her, a luminous nimbus outlining her body through the lace. This couldn't be real and he closed his eyes, willing her to evaporate, but she lingered still.

"Angel?" he whispered, disentangling himself from the woman, pulling the covers over her quickly to shield her from sight.

Springing out of bed he moved to the doorway and his hand closed around Angela's wrist. She was real, flesh and blood, and in his moment of hesitation before thrusting her from the room she struck out at him like an angry cat, trying to claw his face.

"How dare you!" she hissed, twisting in Scott's grasp. Her sharp teeth bit into the arm that was holding her, and without thinking he slapped her across the face, the sound loud in the stunned silence of the room.

Vicious words bubbled to her lips and she kicked him in the shin, shrieking, "You debased animal! How could you bring your whore here—the very bed you and I—"

"Shut up right now, shrew—if you know what's good for you!" Scott's voice was a low dangerous growl. "If I didn't know better, I'd think you were jealous."

With a superhuman effort Angela broke free and stood shaking just inches from him. "Jealous! You can't even begin to imagine how much I hate you!"

Her eyes flashed lightning and he couldn't help but think what a magnificent, feral creature she was, her shaking body almost totally revealed to him. Every thought of Jane vanished before Scott's contemplation of her, and he was angry with himself for feeling such a sharp, overpowering attraction.

Angela continued shouting, unable to stop all the dammed up emotions from overflowing."First you rape me and beat me and get me pregnant! Then you try to kill me—and then desert me! What do you expect me to feel for you—love? You are insane!"

While the battle raged, Jane remained frozen to the bed, her eyes unbelievingly taking in the astonishing scene. This could not possibly be happening! But Angela's angry words stung her into the realization that this was real, penetrating her benumbed mind with a blinding pain. Scott wasn't capable of doing all that, not her loving fiancé—but perhaps the desperate brigand that was his other self could. Hadn't she just seen him strike Angela and heard the ugly accusations that she didn't want to believe were true?

Rape, attempted murder and—no, no! It was too awful to contemplate. As Angela turned slightly the rounded curve of her belly reinforced the worst suspicion of all. Angela was pregnant with Scott's baby! Jane sagged on the bed, stifling a moan of suffering, gnawing doubts assailing her from every side. Her fiancé and her best friend, lovers—evidently of long standing.

Jane was the interloper, and as if in a dream she rose from the bed, hastily grabbing up her cloak and clutching it around her nakedness. She had to get out, had to escape from this room, the bed where they had loved so many times before. Desperately she pushed past them and they both looked at her, surprised, and she saw the fury in Angela's eyes drain away to stunned disbelief as she recognized her.

"Jane, wait for me downstairs!" It was a command from Scott and she broke into a run down the hall, tripping and almost falling on the stairs in her haste, not stopping until she sank into a quivering heap before the dying fire in the drawing room.

Jane sat huddled in her cloak with her face buried against her knees, as the shouting match continued upstairs. The individual voices were clear but what they were saying she couldn't make out and didn't want to—not after what she had already seen and heard.

Then there was silence—and that was much worse.

"What a virago you are! What did you come here for in the first place?"

"What do you think I came for?"

Scott's hand shot out and ripped the delicate nightgown leaving her exposed to his angry gaze. Even with the slight swelling of her abdomen she was dazzling, and her taut breasts peeking from a veil of pitch-black hair inflamed him beyond turning back.

She fought him as one arm went around her waist and Scott pressed her feverish body against his cool skin. Surprised, Angela cried out as his other hand touched her, the inquisitive fingers intently assessing. Ineffectually, she pushed against his chest, trying to get free but at the same time betraying herself by wriggling against his moving fingers.

"You are ready," he observed mockingly, "and you're as hot as a bitch in heat!" Scott's lips met hers, parting them, drowning the frustration of their weeks apart.

They were both lost, engulfed in a riptide of passion. Why resist the impulse? It felt too good.

"I never quite realized what I unleashed in you, Angel," he whispered against her mouth. "What you need is a full-time stud—but I don't mind servicing you this once!"

The caustic remark enraged her and she slapped him hard. "Do you have to be so—so vulgar?"

"Why not, love? Sex is crude and don't try to tell me that what we feel at this moment is anything subtle—it's just raw lust!"

They fell onto the bed together, locked in an unbreakable embrace and Angela gasped in ecstasy at his total possession of her, surging against him, nails tearing at his shoulders and back.

Scott laughed in her ear, caught up in and fully preoccupied by the wanton witch she had become. "Yes—you need a good bout, my little whore. Do you like this—and this?"

He pounded into her like a stormy, angry ocean onto the shore, and she was helpless, unable to resist the momentum and power of the crashing surf. Tossed from the crest of one wave to another she finally reached that one towering tidal wave that shook her and spun her dizzily about, destroying her whole world as she crashed from its height into darkness.

The fury of their mating left both of them stunned. They were such an uncongenial pair yet when it came to the physical part of love they were perfectly attuned—the teacher and pupil, each giving and taking, knowing the secret of pleasing.

Angela fell into an exhausted sleep almost immediately and Scott held her, his hand on her belly where their child was making itself known. This mere slip of a girl brought out more emotion in him than anyone before her had ever been able to—most of the feelings bad. When they fought he wanted to dominate her, bend her to his will, hurt her. Then somehow they always ended up in bed, and after making love to her Scott's feelings veered to the other extreme, tender and possessive. He had given up trying to analyze it, it was too exasperating. Besides, he would be leaving soon and might never see her again.

"Angel, love," he whispered, and her arm curled tightly around his neck and she sighed in her sleep.

Why her, why Angela? Scott could feel her fingernails ripping into his heart like talons, drawing blood, torturing him. It couldn't be allowed to continue or they would destroy each other. Better to be haunted by her distant memory than enslaved by her ethereal person, bound forever by thick silken bonds of midnight hair.

He disentangled himself from her and pulled the covers over her sprawled form. It was better now that their flesh didn't touch, his mind cleared and he was able to think once again. Jane! Scott suddenly remembered that she was waiting for him—or had she left? He didn't want to face her now. What possible explanation could he offer? It was too late, she had heard too much—better to admit the truth and let her know at last the lengths he would go to accomplish his plans.

The candle flickered and almost went out as the door opened and Scott entered the room with her clothes over his arm. Jane looked at him with sorrowful blue eyes that gave evidence she had been crying. There was no mistaking the look on his face, that sated expression he wore after making love. He had been upstairs for a long time.

"How could you. . .make love to her?" Jane asked in a hollow voice as if her body was just a shell vacated by all that made her herself.

"It's the only thing I could do to calm her down, short of knocking her unconscious," he replied moodily dropping the clothes on a chair.

She was hunched up by the fire, sitting on the floor and his answer made some of the life come back into her eyes. "You're as. . .amoral as a. . .a. . .tomcat! I thought I knew you but I don't—you're a stranger. All those horrible things she accused you of—they can't be true. Tell me they aren't!"

"It's all true," he admitted recklessly. "I raped her, many times, until I taught her how to respond. Since then we have been lovers. You saw for yourself how she came to me tonight."

Jane was staring at him, pain in her big accusing eyes. "And the rest—you beat her, you—"

"Damn, Angela deserved it! She shot me and a few weeks later tried to finish the job. I got mad and gave her a good spanking, and I admit that I enjoyed it immensely. She's a spoiled brat, a witch, the bitchiest little—"

"And the mother of your child!" Jane shouted.

"That too," Scott conceded wearily. "While I'm baring my soul to you I might as well tell you that I almost murdered her in a fit of blind rage."

No wonder Angela hated him. All the strange moods and looks of the past returned falling neatly into place, making up a picture that was not pleasing to contemplate. Jane had known from the beginning of their relationship that Scott was in love with Angela, but that they were lovers she had never guessed. How stupid of her to think she could make him forget her. No man would ever forget the mother of his baby. If only she had known before it was too late—but it wasn't too late to break off with him.

"You love her," Jane stated with a surety that surprised him. "No, don't bother to deny it—your eyes give you away. I've known since the night of the ambush, but you're a fool not to admit it to yourself. If you can't be honest with yourself, Scott, then—"

"No!" His fist slammed emphatically onto a table. "I don't love Angela! Never! She's just—a bad habit. . ."

Jane started laughing as if she was vastly amused. "Your father's wife, your stepmother. You deserve that hate. You deserve to be hurt in return for what you have done tc others—to me, to Angela. She hates you!" She drove home the point once again and his eyes flickered briefly with an anguish he didn't even recognize.

"You have been caught in your own trap and will never be free! How fitting to be locked in a prison of your own making—talk about poetic justice!" Jane snatched her clothes up, hurriedly flinging them on. "Take me home," she ordered wearily. "I never want to see you again. I'm only glad I found out about this before I married you!"

"But—but I still want to. . ."

"Never! No matter how much I loved you—no matter how much it hurts. I could never marry a man like you!"

She stormed out of the room.

Life was unsettled, fluid, changing as quickly as the temperamental English weather. The marriage between Jane and Scott was off, even though he had seen her again and tried to convince her to go through with it. She was adamant in her refusal, with a stony resolve that he couldn't sway with words or kisses. The promise that she had made to help him with the jailbreak was the only bond and communication between them now, and when that was over he would be out of her life for good.

It was a relief, for to be saddled with a wife was something Scott had never counted on. He liked his freedom too much, being able to come and go as he wished without answering to anyone. A permanent relationship with a woman would cramp his style and it was inconceivable that he would ever desire anything like that. His six-month entanglement with Angela was enough to convince him of that, as she played havoc with his agitated feelings.

The resumption of their affair had been inevitable. It was almost as if fate was throwing them back together, time after time, laughing at their efforts to resist the irresistible. The only safe alternative was to put an insurmountable distance between them, and Scott meant to do just that. But in the meantime he enjoyed their last days together with a reckless disregard for the future.

Every night he crept into Angela's bed and made love to her with a frantic urgency that puzzled her, but she kept silent and asked no questions. He probably wouldn't answer them even if she did. It was enough that he was there bringing relief from the fiery desires that at times seemed to consume her.

Scott laughed at her, teasing, stroking the swell of her belly. "I thought women with child were supposed to be quiet and subdued, just thinking about the coming event, unruffled by physical cravings. But all you think about is sex!"

"Am I too much for you to handle, Scott?" she taunted. "Have I worn you out?"

"Never," he said, catching her and demonstrating his prowess. "I never get tired of this and I wouldn't have you any other way!"

One night his actions were most bewildering. He came and held her naked against him in bed for a long time and talked to Angela about anything and everything that came into his mind: the May Day fair tomorrow, their baby, his boyhood visits to Scotland. She listened distractedly to the disjointed rambling, frowning at this unusual sharing of his thoughts with her.

Something was wrong, she could sense it, but their frenzied joining wiped every worry from her mind and they talked no more. She lost count of the number of times and the different ways they loved. Scott was indefatigable, his mood changing constantly: serious, playful, brutal, tender, and demanding. Skillfully he used her body like an instrument of passion, perfectly attuned and creating magical music that only they could compose.

Time after time he aroused her until she was ready to scream with the sweet agony of it—wild with excitement, delirious in Scott's embrace—until they were finally one flesh moving in perfect harmony. And Angela was his willing slave, surrendering to his every whim until the fire was finally out.

She was quenched, lying exhausted and vanquished in his arms, knowing that no matter how she tried she would never be able to forget this night—could any other man love quite like that? She didn't think so and it troubled her, for any future lover would have to measure up to his example, and in a way this gave him an odd hold over her.

"I have never met a woman like you before, Angel, and I don't think I ever will again." Scott's eyes were dark and aurous, filled with some mysterious unspoken emotion. "Oh, love—my sweet, wild little vixen!"

Before he left she rose from the bed and he caught her to him, their bodies molded together from shoulder to thigh in one long, final embrace. His mouth fell hard and scalding on Angela's, drinking in her sweetness, and they swayed together for endless moments.

"Good-bye, Angel. Au revoir, my love!" Scott held her away from him for a minute, his eyes containing a sad resignation as he memorized everything about her. He touched her ebony hair and smiled into her aquamarine eyes.

"Scott, I—" But he was gone, vanishing into the shadows like a phantom of the night.

May Day. The whole town was turned out in their Sunday best, bent on thoroughly enjoying the carnival atmosphere of the fair. Booths and amusements had been set up on a flat stretch of ground several miles from the village of Brightlingsea with a beribboned Maypole in the center.

The day was clear and filled with a kaleidoscope of colors: the deep blue of a cloudless sky; the brilliant greens of the grass and newly budding trees; the wild-flowers blooming in a profusion of pink, yellow, white, purple, red—every color imaginable.

Children were everywhere, running, playing, darting in and out of the crowds, teasing and fighting. They were delighted by the holiday, by the rides and food, the gypsies and strong men, the frolicking puppets and tantalizing scents and sounds. Lovers strolled along the banks of the river, absorbed more in themselves than any of the attractions, lost in the spring promise of re-awakening that sent the blood racing faster through their veins. Mothers gathered and showed off their new babies and the men headed en masse for the booth selling beer and cider so strong it bit the tongue and made the head reel.

Keith, Jane, and Angela arrived at noon. After a long revealing talk, the two women had decided that neither of them was at fault for the disastrous encounter in Scott's bedroom. They blamed him, promising one another not to reveal any of the dark secrets that had been so brutally revealed on that night. With tacit understanding they never discussed the matter again, careful to avoid the subject of Scott Harrington. And Angela didn't disclose the fact that they were lovers once more.

Why did she keep thinking of him? It was impossible to get Scott out of her mind. Flashbacks of last night kept coming at the oddest moments, overwhelming Angela with a lost, sad feeling. Their parting had been so strange, he had said good-bye as if he would never see her again. He had never done that before—too many things had happened between them that had never occurred before—a wordless giving, an unfathomable exchange.

Shaking off her uneasiness Angela plunged into the surrounding gaiety. They made the rounds of the whole fair, from the livestock exhibits to the needlework display, stopping to laugh at the amusing dwarfs dressed in outlandish costumes, and having their fortunes told. They gorged themselves on flaky pastries, hot and filled with wild game; scones, dripping with meltea butter and golden honey; steak and kidney pies; cakes, and milk, thick and foaming, fresh from the cow.

In the late afternoon, Jane left to take the basket to the jail. Angela protested that she could let it go for one day but Jane was adamant and fixed her with a piercing look full of mixed emotions. Today was the day.

The basket of food was in the carriage and Jane drove herself the short distance into town. It was deserted in the bright afternoon sunlight, the soldier outside the jail the only one about. He brightened at her approach.

"Good afternoon, Lady Montgomery. I didn't think you had remembered today. You are late."

"The fair kept me," Jane replied with a smile. "It's a pity you couldn't go."

He gave a shrug. "My bad luck to draw guard duty today of all days!"

She went inside and there were four soldiers playing cards, obviously bored with the tiresome assignment. The guard wasn't as heavy today, just as Scott had suspected, most of the dragoons were off enjoying the holiday.

Jane put a hand to her cheek and dropped the basket on the floor and every one of the men leaped to their feet.

"Oh, I feel faint," she sighed as one dragoon took her arm. "It's so stuffy in here—perhaps if the window were open. . ."

They opened the window and solicitously led her over to it but the fresh air didn't help. Jane slumped, falling in a dead faint into the arms of a startled soldier, with the others gathered around. Then the door opened and masked men quickly and silently swarmed into the room catching the soldiers off guard and at a distinct disadvantage.

The dragoons were overpowered and dispatched to unconsciousness by swift blows to their heads. Jane watched the precise movements of the six men through her lashes as they freed the prisoners and tied the soldiers, locking them in the cells.

Scott was bending over her, his breath warm against her cheek. "It's not too late to change your mind, Jane," he whispered.

"No!" she hissed between her teeth trying to lie still and arouse no suspicions, for it was possible one of the dragoons might come to any moment. "I've kept my promise. Go!"

"All right, love—I'm sorry but I'll have to tie you. I can't have anyone know you were in on it!"

He tied and gagged her himself and then carried Jane into a cell and laid her on a pallet recently vacated by one of his men. "Thank you, Jane. I will never forget what you have done. Tell Angela. . ." His voice trailed off at the sudden sparkle of tears in her eyes.

He locked her in and she squirmed uncomfortably as he pocketed the keys and left as quickly as he had come. Scott's devilish laughter at the successful jailbreak rang in her ears, and as the door slammed behind the last man Jane let the tears slip helplessly down her cheeks.

Two hours later the returning soldiers discovered their imprisoned comrades and Jane—and the fact that the smugglers were missing. Time enough for them to have vanished into thin air. The keys couldn't be found and the blacksmith had to be called in to break the cells open.

Captain Latham was in a towering rage, everywhere at once, shouting orders, organizing the searchers, questioning the soldiers that had been attacked. The countryside was scoured, every house searched, no nook or cranny overlooked, but they were nowhere to be found. Unfortunately one of the dragoons had received too hard a crack on the head and never recovered consciousness, so whoever had participated in the escape had murder added to the list of crimes committed today.

Jane was exhausted when she was finally free to return home, and Keith and Angela were waiting for her outside the jail. A half moon illuminated their anxious faces, and after a few initial questions the ride home was silent. When they dropped Angela off at the castle she leaned toward Jane, her mouth close to her ear.

"Is he gone?" she whispered so low that Keith couldn't hear them.

"He sailed on the tide," Jane replied, and Angela closed her eyes in a brief spasm of poignant longing, then went into the house.

The bittersweet memory of last night's loving returned and Angela rushed to her room unable to contain her tears or her ambivalent feelings. Throwing herself on the bed she let the tears flow in a torrent. So it had been good-bye—Scott's way of saying it. She felt abandoned and betrayed.

Her hand touched something under her pillow and still sobbing she withdrew a package and tore off the wrappings. It was a small, gold, heart-shaped locket intricately engraved with her initials. Opening it Angela saw on one side a miniature of him and on the other side a painting of a sailing ship.

The mocking, painted smile was a perfect likeness but it could never equal the vitality of his presence. And two differing emotions fought simultaneously for possession of her. Angela wanted Scott here in her room with her; she also wanted him worlds away.

The tiny gilt letters on the prow of the ship became visible as she held the locket closer to the light.

"The *Dark Lady*," she read, livid with anger. The gesture was just like him—conceited, arrogant! "I hate you, Scott Harrington," she told his image. "Good riddance! I'm glad you're gone!"

Walking to the French doors Angela flung them wide, stepping onto the balcony and into the cool of the night. Gazing in the direction of the sea she felt her baby, their baby, move inside her and her mind repeated over and over again the same word, like a mournful dirge, with each beat of her heart.

Gone, gone, gone. . .

PART TWO

The Fallen Angel

England
1804-1806

Thus am I still provoked to every evil
By this good wicked spirit, sweet angel devil.
—Michael Drayton

It lies not in our power to love or hate,
For will in us is over-ruled by fate.
—Christopher Marlowe

Chapter Seven

The deep purple vault of the sky slowly darkened and tremulous pinpricks of light pierced it, twinkling like candle flames leaping against the night. Cool winds blew the remnants of summer before it, dissipating the last warm traces. It was the dark of the moon and the atmosphere was thick with far-distant memories of a shadowy time.

Angela closed the window and drew the draperies, pressing both hands against her hot cheeks. Unbidden thoughts returned as they always did on nights like this. He would come late, smelling of the sea, to wake her from a sound sleep and heat her with his kisses. They wouldn't speak and only their quickening heartbeats and the crackle of the fire would break the silence.

"No!"

She couldn't let herself dwell on such forbidden memories, for he was gone and wouldn't come again. Instead she went to the small bed and leaned over, touching the black curls of her sleeping daughter, pressing a kiss on the baby-soft cheek. All the excruciating pain of a difficult birth had been worth bearing for Lorna.

She had suckled the baby herself with a fierce protective love she had never felt before. Her firstborn child, the tiny miracle of wonderment and joy that belonged only to her.

A girl! Angela couldn't help smiling, thinking of Scott's presumptuousness in telling her it would positively be a boy. His carefully planned revenge had been foiled by a conspiracy between herself and Lorna. She sobered only when she remembered his threat to return and impregnate her again if she didn't give him a son. It was impossible to go through the agony of childbirth again; even the doctor had warned her against having any more children.

So Lorna was her first child and her last, a sweet little girl too much like her mother for her own good. But how could she be any different when Scott was her father and Angela her mother, mixing that wild blood together once again in their child? Already she showed signs of stubborn willfulness and rebelliousness, so that she had to be watched all the time. And now that she was starting to walk the job of keeping her in sight would increase a hundredfold.

She had taken her first steps today for Keith, and when Lorna had started falling he had swept her up, throwing her high over his head and laughing as she had squealed with delight. Keith. . .Keith. . .there was an inevitableness to their relationship. They weren't lovers, but he was more like a father to Lorna than the aging duke who was confined to his bed, paralyzed since the stroke he had had six months ago. Soon Angela would be free and where else could she turn but to Keith, who made himself more indispensable to her every day?

He loved her but she wasn't sure if she loved him, couldn't even be sure what true love between a man and a woman was like. There was nothing to compare it to but the wild madness that had happened between Scott and herself, and Angela was wise enough to know that had been purely a physical attraction. But there was something to be said in favor of the physical part of love; at least it cooled her blood so that she could sleep at night.

Kissing Lorna again she went to her room where a fragrant fire burned on the hearth. Blowing out all the candles Angela curled up in a big chair, leaning her head back, watching through half-closed eyes the flames reaching upward with eager fingers. Yes, this was one of those nights when sleep wouldn't come but ran baying after a nonexistent moon. There were far too many lonely nights like this with a hot tightness coiled in her belly so that she felt like screaming. She was tired but it would be no use going to bed, no use trying to read or embroider for Angela could concentrate on nothing with such yearnings burning from the inside out.

Perhaps she needed a lover to still the seething in her but there was no one, and hour after hour she sat immobile as the fire on the hearth burned itself out and the other one grew in intensity. Finally able to bear it no longer she changed into her riding habit and stealthily left the sleeping castle.

Angela saddled Pegasus herself, for she could hardly wake the stable boy at three in the morning. They headed toward the lake and the wind cooled her fevered face and brought a semblance of order back to her chaotic thoughts.

The wings of night had descended wrapping the world in a soothing obscurity. With only the brilliant stars for light everything was mysterious and vaguely defined; not even shadows existed. But Angela knew the way for she often ventured out under cover of darkness seeking a solace she never found.

A glimmer of smooth black satin spread before her and she slipped from her mount, slowly removing her clothes. Angela gasped as the icy water clasped her and she swam out toward the center, free, weightless, and deliciously cold. There was nothing like swimming nude in the middle of the night—it was delightfully indecent and invigorating.

For a while she swam and when she got tired, turned over and floated on her back. There was an especially enchanting star near the horizon, not as large as some of the others, but it flashed brilliantly—first blue, then red, now green and amber. Angela watched it for some time until a numbness crept into her bones and she struck out for shore.

Pegasus neighed and she stopped, treading water as the dim shapes of men captured the ghost-white stallion. They laughed as they found her clothes, and the one that towered over his three companions caught up the bundle and made off with her horse. Whatever could she do now? They could be poachers, smugglers, highwaymen or the devilish members of the Hell Fire Club, but whoever they were she must not fall into their clutches.

She would have to swim to the other side of the lake as far from them as possible. But then she heard the sounds of their departure, whispers and galloping horses and she breathed a sigh of relief because Angela wasn't sure she could have made it to the opposite side. Dripping wet and freezing she emerged from the lake with her teeth chattering, no clothes, and a long walk home.

A dark horse appeared out of the gloom, so close that Angela screamed in fright. Wheeling, she ran but he was after her, his boots pounding the ground behind her. Panic made her swift but she was jerked up short as his hand caught her flying hair, and the momentum tumbled them both to the ground.

"What have we here?" he asked turning her over and straddling her twisting body. His hand touched her breast and trailed down. "You don't feel like a highwayman to me."

It was impossible to see his face in the darkness but Angela saw the white flash of teeth and a double row of gleaming buttons marching down his chest. A soldier! Thank heavens!

"Let me go—don't do that!" Angela protested. "I'm the Duchess of Brightling. Stop it!"

"And I'm King George," he countered unbuttoning his breeches and forcing her legs apart.

She screamed, terrified at the intentions of this anonymous soldier who was preparing to rape her as casually as he might take a prostitute. His strength was overpowering and he fell on her, surprisingly still and heavy. Nothing happened and she pushed at him only to have him lifted in the air and thrown down to land in a crumpled heap beside her.

Angela lay shivering, frozen into immobility, only able to stare at the huge figure towering over her. It was the man who had stolen her horse and clothes. Had he rescued her from the dragoon only to turn her over to his companions?

He looked down at her sprawled body, white against the dark ground and laughed shortly. "It's a tempting invitation—and I'm sorry to disappoint you but I don't have the time!"

She was hot again but with anger and embarrassment. As she drew her legs together he grasped her waist jerking her to her feet.

"Here," he said with a deep timbered voice, throwing her clothes at her. "Get dressed—and be quick about it!"

As she donned her dress he watched her closely and then began questioning her. "Do you have a horse?"

"Yes, and you stole it!"

"You'd better not make any foolish accusations or you might find yourself in trouble."

"I'm already in trouble," she yelled, furious at this man, who so far had only saved her. "I am always, continually in some sort of trouble!"

"What's your name?"

"Angela Harrington. I want my horse back and I want to go home!"

"Not yet." He grasped her arm as she took a tentative step away. "Where do you live?"

"Brightling Castle. You are trespassing on my property." She was afraid and defiant at the same time, positive she would never emerge from this situation unscathed or even the same as she was now.

"Your property, my lady? For you must be a lady to own an estate and a castle. Do you have a title, a husband?" There was a lively spark of interest in his voice and she had a feeling he could see like a cat in the dark, observing her while she could not see him.

"I am the Duchess of Brightling and my husband will have your head on a platter for breakfast if you don't release me at once!"

His only answer was a low laugh as he swung her up and over his shoulder as if she were a sack of potatoes and strode off surefootedly into the dead of night. The breath was knocked from Angela's body as the hard shoulder jolted into her ribs, and she was unable to struggle or even call out. She almost fainted with fright but the blood rushed to her head as she dangled upside down, reviving her.

Then with no warning he dumped her unceremoniously on the ground and she sat there staring at the four men as they argued over what to do with her.

Finally, the man that had captured her said, "We've stumbled on a gold mine tonight, boys. We have found ourselves a real, live duchess. She should bring us a sizable ransom—enough to retire on if we want. Let's get going!"

Angela was mounted on Pegasus and her hands were tied to the pommel in front of her, a gag choking off any sounds she tried to make. The tall man held the reins of her horse and led her quickly toward an unknown destination.

They went on for hours, turning and twisting through the trees, galloping along the flat, smooth stretches of terrain. She was cold and lost and her hands were without feeling as the ropes cut into her wrists. What had started out as a lark had turned into a nightmare. She was being abducted! Taken far away from Lorna, her friends and home, held against her will for ransom.

The sky was lightening in the east and a gray mist hung like a shroud concealing the landscape, stroking her face with a clammy wetness. Would they ever stop? Angela, numb with cold and exhaustion dozed off and on, finally waking as she was pulled off Pegasus by the large but strangely gentle hands of her captor.

He deposited her in the bottom of a rowboat that looked hardly big enough to carry them all, but one of the men was dispatched in another direction with the horses. The three remaining men settled themselves in the boat with Angela and they glided into the marsh.

She sat on the bottom of the boat between the leader's knees and she felt his fingers working at the gag and in a moment it was gone. "Turn around," he ordered, moving Angela himself when she didn't respond, untying the ropes binding her wrists.

Involuntary moans of pain choked her as the circulation was restored to her hands, and with unwarranted consideration the man grabbed them and rubbed them vigorously. Angela tried to pull away but collapsed with fatigue and pain against his thigh as he continued his ministrations.

"Feeling better, Duchess?" he asked after a few minutes. And she peered at him through the tangled strands of hair that had fallen over her face.

A smile flashed, lifting the big mustache that drooped over the corners of his mouth, but the light was too dim to make out any more than a craggy face and a large nose. He pushed the hair out of her face and Angela stood up and slapped his hand away.

"Don't touch me!"

"Then sit down, little girl—you're rocking the boat." So she sat at his feet with her stiff back toward him, watching the efforts of the other men as they propelled the boat through the water.

Her head nodded and then jerked upright as she tried to stay awake. They had been traveling in the boat for almost an hour now, and the sun was just making its appearance on the horizon. Fog still hung in thick streamers but it was clearing in places and Angela looked around at the eerie world she had been transported to. It was damp and watery and they slid between hummocks and small islands covered with tall skinny trees and dense undergrowth.

The sun glinted red through the rising mist and there were no landmarks, everything looked the same. At times she found it hard to distinguish between the land and the water. Even if she managed to escape there would be no way to find her way back to civilization.

Observing the two men in front of her through a thick veil of lashes, Angela noted that they looked like father and son. The younger one was tall and rawboned with carrot-red hair and a million freckles. He looked like a farmer with his open honest face, hardly the criminal type. But she learned about faces—they could be deceiving, concealing every thought and passion beneath a calm exterior.

The older man had once been as tall as his son but was now stooped, with grizzled hair. She wondered if the man behind her, the giant with the mustache, was his son, too. Though she couldn't see him and didn't dare turn her head to look at him, he made her uneasy. He hadn't harmed her and had saved her from the advances of the soldier but he had also abducted her.

And now one of his huge hands rested on her shoulder, his fingers unconsciously stroking the soft skin at the base of her throat. Her pulse quickened under his warm touch and he must have become aware of the fact for he laughed softly, holding her still as she tried to squirm away from the heavy weight holding her pinned in the boat.

Helplessness descended upon her, stifling Angela's rage with fear of the unknown. It was happening again, her inability to control her own life, as she was caught up in a current of coincidental meetings and swept along against her will. Her fate was in someone else's hands when she wanted nothing more than to be at home having breakfast with Lorna.

A sob caught in her throat and tears rose unbidden to her eyes. How long would it be before she saw her baby again and held her in her arms? Children grew up too quickly and by the time she returned her daughter might not even know her anymore. She must, she must! And Angela refused to let herself cry, vowing that once she was free she would never again allow any man to control her destiny, or force her to do anything against her will.

She shivered, chilled through, thinking that she would never be warm again, when the man behind her draped his own coat over her shoulders. Half turning, she looked into serene, pewter-gray eyes just inches from her own and suddenly was afraid of him no longer. There was suffering and humor written on his face, but the latter was more in evidence, and as if to reassure her the corners of his mustache quirked upward and lines crinkled, radiating from the corners of his eyes.

"Sleep, little girl," he said with an air of regret and a

certain resignation. "Nothing will hurt you here—I'll see to that."

And she curled up like a kitten between his feet at the bottom of the boat, her head pillowed on her arm. Somehow she believed him, and as she fell into a deep sleep she heard his gentle voice and felt him covering her more tightly with the coat, touching her cheek briefly as if she were a child as young as Lorna.

The sun was directly overhead when they reached their destination, and Angela was shaken out of her sleep. She was groggy and didn't know where she was or who the man was that was lifting her out of the boat. As she was placed on the soggy ground she swayed and his arm shot out clamping around her waist, holding her up.

A frown creased her brow as she looked around at the swirling brown water, the boat departing with father and son, the too tall trees blocking out the sunshine in this damp, shadowy place. Then she looked up, up at the man who must be at least six and a half feet tall and made her shrink to diminutive size. He was broad and powerful with thick silver and black hair and a large hawklike nose. He was old, at least forty, but there was a vitality and youthfulness about him.

"Well, let's go, Duchess. We still have a walk ahead of us." His voice sounded tired and his eyelids hooded his eyes beneath bold black lines of eyebrows.

Angela pulled away from him and started running, she didn't know where, but a panic enveloped her and she wanted to go home. Seconds later he caught her in a grip that crushed her arms.

"I want to go home! Let go—I have to get home to my baby!" she screamed, kicking him. "I don't want to be here alone with you!"

"Come on, Duchess," he said soothingly, "don't go hysterical on me now. I'm not going to hurt you—I promise. There's no place to run because we're on an island, completely surrounded by water and cut off from the rest of the world." He dragged her along after him through the trees.

"Just who do you think you are?" she yelled stumbling after him.

"You can call me Jack," he said with a swift amused glance, setting an even faster pace so that she couldn't talk.

Mire sucked at her feet making each step difficult and when Angela stumbled, losing a shoe, he impatiently picked her up carrying her the rest of the way to a clearing. Perched precariously on the highest ground on the island was a small tumbledown shack completely overwhelmed by trees. Opening the door Jack set her inside the one main room containing only a fireplace, chairs, and a table.

"You can sleep in there." He pointed to a doorway covered with a tattered blanket.

Angela looked around in dismay. "I won't stay here! It's cold and dirty!"

"Well what did you expect for a hideout—a palace?" She could tell from his tone that he was becoming annoyed. "I'll light a fire and it will soon be warmer."

Lifting the blanket he pushed her inside a bedroom smaller than her closet at home. It contained only a bed and washstand.

"Now get some sleep and everything will seem better afterward," Jack admonished.

"But, I can't. . .why there's not even a door. . ." Her voice was trembling and her aquamarine eyes eclipsed her pale face, which was quickly turning pink.

Jack laughed shortly, knowing exactly what was wrong. "Don't worry, Duchess—skinny, dirty, frightened little girls don't appeal to me at all!" With that he left, slamming the door as he went outside to gather firewood.

Angela collapsed on the dusty bed, too tired and confused to think or even attempt an escape. Sleep claimed her instantly, before she could crawl beneath the covers.

Jack Newton returned with an armful of the driest wood he could find and soon had a good fire going. The shack was cold and dirty, he observed, but he usually only spent a few days a year here. Now he was stuck by chance,. for perhaps months, with an unpredictable urchin-duchess as his prisoner. If only he was at home with Amy—he had a terrible feeling he wouldn't see her for a very long time.

Pushing aside the blanket Jack entered the only bedroom and looked down at the bedraggled girl sleeping so peacefully on the narrow bed. Smiling in amusement at the comical picture, he removed her shoe and rolled her under the bankets, brushing the tangled black curls out of her face.

"Why I have sons and daughters older than you, Duchess," he whispered, diverted by the thought.

In sleep she looked so innocent and he couldn't believe she was married with a baby of her own. She was just a child herself, yet she had said she was always in trouble and just one glance at her when she was awake convinced him of that. This girl was too beautiful with her amazing, magnetic eyes and stubborn, sensuous mouth—men would lie, cheat, and kill for someone like her and it was his misfortune to be mixed up with her. If he had known then what he sensed now, he would have run from her as fast as he could, avoiding any entanglement—for she would cause him great distress—that Jack knew positively.

It was dusk before Angela woke, stretching on the bed and ravenously hungry. A delicious aroma of food permeated the cabin and she sat up, running her fingers through her tangled curls, tossing the disordered locks over her shoulders. It was much warmer now and she got out of bed in her stockinged feet, her dress filthy and wrinkled. Her appearance couldn't be helped.

Peeking through the doorway she found Jack stirring a pot hanging over the fire, from which emanated the mouth-watering smells. "I'm starved," she annnounced boldly walking into the room, daring him to try anything with the stubborn tilt of her chin and a wary look from the corner of her eye. "When do we eat?"

"My, Duchess," he greeted mockingly, emphasizing the title of this gypsy-child. "Your nap seems to have revived your spirit and done you worlds of good. You look charming—please," Jack indicated one of the two chairs at the table, "have a seat and I will see if I can induce the cook to speed up preparations for dinner!"

Sitting down she glared at him. "I don't like your tone of voice—and don't call me, Duchess, as if you were. . .making fun of me!"

He was laughing now, filling the room with noise and brightness. "But I am teasing you. How did such a little chit of a thing come by such a grand title?"

He placed bread and cheese on the table and she noticed that the shack had been cleaned, and there were flowers arranged in a milk jug on the table. She couldn't imagine him picking them or cleaning the place and wondered if it had been done for her benefit. In any event it didn't look half bad now.

"Why by marrying a duke," she replied flippantly.

"Of course, how stupid of me. But then. . .I thought you would still be in the nursery. No matter—as long as your husband is willing to pay a pretty penny for his child-bride. I don't mind babysitting for a while!"

"Why you. . .you. . ."

Jack placed a bowl of stew in front of her. "Be quiet or I'll eat it all myself!"

After staring at him for a few speechless moments that's just what she did, wolfing down the simple fare and choking on the strong drink in her mug, but draining it nonetheless. It was the best meal she had ever had, she thought, sopping up the last of the stew with her bread, holding out her mug for more of the fiery liquid that spread hotly through her veins, warming all the way to her toes.

Angela was very warm now, watching Jack watch her with unsuppressed enjoyment. His face wavered through a slight haze and he seemed very far away. Hiccupping, she placed her hand over her mouth and started to giggle.

"Duchess," his voice was stern, "I think you're drunk."

"Am I?" Angela couldn't stop herself from laughing.

"What was that?"

"Whiskey—and at least it makes you happy and makes you forget your haughty manners. Now," he stood up with his hands on his hips and a pleased expression on his face, "I'm going out for a while. Why don't you get yourself cleaned up while I'm gone? But don't go outside, you might fall in the marsh and drown."

Angela sat at the table with her chin propped up on her hand, just staring dreamily into space, unaware that he had left. It was a ridiculous, dangerous situation she was in but somehow she wasn't afraid anymore—Jack had seen to that. After a while she became aware of her surroundings again and noticed that a big wooden barrel had been brought in. It was half filled with cold water and more water was heating in a large kettle over the fire.

At least her abductor was considerate enough to understand her needs and give her some privacy. With a swift look out the door to make sure he was truly gone she stripped off her dirty clothes and dumped the hot water into her improvised bath. It was only lukewarm, but considering the primitive conditions it was the height of luxury and she bathed and washed her hair.

When she had finished she found, much to her dismay, that her clothes were too dirty to put back on, so she wrapped herself in a blanket and washed them out in the barrel. By the time Jack got back her clothes were hanging near the fire and Angela was curled up in a chair, letting her tangled hair dry near the crackling flames.

"I brought you a few things." He dumped a brush and comb into her lap and put her muddy shoe beside the chair. "I forgot about clothes," he said, eying the delicate underclothes swaying close to his nose. "We'll see about that tomorrow."

"Thank you." She had been about to make a smart, sarcastic retort but changed her mind. She might as well be as civil as possible under such conditions. And hadn't he gone to some lengths to make her comfortable, in spite of the fact that he was holding her captive? Things could be far worse than they were.

"Now—if you have recovered from the whiskey—I'd like you to write a letter to your husband."

"But I can't!" she said, watching Jack spread a sheet of paper on the table.

"You must, if you want to leave here, Duchess," he told her sternly.

"Are you threatening me?" Angela sprang to her feet, clutching the blanket securely. "What will you do if I don't—rape me—kill me?"

He shook his head emphatically. How could she think he would harm her? But then she didn't know him. In all the years he had spent as a highwayman, Jack had never once discharged his pistol or even threatened the occupants of the various coaches he had stopped. One look at his massive form looming out of the darkness on a powerful horse, his eyes glittering from the slits of his mask, sent the ladies and gentlemen quaking with terror.

He was selective in what he took, always leaving them enough money to get safely to their destination, thanking them graciously and apologizing for the inconvenience. Sometimes he even let the ladies keep prized jewels, wedding rings, or something of sentimental value, and many times they tearfully thanked him for sparing a treasured heirloom. Gentleman Jack, they had dubbed him, saying it was a pleasure to be robbed by him rather than the assorted riffraff that maimed, killed, and terrorized at night.

His reputation was known far and wide, embellished by his own victims until his deeds were blown all out of proportion. Men new to the profession tried to emulate him but fell far short, and he only laughed when tales of his own exaggerated daring reached his ears.

Jack smiled, his gray eyes unreadable in the flickering light, and Angela took a step backward. "Know once and for all, little girl, that I mean to do you no harm. If you don't want to write the letter now, then you can do it tomorrow or next week." He shrugged his shoulders, looming big and bearlike in the small confines of the room. "I was just thinking of you—of your distaste at staying here and your desire to return home to your husband and baby. The sooner the letter is sent, the quicker you will be free to return home. I think we both want that.

"One more thing—though we may live here for a time, alone and isolated from the world you don't have to fear any advances from me. I won't rape you, as you seem bent on believing, and I won't threaten you. Not all men are as salacious as that soldier I cracked on the head last night—and you hold no appeal for me. I may be a highwayman, but I have my own code of honor."

Angela stared at him openmouthed, not quite believing what he had just said, yet piqued because he found her unattractive. This type of man was beyond her limited experience and she didn't know what to say in reply. If a lion had suddenly spoken, assuring her that he wasn't dangerous at all but a mere kitten, she couldn't have been more astounded.

"Well, my *enfant terrible*—will you write the letter now or later, or not at all?" Jack smiled mockingly at her confusion, one thick eyebrow cocked quizzically at her.

"Now," she said very softly going over to the table and looking down at the blank square of paper. "But I'm afraid I won't be able to write to my husband—you see he is very sick and unable to read it or understand it."

"Oh?"

"He had a stroke, some months past, and is not even able to speak. I will have to write to Keith—he will get the money for you."

"Just how old is the duke—and who is Keith?"

"My husband is seventy-four years old," Angela sighed, seeing the pity leap in Jack's eyes, "and Keith is a friend and neighbor. If anyone can get the ransom, he can."

"Damn—of course! The Duke of Brightling! He's one of the richest—" Jack broke off abruptly looking at

Angela speculatively. She was indeed a pot of gold at the end of the rainbow, and his mind worked swiftly reassessing her potential value.

She wrote at his dictation filling the sheet with delicate, flowing script then paused to look up at him in astonishment. "Fifty thousand pounds! That's ridiculous—impossible! You might as well ask for the. . .the moon!"

"Why not when I'm holding the sun for ransom? Your husband is as rich as Midas and will never miss such an amount—while I. . ." Jack's thoughts turned inward momentarily before he went on. "He's getting you back at a bargain price, little one—or should I say Lord Montgomery is?"

"Shut up!" Angela cried at the implication he was making about her and Keith. "It may take months to get so much money together. I don't want to be stuck in this stinking hole forever!"

"Then write, Duchess, and hope for the best," Jack soothed. "Do you think that I want to stay here any more than you do?"

So she wrote down the astronomical sum and finished the letter, handing it to him for inspection. Jack's eyes flew along the neat lines and she watched him read it, terribly upset, pressing her now shaking hands together. What if Keith couldn't convince the duke's solicitors to come up with so much money? Was she doomed to be kept on this miserable island on the English coast forever?

"Are you cold, Duchess?" Jack asked, noticing the trembling, and she thought he was entirely too observant of her least movement or change of thought. "Go sit beside the fire and it will warm you."

Jack sat down, composing a letter of his own to accompany the one Angela had written. He took a long time over it, scowling blackly as he concentrated, choosing each word with care. By the time he was finished Angela was asleep in the chair near the fireplace, her head fallen upon her arm and a curtain of soot-black hair sweeping the floor.

Jack went to look down on her, shaking his head with despair. Abduction wasn't his forte, he should have stuck with robbery. An uneasy feeling enveloped him, emanating from the small defenseless form sprawled before him. That girl would be his downfall, utterly destroying Gentleman Jack—but he was past doing anything to remedy the situation. It was too late now, everything had been set in motion and whatever followed was as inevitable as the changing seasons.

Touching Angela's shoulder he shook her, gently at first then harder, trying to rouse her. He should let her sleep in the chair and use the bed himself this night, but he couldn't. Picking her up, he strode into the bedroom placing her on the bed and inadvertently banging her head slightly against the wall.

Angela's eyes flew open and for one suspended moment she was paralyzed, forgetting his vow not to touch her. He was bending over her, one of his arms beneath her and the blanket that she had so carefully wrapped herself in had fallen away, exposing the whole length of her body. She saw the quick, involuntary way his cool gray eyes traveled over her young curves, pausing briefly at her bosom, then back up to her shocked aqua eyes. Before she could voice any protestation Jack impatiently jerked the blanket back over her shrinking flesh and left her alone in the room.

He was shaking with desire for the girl that just this morning he had denounced as a skinny, annoying child. What was there about her that had changed his opinion so suddenly and irrevocably? That brief glance had assured him that she was every inch a woman and definitely not skinny—and her breasts! He closed his eyes with a low sound somewhere between a moan and a groan, seeing those full white curves, pink-tipped and splendid beyond imagining.

She was crying in the next room, sobs that called out for comforting. But he steeled himself, clamping both hands over his ears to block out the sounds that insidiously crept through his fingers. She was frightened of him, he had read it in her eyes. He had just assured her that he wouldn't touch her. How foolish his words sounded to him now—no wonder she hadn't believed him.

"Amy," Jack whispered hoarsely, trying to conjure her blond image to his bedazzled mind. "Help me, Amy."

Chapter Eight

Two weeks passed and they waited for news from the outside world, word that the ransom had been met. In the interval there was a wordless reaching out toward one another across a deep, wide chasm that was never physically breached. Oddly, they became friends, and at the same time Angela felt that in spite of all they shared there was a change, a withdrawal in Jack.

She liked him very much—too much. How could she help it? He was big and colorful, wicked and at times more naive than she was—and no one could make her laugh like Jack. On the chilly autumn evenings after dinner they would sit before the fire and he would spin long rollicking tales, half of which Angela didn't believe. He was quite a storyteller, and she learned a lot about him by the casual, offhanded questions she sometimes asked.

He was the illegitimate son of the daughter of an earl and a groom. That was as much as he knew of his parentage; not even their names had been revealed to him. His anonymous mother had paid for his keep at Zachery Newton's farm since Jack had been a few days old and he grew up as a farmer's son—until he was ten years old.

Then he learned the stark, unvarnished truth, that the Newtons weren't his real parents, and he was no kin to his brothers and sisters. And as if that shock wasn't great enough, he was then sent away from the only family he had known to begin his education.

Somehow word got out, as it always did, no matter how many schools he attended. Bastard, they branded him, making him the butt of their jokes, treating him like the lowest scum with a cruelty that children learn at an early age from their prejudiced parents. Jack became a loner, absorbed in his studies, the top student in his school, his only pleasure the contemplation of the summers with the Newtons.

Upon graduation from a university Jack quickly learned that society had no place for the likes of him. The money from his mother was cut off and he had the choice of returning to Essex to be a farmer or finding a job somewhere in the large, sprawling city of London. Opting for the latter he found a job as a clerk in a large law office. If he had been legitimate he would have been made a partner, as it was he was fortunate to have found any work.

For two years he drudged with no chance of advancement, at work by seven and sometimes still at his desk at ten at night. Sunday was his only day to get outside and feel the sun and rain and snow, depending on the season—for every Sunday without fail he rambled through the parks of the city.

He met Amy there among the flowers, proud and beautiful in spite of her position as governess to the seven children of a prominent London family. Their romance was long and slow, drawn out over more than a year until the night she sought him out in his room, overcome by tears. The marquess had taken advantage of his wife's absence to try and seduce Amy, and when that failed had resorted to force. Somehow she had escaped and ran to the only haven she knew. A week later they were married.

For two years they scraped by, both working and living a hair's breadth away from poverty, until Amy became pregnant. It was then that a desperate Jack had turned highwayman, reaping more in a week than he had in one year. He gained money, a reputation, and a price on his head, but Amy knew nothing about it. Jack fobbed her off with a fictitious business he had dreamed up, and they prospered, moving to a modest, respectable section of the city.

After that the children came like clockwork and he never regretted the life of crime which circumstances had forced him into. Jack's only concern had been the lies he was forced to tell Amy and the children in order to protect them, that and the dreadful prospect of being caught and having them find out exactly what he was.

Jack loved his wife, he had told Angela that, but she also knew that there was a wonderful warm relationship growing between them. He tried to hide it, but she didn't, caught up in some tender, inexplicable longing new to her. It was more emotional than physical, but that element was always present too, even though he never touched her, treating her with the utmost respect.

There was something fascinating about Jack, an excitement that communicated itself to Angela even when he was away. The tension between them built. As each day passed she realized that she wanted him more and she waited—for a sign, a touch, or just a look that would indicate his need of her—but he remained aloof.

Time was suspended, and Angela was unaware of each day slipping lazily by. She was perfectly happy except for wanting to see Lorna, every need but one filled by Jack. It couldn't continue in the same halcyon way indefinitely, so she reached out, trying to hold onto her elusive happiness with both hands, throwing Jack into a dilemma that had only one solution.

In the daytime he usually disappeared for hours, his destination unknown, but Angela suspected he was at the Newtons' farm. She spent her time keeping the cabin clean, cooking, and walking for hours outside when the weather was good; always keeping close to the house, for Jack had warned her repeatedly about the treacherous, swampy places.

But it didn't look so forbidding now, the tall trees on fire with the brilliant apparel of fall. Leaves of every color lit up the once gray world giving it a jaunty gayness, and Jack appeared beneath the trees with a smile that warmed Angela's heart.

She went to meet him eagerly, showing too much of the happiness that he inspired. "Jack, are you hungry?"

"I'm always hungry, little girl. Is dinner ready?"

"Almost," she replied, content just to walk beside

him. "What's in the basket?" She tried to take it but he switched it to his other arm keeping it beyond her reach.

"A present," he said laughing down into her surprised aqua eyes, "but you can't have it till we get to the house."

"Then hurry," Angela urged, taking his hand and breaking into a run, dragging him behind her. "I can't wait! I love surprises!"

They burst into the room laughing and he teased her, holding the basket beyond Angela's reach, his eyes sparkling with silver glints of tender indulgence. On tiptoe, straining she reached for it only to have her fingers graze the basket as Jack lowered it tantalizingly.

"Beast!" she cried in mock anger hammering lightly on his chest with her fists. "Wretched highwayman! Stand and deliver!"

"And what shall I deliver, Duchess—my jewels, my horse, myself, this basket?"

"Whatever you are willing to give," Angela whispered and the playfulness went out of them both.

Impenetrable shutters came down over the susceptible emotions that a moment before she had seen in his eyes. He was shutting her out as he had done before, wary of any involvement, at the sudden realization of his own fluctuating feelings. Jack placed the basket in her hands turning away to busy himself with something else, anything, so he wouldn't think about Angela.

He lifted the lid on the pot sniffing appreciatively and when he turned around again, sure of his regained determination and strength she was just standing there with the basket in her outstretched hands and her luminous eyes fixed unwaveringly on him. The corners of her mouth were quivering, and he was afraid of what she might say or do. For with the barrier between them—of unspoken words and unacknowledged feelings—there was safety, something behind which he could hide. But each day was becoming more difficult as cracks appeared in that separating wall and he couldn't even think about what might happen when it crumbled and collapsed.

With a supreme effort Angela drew herself up, gathering back the wild outburst that had been trembling on her lips. It could only make things worse, the airing of her secret thoughts that Jack knew already but was unwilling to admit. She gave him a pathetically weak little smile and set the basket on the table.

"Thank you," she said breathlessly, noting his relief. "I do love. . .presents."

Angela lifted the lid and found a kitten curled up sound asleep inside. "Oh!" She touched the soft ball of blue-gray fur and it stretched, opening curious yellow eyes. The setting sun shone through the window turning the drop on her cheek to gold and Jack reached out to reassure her, but Angela snatched the kitten from the basket and fled to the bedroom.

Jack's hand encountered only the vibrating air, his fingers closing upon nothingness and a bittersweet pain shot through him. It was better that she had left, his mind told him, but his treacherous heart urged him to go after her and still the silent weeping that permeated the atmosphere. He couldn't hear her sobs, but they shook him, all the more violent for being suppressed, and he sat down helplessly, gripping the arms of the chair for support.

If he had known the kitten was going to precipitate such a potentially dangerous situation he would never have brought it. It wasn't the gift that was the cause of the trouble but his own striving against the impossible, against the inescapable surety of his love for Angela. Not that he loved his wife any less, but rather found that his heart was larger than expected, able to love two women of differing natures with two different degrees of intensity. What an infernal predicament!

Hesitantly, Angela emerged from the darkness of the bedroom, under control once more. Her eyes were red and her cheeks flushed but other than that there was no sign that anything had happened. "Is dinner ruined?"

"No," Jack answered admiring her restraint. "I waited for you. Are you hungry?"

"Not really," she admitted, busying herself with preparations for the meal. When the table was set she stopped, looking helplessly at him. "I'm sorry I made a scene and ruined your surprise — but I couldn't help it. I don't know what came over me and I feel so foolish. It won't happen again!"

"Don't apologize, Duchess. I'm the one that's a fool —the biggest one alive!" Angela gave a short laugh and he smiled sadly. "We won't mention it again—forget it!"

"Yes," Angela echoed unconvinced. "Forget it ever happened." She brightened visibly, forcing a lightness into her tone. "We must think of a name for my new kitten, Jack! Thank you—I do like the surprise so. Can I take her when I leave? Lorna would adore it!"

"You can do whatever you want—you always do anyway, don't you?"

"Yes," she said impishly, "and that's what gets me into trouble. I have bad blood and you would be wise to beware of me, Gentleman Jack!"

They had a jovial dinner, talking incessantly, for the silence whispered of things unmentionable. And when the dishes were cleaned up and they sat in front of the fire as usual, the silence loomed as huge and impenetrable as the night and they watched the antics of the kitten as it played with a rag Angela had tied into a tight knot.

The tiny paws batted the toy back and forth across the floor, clawing and clutching, and Angela felt as if she were that bit of rag, tightly coiled and buffeted against the walls.

"Pandora!" Jack said breaking the quiet and making Angela jump.

"What?"

"That cat's name—Pandora."

"Yes," Angela said finally, after contemplating the name, "the curious one. Would it have been better if she had never opened the box?"

"I don't know, perhaps." He got to his feet and went to the door. "I'm going for a walk, Duchess—good night."

"Perhaps it's better if we never knew," she whispered, quickly averting her face as he glanced sharply at her. "Have a nice walk."

The door banged closed and he was gone, leaving behind a desolate hunger in Angela that grew more voracious as the minutes passed. She laughed bitterly and scooped up Pandora, pressing her cheek against the long silky fur.

"Why is it that men can't leave me alone?" she wondered aloud, stroking the kitten until it purred. "Yet, when I want them they disappear forever, and I'm always alone."

Sighing deeply with resignation Angela went into the bedroom and changed into the old, worn nightgown that Jack had acquired somewhere. Would he consider her more attractive in silk and lace, in elegant surroundings of crystal, rich wood, velvet, and silver? She snuggled down beneath the cold covers and the kitten curled up beside her, eyes glowing like twin nightlights in the darkness of the room. The feeble firelight from the main room diffused softly through the holes in the blanket covering the doorway—such a flimsy excuse for privacy, but it had kept Jack away.

"I love him," Angela whispered with a dawning sense of wonder. "I'm in love with a notorious highwayman, and neither of us is free! Nothing can ever come of it —nothing!"

Tears prickled like needles behind her closed eyelids and a lump rose in her throat. What should have been simple and free was complicated by others—husbands, wives, children, and families. But forbidden, it struggled to break free of the bounds of convention, the span of intervening years and the circumstance of birth.

"I want him, Pandora—you don't know how much. But I won't cry again—I can't! It hurts too much!"

Exhausted by the battle Angela fell asleep, waking in the middle of the night to a single candle flaming in the room. The cold kissed her face and her fingers sought the thickness of his hair.

"Scott?"

There was silence, and her eyes opened to troubled smoky-gray ones as Jack lifted his head. Reality made a swift trip from Brightling Castle to a small cabin, jolting her from the arms of a lover into the arms of the man she loved.

"Jack!" Angela touched his face tracing the black and silver mustache, with one arm still about his neck.

His lips swooped down as swiftly as a bird of prey, opening hers, tasting the ambrosia of her yielding kiss. Sleep fled before the assault, and Angela was all fire and light, burning away the chill darkness of the night. The last barrier between them ignited, flaming like a silken curtain billowing in the wind, obliterating every obstacle.

Their tongues touched, caressed for the first time, and Angela sighed with the soaring pleasure of it as Jack gently but firmly explored her mouth. Her frantic fingers clutched his massive shoulders and as his hand closed over her breast, touching it through the thin linen nightgown, she surged upward, softly biting his lips and moaning her urgent need of him.

Abruptly Jack broke the embrace sitting upright on the bed and she cried out in protest, her body achingly wanting the weight of his upon her.

"We must not! We can't! Help me, Angela—help me fight the terrible yearnings before they destroy me!" he pleaded with desperation. "We are married—both of us to different people—but this seems so right."

"It is right!" she cried, reaching out for him, irresistible in dishabille with her hair floating loosely over the pillows, blending with the night. "I love you, Jack—it's no use pretending I don't—no use resisting the impossible."

"No!" He tried to stand up, to flee from the temptation of her green-blue eyes and her desire-reddened lips that were saying unspeakable things, but it was useless. "You have to help me—let me go!"

"I can't help you! How can I when I can't even help myself?"

With every ounce of strength in his powerful body he

stumbled to his feet, dark eyebrows drawn together in a scowl at the painful effort it took. One look at her crest-fallen expression, at the tears welling in her enormous eyes stopped him, but his conscience impelled him onward.

"Jack!"

The cost of leaving her was too high in emotional as well as physical agony and Jack collapsed outside the bedroom door, shaking with his need to return. But could he betray Amy, his loving wife, the mother of his six children, for a brief illicit affair with a girl young enough to be his daughter? For it couldn't last and nothing good would ever come of it, except a fleeting ecstasy so intense that just one kiss destroyed him.

Angela was crying again, for the second time today, and it was all his fault. Like a man caught in a burning house he clawed his way to the door and out into the misty night. The frosty air drove into Jack's tortured lungs like knives and he staggered toward the boat like a drunkard, needing to put distance between him and the bewitching girl that had him tied in knots.

As he shoved off vowing never to touch her again or even think about it, he saw the light spilling through the trees from the open doorway. In the distance she called to him like a siren beguiling him to return. It was a blessed relief to be so far away, for now he could regain his sanity and do what was right. The fog drifted between them, swaddling him in a separate, peaceful world where Angela did not exist, except in his mind and heart.

He came with the dawn, and just as quietly, to assure himself that Angela was all right. She was huddled on his pallet before a cold fireplace, thankfully asleep. Pandora was in the crook of her arm and her bare feet peeped out from under her thin nightgown making him more aware than ever of how very young she was—and how desirable. After covering her, Jack wrote a brief note and left it for her on the table.

His instincts had been right, she was bringing calamity upon him, throwing his well-ordered life into total confusion. But was he doing any less to her? She loved him! Jack could hardly believe he had heard her say those words last night, and what they had done to him was amazing. Should he continue with his plan—wait out the time needed to acquire a fortune for her, or should he be done with it and her once and for all? It would be so easy to return Angela to Brightling Castle right now without further complications.

Not able to resist a final glance he looked down at Angela, letting everything he felt for her show in his eyes, holding nothing back. There could be no harm in that, she was asleep and would never know. Traces of tears lingered on her cheeks and spiky black lashes, and the lips he had dared to kiss were softly parted revealing just a glimpse of even white teeth. Jack shook himself and tore his eyes away from her luxuriantly flowing hair. In another minute he would be kissing her again and that would never do.

When Angela awoke she found his note and spent the better part of the day fluctuating between despair and joy. At least he hadn't left her, and he was returning for dinner. They would either become lovers or never see each other again, there could be no middle ground where they were concerned.

She breathed deeply of the cool, crisp air and continued picking the ripe blackberries off a thorny bush. Her mouth was purple from their plump sweetness but she had eaten far too many. The basket dangling from her arm wasn't even half full, and if she wanted enough to make a pie for dessert she would have to hurry.

The bush Angela was working on had been picked clean and she looked around impatiently for another. She found a big clump of them farther into the woods and began plucking the berries and dropping them into her basket.

The rays of the sun pierced through the trees like golden arrows, shooting alternate bands of shadow and brilliant light over the fallen leaves whispering softly under her feet. As she reached for an especially large berry she almost lost her balance and fell, righting herself at the last minute.

Angela was rooted to the spot. Her shoes had sunk into the leaves and she couldn't move. Struggling to free herself only worsened conditions, and a cold slime clutched her ankles, firmly refusing to let go. The basket fell unnoticed to the ground spilling the precious contents into a heap and she watched in horror as the basket was slowly sucked downward until it vanished from sight.

Quicksand! She had heard about it before. It engulfed any animal or human foolish enough to step onto it, slowly sucking them under to a ghastly death. Panic spurted through her and she started screaming, calling for Jack. Where was he? He had to get back in time. If he didn't it wouldn't matter what decision he had come to—she would be dead!

Angela went down faster when she struggled so she tried to stay calm and still, but it was beyond her endurance. Reaching out, she grasped the blackberry bush, crying out as the long sharp thorns cut into her hands. Still she tried to ignore the jabbing needles, pulling with all her strength, but they gave way under her weight and she only succeeded in tearing the soft flesh of her palms.

Tears streamed down her cheeks, gushing from her eyes in pain and frustration, and she wiped them away leaving blood smears on her face. Her heart was pounding, threatening to burst in her chest as the cold, wet fingers of death tugged insidiously at her knees. It was winning—slowly, ever so slowly—drawing her down into the earth.

A cold sweat broke out all over her and as she continued shouting for help she went through differing stages of choking terror and icy calm. Every sensation was intensified, and Angela was acutely aware of the singing birds, the sharp breath of fall, and the ever changing colors of the sunset against a turquoise sky.

"I don't want to die!"

She had so much to live for, so much to do—this couldn't be the end. Without her Lorna would be an orphan with no memory of her, and the thought of never seeing her daughter again filled her with anguish.

Fear grasped Angela in a lover's embrace as the sands reached her waist, crushing and sucking, stronger than before. She was in a nightmare, a living hell where the only reality was imminent death. The half of her that was under the sand felt as cold and lifeless as the grave.

"Jack! Jack!" she screamed and the hysteria engulfed her. "Keith! Jack! Help me—please! Scott! Scott! Scott!"

Jack appeared out of the trees as the sand reached her arm pits. Stopping abruptly he took in the situation with a glance. It was a miracle he was in time! He had heard her screams even before he had landed the boat and had never moved so fast in his life.

Taking off his thick leather belt, he lay flat on the ground and inched his way toward Angela, testing the surface as he went. When he was close enough he cast one end toward her and Angela reached out, eagerly grabbing it. She winced in pain as her bloody hands closed tightly around the leather, the only solid thing in her now precarious world. Jack pulled with all his might but the belt slipped from her grasp.

"It's not going to work. Angela," his voice was dead calm, "don't move. I'll be back in two minutes. Keep your arms free and don't move!"

"Jack," she cried as he left, "don't leave me! Come back!" All hope went with him but his instructions must have sunk into her mind for she remained still, resting her aching arms on her head to keep them from the quicksand.

Jack was back in just moments but it seemed like hours to Angela in that deathlike grip. He had a long stout rope with a large loop at one end, and as he threw it toward her she noticed how white his face was and how his eyes glowed with a terrible urgency. It took several throws before the rope fell close enough for her to reach.

"Put it over your head and under your arms and hold on."

She obeyed his order. Each movement was agonizingly slow. The loop closed around her, bruising her as it became taut. Jack ran the rope around a tree and then pulled steadily with all his strength. Slowly Angela began moving, but the quicksand didn't want to give up its victim easily. Finally with a loud, obscene, sucking sound it released her and she was caught up in Jack's strong arms pale and half fainting from the ordeal.

He carried her back to the cabin, his face ashen with the thought of what would have happened if he had returned even a few minutes later. And it would be his fault if Angela was dead now. Laying her in front of the fire he stripped the wet, filthy clothes from her and rubbed her cold limbs briskly with a rough blanket.

Angela was in shock from the ordeal, unaware of what was happening except for the reassuring presence of Jack. It wasn't until he immersed her in a hot bath that the color started to return to her cheeks and her eyelids fluttered open. The heat soaked into her body but she still shivered uncontrollably, and he held her up with one arm while he washed her.

She was safe, being tended as gently as a child by this amazing man she had only known for a few weeks. But what did the short time of their acquaintance matter when her heart betrayed an alien buoyancy, an elation never before experienced? One day had been long enough to fall in love, one hour to recognize the unusual influence that emanated from Jack, touching everyone he met, especially her. He had saved her life, she couldn't let him go.

"My sweet little girl," he said, his voice cracking with emotion. "I should never have left you alone. You are too precious to lose, too beautiful to resist."

His pearl-gray eyes filled with indecision and an inner turmoil, caught helplessly in the deep-jeweled sparkle of hers. Angela smiled with her overflowing heart in her eyes, and all his carefully thought out plans vaporized, dissipating swiftly before the heat of her gaze.

"I was going to take you home tomorrow, Duchess. I

was going to run away from you and every danger you represent."

"But not now, Jack. Nothing can keep us apart—it was foreordained in ages past. We were meant to be in spite of every obstacle. We had to love no matter what the consequences."

"Yes, I knew it from the beginning—there is no help for us, no use resisting it. I am weak before the illogical beating of my own foolish heart."

The tips of his fingers traced over her body beneath the water, imparting a warmth of such quick intensity she couldn't keep the tremors from coursing through her. That old familiar burning returned, the sensual yearning so long denied, bursting forth with volcanic force, wiping out all thoughts of her recent brush with death. Jack smiled as he felt her respond, capturing her slippery breasts in his large hands and massaging them until Angela's hands caught his pressing them closer.

"Jack, Jack!" she whispered, her head falling limply against the rim of the barrel.

He kissed her cheek and then her inviting lips, and his mustache prickled against her mouth sending shivers of disquietude down her spine. Angela's wet arms went around his neck clinging tightly as Jack explored her body with lambent touches, all the more arousing because of his patience and the wish to prolong their pleasure.

"You taste of blackberries," he said, lifting her dripping from the improvised tub. "Whenever I think of them, I will think of you."

She was a vision of pink and white loveliness lying before the fireplace, and as he undressed he watched her loosen the knot of hair and shake her head sending blue-black, lashing curls dancing everywhere. Jack knelt beside her reverently touching her hair, tracing the line of her cheek, brow, and lips.

"I love you, Angela, in a way that amazes and frightens me. You are as lovely as the twilight, little one, and so delicate—you must stop me if I hurt you, for I would rather die than cause you any pain."

She touched his broad chest and smiled beguilingly up at him. "I am flesh and blood, Jack, and won't break if you make love to me. The time for waiting is past. I want you—all of you—without restraint!"

Angela's breasts rose and fell enticingly, timed to her ragged breathing, and his eyes darkened, drawn to the tiny puckered rosettes just begging to be plucked. It was beyond all endurance to withstand any more and his mouth lowered, fastening over one of the pouting breasts, tasting and feeling the fine-grained texture of her skin.

She arched up as flickering tongues of lightning played over her, and caught his great leonine head closer, moaning as her fingers tangled in his hair. Every touch made her wild blood sizzle and boil, astonishing Jack with the ferocity of her reciprocation. His very gentleness drove her to acts of passionate rashness that in turn stirred him with a rapture beyond believing.

"Now, Jack—now!"

She was radiant with the glow of joy, reaching out to bring him to her. And when his flaming flesh touched hers he paused, trembling on the brink of a discovery that would leave both of them forever changed.

A small voice in the back of his mind mocked him, whispering that this was one more act in a strange chain of events that would be his downfall. The warning could be ignored, but not Angela, and he stilled the voice. Every man should have such a glorious defeat!

Angela's frenzy was not to be denied and their coalition was slow and profoundly tender as she accommodated him eagerly. Only then did she drive him past all control, past all thoughts of her fragility, and the incalescent movements overpowered her, sweeping her along with the force of a hurricane. She was helpless —drowning, soaring, dying in the cataclysm of desire, the ecstasy of bursting lights, roaring winds, and the tempest that shook her to the very core.

Every latent emotion had been laid bare, shared with the total committment of their bodies and hearts. Jack cradled her against his shoulder as the tumult vanished slowly, admitting silently to himself that no other woman had ever loved him so well. Kissing her moist mouth he marveled at the savagery of her lovemaking, wondering if she was always so intense. There would be time to find out, to explore this mysterious relationship further, for how could he return her to her home after this? They must at least have a short time together.

"Are you happy, little girl? I am. To love you and then die would not be too great a price to pay."

"Jack, Jack," Angela murmured drowsily, smoothing down his rumpled hair. "You are so good for me, so very good! What will I ever do without you? I never want this to end!"

"Shh," he whispered in her ear, tightening his arms about her. "Don't talk of endings—think of now, of the wonderful beginning we have just had!"

The end began three weeks later when Jack told her with a pained expression on his face that the ransom had been raised and the exchange was to take place in a few days. Angela's eyes were bright with unshed tears as she absorbed this new information. She had known their time together would be brief, but not this short.

Their relationship was a wonder to her, affectionate and warm with a devotion only Jack could have brought. He was a considerate lover and gentle friend, stilling her unvoiced fears that no one could ever replace Scott as a lover. They were two different men with different methods but the end was the same—that wild, mindless forgetfulness where nothing but pleasurable sensations existed.

But Jack was much more than Scott had been because they loved each other, and his only concern was for her happiness. In comparing them, the superficial affair with Scott paled to insignificance and faded with time.

"We could still see each other sometime, after this is over," Angela suggested hopefully. "I could open the house in London and—"

"No!" he shouted and she looked at him with wide hurt eyes. "I'm sorry, Duchess—I shouldn't have yelled at you. I was just giving way to my own disappointment. Don't you think our parting will be just as difficult for me? Do you think I want our affair to end now when I am just discovering—" He didn't finish, shaking his head and clasping her tightly to him. "The money means nothing now—nothing! I would give it all for one hour with you. Oh, my sweet little girl—how can I bear to let you go?"

They made love with a desperation born of sorrow and loss—the loss of a rare and precious time that would never be repeated. And their passion was all the sweeter for the knowledge that this magnificent madness must end. The world had stopped briefly for them and allowed them a respite but would wait no longer. Time was flowing on and they were caught inexorably in its clutches, being torn from each other's arms by a power greater than their love.

Jack held her as sobs racked her body, trying to comfort her and stem the outpouring of grief. "Shh, little one—crying won't help. It can't change what must be."

Kissing her salt-wet lips Jack distracted her, and Angela began kissing him back, half laughing, half sobbing as he whispered outrageous endearments against her mouth. Pulling slightly away, he looked down at her, running one finger lightly over the tips of her tear-spangled lashes.

"That's better," smiled Jack, kissing each dimpled cheek. "I like it when you're happy—when you laugh. Let's make all our time together count now."

"Just tell me why—why we can't continue afterwards as we are now."

"I have a wife and family to return to, and you are married with a daughter of your own. Surely you can understand that. We both have obligations to fulfill."

"I don't care—"

"I love my wife, Duchess, and I will not have her hurt." His eyes were dark and serious as he continued, "I have never betrayed Amy before and I won't do it again. She must never find out about this—or you. If we see one another in London and continue our liaison she will suspect something, and that will never do."

"But you love me!" Angela insisted, reassured by his tender smile and the soft brush of his mustache against her breasts.

"Yes—that I can't deny, any more than I can deny that the sun will rise in the morning. But we have to be realistic—I can live without you but not without Amy. She is my wife, the mother of my children, and we have lived together for twenty-three years." Jack sighed as if a great weight had suddenly descended upon him. "I love you both and have to choose between you. The decision is easy—the only logical one to make, but the telling is hard. See, you are starting to cry again."

"I'm sorry," Angela said forcing back the tears and putting her hands over her face. "I am not as strong as you think I am—I can be hurt too!"

"I know, love, I know. But be brave—for me. When we leave here it will be over—forever, for good. We will not meet in London or anywhere else. We will never meet again."

Jack buried his face in her sweet-smelling hair, hating himself for causing her such pain. "It would be harder to keep on seeing each other. This way it will be a clean break with no regrets. Each of us will go our own separate way, but there will always be the memories and our love. No one can destroy what we have had and I will never forget you no matter how hard I try. I love you, Angela, and always will—in a secret corner of my heart that will always be filled with joy and laughter and you!"

Chapter Nine

It had rained all night, a cold stinging downpour not fit for man or beast to be abroad in. But six boats glided silently through the gray predawn gloom, crimson-coated soldiers huddled miserably against the chill. They perked up as their final objective came into sight—a small, tree-obscured island floating wretchedly on forbidding waters.

Keith pulled his pistols from beneath his coat, carefully checking them in the pale glimmer of light just becoming visible on the horizon. This trip was the culmination of five frantic weeks of planning and mental anguish to get Angela back. Half-maddened by the thought of her hurt or dead, he had worked day and night to raise the price of her release, vowing to kill the man that had taken her.

The fortune he had offered for information leading to her discovery had done the trick, and Sam Newton, Gentleman Jack's foster brother, turned to him with an expectant grin. Any amount would be worth getting Angela back.

The boat touched the shore and Keith leaped out, running along the ill-defined path in the pale morning light. He heard a furious grunt from Captain Latham for disobeying the order to keep well behind the dragoons, but the cold, gut-churning anger that had resided in him all night suddenly blazed red-hot, knocking every thought of caution from his mind.

Oblivious to the danger to himself he kicked open the door of the pitiful shack and entered it, a pistol in each hand. What a hovel! How could Angela have endured such squalor for so long? Keith's quick glance found the barely covered doorway and a kitten rubbed against his leg. Impatiently he shoved it away, every nerve and fiber of his body straining toward one end.

Angela was jerked out of a sound sleep by a loud crash to find Jack already on his feet grabbing for his pistol. Their eyes met and held for an endless moment of eternity, his gray ones calm with total acceptance of whatever was about to come. She started to rise up and go to him, but one gesture stilled her instinctive response, and she huddled on the bed as the tattered blanket moved and Keith appeared in the doorway.

An instantaneous flash of brilliant light and a simultaneous roar filled the tiny room, gone as swiftly as lightning. Jack staggered, streaked with blood and the pistol fell from his suddenly nerveless fingers. Angela screamed as his blood gushed in a crimson river from a gaping wound in his shoulder.

"Now," Keith growled between clenched teeth, leveling the other pistol at Jack's heart. "I'm going to finish you off—you bastard!"

In one instant Angela was between them shielding Jack with her own small body. Her back was pressed against him and she felt the sticky warmth of blood and the strength slowly seeping from his powerful frame.

"Put it down, Keith, unless you mean to shoot me first." Angela's mind worked frantically. How in the world had he found them? Surely Keith couldn't be alone. As soon as the thought entered her mind the soldiers appeared, crowding into the doorway behind Keith.

"Damn you, man—I told you to wait!" Captain Latham's jaw dropped at the sight before his unbelieving eyes. For there against the wall was a naked, black-haired gypsy, magnificent in her fury, all blazing eyes and claws, defending an equally unclad giant dripping with blood. That couldn't be the Duchess of Brightling —it was impossible!

"Take him!" Keith motioned to Jack and two dragoons piled into the room intent on capturing the highwayman.

The room was crowded and dark, and in the ensuing

confusion Angela swept Jack's pistol up from the floor, pointing it straight at the captain's head.

"Stop!" she ordered in a loud, calm voice. "One more step and I'll blow the captain's head off." She couldn't help smiling at the look of shock on all their faces. "Now I want everyone to drop their pistols slowly, and very carefully back out of the room."

They did as the madwoman said, positive she would not hesitate to fulfill her threat. Captain Latham stood stock still with an ashen face, his breathing ragged as he stared down the barrel of her perfectly aimed weapon. What was going on? He had counted on every unexpected angle but this and now he was going to die.

Keith stood solidly where he was, staring at the perfect embodiment of all his dreams come to life. Her breasts thrust between inky locks of gleaming hair, quivering with her inner turmoil, and his eyes were drawn down to her slender waist and flat belly that gave no evidence of her ever carrying a child. Sylphlike in aspect, he knew the strength that resided within her, and when her eyes flashed at him, motioning him to leave, he hesitated.

"Get out, Keith—now!"

"Hell, Angela," he exploded, "are you crazy? What has he done to you? I've come to rescue you from—"

"From what?" she taunted angrily. "A fate worse than death? As you can see I don't need rescuing. I'm perfectly able to take care of myself—so go play your knight in shining armor games with someone else! I'm sick and tired of people interfering in my life—get out and leave us alone!"

"Duchess, the game is up," Jack whispered. "You have one shot and as soon as you pull the trigger they will take us. There's no way out of this for me, but I won't see you hang alongside me!"

Jack grabbed at the pistol and the shot went wild, energizing the frozen scene to life. Chaos ensued as soldiers poured into the room and Angela clutched at Jack, crying and attacking anyone that came within reach. It took three men to drag them apart, and she bloodied them with her nails and teeth before Captain Latham shoved her at Keith.

"Do something with her!" the captain shouted, his hand over the deep furrows she had clawed down his cheek.

The slap exploded through her head stinging her into awareness that they were alone in the hut. She touched her numb cheek cognizant only of the fact that Jack was gone and wounded, needing her more than ever.

"Angela, Angela, what has gotten into you? I can't understand why you acted like that. What hold does that man have over you?" Keith was pale and shaken, looking at the cruel mark on her face. "I have never struck a woman before in my life! Lord, what you do to me! You manage to bring out all of my worst qualities."

Tears seeped from beneath her lashes, enraging him because they were for another man. Losing all control, Keith kissed her hard and passionately, trying to wipe out all the other kisses she had willingly given to Jack. They struggled silently and he slammed her against the wall, pressing against her so tightly that her breasts flattened against his chest, cruelly imprinted with the buttons on his coat.

She couldn't breathe, couldn't fight him anymore, and she sobbed as he ravished her mouth, bruising the lips that only hours ago had been glued to Jack's. They would kill him, he had known it even as they had struggled with the pistol. They would hang him in London before a holiday crowd of thousands of people eager to see Gentleman Jack dance at the end of a rope.

"See what you do to me!" Keith said, thrusting away from her, running his hands over his face. "I'm sorry, Angela—I'm sorry."

"Get out, son of a bitch! I want to get dressed and go with Jack!"

He winced at her words but made no move to leave. With jerky movements Angela crossed the room and snatched up her dress holding it in front of her, shielding herself from his roving eyes. Finally he turned and went to stand just beyond the blanket, hearing her swift toilette and the whisper of clothes as she shut that lovely body away from his view.

She was pale with all the fire gone out of her when she confronted Keith. "I won't testify against him, so you might as well let him go."

"You will be summoned before the court and will have to swear to tell the truth," Keith replied sternly. "Besides even if he isn't convicted for your abduction, Gentleman Jack is wanted for various other crimes. I'll even get a forty-pound reward for capturing a highwayman, which I can deduct from the two thousand I offered to find you!"

"Do you mean to tell me that someone is collecting that reward—someone led you here?" Angela was incredulous, some of the spirit returning to her again.

"Yes. There's no other way I could have found you in this godforsaken place."

"Who?" Her voice was venomous, and Keith didn't like the look in her eyes.

"His name is Samuel Newton, Gentleman Jack's foster brother."

"The traitor!" She stamped her foot in rage. "Where is he? I'll kill him!"

Angela pushed her way past him, stopping short just outside. A few dragoons sat wearily beneath the trees, waiting for them, but the rest had gone and Jack was nowhere in sight.

"Why. . .everyone is gone," she murmured dejectedly. "Where is Jack—where have they taken him?"

"To the boats, Angela. Why don't you get your things together so we can get out of this dump?"

She had nothing to gather except for a frightened Pandora that hissed at Keith before Angela popped her into a basket. One last time she looked around, and the cabin was dismal and empty without Jack's presence. In a few days it would look exactly the way it had on their arrival, but in her memory it would remain a bright and shining place, filled with love and a magical aura of tranquility.

Jack was only half-conscious, lying in one of the boats, but Captain Latham wouldn't let Angela travel with him for fear of another outburst. The clumsy bandage was scarlet and she longed to change it, to cradle his head on her lap on the long journey home. But Keith forced her into another boat, where she sat stiff-backed, gazing longingly at the boat behind theirs.

He was sitting halfway up, slumped against the side of the boat, and she leaned toward him, reaching out a hand as if to touch him. Teeth flashed beneath his moustache in a grimace of a smile, and Keith snatched her back into the boat before she fell into the water. Soon he would have a doctor, the best of care, and Angela shook off the hands of the man that had shot him.

There were lackeys and more soldiers waiting on the shore, horses and a carriage from the castle. The carriage was for her use but she insisted that Jack be transported in it, and Captain Latham gave in to the haughty, determined woman that was a far cry from the shrew that had scarred his face. She even looked different with her white face and subdued nature and her hair pulled back away from her face. But when she insisted on a few minutes alone with the prisoner and he denied the request, her aquamarine eyes flashed dangerously, and he took a quick step back.

"Two minutes—no longer," Captain Latham relented, and she disappeared from his sight before he could blink.

"Jack, Jack," Angela called, putting her hand on his cold, wan face.

Her lips touched his briefly, breathing warmth into him and his pewter-gray eyes opened slowly, wearily. They didn't speak as she removed the soaked bandage and bound the wound tightly with hastily torn strips of her petticoat. Above all else she couldn't let him bleed to death on his way back to London.

The two minutes had passed and still Captain Latham had made no attempt to interrupt their privacy in the seclusion of the carriage. Angela made him drink some wine from the hamper of food Keith had ordered brought, and a little color returned to Jack's face.

"My little girl," he said, his breathing labored, touching the soft oval of her face. "You are so good, Angela, so sweet."

"Don't talk—save your strength," she admonished, covering him with every blanket she could find. "Everything will be all right. I will find the best barristers in all of England to defend you—doctors to tend your wound. In a few months you will be well and free with. . ." she choked on her own words, "with Amy. Close your eyes, Jack—sleep."

"I love you, Duchess," he sighed, giving way to the darkness descending upon him. "Never forget. . ."

"No, no! I will never forget, my love—how could I?"

The door opened and it was Keith sent in the captain's stead. "It's time to go, Angela. You have had fifteen minutes instead of two—they have to take him now."

He stiffened as she kissed the highwayman's cheeks and lips, and his hand was cold as he helped her from the vehicle. She had given Jack what he had so long denied himself—her supple body, and he cursed himself for not taking advantage of her and accepting what she had so charmingly offered on several occasions. But Keith had been holding out for the ultimate prize—her love—and it seemed that she had not withheld that either, from a criminal deserving only of death.

They continued back to Brightling Castle unescorted, and every time Keith nudged his horse close to hers to question her, Angela cut him short and tried to ignore the reproachful looks he gave her. Before they reached the castle he forced his horse to a standstill; her sapphire eyes narrowed belligerently.

"We have to talk now, before you get home and lock me out of your life!" She looked at the ground with stormy eyes, and Keith took her chin in his hand, forcing her to face his resentment. "Tell me about it."

"I owe you no explanation," she said obstinately, pushing his hand away. "The subject is private and closed!"

"You do owe me an explanation and will give it here and now!" Keith dismounted, not relinquishing his hold on her reins and forcibly dragged her from her mount. "I risked my life to rescue you—spent a small fortune to get you back!"

"I will reimburse you."

"It's not that!" he shouted, exasperated by her lack of feeling.

"What then? Tell me and get it over with! I want to go home."

Keith's fingers dug into her shoulders and he shook her like an obtuse child, trying to waken Angela from the depression that had settled over her like a cloud.

"I love you! How did I know you didn't want to be set free from your—captor? The ransom note demanded money, or else. . .oh, lord! They would start sending pieces of you—a finger, an eye, a breast—to prove they were serious." Keith's face was drawn with the horror of remembered threats but still he continued, "I had to find you—I couldn't eat or sleep or think of anything but you—alone and hurt, of them mutilating your beautiful body!"

"Keith. . .I didn't know. . ."

He had shocked her. So that was why Jack hadn't let her see the note, telling her it would be better if she didn't read it. "But Jack would never have hurt me—it was an empty threat, a lie."

This new twist to the adventure showed Keith in a different light, wanting only her safety. She had been thinking only of herself and Jack, ignoring all day the feelings of others—Keith, Jane, her parents—they must have been frantic. Everything he was saying was true, and she owed him the truth, no matter how much it hurt him.

"Then," Keith accused, continuing his tirade, "I found you in bed with. . .with. . .your lover! And you tried to protect him—you fought like a wildcat for him. Why? I don't understand anything. Why, Angela?"

She looked up at him with star-bright eyes and said through quivering lips, "I love Jack. I don't know how or when it happened but—"

"You can't! I won't let you!"

She had never seen Keith so angry, not even when he had shot Jack. It had been a mistake to tell him, even though he had guessed it already. But putting it into words had only incensed him further, and Angela had an ominous feeling in the pit of her stomach that Keith would make her pay for those words.

Jealousy and rage churned in Keith, making him want to punish Angela for the torment she was heaping upon him. There was no rational thought in his head as he grabbed a handful of her onyx curls and let the furious emotions boil to the surface. It was a few short steps to the woods and he jerked Angela's head back and ground his mouth down on hers, purposely bruising her treacherous lips.

This time she was limp in his arms, unresisting but for an unsuppressible moan that maddened him even more. Pushing her away from him so suddenly that she almost fell, Keith caught the top of her bodice, ripping it down to the waist.

"Fight me, damn you! What's the matter with you?"

Angela's swollen mouth trembled uncontrollably and she caught her bottom lip between her teeth. A hard hand closed over her breast and she winced as Keith squeezed it viciously. He wanted her to fight so he could humiliate and subjugate her, but she refused to play his game.

Looking steadily into his glazed blue eyes, she shook her head vigorously. "I've had enough fighting and violence to last me a lifetime! I'm sick of resisting lust-crazed men—tired of being raped! Do what you want with me, Keith—you're stronger. I will only lose in the end anyway!"

He threw her to the ground with such force that she lost consciousness for a few seconds, but by then all the antagonism and brutality that had been unleashed in Keith was beyond stopping. Angela couldn't help screaming at his attack, as he tore into her body that Jack had loved so gently and so well.

It was over in minutes and she was angry and sad, pitying and detesting him at the same time. Cool, collected Keith Montgomery had finally lost all control, destroying his own exemplary code of behavior with unprecedented violence.

He raised his golden head, eyes full of regret and tears. "I'm sorry, Angela—so sorry! I don't know what. . .never meant to. . .please don't cry!"

She had always thought Keith rather unreachable and godlike but he had proved himself just as human as she. And what was she? In the same breath Scott had called her an angel and a slut, his love and his enemy; Jack had told her she was sweet and wild, a child-woman he could never get enough of; and Keith could only murmur that he was sorry—sorry he loved her, sorry he raped her. Was she that contradictory, that changeable? Ever since her marriage her behavior had been completely irrational, surprising even her.

Thoughts swirled crazily through her head. What did she want? That was the important thing. Love, a husband and family or independence, choosing her own lovers to suit her moods? At the moment she wanted only Jack but he was beyond her reach; Keith wanted her and had just had her body, but nothing else; Scott wanted to be the father of her children, but she hated him.

Life was so mixed up and complicated. She longed for the simplicity of earlier days.

It was wonderful to be back home again even though a part of Angela longed to be with Jack. Her parents had come from Italy as soon as Keith had notified them of her abduction and that had been a welcome surprise. But above everyone, she had missed Lorna the most and couldn't cuddle and hold her enough, marveling at how much she had grown in a few weeks.

She was walking now and into everything just as Angela had known she would be. The servants spoiled her, much to Molly's displeasure, and now Angela couldn't help coddling her daughter for just a little while to make up for her long absence. Children were such delights and she longed for another baby, knowing it was impossible.

Angela was settling back into domesticity very well, considering her unsettled thoughts. Jack was in London awaiting trial and she longed to fly to him, but what could she tell her parents? If she could only keep that one small detail of her abduction from them—that they had been lovers—she would be content. Perhaps when they returned to Italy in a few weeks the gossip that was sure to erupt during the trial would not get that far. She fervently hoped so for her mother's sake.

With a small knock on the door Molly swept into the bedroom with Angela's breakfast tray. "Milady, someone sent you a lovely surprise. Shall I bring it in now or later?"

"Now, Molly," she said, curious but remembering another surprise that tinged her pleasure with sadness.

"Mama, Mama!" Lorna ran into the room still dressed in her nightgown with Pandora under one arm. The kitten seemed perfectly contented to be dragged around by an adoring little girl and purred loudly in spite of its awkward position.

Relief lit up Lorna's small face as she saw Angela sitting in a chair sipping chocolate. She ran to her and Angela swept her onto her lap, kissing each deep dimple and smoothing down the wayward, dark curls so like her own.

"Oh, my baby," she whispered against her hair. "I'm so glad to be home with you again."

Her absence had affected Lorna adversely, and she woke up screaming for her mother in the night. Only Angela could soothe her back to sleep, rocking and singing until the turquoise eyes fluttered closed. And sometimes she sat there for hours holding her sleeping child as if she would never let her go.

"Stay, Mama—stay!" She threw her plump arms around Angela's neck pressing her face against her breast.

"My sweet little Lorna—I'll never leave you again. I

promise—nothing will ever separate us again!"

Molly returned with a large crystal vase of delicate pink roses.

"They are lovely," Angela said, "but who sent them?"

"This came with them, milady." Molly handed her the message, and after settling Lorna more comfortably on her lap she tore it open.

A brief glance at the end assured her it was from Keith and she hesitated, not wanting to even think about him. She didn't know how to react to him anymore, and the only sane thing to do would be to forgive him and put their relationship back where it had been before he had raped her.

Scanning the letter, she frowned at the ambiguity of one statement. He was sorry for raping her but glad he at last possessed her. Then her eyes found the other sentence: "I'm only sorry that I didn't pleasure you the way you pleasured me." She sniffed disdainfully, spilling some chocolate on the tray. He was just as conceited as every other man, even more so! As if he could cause her to betray the love she felt for Jack, given the time and opportunity—ridiculous!

She would set him straight, and the sooner the better. "Molly, order the carriage. Lorna and I are going to pay a call on Jane today." There was no need to mention Keith's name; she could see from Molly's smile that it was understood.

Angela dressed with care in one of her simplest gowns: peach-colored velvet trimmed with chocolate-brown braid. The neckline was extremely modest, and Molly did her hair in a simple chignon. But by the time she was ready to leave several tendrils of hair had pulled loose, framing her face charmingly. Irritated, she smoothed the curls back only to have them spring right back again.

Lorna looked like a doll in her ruffled white dress and blue sash. "Pretty," she observed, pirouetting before the mirror in Angela's room.

"I'm afraid you're vain already, my girl," laughed

Angela, tying the blue satin ribbon around her daughter's short curls. "Come, we're going to see Aunt Jane and Uncle Keith."

The day was lovely, bright and sunny with a crisp bite in the air that set Angela's blood racing. As they drove through the wind-whipped trees she wished she was three people, then she could go for a gallop on Pegasus, pay a call on Keith, and be with Jack in London all at the same time. She smiled at her indulgent fantasy and at Lorna.

Her reverie was interrupted as the carriage came to a halt before Bentwood, and even before they reached the door it was flung open and Jane rushed out all smiles. She hugged Angela, kissing her on both cheeks in an enthusiastic welcome.

"Oh, Angela, I'm so glad you're back again! I was going to call yesterday but I thought you would probably want some time alone with Lorna and your parents after your ordeal. You'll have to tell me about it—everything! Keith has been so distant and close-mouthed about your rescue—I could barely get one word out of him. Was it exciting? Were you scared? Just imagine being abducted by the most dashing, mysterious highwayman in England. Was he handsome? But I'm keeping you standing outside," Jane laughed, ushering them into the house with a nonstop stream of conversation.

"You don't know how worried we all were while you were gone. And Keith—I have never seen him in such a black mood. I had to tiptoe around the house for weeks for fear he would bite my head off if I even looked at him the wrong way! Lorna, how pretty you look—"

"Jane!" interrupted Angela, shaking her head and laughing at her friend's loquacity. "You never change."

"Is that bad?"

"No, you are wonderful and I wouldn't have you any other way. You're irrepressible!" Angela frowned at Lorna who was bouncing up and down on a thickly cushioned sofa, and she subsided with a little pout. "Besides, Jane, if you do all the talking then I won't have to answer any of your questions."

"But you must! Here I sit at home doing the same things every day while my best friend is off on an adventure—it would be cruel not to share such excitement."

"I'm afraid the whole world will soon know all about my—escapades," sighed Angela sobering at the thought. "Jane, what happened was very. . .improper. A lot of people are going to be in for a big shock."

"Not me. It couldn't be worse than. . ." she leaned closer and whispered with wide eyes, "Scott!"

"It could come close." She closed her eyes briefly, and a fleeting look of pain crossed her face.

Keith's unexpected arrival in the doorway precluded any more soul-searching questions and Angela felt a vast relief. Lorna squealed with delight and launched herself at the uncle she adored. He caught her up with undisguised pleasure, and as Angela watched the spontaneous affection, and saw Keith kiss her daughter, she knew that he loved her child as much as she did.

Keith should be Lorna's father instead of Scott, she told herself, and she looked at him so intently that he returned the look as if there was no one in the room but her. Angela blushed, she couldn't help it, as unbidden thoughts of the last time she had seen him rose to haunt her. How cruel he had been, yet, she had to admit, he had been goaded into it. Could she hold one mistake against him when at all other times he was the most polite and considerate of all the gentlemen she knew? They had been good friends before but could they ever be just friends again?

"Thank you for the roses," Angela managed to get out. "They were lovely, Keith."

"You are welcome," he replied, sitting down next to her with Lorna perched on his knee playing with his pocket watch. "But I'm sure they paled and wilted before your beauty."

The formal words belied his look and his blue eyes raked over her knowingly, remembering every firm line and soft curve of her exquisite body. Angela turned crimson with embarrassment and Jane glanced at her with an amused, knowing smile and uplifted eyebrows. She was nobody's fool!

Abruptly Angela stood up, breaking the pregnant silence and blurting out, "Jane, would you mind watching Lorna for a while? Keith and I have some—business to discuss."

"Of course not! You two run along—and take your time."

They didn't speak until they were alone in his study and then Angela turned to him, still prettily flushed from their silent encounter. "I won't have you looking at me like that any more! Jane has noticed that something is going on between us and I won't have it!" She stamped her foot with emphasis.

Keith just continued smiling, his eyes amused at her outburst. "So you haven't forgiven me yet. But there's nothing going on between us—how could there be after that unfortunate incident a few days ago? As for the way I look at you," he shrugged his shoulders, "I can't help it. I'm in love with you, sweetheart, and it shows. Everyone has been aware of it for years, including you, so why does it suddenly seem to irritate you?"

"Because things have changed. You seem to take it for granted that we will become lovers. I'm not a fool—I can read between the lines."

"But I take nothing for granted when it comes to you—I never have. Angela, Angela, I love you so much that it hurts. Can you understand that—have you ever felt that—" He broke off at the desperate look on her face, touched her cheek with a finger.

"Don't touch me!" she shouted, moving away from him. "I'm in love with someone else, and what happened Thursday can never be repeated. We can either go back to being friends—or nothing. The choice is yours."

"All right—whatever you want," Keith replied catching her by surprise. She had been ready for a long argument but he had given in almost too easily, and there was no time to analyze her feelings. "I'm willing to take as much or as little as you are willing to give me!"

The space between them closed and he caught her, tilting her face up for his kiss.

"I'll scream!"

"I don't think so."

Angela tried to twist from his grasp, opened her mouth to make good her threat but Keith's lips covered hers, clinging and moving insidiously. The hot rush of rage was not a far cry from passion, and her head fell back heavily against his arm as she was overpowered by his onslaught. Now, he was kissing her like a lover, not with the brutality of before, and every thought flew out of her head except for the first time he had kissed her, so long ago in the snow.

A slow hunger began and grew in spite of her desire to resist. And then she didn't want to resist at all, as her legs went weak and the ache began where he had ravished her before. She held him to her and met his thrusting tongue with her own, sweet and slippery with passion.

"No, no!" she moaned against his mouth, suddenly aware of, through all those layers of clothes, what the kiss was doing to Keith.

He released her and Angela flew to the French doors throwing them open to swallow the cold reviving air. The wind caressed her burning cheeks, and she put her hand to her bosom to try and still her heart and the panting tremors that gave her away.

An arm encircled her waist beneath her heaving breasts, and Keith pulled her back into the room. "I just wanted to prove a point to you, sweetheart. You can be as childlike as Lorna sometimes, not knowing what you want but underneath all those clothes you're a warm, loving, passionate woman. Don't try to run away from what you are or what you really feel like doing.

"I know you are confused right now and need time to think things through. Well, I'm willing to wait as long as you are—longer! I'll never stop loving or wanting you, but I will never take advantage of you again. I'll just be here—waiting—whenever you need me, my love!"

Keith moved away from her and she didn't realize he was gone until the wind slammed the door shut and she turned to find an empty room. Overnight he had changed, making new demands on her that Angela was unwilling to acknowledge. He was sure of himself once again and sure that eventually she would turn to him in desperation. Yet he could have taken her today, willingly, and she wouldn't have screamed. Perhaps he knew her better than she had suspected, but in any event she wouldn't underestimate Keith again.

A short ironic laugh escaped her. She had been going to clear the air and set things straight between them, putting their relationship neatly in a pigeonhole marked *friendship*. Things were even more unsettled now than they had been before.

Chapter Ten

The summons to appear at Jack's trial came, just as Keith had warned her it would, and Angela had no choice but to obey it. With her parents returning to Italy she ordered the London house opened, relieved that Nigel and Clarissa hadn't learned of the scandal already rocking the capital.

The first time she had seen one of the prints she had looked at it uncomprehendingly, for the woman pictured looked nothing like her. Only the long black hair was right, strategically covering certain portions of the anatomy. There were at least a dozen like that one, caricatures of her and Jack holding off the dragoons, and she was always gloriously naked, and he was liberally dripping with blood.

Then there were the broadsheets, articles, and chapbooks each claiming to tell the real story of The Duchess and The Highwayman. One of the more far-fetched claimed that she had known Jack for years and Lorna was the daughter of their longstanding love affair. The object of the abduction, they said, was to get money so they could elope, leave England, and start a new life together.

The libelous publicity infuriated Angela but there was nothing she could do but ignore it. Not only was she dishonoring the ancient Harrington name but now a shadow hung over Lorna's life as well. But she could not regret the halcyon days with Jack and she admitted to Jane that she was an unrepentant sinner, only sorry that she had been caught.

Keith and Jane were opening their townhouse for the duration of the trial, for moral support, Keith had said, but Angela knew differently. He wasn't about to let her out of his sight and miss his opportunity to become her lover. His friendly, waiting attitude grated on her nerves, as he stalked her as patiently as a hunter after some rare, exotic animal.

London swallowed up the luxuriously appointed coach they were traveling in, and Angela became just another person in the endless stream of people moving to and fro continually in the noisy, busy city. The buildings were suffocatingly close for one used to the spacious countryside, and they seemed about to topple in on Angela. She didn't particularly like large cities and hoped that the trial would be over soon so that she could go home.

Thoughts of Jack confined to a tiny, dirty cell in the midst of Newgate prison brought tears to her eyes. She had sent money for a doctor but had no idea of whether he had received it. Somehow Angela had to get him out, set him free, because a man like Jack didn't belong in a cage.

The coach clattered over the wet cobblestone streets and finally slowed, halting before an elegant house in St. James's Square. The doors were flung open, spilling cheerful light like golden puddles into the darkness of a rainy pre-winter dusk. Scrubbed, starched servants were lined up and stood rigidly at attention, awaiting Angela's inspection as she entered the main hall. She went through the interminable introductions and promptly forgot every name, glad when at last the housekeeper showed her to her rooms.

Angela shook her head in disgust at the opulent master suite. Everything was red; the carpet, draperies, and bed hangings, and the gilt rococo furnishings added the last touch of vulgarity. Compared to the rest of the elegant house this room was entirely out of taste. The heavy-handed, ornate treatment could only be a joke and she picked up a candle to inspect one of the paintings on the wall.

She almost dropped the candlestick in surprise, cheeks blushing as scarlet as the decor, as she discovered the theme of the bedroom. The main figure in the painting was Bacchus and surrounding him in silent revelry was a sylvan orgy, replete with satyrs and nymphs in imaginative, realistic poses. For a moment Angela stood rooted to the dreadful carpet, then slowly walked around the room examining the other paintings.

Every one of them was mythological and obscene with an excess of plump, pink and white flesh intertwined with explicit reality. But the painting on the ceiling surpassed all the others—Leda and Zeus, in the guise of a swan, done in life-sized proportions and executed with loving detail.

This was really unbelievable! The room was an erotic fantasy, designed to shock or titillate—or perhaps stir the flagging desires of an old roué with a very young, very beautiful new wife. That had to be it! The closer she looked the more she realized that the room was newly decorated.

Percy was disgusting! Of all the nerve! He had expected to bring her here and indulge in a sexual flight of fancy, and she wondered whether the lurid decor was for his benefit or hers.

"The filthy old lecher!" she said, shuddering with revulsion and flinging herself angrily onto the bed. "This is really too much! I'm glad he had a stroke, glad I was never here with him."

Someone moved above her and Angela stifled a scream, half sitting up, then she flopped back down weakly. It was only her own image reflected back at her in the mirror covering the whole ceiling above the bed. She hadn't seen it before because of the concealing canopy, and she stared at herself and the gigantic expanse of garish red velvet that she lay on.

This might have been her husband's dream world but the thought of them together in this bed was a nightmare. The one close encounter with him had been totally revolting and she pushed the memory aside, glad she didn't have to worry about his attentions anymore. Slowly Angela's lips curved into a smile, and laughter bubbled up out of her like a clear mountain spring. It was too, too funny—the thought of Percy, old, fat, and bald, posturing for her benefit beneath the mirror, as if

it could possibly arouse her or any other woman.
"The place looks like a whore house!" she observed.

The elegantly liveried footman glanced curiously out of the corner of his eye as the duchess went by. The rumor that their new mistress was slightly daft had made the rounds even before breakfast, and that, coupled with the notoriety of her liaison with the highwayman, made it hard not to stare. For one of the upstairs maids had reported, that upon struggling into the master suite with hot water for milady's bath, she had found her sprawled on the big bed giggling helplessly. And everyone had heard about that bed, that room!

Yet this morning she seemed sane enough, and beautiful enough to capture the heart of any man she turned her aquamarine eyes on, from king to chimney sweep. She was dressed richly but soberly in a dove gray, moire dress with exquisite handmade white lace at the cuffs and high neck. She seemed a bit preoccupied as her maid hurried after her with a dark cloak and she entered the coach.

Angela shivered as much from anticipation as from the chill in the air and she snuggled deeper into her fur-lined cloak dreading the task ahead of her. He had said they should never see each other again but she had to go. It was imperative that she find out if he was all right and well looked after. She had to arrange for legal counsel for his defense. If she didn't see Jack then she would have to seek out Amy, and that could only be a last resort.

Leaning her head back against the cushioned seat, Angela closed her shadowed eyes wearily. She had hardly slept well last night in the strange room with city noises outside and her own tumultuous thoughts inside. Her hands clutched tightly at the heavy leather purse concealed inside her muff, the gold to bribe her way in to see Jack. Would he be glad to see her or would he tell her to go? Was he well or sick? Did he still love her or had Amy recaptured all of his affections? There were so many questions needing answers and so much to do.

As the coach approached the great, gray hulk of Newgate, Angela pulled the hood of the cloak closer about her face, adjusting the veil that would shield her from any possible identification. All she needed now was for the gossipmongers to find out she had visited Jack. They would be off on fresh speculations dreaming up new plots and angles.

A damp chill enveloped Angela as she entered the horror that passed for a prison, unescorted. It was colder inside than out, and she pressed a scented handkerchief against her nose and mouth as the stench of unwashed bodies and centuries of sickness and death assailed her, threatening to make her retch.

The turnkey escorted her into a small room and she was surprised to find it crowded with ladies and gentlemen as finely dressed as herself. They were brilliantly colored butterflies, flitting against the gloom of the slimy stone walls. Entirely out of place, they chatted gaily, laughing and greeting one another as if at a party. They eyed the incognito new arrival with sly smiles, whispering behind waving handkerchiefs and bejeweled hands. There was a maliciousness to their scrutiny, and Angela shrank into a corner glad they couldn't see her face.

"Three and six pence, dearie."

An ugly, stocky man built like a wrestler was accosting her. She took a step back repelled by his battered appearance, at the shapeless lump of a nose flattened against his face and those colorless eyes, glinting evilly through puffy slits, quickly appraising her. He repeated the request in a harsh, guttural voice, and his brawny arm shot out toward her, palm up.

She jumped in surprise and for a moment thought that he might touch her and that made her feel sick and shaky.

"I want to see Jack Newton," she said, her voice quavering, threatening to crack.

"Aha! Another lady to see Gentleman Jack. 'E does make 'em drool, doesn't 'e? Like I said, sweetheart, that 'ill be three shillin's and six pence—everyone pays the same." He smiled at her confusion and she pressed the handkerchief tighter as his fetid breath polluted the air. "'Aven't been 'ere before, 'ave you, dearie? I can always tell. As soon as a few more swells pay I'll take everyone on a nice guided tour to see the gallow's bait."

She stared at him, transfixed as a horrible realization dawned on her, piercing her stunned mind. All these people were here for only one purpose—to see Jack. Like a circus or a freak show they all wanted a glimpse of the notorious highwayman, caught at last. It was barbaric—cruel! People gaping at him through prison bars, poking fun as if he was an animal.

Angela could sense the anticipation in them and felt like screaming at them all to get out and leave Jack in peace. Instead she bit her lip, suppressing an outburst that would accomplish nothing and might prove damaging not only to Jack but to herself.

"I got to make a livin', dearie, so pay up or get out." His words thudded her back to reality. "Can't take no charity cases!"

"I want to see him. . .alone."

"Well. . ." the turnkey hedged, scratching the sparse hair on his sweating skull. "Alone. . .that'll cost a bit more."

Inside the muff she grabbed a handful of coins and held them out for his inspection. A grin split his beefy face as he nodded, and she dropped the coins into his hand careful not to touch him.

"I want to see Jack Newton now, alone!"

"Yes, yer ladyship! Follow me."

Angela trailed after him through dark, narrow stone passageways lit fitfully by torches attached to the walls. Groans echoed down the corridors and she shivered as the dusty cobwebs, hanging like tattered lace curtains, swayed with their passage. Something large and furry darted in front of her and she stopped dead, stifling a scream.

"Ain't nothin' but a rat," he reassured her, kicking at the evil creature. It scurried off and he laughed. "Prisoners 'ere keep 'em as pets!"

It seemed like they had walked for hours going up and down steps, twisting and turning in every direction, when the turnkey finally stopped, fumbling at his belt for the keys. Angela tried to still her breathing and the hasty beating of her heart, composing her face into serene lines. It wouldn't do to upset Jack and above all she had to remain calm. The key turned in the lock and he flung open a heavy door.

"'Ave a nice visit," he laughed with devilish amusement as she went through the doorway.

She ripped aside the veil as the door banged shut and their eyes met across the space of the room, changing it, warming the air, lightening the gloomy cell. They reached out to each other only to be stopped by the solidity of bars. Angela's hands closed around them to support her trembling knees.

"Jack—oh, Jack!"

Tears stood in her huge eyes as she smiled up at his beloved face, paler from being wounded and imprisoned but just as bold and strong. Crystalline drops spilled at the rattle of chains, the sight of manacles even upon the arm in the sling.

"Duchess, my sweet little girl! Surely I'm dreaming!"

His hand reached through the bars, brushing back her hood, touching her hair, face, tears—like a blind man trying to see. Their mouths met and clung, sweetly scalding, and Angela could have melted through the bars at the soft brush of his mustache and the way his tongue engaged hers in an ardent joust. She was warmed by him, even as her heart broke with the knowledge that they would never be lovers again.

The kiss lasted breathless seconds, hours, and then he drew away, his slate-gray eyes filled with unknowable sadness. He smiled that flash of white teeth, self-assured, even jaunty in spite of his situation.

"You shouldn't have come, little one—but I'm so glad you did. Do you see how contradictory you make me?"

"And you do the same thing to me—more!" Angela reached out and touched him and he clasped her small hand in his. "Oh, Jack! Are you all right? Your wound, the bars and chains—it's awful!"

"I'm fine, my love—mending well thanks to the doctor you sent and I haven't had a chance to become bored. You should see all the illustrious visitors I've had. Fine ladies and gentlemen—"

"It's terrible, those sick people staring at you like. . . like sadistic monsters. I saw them out there waiting—"

"Shh! Don't be upset, Angela. That's the way things are around here. They come to see a famous rogue that has perhaps robbed one of them at some time. It's a diversion in their own empty lives and I feel sorry for those pitiful people because I have had so much."

"I would have come sooner but my parents were here—I couldn't let them find out what everyone else already knows." There was a pleading in her sparkling eyes, begging him to understand and she knew from the look of quiet understanding that he did and wanted no explanations.

"I've been worried about you, Duchess—all alone to face the gossip and the terrible lies that are spreading through the city."

"That part doesn't matter, Jack. It's you that matters, locked up in this dark dungeon. We have to get you out and that's why I came. I'll get the best counsel in England to defend you—and decent food. . .and a real bed."

Her hand tightened in his as he shook his head, and silver glints shone in his dark hair.

"Angela, I could never accept all that, your money—no! It's out of the question. I'll get by just fine—Amy and I have some money saved. . ."

"But not as much as you will need for this!" she said emphatically. "Your life is at stake. If you don't have the very best you could die! The thought of you hanging—"

"No!" Jack broke away from the bars, pacing angrily up and down the cell as far as the clinking chains would let him go.

"Damn your pride, Gentleman Jack! No one will

know—besides it's not as if you haven't taken money, and jewels from women before, and you did hold me for ransom. To me the difference is the same, no difference at all! You need my help and I can give it. If our positions were reversed I would accept your help!"

"Don't try and bully me, Lady Harrington!"

All the anger and haughtiness left Angela in a flood and her voice became soft and cajoling as only a woman sure of her man's love can request her own way. "Then do it for me, my dearest—because I love you." She had his undivided attention now, saw the softening effect of her words and pressed home the advantage. "Shall I beg you, Jack—get down on my knees and—"

"No! Never on your knees, not you, not for any man!"

Jack grabbed her, pulling her up against the bars, devouring her mouth with kisses of such wild insistence she would have endured imprisonment and torture if she could be with him. With a groan of frustration he wrenched his lips free of hers, banging angrily against the bars.

"If it wasn't for these damned bars," Jack growled with a pained scowl on his face, "we wouldn't be talking at all."

Angela's lips hurt with the loss of the delicious pressure of his but she managed a weak, somewhat reassuring smile. "I still have some gold left. Should I see if the turnkey can be bribed further? Do you think he could be induced to let me share your prison for an hour?"

"Yes, and he would probably parade fifty people through here to see the show—"

"Imagine what the print makers would do with that juicy scene!" She couldn't help laughing, in spite of her concupiscent yearnings, and Jack joined her, the air between them clearing of quarrels.

"How can I not give in to you, Angela? You always get your way. You cry or laugh and wrap me around your finger. But promise me one thing—"

"Anything!" she cried straining against the ever-present bars.

"First, you won't come to see me again. Second, you won't see or talk to Amy. She's been through enough hell in the past few weeks to last a lifetime. I'm only grateful that she's a strong woman—and that she still loves me."

"Yes to the second, but—" Angela wavered.

"I don't want you to come again, little girl. Don't you see how bad it is for us both?" A moment before he had been vibrating with passion, now there was only resignation written on his face. "Make your arrangements for barristers and whatever else you want. If you must communicate with me, send a note but please don't come again!"

"But—"

"You must do as I say, Duchess, for your own good and mine. I love my wife and I can't hurt her anymore. She knows all about us—"

"Surely not everything, Jack!"

"Almost everything. But if she finds we have been seeing each other—" He let the sentence dangle, unsure himself of what would happen. "What we had was wonderful while it lasted, but it's over now. Hide it away in a dark corner of your heart and someday it will be as brittle and faded as a pressed flower."

"No—I love you—now, always!"

"Not always, Angela—just for a few fleeting weeks. You were infatuated, fascinated by something new and different, by love itself. Don't try and fool yourself."

She was wounded and mystified by his sudden rejection and he saw it on her face but couldn't stop. He had to cut her free, let her go, though he longed only to clasp her tighter. Angela had her own life to live and only by hurting her now with a swift sharp stroke could he release her from the useless dead weight of his love. It was almost like learning to let go of a child, but much more difficult.

"I think you are already in love with another man but just won't face up to it. With me you felt safe because you knew it had to end, but with him you felt threatened in some way. At first I thought it was Keith Montgomery, but now—"

"Shut up! I don't know what you are talking about!" Angela leaned her forehead wearily against the bars, bereft of all vitality. She trembled, wanting to close her ears against Jack's sudden accusations.

"I'm talking about Scott!" Jack said evenly.

"Scott!" Just the hated name revived her fury. The color mounted in her cheeks and her eyes were flames of shooting rage. "How in the world—" She hadn't told Jack about that, never even mouthed his name.

"The name you whispered in your sleep and when I held you in my arms—the man you screamed for, to rescue you from death. . ."

"No, no! I hate him!"

"Who is he, Duchess? Who is Scott?"

She had moved away from Jack, trying to escape from the words that would not stop. The outer door was against her back and Angela shook all over, pressing herself against the wood. There were voices outside, the rattle of keys, high-pitched laughter and in a moment the tour would begin.

"Who is Scott?"

Her tear-filled aqua eyes couldn't look away from the gray ones, couldn't fathom why he was doing this to her. Trying to speak, she couldn't and after several attempts Angela found her voice.

"A smuggler. My taste seems to run to criminals."

Every person in London seemed to be packed into the courtroom and a thousand more milled around outside. Angela adjusted her bonnet and took Keith's hand, descending from the carriage into a scene of unrestrained turmoil. Every eye was on her as they made their way through the press and into the courtroom.

Tiers of galleries rose on three sides of the room, newly erected, and packed with the people who had been trying for weeks to get tickets to the most highly publicized event of the year. Jack Newton, known highwayman, accused abductor of the Duchess of Brightling, was worth getting up at four in the morning to see.

Silks, satins, and velvets vied with rough homespun as they sat shoulder to shoulder, and the movement was continual. They laughed, talked, and waved to one another, eating and yawning behind waving lace handkerchiefs. Girls with baskets of fruit and pastries did a booming business and added to the carnival-like atmosphere.

The gossip and rumors had come to a boil during the past months, fueled by the newspapers, ballads, poems, and broadsheets eagerly digested by everyone from scullery maids to the highest peers in the land. Every man, woman, and child in the city knew who Lady Harrington was, and industrious, money-hungry imaginations played the situation for all it was worth, commemorating the fictionalized events in print until they bore no resemblance to reality.

Angela sat quietly between Jane and Keith studying her tightly clasped, gloved hands, trying to ignore the blatant stares. Her cheeks were crimson at the crude remarks and catcalls they had shouted as she had made her way through the crowds, and her stomach was full of fluttering butterflies. This was a million times worse than the scene at the prison, for at least there she had been disguised. She felt as if she were on trial alongside Jack, and this was just the first day.

Keith's face was a polite mask of forced impassivity, but a muscle twitching in his cheek betrayed him. They had argued violently last night over whether he should accompany her, Angela insisting on going alone. But he had been just as insistent and now she was glad she had lost, for he was as solid as a rock, supporting her and getting her through the mob in one piece. He could always be depended upon to do what was best for her, her safety and happiness always paramount in his mind.

She touched his hand and he glanced at her with sharp sapphire eyes. "I'm glad you came with me, Keith," she confessed. "Thank you for believing in me—no one else seems to."

The frozen silence and wall of transparent ice that had been between them cracked, shattered into tiny melting pieces as if it had never existed. He managed a stiff smile filled with acute longing, and he squeezed Angela's hand reassuringly. With surprise she snatched it away and sat stiffly, staring straight ahead in shock.

Keith truly loved her with his whole body and soul, and it struck home for the first time today. His was not a physical love like Scott's or even the idealistic love she had known with Jack—it was total, completely undivided, focused only on her with an all-consuming loyalty that scared her. It didn't matter that she had had an affair with Jack or that she was infamous in the eyes of the world. And if he knew about Scott and the fact that Lorna was illegitimate, that would also mean nothing. Knowing the worst about her he still wanted her, waiting patiently in the backgrouind, not rushing her—except for that one very human slip. If she were the lowest prostitute in the city's gutters he would still love her.

All along, without consciously knowing it, Angela had exploited his love, turning to him for friendship or only when she required him, ignoring him when it suited her mood. What a totally selfish creature she had been, caught up in her own problems to the exclusion of Keith's, wiping her muddied feet on the spotless carpet of his feelings. In her own way she had treated him the way Scott had treated her, casually and with no regard.

Another stir went through the audience, distracting Angela's attention from her own troublesome musings, and she stiffened as the barristers she had hired for Jack's defense took their places. They were not the disturbing element, it was the woman with them, Amy Newton. Nothing missed Angela's attention as she studied her rival covertly from under lowered lashes, twisting the cord on her reticule beyond recognition.

She was a tall, voluptuous blond that had kept her figure in spite of bearing six children. Dark brown eyes sparkling with vitality met Angela's and stopped, examining her with no hostility but a lively curiosity. Amy smiled very briefly, very slightly, with a mouth too wide for classical beauty but blending charmingly with the dignity and grace of her countenance. With a quick inclination of her head she acknowledged Angela and then sat down, but still suspended in the air between them was that unmistakable look.

Pity! Amy Newton pitied her, and Angela had all she could do to keep from bursting into tears. How strong and confident she must be to be able to dismiss her so lightly, as a rival of little consequence. How sure Amy must be of Jack's love and devotion, sure that he would never leave her for another woman. And she was right. The fling had been short-lived and she had her husband back while Angela was deserted—pity because the duchess who had everything in the world could not have love.

Now Amy had another battle to fight and a more formidable opponent—the law courts. But she was determined that after all they had been through she would win him back from the very shadow of the hangman's noose, knowing without a doubt that she could not lose him now. After twenty-three years together their lives had just begun and she loved him more now, in spite of his transgressions, than she ever had before.

Everyone scrambled for a look as the prisoner was brought in chained between two guards. Angela's eyes devoured Jack, making up for the months since that brief terrible visit in his cell when he had been brutally honest with her. At least her bribes had been successful, he was healthy and well dressed, as big as ever with his leonine head shining with even more silver than she could remember.

Jack didn't look at her, only Amy, smiling with a quirk of his mustache that shattered Angela's heart into fragments. So he really did love his wife, more than he loved her, and she closed her eyes against the knowledge, against the looks flowing between them. Pain was the only thing making her believe that this wasn't a nightmare, and she bit the inside of her cheek to keep herself from breaking down, for there were people watching her, just waiting for any sign of emotional fireworks.

Jane touched her arm as the judge entered the room black robed, white wigged, and everyone rose as the court was called to order. There was relative silence now as everyone listened to the proceedings but the day dragged on and on through complicated legal technicalities, just a prelude to all the excitement the people in the galleries waited for.

Early winter dusk was falling as they left the courtroom, and Angela's head pounded with a fierce headache from her concentration on the trial. Jane had left earlier so she and Keith returned alone, blessedly cut off from prying eyes inside the carriage. As they were whisked away he turned to her, concerned over her strained white face.

"Are you all right, Angela?"

"It's just a headache—I'll be fine in the morning. Keith. . ." Her voice changed and she looked up at him with a look he had never seen before. "I'm sorry!"

"For what?"

But Angela wouldn't say, and unexpectedly she slipped her arm through his, interlacing their fingers, and laid her head wearily on his shoulder. She felt his involuntary reaction, as if she had burned him, but then he relaxed, gazing silently out the window at the street lamps being lit, her head a wonderfully light burden on his shoulder.

"Did you hear what they were saying?" she asked sometime later when he was sure she was asleep.

"Who?"

"All those people. They think you are my latest lover—why one man was laying bets on it!"

Keith sniffed. "I wouldn't bet on it myself—the odds are against it." Then gently, "Don't listen to anything they say—bunch of scandalmongers! I'm afraid it's going to get a lot worse before it gets better."

"Yes," said Angela, snuggling closer to him in the dark, "but it's not so bad when you are with me."

Keith tried to see her face but only the top of her head was visible. What change had come over her today? There was something new that he couldn't quite comprehend, but the odds seemed to be improving and he smiled secretly, his pulse leaping at the thought.

Angela went directly to the master suite; she still couldn't think of it as her room but didn't feel like going through the trouble of moving while she was so preoccupied. At least it was warm with a cheery fire and a steaming bath awaiting her return. Even though she hadn't eaten all day the dinner tray looked unappetizing and the very thought of eating was repulsive. So she soaked in the tub, letting herself drift, and the convoluted pathways her thoughts insisted on taking only made her head hurt worse.

The darkness came so early in the winter and lasted so long. She caught her breath at the reminder of the winter nights two years ago, an eternity ago. Scott! Jack had been wrong, she still hated him though the memory of his lovemaking could warm her blood. That was the difference—Jack had warmed her heart.

It was early, not even seven yet, but Angela was exhausted, and she put on her nightgown without even combing her hair and climbed into bed. She nestled into the covers, the flannel-wrapped bricks at her feet sending a soothing warmth through her tired body. Alone, but for her own reflection above, she closed her eyes and let sleep claim her with thankful oblivion.

A log fell apart in the heart of the dying fire and red glowing sparks flew up the chimney, rushing to their death in the freezing night air. Angela stretched languorously like a waking cat, yawning and touching the pillow beside her. There was no one there and never had been, she hadn't shared this bed with any man. A more immediate need required her attention as her empty stomach protested vigorously and she discovered that she was ravenously hungry.

Lighting a candle she saw that Molly had removed the dinner tray and Angela reached for the bell pull, then stopped. What time was it anyway? She felt wonderfully rested and her headache was gone so it must be close to dawn but a glance at the clock told her she was wrong. It was only a little after two and the whole household was asleep.

Belting a pale yellow robe around her waist, she glided silently down the hallway and opened the nursery door. A dim night light flickered, casting long golden shadows through the colored glass. Kneeling beside Lorna, she adjusted the covers, smoothing her curls back from her forehead.

"My sweet baby," she whispered with a gentle smile. "I am not alone after all am I? I will always have you—my own little girl."

She knelt there for some time just watching her breathe through softly parted lips, seeing her lashes flicker as she dreamed. Pandora stirred and came to rub against the yellow velvet, and she scooped the kitten into her lap, scratching beneath her gray-furred chin. There was peace and tranquility here in this room, undisturbed by the commotion of the day. It was a haven from which Angela could emerge refreshed and revitalized with all her dreams and ideals intact once more.

With a parting kiss for Lorna she put the cat at the foot of the bed and made her way down to the kitchen. It was odd to see the great house dark and deserted, her candle the only point of light in the vast elegant interior. It was cozier in the kitchen, and she rummaged through the larder until she found what she wanted. Thick slices of meat and cheese tantalized Angela and she put them on a plate along with some fruit and bread. On the way back to her room she pilfered a bottle of wine from the liquor cabinet in the library to complete the improvised meal.

Putting the tray on a table near the fireplace she built up the fire to a gentle roar and sat down curling into a red velvet chair. A sense of warm well-being encompassed her as she poured the wine, instantly dispelled as she looked at the food. It was enough for two people and she could never finish it all herself.

An overwhelming loneliness descended upon Angela like a great dark blanket wrapping her, hiding her away from the rest of the world. She needed someone to share her life with, the good moments as well as the bad. She needed a man to love her and spoil her and put her in her place when she was wrong.

"Alone," she said sipping the wine. "Why, I'm even starting to talk to myself!"

A burst of pebbles against the window startled her up out of the chair. Cautiously parting the draperies, she saw a man below in the garden. The moon turned his hair to a platinum blaze and she jerked the curtain shut. Keith! Her heart hammered crazily against her ribs and she didn't even stop to assess the situation. Of their own volition her feet moved, flying down the stairs. This was folly, but she knew she couldn't stop herself, and she opened the French doors, aware only of her need for companionship and the need to dispell her loneliness.

"Keith!" She hurled herself into his arms, and they closed around her strong and comforting without making any demands. "Hold me—just hold me!"

Her quivering body molded softly, tightly against his and he stroked her hair in wonder at the unexpectedness of her actions. She put her arms around his waist, hugging him to her as if he would thrust her away and disappear again into the darkness.

"I didn't wake you did I, sweetheart? I saw the light through a crack in the curtains. I don't know why I came—just an urge. . ."

"I'm glad you came—glad!" Her face was a white blur in the moonlight. "I needed you so. Oh, Keith, Keith—what would I do without you?"

Her lips tasted of wine, warm and heady, opening eagerly beneath his. They swayed dizzily, lost to the night, and he forgot that she didn't love him because her body did. There was no mistaking the sinuous movement of her hips pressing against him, and her nipples were hard buttons of desire, thrusting against his chest even through her clothes.

Angela broke free, laughing throatily, pulling him

into the house. "Shh! Everyone is asleep." And they stole up the stairs like naughty children on a prank.

She leaned breathlessly against the closed door, her lips curved in an enchantress's smile, and Keith could not tear his eyes away. Flames of fire reflected in her eyes, dancing in the dark pupils and her hair was a coal-black thundercloud, sleep-tousled, foaming around her shoulders, falling on soft velvet to swirl around her slim hips. He reached for her and she slipped through his fingers like a breeze.

"I'm starving," she laughed, half apologetically as she plopped down in a chair. "I haven't eaten all day and I was about to start when you came. Keith, don't just stand there staring. Take off your coat and sit down—help me eat all this food."

They shared wine from the same goblet, the only one, but Keith just nibbled at the food, watching her devour it hungrily. He couldn't believe he was alone with Angela sharing an intimate middle-of-the-night supper. The impossible might be attainable tonight. And when she was finished she leaned back in the chair replete and pleasantly relaxed. Just having someone with her made her feel better, and she stared dreamily into the fire, slowly sipping the last of the wine.

The robe had come partly open but Angela seemed unaware of it and Keith could not keep his eyes from her perfectly formed breasts swelling against the thin embroidered silk of her nightgown. As she twirled the stem of the almost empty goblet between her fingers, the cut crystal caught and fractured the firelight, reflecting tiny rainbows against the graceful curve of her neck and bosom.

He was hypnotized by the delicate moving colors traveling over her flushed skin. If he didn't leave now, right this minute, then he would stay the night whether she wanted him or not. But he couldn't afford to rape her again, that particular act had cost him dearly, alienating Angela to such a point that he had despaired of ever winning her love.

Keith stood up abruptly reaching for his coat. "Good

night, Angela. I will see you in the morning."

"Don't go!"

He couldn't believe that her parted lips had uttered those words and he went to stand in front of her gazing down at her upturned face.

"If I stay—then I will love you," Keith stated simply. "I want you to come to me of your own free will, with no reservations and no regrets. Angela, I promised that I would never take advantage of you again and I mean to keep it. So if you have any doubts then tell me to go—now."

She would be betraying her love for Jack if Keith stayed, but he had already broken that bond by rejecting her in favor of his wife. Spending the rest of her life alone, even the remainder of the night alone was not a pleasant prospect, and Angela had learned by now how weak her flesh could be.

"Stay," she said standing, swaying inches from him.

Still he didn't touch her and Angela loosened the belt of her robe and let the garment fall to the floor. She looked like a virgin bride with her skin gleaming through the white diaphanous silk, and Keith could almost imagine it was their wedding night. Taking his hand she placed it against her breast.

The taut, firm flesh tingled against his fingers, and he felt the quick leaping of her heart and drew Angela slowly to him. Her wine-scented lips were smooth and moist, and as his tongue explored the paradise that opened to him, liquid fire exploded through his veins. Angela fell against him with a moan of pent-up desire circling his neck with her arms, ruffling his gilded hair.

He was going slowly, too slowly for her but Angela couldn't seem to rush him. She wanted him now, but maddeningly he undid the yellow ribbons holding the front of her nightgown together, one at a time, and there were at least a dozen! Her breasts sprang free and he pressed hot kisses against her face and throat, every touch leaving behind shivers of pleasure.

Then his mouth brushed the cleft between her breasts, moved to lick her nipples until they were swollen and aching, until she had to cover her mouth with her hand to stifle the sounds she couldn't help. Keith's hands traced down her spine cupping her buttocks, making every nerve in her body scream for relief. It was then that her legs gave way and she fell to her knees, her cheek against the hardness of his loins.

She reached up to him in supplication and he lifted her effortlessly, tumbling out onto the big bed. The mirrored ceiling reflected their entwined bodies, magnifying every caress with the added dimension of sight, and Angela could hardly believe what she was seeing. Keith adored her body lingeringly with his fingertips and lips, kissing and stroking the porcelain-fine texture of her skin.

Passion's storm whirled like a tempest through her until she was delirious with the rising heat, intoxicated under his patient touch. She begged Keith to take her but he continued on and on until she couldn't even speak. The only sounds coming from Angela's lips now were low moans and she muffled them against his shoulder lest someone hear what was happening behind her closed door.

At last he couldn't hold out any more and he possessed her, filling Angela's softness with slow, hard strokes, smiling at his own victory as her head lashed back and forth and her fingernails dug furrows into his back. It was worth the wait, the agony, to transform her into a demanding, mindless wanton heaving like a restless sea beneath him, drowning him in ecstasy.

Angela's wide eyes were glued to the image of their mating above her, to the wild movements, the swift plunges, that was more erotic than any of the paintings in the room. He drove her to the precipice of desire, casting her screaming body into turbulent darkness lit only by exploding stars of sensation.

What to wear! Angela looked frantically through her closet for the third time, rejecting almost every dress. It had to be something vivid, flamboyant, something so distracting that the people at the trial wouldn't even glance at her face.

Keith had left an hour before dawn, before the servants began stirring, but not before making love to her again. She closed her eyes, cupping her breasts, remembering the feel of his mouth on her skin. Today her whole body felt light and buoyant, as if a great weight had been lifted from her shoulders.

That was the problem. Not only did she feel different, she looked different too. The faintest of mauve shadows were smudged beneath heavy-lidded aqua eyes that glittered with too much brilliance. Her cheeks bloomed with color, but worst of all was her mouth, red and kiss-stung with an absurd tendency to curve into a secret smile.

Cold compresses hadn't helped at all, she bore the unmistakable look of a woman that had been thoroughly made love to. And when she walked into the courtroom on Keith's arm everyone would know her secret. Well there was nothing she could do about it now short of staying home.

"Damn!" Angela kicked a footstool and winced at the pain. "I look like a country girl who has just been tumbled in a haystack!"

She finally settled on a Chinese-red brocade dress that rivaled even the color of her lips and a frivolous coiffure that distracted attention from her face. They had branded her as a scarlet woman already, she might as well live up to expectations.

Keith greeted her, as always proper and formal in front of the servants, but his deep blue eyes held an amused sparkle. They had breakfast together in the morning room with no opportunity for anything but small talk. Yet only a few hours ago they had lain entwined and spent, and he had whispered passionate love words in her ear.

When they were alone in the carriage Keith jerked the curtains closed, kissing her soundly in the semidarkness.

"I love you, sweetheart," he said against her cheek. "What you did to me last night was beyond anything I've ever even dreamed!"

Angela pushed him away. "Stop, Keith! Don't kiss me anymore. You will make me look even more like. . like. . ."

He threw back his head and laughed genuinely amused at her worry. "If that's what is bothering you, Angela—you can forget it. The damage has already been done. You look ravishing and very desirable."

"I look ravished!" she said, smoothing her hair back into place. "Every person there will examine me like a bug under a magnifying glass—and do you know what they will see?"

"The most beautiful woman in England—in the world! Looking like a cat that has just stolen a dish of cream." Keith glanced at her distressed expression fondly. "The women will wonder at the secret of your success and the men will wish they were in my place."

She couldn't help laughing. "And then everyone will rush off to their oddsmakers to collect on their bets!"

"Yes, but I gambled for higher stakes than any of them—and won it all!"

Not quite all, she silently corrected him.

The scandal sheets now portrayed Angela as the faithless lover gallivanting around London with her golden-haired paramour while Jack rotted in prison with his faithful wife a shadow in the background. There was even a play at Covent Garden entitled *The Bandit and The Lady*, and every night it ended differently depending upon the proceedings of the day. It only awaited the outcome of the trial for a proper ending.

The trial dragged out slowly for over two weeks. Jack's traitorous foster brother testified, along with Captain Latham and every one of the soldiers that had been present. They rehashed every detail at least a dozen times, and then it was Keith's turn to testify. As he told his version the crowds sat enthralled, looking from him to Angela in order not to miss the slightest reaction. But they were disappointed at the iron-willed control the duchess had acquired since the start of the trial, and

Angela didn't betray any emotion with so much as a flick of her lashes.

They saved Angela for last, and on the day that she was required to testify the crowds had swelled to twice the usual size. It could have been a national holiday, considering the huge mob that seethed outside and inside.

There was complete silence as she stood in the witness box and placed her hand on the big leather-bound Bible. Every eye was on her as she repeated the oath in a clear composed voice but her delicate face was pale. Only those in the audience that knew her and saw the stubborn set of her chin and the firm determination of her mouth knew what she was feeling.

For all her cool exterior her insides were quaking, and her knees shook and seemed about to fail her at any moment. Everyone was a blur before her eyes, and in her tightly clutched, gloved hand was a tiny bottle of smelling salts that she prayed she wouldn't have to use. What Angela said in the next minutes could either save or condemn Jack, and the weight of it rested fully on her frail, squared shoulders.

Her vision cleared as she looked at Keith, and he smiled encouragingly even though he didn't agree with her decision to be a witness for the defense. Jane winked impishly when she caught Angela's eye and somehow their support helped.

Taking a deep breath, she turned her full attention on Mr. Green, one of the barristers she had hired for Jack's defense. He was supposed to be one of the best in England, and Angela only hoped he lived up to his reputation.

With patience and careful questions Mr. Green drew the answers from her, expertly dwelling on the points important to the defense. Aspects that were detrimental to the case were carefully glossed over or else left out entirely. As Angela told her version of the abduction and her six weeks of captivity a hush descended and the audience was spellbound.

As Mr. Green finished his questioning the people

stirred and then fell silent again as the prosecutor approached the box. His beady, black eyes bored into Angela for a few endless moments before he began the cross-examination. Her hand clutched the railing in front of her so tightly that she was sure its imprint would remain in the polished wood, but aside from that one outward sign of agitation she seemed unruffled.

He made her repeat the whole story again listening intently for any contradiction, then began his insidious questioning, dwelling on her affair with Jack. Every intimate detail of their relationship was dragged out and laid bare, and the crowds lapped it up waiting for more. There was a lengthy theatrical pause as he paced back and forth in front of her, apparently deep in thought.

"What are your feelings for Jack Newton?" The question broke the silence like the boom of a cannon.

"Why I. . ." Angela faltered, thinking of the oath she had taken. "After a period of time we became friends."

"Friends! Friends with the criminal that abducted you?" His tone was totally disbelieving.

"Yes. I realized that Jack would never harm me and when he saved my life it only reinforced our friendship."

"You used that same word again, Lady Harrington. Am I to assume that you conduct illicit affairs with all your male. . .friends?"

Angela's eyes snapped at him with fury and she retorted sharply, "You, sir, are supposed to assume nothing!"

The courtroom broke into chaos, some of the people applauding her spunk and others shouting obscenities. Angela stood motionless until order was restored.

The prosecutor gave a thin imitation of a smile and came to the point. "Are you in love with the defendant, Jack Newton."

Two spots of color appeared on her cheeks and she drew a hot angry breath. "I refuse to answer that question!"

The room stirred again and the judge sternly

reminded her that she was under oath and must answer the question. The audience strained forward.

"Are you in love with Jack Newton?" His voice was triumphant.

What could she say? Jack was looking straight at her, his gray eyes as cold as ice—Keith's face was once again that stiff mask that he assumed when he was terribly upset, and even from the witness box she could see the muscle twitching along his jaw. Amy Newton's head was bowed and all Angela could see was the top of her bonnet. No matter what she said it would be wrong, so she might as well tell the truth.

"Yes!" Angela answered haughtily, daring anyone to gainsay her.

The courtroom broke into pandemonium again, and this time order could not be restored. In disgust the judge adjourned for the rest of the day.

The next morning Angela didn't have to testify any further. The prosecutor had made his point. All that was left were the summations and they were quickly over.

The outlook was not very bright when the jury adjourned to decide Jack's fate, and Angela refused to leave the courtroom, sitting tensely in her chair, staring off into space. Not even Jane's chatter could break the strained atmosphere, and she finally gave up and kept silent.

The jury was out for only two hours, and when they returned everyone scrambled for their seats. The silence became as thick as a London fog as everyone waited expectantly, and Jack stood tall and proud facing the twelve men as the verdict was read.

"We the jury find the defendant, Jack Newton—guilty!"

Angela sat stiff with shock as the words jolted through her like lightning. Guilty! Her eyes, wide and unblinking, were focused on Jack's broad back.

Then the judge's voice rang out through the room, "The defendant, Jack Newton, having been found guilty of the aforementioned crimes is hereby sentenced to be hung by the neck until dead. The public execution will take place one month from today at noon."

They had to have an armed escort to get through the agitated mob to the carriage. Angela sat still and silent, stunned by the verdict, and Keith was just as quiet. Anything he said now would be inappropriate.

Hung! They were going to hang Jack in a few short weeks. She couldn't believe it, couldn't begin to accept the fact that he was going to be executed. A world without him would be a darker place, and if she could just know that he would be alive somewhere she would let him go without a murmur.

Keith escorted her into the house and an agitated Molly accosted them in the hall. "Milady, a messenger arrived one hour ago on urgent business from the castle. He brought you this." She handed Angela a letter and stood waiting expectantly.

Angela stared uncomprehendingly at the letter in her hand, gazing glassy-eyed at the blob of red sealing wax imprinted with the Harrington coat of arms. They waited and she made no move to open it.

"Angela, aren't you going to open the letter?" Keith asked but she didn't seem to hear him. "Angela!"

Then she thrust it into his hand and he hesitated, then ripped it open. He scanned the contents quickly and then read it all through again, disbelief marring his face.

"Angela," he said in a cold, hushed voice. "The duke—your husband—is dead."

Chapter Eleven

"We have been through all this before! I'm just not ready to get married again."

"But, Angela, it's been almost two years! For all intents and purposes we are married. We sleep together and spend most of our time together—why Lorna thinks of me as her father."

"Please, Keith, don't go on any more," Angela said, changing the subject. "Let's finish our walk. Isn't it a marvelous day? Jane told me that there are wild daffodils by the lake and I'd like to take some back—"

"It's him!" said Keith angrily, stripping the new buds from a low hanging branch, throwing them to the ground. "After all this time his ghost is still between us."

"We agreed never to mention Jack again! He's dead—that's the end of it!" But there was a trace of anguish in her voice.

If Keith only knew that Jack's memory meant more to her than his very real presence, that sometimes when he made love to her, she indulged herself, pretending it was another man—silver and black hair instead of blond, the soft tickle of a mustache, such tenderness!

"Stop it!" she shouted, startling Keith, surprising herself, because he had said nothing else. Angela was trying to still her own imagination.

If only there was a man that could wipe out the memory, if only it was Keith! But it wasn't and she wondered if it ever could be.

There had to be some man in this vast, wide world that could do it; she clung to that thought to keep herself going. But she would never find him if she stayed tucked away in the country, rusticating with her golden lover.

Distraction was what she needed, for she was on the verge of tears. Angela took it out on Keith. "Damn you! Go to hell, Keith—go anywhere, but leave me alone!" She flounced off through the trees and he let her go.

He had really done it now! This wasn't the first time they had argued about their relationship but he was a fool to have mentioned Gentleman Jack. Through narrowed eyes he watched her walk away, her slim hips swaying provocatively beneath the blue and yellow embroidered gown. He almost went after her, enticed, as always, by her marvelous body. She gave that freely enough but he wanted more.

It would be better to leave her alone right now. Keith knew her moods, and she had just gone off into her private world where words, anger, even physical contact could not stir her. Later Angela would be herself again, warm and passionate, and he smiled thinking of how sweet their making up would be.

It grew breezy as she neared the lake, and Angela held her skirt out like sails on either side of her, running down a slope before the wind. It pushed her faster and faster and she flew like a brightly colored bird skimming across an emerald carpet. Anger dissolved as she laughed out loud, letting the wind blow all the cobwebs from her mind.

A chorus of birds rent the azure fabric of the sky. Thrushes, blackbirds, and cock blackcaps busily prepared nests in the bare and budding trees. In another month the countryside would be in full bloom but now only the daring flowers appeared: dog violets, lords and ladies, windflowers, and daffodils. They were delicate splashes of color in the woods, a lovely prelude of what would come.

The dew-wet grass was ablaze with crystals catching the early sunbeams and refracting their rays. Angela bent and picked some wildflowers, twisting their stems together and tucking the bouquet into her bodice. The air wafted sweet with awakening scents, and a strange instantaneous feeling of exaltation filled her for no apparent reason. She felt wonderful, energized and excited, and happiness bubbled in her like a clear mountain spring.

She had forgotten the quarrel with Keith and her sadness over Jack, and she skipped carefree around a clump of green and black hawthorns. She stopped, the breath catching in her throat, her green-blue eyes wide with amazement at the unbelievable panorama. It couldn't be real—a lovely fantasy perhaps, or an imaginary painting.

Acres and acres of them ruffled the shore of the lapis lazuli lake, an endless belt of daffodils fluttering in the breeze. How merrily they danced as she hurried toward them, so carefree, like ethereal fairies responding to some magical, unheard music known only to them.

"How lovely! How magnificent!" Angela cried as she entered their separate enchanted world.

She sank down among the golden waves, heedless of the dew soaking her dress. Their beauty intoxicated her, the delicate yellow petals translucent in the sunlight. She pulled off the hat that was supposed to shield her complexion from the sun and sent it soaring out over the expanse of the lake. It landed on the surface like a white swan, and as she watched the wind play with it she pulled the pins from her hair, letting the heavy ebony tresses slip down her back.

Running her fingers through her freed curls, Angela tossed her head laughing, letting the wind tug and tangle it like a man's hands. And then a dark shadow swept through the sky, surprising her with its suddenness. It fell just inches short of her hat floating on the rippling lake—a black hat, a man's hat!

She jumped up whirling around and saw him in the distance beneath the shade of a willow tree. How long had he stood there watching her with his arms folded over his chest while his horse cropped the new grass? The peace of this place was shattered and she was frightened, because now he was walking toward her and there was something very familiar about his lithe, self-assured movements.

He was closer and the sun glinted on his hair, turning it to polished bronze. She couldn't breathe, couldn't move as recognition flooded her like the hot flush of the summer sun. He was back!

"Who needs a hat on a day like this?" he asked.

His liquid-brown eyes swam with golden flecks, resting warmly on her face and he flashed that familiar boyish smile that crinkled the corners of his eyes and made Angela start breathing again.

Her lips soundlessly formed his name and her mind shrank from the things his gaze did to her. A deliquescence began deep inside her, a glow that increased as he reached for her. His hands spanned her waist and he drew her gently, inexorably to him.

He pressed a kiss against her temple, then her softly flushed cheek, and Angela stood unresisting, spellbound at this assault on her senses. She swayed against him and his mouth found hers like a long awaited treasure. His tongue probed her mouth, savoring the honey sweetness he had been starved of, had been forced to return to lest he die of wanting her.

She sighed, that half-breathless little protest, before giving in, and he probed deeper until she opened to him like a flower bursting into bloom. Angela's arms circled his neck, her fevered body leaning into his, the spark of her pleasure bursting and crackling like a fire. How could he do this to her? She had forgotten with the passing of years and other lovers the way it had been between them—but now there was no gainsaying it and he wiped every thought but his presence from her giddy head.

"Angel, Angel—you are as beautiful as a dream. My heart—my sweet little love."

Scott's lips discovered the pulsing hollow of her arched throat where the skin was the texture of rose petals. His nostrils flared at the remembered woman-scent of her, sweet and spicy, smelling of wildflowers.

Slowly his hands moved up her slender back unfastening her gown and the wind gusted, twining her loose luxuriant hair around them both, binding them together as one.

How long he had waited for this moment, endless seas of waiting. And Scott forced himself to go slowly, carefully so he wouldn't break the sensuous spell that enwrapped her and once again invoke her wrath. He had finally been forced to admit to himself how abominably he had treated her in the past. No wonder Angela had spewed forth her hatred on almost every occasion they had been together. But there had been a few, very few moments of tender capitulation and he hoped that more than three and a half years of being apart had softened her attitude toward him.

She was even more beautiful than he remembered, if that was possible, lovelier than those hauntingly elusive dreams that had tormented him to total distraction with such exquisite pain. In Jamaica Scott had drowned himself in willing women, trying to forget her, but the excesses he drove himself to only made Angela more desirable, more unattainable. For he had learned that pleasure was more than a transient, split-second slaking of passion, that there was more to loving than the mere satisfaction of the flesh. It was a total commitment—body, heart, and soul; an endless giving and taking, an unfathomable flow of emotion between a man and a woman.

Angela was the quintessence of all his feelings, of every woman in the world, and he loved her. There was no rhyme or reason to it, and try though he had there was no changing it. Scott admitted his defeat, bowed before the illogic of the situation, for he was crazily, irrevocably in love with a woman who hated him.

"Angel, love—the things you do to me!" he said huskily against her hair. "Your lips are sweeter than the wine of the gods and I'm drunk with wanting you. Your hair is like the silken strands of night and your skin is softer than velvet. You are perfection, an enchantress weaving a spell over me. Have pity, my adorable little Aphrodite, on a mere mortal man—let me worship at your temple of love."

What was he saying and doing to her? The startling

realization that he was seducing her broke through the mists of her befogged mind. She pushed him away and his eyes fastened on her chemise, that thin silk and lace confection that barely confined the swelling curves of her glorious breasts. Cheeks flaming with shame and embarrassment, she covered her exposed bosom with her hands.

"Scott. . .I don't think. . ."

"That's right, love—don't think right now. The time for feeling is here—and please don't hide yourself from me. Shall I put my hands where yours are? I could do such exquisite—"

"Please—stop!" But in spite of her protest she didn't move, just stood there staring at him as he said more outrageous things.

"But they are such ripe, delectable looking little fruit and I would like to sample them."

He put his words into action pulling her arms away and lowering his lips to a delicate, rosy nipple. Mouthing it through the web of silk, he felt it pucker and harden against his tongue, heard her ragged breathing and the pounding of her heart. Leaving a wet spot on her chemise Scott exposed her other breast, teasing it till it blossomed and thrust achingly into his mouth.

Almost laughing with jubilation, he felt Angela's hands catch in his hair pulling and pressing his face hard against her curves. His mouth was a hot shock against her bare flesh, and the small reluctance she had gave way to blind rapture before his bold reclaiming of her.

"Your breasts taste just like cherries."

This had happened before, some time, some place—eons ago, yesterday. And it was happening again and she wanted it, had a nonsensical thought that it was destined to be repeated forever.

The soft green grass was their bed, the curved expanse of sky their canopy, and the soft rustling daffodils were curtains shielding them from view.

An aching joy filled Angela at the fusion of their flesh, an ecstasy that made her body his and hurled every thought from her mind. Their motion was at one with nature: the slowly moving clouds, the reeling flowers, the erratic gusts of wind, and the rippling lake.

Time ceased to exist as they hurtled upward into the starflung realms of deepest night, finding together the empyreal heights.

"Angel—love!"

They were back on the earth once more and Scott lay beside her, leaning over her with one leg thrown over hers to keep her still. She was as restless as the gusty breezes but he wouldn't let her go. He had felt her pleasure and knew the way to enslave her, but once it was over she was herself again, suspicious and rapidly withdrawing from him. How could he win her love and trust? How could he make her want him the way he desired her?

If this was the only way then so be it. He would concentrate on rekindling the physical bond between them until once more her lissome body was addicted to what only he could do for it. Angela had a streak of sensuality that made her vulnerable, and he would play on this one weakness.

"Your eyes are just like the sea, mysterious and ever changing."

His fingers captured a long black curl and he drew it teasingly down her neck and across her breasts. She didn't say anything, hadn't since her halfhearted objections, and Scott wondered what was going on inside her head. Did she regret what had just happened? He never could. All of his senses were full of her and his dark eyes glowed with satisfaction at his new exploration of her charms.

Angela had been a child before and now her body was a woman's. Her small breasts had filled out round and voluptuous but her waist and hips were just as slender. Scott's hand moved caressingly over her hard-muscled thighs and then wandered back up to rest on her flat belly.

"Our child," Scott murmured contemplatively, "he must be almost. . .three years old now."

That brought a smile to her somber face and a twinkle to her eye. "Yes, she will be three in the fall."

"A girl!"

Angela laughed at the perplexed expression on his face. "I told you our baby would be a girl—that I would be the one to spoil your plans."

"You don't have to look so pleased, my love. Do you remember what I promised if you didn't give me a son?" Scott pressed his loins against her making the threat, reminding them both of his words of long ago.

It was his turn to laugh now at the panic on her face as she tried to push him away. "No! Never! I cannot have another child—I won't!"

"And what's to prevent it, my little wildflower?" he drawled wickedly. "Such sweet pastimes were meant for that purpose, and I have already proved that my seed is strong—"

"No! There is no need—no point to it now. Your father is dead and half of everything is yours—the castle, estates, the money. You are rich—you are the Duke of Brightling!"

"But. . ."

"But nothing!" Her words tumbled out quickly; she feared the consequences of another encounter, seeking to distract him. "No matter how much bad blood there was between you and Percy, you were still his only male heir and he knew it."

"I suppose the other half is yours?" Scott was frowning and his voice became urgent. "You haven't married again—tell me you haven't! I couldn't bear that!"

He was shaking her, half insane with jealousy at the thought that his Angela might now belong to someone else—a young, virile husband who could satisfy her yearnings, a man she loved.

"No. . ." Angela hesitated, not knowing what to make of his rapid change in mood, at the relief flooding his lean, brown face. "But I do have plans. . .Keith and I—"

"Damn Keith and to hell with all your plans!" he

growled, his eyes stabbing her with anger. "You belong to me! And it's me you are going to marry—no one else! I'll see to that!"

Tearing herself from his grasp Angela sprang to her feet, arms akimbo, magnificent in her rage. "You!" she screamed. "No woman in her right mind would marry you! Not even Jane would be your wife.

"Do you think you can come back here after almost four years and just take up where you left off? Why you arrogant, patronizing son of a bitch! I hate you! I hate everything about you—"

Her words sparked his anger, and before Scott even thought he was on his feet, temper afire. His arms shot out shoving her backwards, tumbling her into the lake.

Angela came sputtering to the surface to find him laughing at her. Laughing!

"Did that cool you off, Duchess?" he taunted.

"You bastard," she shrieked, her anger far from doused. "I know what you're after—I know the devious pathways your diabolical mind takes! You want everything—not just half and the only way you can get it is to marry me. You—you—"

He dove into the water cutting it cleanly with his sunburnished body, emerging just feet from Angela. Laughing he shook his head scattering a storm of water droplets through the air, the icy chill of the water unable to freeze his avid lust.

"You little fool. . .vixen. . .angel!" he said reaching for her. "It's you I want, not castles or estates or titles. You and our daughter—and all the other children we will make."

"Liar! I don't believe you, Scott Harrington—you will never have me—never!"

"But I will, you little hellcat—and it's just as easy as this."

Deftly Scott grabbed her, kissing her wet lips thoroughly until she stopped pounding at him with her fists.

"See how right it is—and how natural this is?"

He slid his hands down her back and over her hips

grasping her thighs, lifting her toward him. Angela gasped, throwing her arms around his neck to keep from falling backward into the water. The blue surface of the lake churned white with their silent struggle.

"No! Don't!"

But he ignored her pleas, and with one fluid movement breached her hotly, grinning at the look of pained surprise in her incredulous aquamarine eyes. His hands cupped her buttocks supporting her almost weightless body and he moved her flesh against his, lunging with a power she couldn't ignore.

"Beast!" hissed Angela. "You're hurting me."

"You are so tense, sweetheart," Scott cajoled. "Just relax and you will enjoy it."

"How can I when you are raping me?" she cried, twisting and turning to free herself of his very real, unwanted presence. But it didn't seem to help, in fact Angela only succeeded in inciting him further.

"You're so eager, love," Scott whispered, nibbling at her ear lobe. "I think you do like it in spite of your protests."

He fit her more closely to him, moaning as she bit into the side of his neck in self-defense, gasping at the simultaneous pain and pleasure, at his tight fevered prison.

"Sheathe me, darling—all the way! I know you can do it. Don't be stubborn, Angel."

She screamed in outrage as he accomplished his end. "I hate you, Scott, and always will!"

"I have become uncommonly fond of the way you hate me."

Fastening his mouth on hers, Scott stopped the conversation but she jerked her head back, pale eyes glittering in the reflected sunlight of the lake. "I want to go home!" she told him adamantly. "Let me go—now!"

"Make me," he teased, stealing another quick hard kiss from her quivering mouth.

"I can't—you know I can't!" Angela cried helplessly. "You are stronger than I am—you are a brute!"

Her eyes were incredibly round and large and her stubborn chin was trembling, giving her the vulnerable look of a lost child. Tears welled up out of those wide, unblinking eyes and dissolved slowly down her cheeks. Scott couldn't believe the change. A moment ago she had been a screaming fighting spitfire, now she was all soft and defenseless making him feel like an idiot for forcing her.

"What's the matter now?" he asked, exasperated at himself for being moved by her distress. But Angela only shook her head unable to speak.

"All right then—I'll let you go!" he told her, damning himself as ten kinds of a fool.

But as Scott moved to let her down, perversely she clung to him, sending a fleeting frown across his face. She pressed her soft, salt-wet lips against his and he almost dropped her in surprise as her tongue flamed into his mouth to meet his. He couldn't understand her—changing in one breath from a blizzard to a heat wave—making his blood boil in spite of the chill of the lake.

Still, she made little sobbing noises in the back of her throat, but she seemed disinclined to break the long soul kiss that turned her world completely upside down. Scott wasn't hurting her now, just the opposite, as a beatific haze settled over her.

Why she had changed so abruptly was just as much a mystery to Angela as it was to Scott. But when he had made the move to set her free the thought of parting with his vigorous invasion of her, that sent her mind reeling in spite of her protests, had been unthinkable. Now wonderful ripples of pleasure jostled her.

Angela wept uncontrollably and buried her face against his neck, digging her nails into the tense muscles of his wide shoulders. She urged him on as he sent her skyrocketing into a seething, boiling cauldron of desire that engulfed her and erupted within her like an exploding volcano.

Her nails raked his back as he arched against her, and he didn't even notice it, consumed as he was in the earthshaking tremors that lashed through him, threatening to send them both plunging beneath the water.

They used his shirt to dry themselves with and he hooked her back into her dress taking much longer to do Angela up than he had spent undressing her. Regretfully, Scott finished the last hook and dropped a gentle kiss on the nape of her neck where the hair curled damply.

Letting her wet shining hair drop down her back, Angela faced him with a dubious expression on her face. Smiling reassuringly, he let his gaze stray to her mouth still soft from his kisses in spite of her hardening attitude.

"Are you hungry?" he asked.

"Hungry?" She repeated the word as if she had never heard it before, still in a partial daze.

"I have some food in my saddlebags," Scott explained, "and I am starving."

"I know!"

Ignoring the barb he walked to his horse, and Angela's eyes were drawn to his retreating figure dressed only in breeches and boots. He really was a magnificent animal, she admitted reluctantly to herself, but like all wild things, dangerous. The marks she had made on his powerful shoulders stood out scarlet and raw against his mahogany skin, and she couldn't help admiring his physique, which if anything was even more splendid than before.

As Scott busied himself with the saddlebags he caught her open gaze upon him out of the corner of his eye. What an amusing child she was, unable to hide her curiosity. Well, he would gladly satisfy that inquisitiveness at any time!

When she sensed his observation of her Angela quickly turned away and busied herself hanging his sopping shirt up to dry. Then she ignored him totally and set about gathering a huge armful of daffodils to occupy her vacillating mind. How could he? How could she? There was no sense to it—absolute madness! She felt as if she were another person, a stranger that she didn't understand and had no control over. Where Scott was concerned her body took over and her mind took flight. Beware! Hadn't she told herself that before?

He spread his brown wool cloak on the grass and they sat cross-legged, hungrily devouring the food she had placed between them. So she was wary of him again and with good cause, for he meant to have her any way he could get her. Scott had her halfway to giving in already, and if they could both manage to keep their tempers it would work. Only his first day back and they had made love twice—things were progressing nicely.

The brandy from the silver flask burned down into Angela's stomach curling warmly through her veins. She started to relax but then sat up erect; she must not let her guard down.

"I hope you don't mind dining al fresco," Scott said, his smile warm and lazy.

"No," she retorted, "I love picnics—as long as they are held in the right place and with the right people. Now the spot is perfect but. . ."

Her sarcasm went unnoticed as Scott pulled a slim velvet-covered case out of his coat. Silently he handed it to her, his compelling eyes never leaving her face.

"What is it?" she asked frowning slightly.

"If you would open it, love, you would find out."

Hesitantly she opened it and caught her breath at the exquisite jewels glittering in the noonday sun. There was a necklace and bracelet of large aquamarines and tiny diamonds set in finely wrought gold. She touched the sparkling stones with the tip of one finger and then looked up at him questioningly.

"They are for you, Angel. I saw them in Kingston and knew that no other woman could ever wear them."

"But. . .I couldn't. . .accept them. It wouldn't be. . .proper," she stammered.

He raised one dark eyebrow and asked sardonically, "Since when have you been the proper lady? It is my gift to you, rather belatedly, on the birth of our daughter."

Taking the bracelet from the case he clasped it around her dainty wrist. "Turn around," Scott ordered. "Let me help you fasten the necklace."

The stones slid coldly around her neck but his fingers were warm and caressing as he lifted her hair. He fastened the clasp and she turned to him, a bemused smile on her face.

"I knew it!" Scott said softly, his eyes plumbing the depths of hers. "The exact color of your eyes. On sunny days the Caribbean is the same sparkling greenish-blue, and then I always thought of you—wished you could be there with me."

"Thank you, Scott," she said simply. "They are lovely."

"Will you wear them at dinner tonight?"

"Are we dining together?" Angela inquired suspiciously.

"You said that half the castle is mine. So that means I won't have to move back into the dower house."

"You can't! What would people think if we lived in the same place together?"

"I don't care what they think but you could marry me if you're so concerned about respectability."

"I told you no!"

"Then you really do care about gossip?"

"People can be very cruel," Angela replied, her eyes cloudy with the remembered hurt of the slander during the trial.

Scott studied the averted cameo of her face, wondering at those cryptic words and the mood of sadness that emanated from her. "Have people been cruel to you, sweetheart?"

She shuddered inwardly to think of what Scott's reaction would be when he found out about Jack. Anger, surely, and jealousy, perhaps, but there would be no one for him to take it out on but her.

"Yes," Angela blurted out, her eyes flashing and her chin stubborn. "Everyone was cruel except for Jane and Keith and Molly. And I hope you find out about it right away—today—because then you will stop your foolish talk about marrying me!"

"Whatever are you talking about?"

"If you think I'm going to tell you you're mad! You will find out soon enough and I don't want to be around when you do." Standing up she quickly gathered the daffodils she had picked. "I'm going home now and I am going to forget what happened here today. When you arrive—much later, I will be just as surprised as everyone else to see that the prodigal son has returned."

She started into the woods but then stopped and whirled around, eyes snapping. "And don't you dare tell Lorna that you are her father. I won't have it!"

Scott laughed as she ran off in a huff and said to himself, "Angel, Angel—you have a lot to learn about the way things will be—and I will be the one to teach you!"

Angus busied himself unpacking Scott's trunk and valises. It was wonderful to be back in a decent climate again. Jamaica had not been to his taste at all, too humid and hot for the dour Scotsman used to cooler weather. Perhaps he could even convince the lad to go up to the Highlands for a while. But in any event England was better than that infernal island.

It had taken almost a year and a half to turn the rundown plantation, Bluehills, back into a money-making investment. But the land was lush and fertile, and once the encroaching rain forests had been beaten back it started shaping up. Angus shook his head in disgust at the picture of Scott working right alongside the slaves, bare-chested and sweating in the hot tropical sun.

He had to admit though, that under the tutelage of their new master the slaves had become good workers, respecting Scott who was never too busy to show them how to do a particular job.

The house had been in better shape. Shut up for several years all it had needed was a good cleaning, new paint and some slaves to keep it running. The rambling one-story building was situated high on a hill overlooking a sandy cove, perfectly designed to catch every ocean breeze. And they had needed the tradewinds in that torrid place.

Once things had been put to rights Scott had

expanded his holdings, planting not just sugar cane but pimento, banana trees, and coffee. He also set up a small factory for making rum, the favorite drink in the islands.

When everything was running smoothly the new overseer took over and Scott went off adventuring on the *Dark Lady*. The voyages to Cuba, South America, and the United States had increased his profits day by day and kept him busy and out of trouble. But when he returned to Bluehills boredom set in.

Angus rolled his eyes heavenward at the thought of the endless stream of women—black, white, yellow, and café au lait—that had graced Scott's bed. But none of them had stayed longer than a few days. No, Angus corrected his memory, there had been one, a fragile petite girl with black hair and blue eyes that had stayed for over a month. When Scott had tired of her he went on a drinking and gambling binge the likes of which Angus had never seen before. After he finally sobered up they set sail for home.

The last straw for Angus's unadventurous spirit had been the attack on the ship by a nasty little Frenchy pirate. But after he had tangled with Scott there wasn't much fight left in him. His crew spirited him away, face slashed and leg laid open from thigh to ankle. If he lived he would probably never walk again.

"Angus!" Scott's energetic entrance broke his reverie. "Lay out my clothes for tonight. I'm dining with Angela and the Montgomerys and later who knows? Damn what a day!"

"Wha' are ye talking aboot, lad?"

"I'm going to marry Angela as soon as possible."

"Are ye daft?" Angus exploded. "Din'na ye know wha' she has been up to while ye ha' been gone? Ye would na wan' to marry with the likes of her!"

Going over to a chest of drawers Angus pulled one open and grabbed a handful of papers. "Here!" He thrust them at Scott and went back to unpacking.

Newspaper clippings, prints, broadsheets, poems, a theater program, everything the gutters of London could dredge up he held in his hand. The grim lines of a thunderstorm settled on Scott's face as he looked slowly through them, reading every word. A sharp pain knifed into him, turning in his gut, but he could not put them down.

"Where. . .did you. . .get. . ." he was almost incoherent in his rage.

"One of the servants—a troublemaker to be sure. But do na ask me his name for I will na tell ye."

"Is it true?"

"How do I know—I was na here was I? But there's never smoke without a fire."

She had betrayed him! How dare that little slut carry on so! Scott crumpled the papers and hurled them to the floor. His hands balled into fists and Angus hastily fled the room lest he be the one to get in his way.

No wonder she hadn't wanted to be around when he found out! Scott's hands itched to fasten themselves around her slim white throat and press till he crushed all the lies and deception out of her. Angela! He could see her in his mind, struggling, gasping for breath, her eyes wide with terror, lips turning blue from lack of air.

"No!" He swung out blindly, sending a table crashing across the room. No—no he didn't want her dead. Let her live so he could torture her the way she was torturing him. He would use her, get her out of his system once and for all and then discard her like the whore she was.

Scott flung open the door to go—he didn't know where. Standing in the hall was a disheveled little girl with both hands full of cookies. Crumbs spilled down the front of her green muslin dress and her pink mouth was opened in an astonished O.

"Don't tell," she said, "I am not supposed to eat now." She held out one hand, offering him a cookie with the air of a conspirator. "Want one?"

He burst out laughing and took one, popping it into his mouth, his anger vanishing momentarily as he inspected his daughter. It could be no one else but Lorna for she was exactly like Angela—the same hair and eyes, enchanting dimples, and it seemed, the same rebellious quality that got her mother into trouble. Scott had never been around children and knew nothing about them but suddenly, surprisingly he wanted to know everything about his daughter. How did one treat a child? He didn't have the vaguest idea.

"I'm Lorna—who are you?"

"Well, Lorna," Scott said picking her up so that her face was level with his, "I'm your father." Let Angela explain her way out of that one.

"No." Lorna's forehead wrinkled with concentration. "My papa is dead. I don't remember him but Mama said he died."

"That was my father—your grandfather that died," explained Scott. "Your mother was married to him but . . ." How could he possibly explain it to a child? "He pretended to be your father while I was away. But now I'm back and I'm your real father."

"Are you really?" Joy lit up her small face and when he nodded Lorna threw her arm around his neck and planted a wet kiss on his cheek.

Scott's heart lurched in his chest and he set her down quickly, surprised at the strength of his own emotions.

"Look," he said, taking her hand and leading her over to the open trunk. "I brought you a present."

Together they ripped off the string and wrapping paper and Lorna lifted the lid of the box. There was a moment of doubt when he thought of the toy he had brought his son. He should have brought a doll too, just to be on the safe side.

Scott's fears abated as Lorna squealed with delight, reaching into the box and carefully taking out the miniature sailing ship. It was a replica of the *Dark Lady* that he had had specially made.

"Oh, Papa, Papa! Thank you!"

How quickly children accepted changes, already calling him papa. A flooding warmth of feeling filled Scott, washing away any doubts he might have had about being a parent and the odd, wonderful joy that had begun when he had learned that Angela was pregnant was fulfilled. This tiny girl was part of him, the same flesh and blood—she belonged to him, depended on him, and he could never forget it.

"Does it float?" inquired Lorna, entranced by all the sails.

"It sure does, baby," he told her enthusiastically. "I tried it out myself in Jamaica."

"Where's that?"

"I'll tell you all about it. Would you like to sail it now, on the lake? We will ride there on my horse and you can sit in front of me and hold the reins."

Excitedly, Lorna clapped her hands and Scott snatched his laughing, black-haired daughter into his arms, everything forgotten but her pleasure. And as he bounded down the stairs two at a time he said, "And someday, Lorna, I'll take you on a real ship—right out in the ocean."

If a spark had been struck in the room it would have exploded. Scott and Angela glared at each other from opposite ends of the table with Keith and Jane keeping up a pretense of conversation. The servants moved silently from kitchen to table, serving the courses with knowing eyes. Neither of them was eating and Scott's wine glass was continually being refilled.

The gall of him! Telling Lorna he was her father after she had specifically told him not to. Then to make matters worse he had spirited her away to go sailing boats on the lake. Lorna had returned exhausted and overwrought with her head full of pirates, island plantations, ships, and slaves! There was no telling what Scott would do next.

And worst of all the child was clearly under Scott's spell and absolutely adored him. She had refused to go to bed until her handsome father gave her a wild piggyback ride through the house, told her another pirate story, and tucked her in for the night, kissing her several times before leaving. He was spoiling her rotten on only the first day back, and Angela shuddered to think of how unmanageable Lorna would be after a week of such treatment.

Molly was horrified to find her little darling was Scott's by-blow, and every single servant in the place was talking about it. Leave it to them to be the first to find out—and the first to tell. The gossip had spread like wildfire.

How dare he roar back into her life like a stormy north wind, turning her carefully ordered life into utter chaos! Her dark secrets were revealed to the world and soon everyone would be agog with her latest sins. For in some circles it would be considered incest, and the fact that they had a child by their union only added an extra fillip to the story.

Angela felt like screaming and crying, like breaking everything in the room and then clawing the smirk off Scott's face. If he thought he could breeze back into her life, tumble her among the flowers, yell Lorna's illegitimacy from the rooftops and then marry her in order to get everything he wanted he had another thing coming.

He was trying to trap her! The thought slammed into her mind, making it spin. Informing the world of Lorna's paternity was the first step toward forcing her to the altar. He thought a little gossip would shame her into knuckling under to his demands! And he talked of more children, so did he perhaps think to trap her by getting her pregnant again? That would be harder to ignore than gossip and much more visible. Good heavens! What if she was already? And she squirmed beneath the table, touching her abdomen where she could still feel the ache of his powerful invasion.

Scott tossed off another glass of wine, but a cold rage curled in the pit of his stomach in spite of all he was drinking. Her golden lover, is what the gossipmongers had branded Keith, following hot on the heels of her highwayman! Everyone in England knew about Angela's bedroom acrobatics—the details had been publicly aired, dragged through the courtroom and the muddy streets. And in spite of it all she was more beautiful and more desirable than ever.

His eyes slid back to Angela again. Her eyes were

wide and innocent but there was a pout on her sensual lips, and she really did look like an angel viewed through the flickering flames of the candelabra. But Scott knew better. She was a little demon, the Devil's daughter, a shining fallen angel.

She had even had the effrontery to wear the aquamarines tonight, and they blazed like an insult against her skin. All those months, years of wanting her, loving her, to have it shattered like this. But Angela was not in love with him, that was very clear, and he had only made an idiot out of himself by asking her to marry him.

But in spite of everything, knowing the very worst about her, he still wanted her—why not admit it? He would do anything to stop wanting her, anything to cut the treacherous little bitch out of his heart—anything to make her his again, to lie glued together with passion and hear her admit that she loved him.

Scott left right after dinner, and Angela was left in the sitting room with two very puzzled friends. Jane said nothing as she sipped her coffee. That in itself was more eloquent than any question. It was Keith that brought everything to a head.

"What was that all about?"

Jane shot him a frown and shook her head slightly but he ignored her. She at least had an inkling of what was happening although she hadn't heard the gossip yet. Wasn't she aware of past secrets that her brother knew nothing of? Why couldn't Keith be quiet and forget the tense evening?

Angela's cup rattled against the saucer and she hastily set it down. It would be only a matter of time before Keith found out the ugly truth.

"I suppose I should tell you now," she said, dreading what his reaction would be, "before you hear about it from someone else. Sit down, Keith—you're not going to like what I have to say."

He did as she said, a cold foreboding deep within him. Since this afternoon an invisible barrier had slammed down between them and he didn't think it was all because of their quarrel. He was going to lose her! The sure knowledge struck him with the force of a bomb going off beneath his chair.

"I'll leave you two alone," said Jane, starting to rise.

"No, stay. You already know most of it, Jane, but not what happened today." Angela took a deep breath and plunged in. "Scott wants me to marry him—"

"Never!" shouted Keith jumping to his feet, his face livid with fury. "I'll kill him—I'll—"

"Keith, I have refused his proposal. But now he is trying to force the issue, make me give in by telling everyone that. . .Lorna is. . .his child."

"The liar! That filthy deceitful son of a bitch!"

"He may be almost everything that you called him but he isn't a liar."

"Wha—what!" All the starch went out of Keith and he slumped back into the chair, his wounded eyes impaling her with silent pleading.

"Lorna is Scott Harrington's child."

"How could you, Angela?" His amazed voice was accusing. "The highwayman was bad enough, but this—this is the worst betrayal! How could you stoop as low as Scott Harrington? Lovers! I can't believe it—could never forgive—"

"I didn't ask for your forgiveness, did I, Keith?" she snapped. "What happened wasn't my fault. Scott drugged Percy and raped me on my wedding night."

Jane gasped at this new revelation, her eyes helplessly shifting from her brother's tortured face to Angela's glittering eyes. The more she learned about the man she still loved the worse his reputation became, and she wanted to close her ears to this conversation.

"Why didn't you tell me, Angela? I would have killed him!"

"You forget—we didn't know each other then and I couldn't tell anyone of my shame. I have no doubt Percy would have annulled the marriage if I had told him, so there was no one but myself to avenge what he did. I shot him the next day and he must have thought I was dangerous because the next time he felt like bedding me he drugged me."

The enmity that Keith had always felt for Scott crystalized into hatred, and every strange event and tortured look of Angela's past became clear. He was calm now with the frozen iceberg of revenge overpowering every other emotion.

"I will call him out."

"What—and get yourself killed?" Angela exclaimed. "You will not duel with him because he fights dirty and would gladly get rid of you—his rival. Be sensible, Keith—it's past history and happened long ago."

But she didn't dare tell either of them that history was repeating itself and that even now she was falling under Scott's power. Her wild blood longed for what he could do to her and his very wickedness attracted her like a moth to a flame—though she knew it could destroy her.

Chapter Twelve

Rain slashed the night and silver daggers of lightning pierced the darkness, sending the wind howling in protest and pain. It rattled the shutters seeking refuge but there was no escape from the jagged fingers of fire that sizzled and ravaged the storm.

The shutters on one window were not closed and the tempest beat mercilessly against the crystal panes. Scott stood watching the gloom and quick illumination, so startling in contrast it almost blinded him. Brandy burned warmly into his stomach and on a night like this one he needed it. It was very late and the household was asleep but he had waited purposely for this moment.

He had been home for just two weeks and the whole time, except for those first few hours by the lake, had been an armed truce. Carefully, he made sure he and Angela were never alone and when they chanced to meet they spoke to each other only when absolutely necessary, then in monosyllables. There was a purpose behind his avoidance of her—he had to have time to think. Besides, a confrontation in the early days after his discovery of her betrayal would have resulted in a flare of tempers as loud and bright as fireworks. But the battle would have to be fought eventually, if only to clear the air between them, and Scott had determined that he would choose the time and the place.

Now was the time but first he would subdue and tame her, in flesh if not in spirit. Then they could battle it out, after he had tasted her lips and quenched his passion in her yielding flesh.

On silent feet he made his way through the sleeping house with the storm lashing outside like a wild thing. Huge claps of thunder punctuated the moans of the wind and reverberated down the hallways he trod. The door to her sitting room was open, and he passed through it in the dark and paused outside the bedroom door.

What was that sound? Could it be voices? Noiselessly Scott turned the crystal doorknob. It was locked! But there was more than one way into Angela's bedroom, a fact they both knew well. So he retraced his steps, making a detour to the library where a sliding panel admitted him to the secret maze.

He slid along the passageways in the dark for he hadn't stopped to get a candle. He knew every turn, each step by heart. Stopping, he searched for a moment until his fingers found the catch and he smiled to think of the surprise in store for Angela. The door opened toward him without a sound, and Scott gently pushed his way past the gowns hanging in the closet, only the whisper of rich materials heralding his approach.

Good, the door between the dressing room and bedroom was unlocked. A crack of light filtered through the darkness to where he stood listening intently with a frown furrowing his brow. Muffled sounds drew him on —had it been a sigh, a moan?

The door yielded and Scott's blood congealed in his veins, his eyes dark pools of agony reflecting the flickering candle beside the bed. But the tiny flame was sufficient to light the scene of Scott's torment and as he stood petrified, still unable to comprehend what he did not want to believe, something snapped inside of him. The cold, deadly anger that had been an intrinsic part of him for the past weeks gave way before the torrential, all-encompassing fury that swept through him, seeking a violent release.

Black and gold hair was a startling contrast in the flickering light, and Angela's fragile body was pressed into the bed by the full weight of Keith's. Although the covers were over them there was no doubt in Scott's mind as to what they were doing—the movement was too familiar. Her thrashings had all too recently been done for his benefit and her moans had been echoes of his own. Scott had thought her betrayal before total, but this was the ultimate deception!

Angela panted, her body tense and restlessly moving. This was the first time they had been together since Scott's return and she tried to block out the horrible thoughts that kept hammering at her brain even now. How she had wished to wipe Jack's memory from her mind and body at times like this, and now she had accomplished it—but at what price?

Scott had effectively banished Jack's ghost from her bedroom but in doing so had taken his place, and now it was his face as she saw behind her closed eyelids. During the whole time with Keith her mind kept creeping back to Scott—the way he made her feel when they lay together, how his lips moved upon hers, his total command of her senses.

No matter how often she dismissed the thoughts they returned, and she found herself comparing lovers, finding something lacking in Keith. She knew it was unfair but couldn't seem to control her ruminations. Was it because Scott was by far the most accomplished of her lovers that he pushed aside even her tender feelings for Jack? At a time like this she didn't know and couldn't think, needing the release that her golden lover couldn't seem to accomplish, growing more frantic as her ghost-lover insisted on taking over.

They were on the threshold of fulfillment when Keith jerked free of her, and Angela half rose on her elbows, protest dying on her lips. The rapidly moving scenes happened in slow motion and she stared in horror at the confrontation between her two lovers, not quite able to believe what was happening.

Scott had the advantage of surprise and in succession punched Keith in the stomach and the jaw, then brought his knee up between his legs. As he crumpled to the floor Angela came at Scott like an enraged tigress, her nails curved into claws, but he caught the movement from the corner of his eye. With an effortless motion he backhanded her and stars of pain exploded in her head as she fell beside the bed. Black dots danced before her eyes but before she fainted she saw very far away, through a dim tunnel, Scott's booted foot kicking Keith in the stomach, ribs, and face until he was bloody and unmoving.

There was blood in her mouth and she felt as if she was going to be sick. Angela opened her eyes a crack and the dim light sent waves of pain crashing through her head. Where was she, and what had happened? She couldn't seem to think, and the lapping waves of blackness were comforting as they engulfed her once more. But consciousness kept interrupting the blessed nothingness and someone passed a cloth, wet with icy water over her face. Trying to brush the annoying thing away she found that she couldn't move her arms and this time opened her eyes all the way.

Her vision was filled distressingly by Scott's hardened, dangerous face. Brown eyes as hard and unyielding as diamonds pierced her with hatred and anger, filling her with dread.

"Good," he growled, his mouth grim. "You are coming around. I wanted you to be conscious for the rest of this night—for your punishment, you lying little whore!"

Angela struggled to get free, but her arms were stretched tautly over her head, tied to the bed with the silken drapery cords. The firm sailor's knots tightened around her wrists, making her hands throb protestingly. Keith! In a panic she turned her head and located his body in a darkened corner of the room. He too was bound but that hadn't been necessary, for he was motionless and she wondered if he was dead.

"Don't worry about your lover—he's still alive, but he won't look so pretty after tonight."

"Let me go! Please, Scott. . ." But a grim smirk told her she might as well have pleaded for mercy with the Devil. "You have no right—no claim on me! What I do and who I see is none of your concern. I know you're angry—mad because you found out about Keith. . .and Jack, but I don't belong to you. I can do as I please!"

"You are wrong, Angela. Everything you do

concerns me because you are going to be my wife. That makes you my fiancée, and when you betray me it is very much my business." He explained it slowly and simply as if speaking to a child. "Did you think I would let this episode pass unpunished? You deserve whatever I do to you—and you know it."

"No, you're crazy! I told you I wouldn't marry you. I refuse to be your wife—or anything else!"

"But you will be," Scott replied ominously, standing over her and stripping his clothes off. "And when you are my wife I will keep you in your place, and if you ever betray me again I will kill you."

Terror gripped her at the cold, dispassionate way his eyes moved over her, and all the remembered cruelties of the past returned with new impact. "Wha—what are you . . . going . . . to do?" Her voice quavered pathetically, but neither that or the pleading, frightened look in her eyes touched him.

His body was a cold shell housing only emptiness inside. The heat of anger had concentrated into ice and what was about to happen was inevitable. Even if it spoiled all of his carefully laid plans Scott was helpless to stop himself, for the hurt in him went so deep that the only way to exorcise it and make himself whole again was to inflict even more pain on Angela.

"What I should have done long ago, love," he said falling onto the bed beside her. Tangling his fingers in her hair he jerked her face viciously toward his, covering her mouth with his but not in a kiss. Scott's teeth bit into her lips and then moved down over her neck and shoulders inflicting the same punishment, leaving ugly marks on her skin.

Angela writhed beneath him and he dug his fingers cruelly into her breasts to keep her still. She tried not to moan as her flesh throbbed in protest at his sadistic attack, but when his sharp teeth followed his hands biting into the tender flesh of her nipples she arched in shock, barely able to suppress a scream.

"That's right, slut—scream!" he said his face contorted as if he were the one being tortured. "Scream,

Angela—I want to hear you scream!"

It went on and on, Scott's hands and teeth abusing every part of her body until there was nothing but agony and she wished she could faint. Drops of blood smeared over her skin, and Angela closed her eyes, clenching her teeth so tightly she thought they would disintegrate. She might be helpless and totally within his power but he wasn't going to have the satisfaction of hearing her scream for mercy, and her obstinacy seemed to incite him to further acts of violence.

He was a fiend, humiliating her, breaching her last pitiful attempts at defending herself with ease. The ferocity of this rape exceeded even her wedding night, and groans escaped from between Angela's teeth as intense shocks cut into her, ripping through her belly. Her fingers clenched the silken ropes tightening spasmodically as he battered her delicate body taking his time over the task of subduing her.

He was killing her, tearing her to pieces each time his body thrust against hers and through a haze of shock and anguish Angela heard his grunts in her ear as if he were on the rack. When she curled her spine away from him, trying to elude more suffering, he just reached a hand beneath her shoving her raw flesh against the instrument of her torture.

It was over at last and Angela went limp with relief and fatigue as he strode through the dressing room door. She ached all over but it was nothing compared to the sheer terror of a few minutes ago. A gasp of despair passed her swollen lips as Scott returned with her quirt in his hand. So it wasn't over after all; she had underestimated him again. The evening had only begun.

Her bound arms twisted and felt as if they were being pulled from their sockets as Scott turned her over. Angela bit into the pillow as he beat her, half smothering herself as the braided leather lash welted her back, buttocks, and thighs. It was impossible to keep her body from jerking as each stroke raised new wheals on her skin, criss-crossing her fair skin with red stripes.

He alternately raped and beat her until dawn lightened the stormy sky and she had given up hoping for relief. But now it seemed he was going, for he got dressed with his eyes averted from the damage he had done her.

In pain-clouded confusion Angela looked into Keith's wide open eyes, then at Scott as he pulled a ring from his finger. Wrapping part of it with his handkerchief, he held it in the flame of the candle. She jerked in shock as he pressed the glowing signet ring into the broken flesh of one round buttock, searing her flesh with one final excruciating pain.

"Now you belong to me," he growled in a strange hoarse voice. "I have set my seal on your flesh forever!" Then he released her wrists and left without a backward glance.

Angela didn't know how long she lay there half conscious with his words still ringing in her ears. The only reality was an ocean of pain drowning her, burning into her, covering every inch of her body. Hatred seared into her heart like the brand he had placed on her skin, and she struggled against the oblivion she had prayed for before.

Stiffly she moved to the edge of the bed—she must get to Keith. But her legs collapsed under her and she fell to her knees, doubled over, both hands pressed against the piercing agony in her belly. Nothing Scott had ever done to her before even came close to equaling this, and the unsuppressed violence she felt for him mobilized her.

She crawled over to Keith on her hands and knees muttering vindictive curses under her breath. Every movement was clumsy and slow and it took fifteen minutes before she got his arms free.

"I'm going to kill the bastard!" Keith groaned through smashed lips, adding a long string of profanities the like of which she had never heard from him before.

"Yes!" she agreed. "Kill Scott! Kill him for me!"

Then the darkness that she had been fighting overwhelmed her, crashing down on her with stunning force. Angela collapsed beside Keith as if she were mortally wounded, and even in unconsciousness her teeth were clenched against the moans that came unbidden to her lips.

She awakened, not wanting to return to reality but disturbed by the loud pounding on the door. Angela was in bed and Keith was sprawled beside her, his face unrecognizable and covered with dried blood. Would the noise ever stop?

"Who is it?" she called in a voice very unlike her own not daring to move her wounded body.

"It's Molly, milady, with your breakfast."

"Go away! No breakfast—don't want to be disturbed." Rolling onto her stomach she slept.

There was knocking on the door again. "Why can't they leave me alone," she groaned opening her eyes slowly. The room was dim with twilight and Angela realized she had slept the day through.

"Angela—Angela!" The knocking was insistent. "Please—open the door. It's Jane and I must talk to you. Angela—are you all right?"

She could hardly move but somehow managed to stagger to the door, reeling and clutching at pieces of furniture for support. Jane was her friend and she needed help. She could depend on her for that and keeping her mouth shut about what had happened.

"Are you alone?" Angela inquired, leaning heavily on the door. Her fingers trembled on the key.

"Yes. Angela, I'm so worried about Keith—he never came home last night and has been missing all day. I thought—"

The door opened and the light from the sitting room fell on Angela revealing the atrocities that Scott had inflicted on her. Jane took a step backward in horror one hand pressed to her mouth.

"Oh, lord!" she choked, appalled at the bloody, bruised creature that had to be Angela because of her long black hair. Every thought of Keith vanished before the distress in her sunken aqua eyes.

"What happened?" Without waiting for an answer Jane put her arms around Angela's cringing form and half-dragged, half-carried her back to the bed. She fumbled for a candle in the dimness. "Who did that—who would dare?"

"Scott!" Angela's voice was filled with hatred and revulsion as she spat out the vile name.

The candle flared and Jane saw her brother lying on the bed. His chest moved shallowly. Thank heavens he was still alive! She looked from him to Angela in total bewilderment, wondering who to assist first.

"You must help us, Jane. Keith—he's unconscious. Scott found us together last night and beat us. He tied me up—he raped me and. . .and. . ."

"Don't talk now," soothed Jane. "I'm here and will take care of everything. Everything will be all right."

"Don't tell. . ."

"No—I won't tell anyone. Shh! Lie still."

"Do Keith first," Angela said as Jane covered her lightly with a blanket. "I think he. . .is worse off than me."

Scott sat sprawled in a chair in his bedroom, his face in his hands and his head throbbing. After he had finished with Angela he had proceeded to drink himself into a stupor to erase the vision of what he had done to her from his mind. But it had done no good, even in his sleep he saw her delicate mistreated body swollen and bruised, those reproachful green-blue eyes dull with pain. She had been so brave, hardly uttering a sound.

He had been beyond rage, and each hurt he had inflicted on her had torn through his body as if he was flagellating his own flesh. Why did he do it when it had only hurt them both? How could he have let himself spoil their whole relationship? To say that he was sorry now could never undo what he had done and Angela would never forgive him. It was too late for regrets, too late for a great many things.

"I hate you!" Her words echoed in his ears becoming real for the first time.

The door was flung open with such force that it crashed against the wall knocking a painting to the floor. Scott stood up as Jane stormed into the room, her face blazing with fury, the quirt he had used on Angela clutched in her hand.

With one sweeping glance she took in the empty liquor bottles and the disordered room. Scott was wearing only a robe and the hair on his chest gleamed in the candlelight. There were dark, sunken shadows beneath his eyes and lines etched into his haggard face. Her gaze returned to his eyes, they were horrible—as if he was dead—and he was unsteady on his feet, running a hand over the stubble on his chin and through his tousled hair.

Jane raised her arm and swung the quirt and it made sickening sounds as it struck his face and chest. She struck him again and again leaving marks on his unprotected skin, and he didn't even wince or make any move to stop her. It was almost as if he welcomed the pain like a lover's caress, needing it to exonerate him for the evil he had done.

Sobbing and disgusted with herself, Jane threw the quirt on the floor. "How could you?" she shouted, dashing the tears from her eyes. "What manner of man could. . .could do such a thing?"

"Is she all right?" His voice was dull and lifeless.

"All right! After what you did to her? You. . . you're a monster—a perverted, sadistic fiend straight out of hell! If I were a man I would kill you.

"I can never, never forgive you for what you have done to Keith and Angela. You had absolutely no right to. . ."

"I was mad—mad with jealousy and the fear that I had lost her to your brother. But now," his voice was thick with despair, "I have lost her for good.

"I found them together—in bed making love. Can you even comprehend how I felt. . ."

"I was in a similar position myself—once."

He looked at her and had the grace to flush at her words. How could he have forgotten that night? Then with all the logic of a child he said, "I love her and yet I had it in me to almost destroy Angela, because she doesn't love me. You were right, Jane, so right! Caught in my own trap with no way out."

Scott's face was screwed up with grief, and Jane stared astounded as he turned his back to her, leaning on the mantel with his face in the crook of his arm. His shoulders shook but the only sound in the room was the crackling of the fire, and she stood rooted to the carpet watching his silent agony. She had never seen a man cry before.

Jane smuggled Keith out of Brightling Castle under cover of darkness a few days later. For the next few weeks she flew back and forth like a shuttle between the two houses, tending to the hurts of her brother and her best friend. And every day, as Keith's broken nose and cracked ribs slowly healed, she had to calm him as he chafed against the enforced bed rest, wanting to see Angela, longing for the moment when he would kill Scott on the field of honor.

Angela's body mended too, until the only sign to remind her of that night was the small reddish-purple scar his ring had left on her smooth white skin. The first time she looked at it in the pier glass she screamed in rage at his branding of her with his initials like an animal. He wanted to own her completely, and in a rage she threw her silver-backed brush through the mirror shattering it into a million pieces.

She would have that scar for the rest of her life, but that didn't make her Scott's property. To the contrary, whenever she thought of it she became angrier, adamant that he would never touch her again. And when she visited Keith he assured her that he would kill the man that had almost destroyed them both. Now she had a champion, someone besides herself to depend on, but she would have relished the thought of killing Scott herself.

One afternoon as Angela and Lorna were leaving the house for a walk they ran smack into Scott returning after a month's absence. The surprise of seeing him again left her speechless for a moment, but Lorna made up for her silence, greeting her father enthusiastically.

"Papa—Papa! You came home," she cried as he picked her up. She threw her arms around his neck and Scott peered at Angela's stunned countenance over his daughter's head.

Her cheeks were red and her eyes glittered but she was just as lovely as ever. The picture of a ruined beauty that he had carried with him for the past weeks disappeared, but he could never forget what he had done to her. So she had recovered; Scott breathed a silent sigh of relief, wondering if the other marks had faded. But there was one thing that had only intensified and that was the hatred blazing from her pale eyes.

"Take me for a ride on Styx, Papa. Tell me a story."

"Bastard!" Angela hissed at him, snatching Lorna right out of his arms and holding her protectively against her bosom. "Get out of my house—I don't ever want to see you again!"

"You seem to forget, Angel," Scott reminded her, holding his ground, "that half of this place is mine. You can't order me out, unless you want to fight it out in court. But I doubt if you would win—and you are a very bad loser."

Angela bit her lip to keep from swearing at him in front of Lorna. "I knew you would come back," she told him scathingly. "Any other man would have blown his brains out in disgrace over what happened—but not you! You come swaggering in here as if you own the castle and everything you see. Well you don't own me or my daughter, and if you insist on living here then I will move out!"

He didn't say anything as he walked down the hall, ignoring her tirade, but after a few strides he stopped and turned, his gold-spangled eyes serious. "By the way," Scott said offhandedly. "I'm sorry about what happened the last time we met. I hope you are feeling better." His voice was as unemotional as if he had just inquired about the weather.

"You're sorry! Sorry!" Angela's voice rose to a shriek. "You are a beast, Scott Harrington—no I do the animals an injustice comparing something as low as you are to them! You are the scum of the earth—a—"

"Mama," Lorna said, peering apprehensively at her mother's distorted face, "are you angry with Papa?"

Angela flounced out of the house, slamming the door, and the sound shook the hall like distant thunder.

The servants' grapevine was as efficient as ever. Within minutes of their quarrel it was being whispered about all over the castle as wild speculations as to what had passed between them at their last meeting were the main topic of the day. Excitement was never far away when the duke was around, and where his stepmother was concerned there were sure to be violent clashes.

Scott had barely settled back into his rooms when Sandler the butler knocked on his door, informing him that he had a visitor.

"I put Lord Montgomery in the morning room," Sandler informed him.

"Very well. I will be down shortly."

So Angela had run to Bentwood, straight to Keith as soon as she had seen his face. There was only one reason he would want to see him and Scott knew exactly what that was. This would be his chance to kill Keith—or win Angela—and he wondered if he could still his natural impulses. It would be difficult, very difficult, and he might end up dead with Keith winning everything. He would just have to trust in luck and hope Keith was nervous and a bad shot.

Scott tied his cravat and examined it critically. He might as well get the formalities over with as soon as possible, with the same speed he had surmounted the obstacle of his first meeting with Angela. She had been so desirable and so angry, with her eyes flashing like the aquamarines he had given her. The need to fold her tenderly in his arms and beg her forgiveness had been overpowering, but she had been as prickly as a cactus.

He should have known there would be an audience. As Scott entered the room three pairs of eyes bored into him and only Jane's were in the least sympathetic. No one spoke as Keith strode up to him. The slap rang out in the silence of the room, harder than etiquette demanded, so forceful that Scott's head snapped to one side.

"My seconds will call on you tomorrow," Keith said, noting with satisfaction the mark of his blow on Scott's grim face. "You have the choice of weapons, of course."

"Yes," drawled Scott, apparently bored with the whole scene. "Pistols at twenty paces."

Angela's gaze pinioned him with its malevolence. "Keith is going to kill you—you know!"

"We will see," he replied, slowly turning and leaving the room.

"And if he doesn't then I will," she shouted after him.

The day was unusually warm and the sun wasn't even up yet. Not a breath of air stirred the leafy green branches of the trees where birds were singing sweetly to one another, unaware of the drama being enacted below.

Two groups of men stood quietly, waiting for the first light of morning to banish the pale stars. Keith had never fought a duel before and he was extremely nervous. The fact that Scott was cool and utterly confident didn't help matters any and he surreptitiously wiped the sweat from his brow. He was desperate. He had to kill Scott and avenge the abuse that had been done. But of greater importance he had to protect Angela and assure them both that she would never have to fear being manhandled by him again.

It obviously wasn't Scott's first duel, and Keith wondered if he had ever killed another man. Yes, he decided, the man was a brute, completely without morals or honor. It would be a pleasure to rid the world of his presence—or die trying.

They went over the instructions again, and as the sun flooded the summer day each man chose a pistol. Back to back they stood stiffly, waiting, and then the voice rang out clearly counting in the dawn hush. Keith paced off the distance with the scene of Scott raping Angela foremost in his mind. When he visualized that he was angry enough to kill, and every muscle and nerve in his body was attuned to that one all-encompassing thought: to see Scott Harrington lying dead in a pool of blood.

At the final count they both whirled and Keith quickly took aim, squeezing the trigger gently. A sharp retort cracked the peace of the day and the acrid smell of gunpowder stung his nose.

Scott lurched and almost fell as a fiery pain streaked through his body. Trying to ignore the hot gush of blood that stained his shirt crimson, he straightened and took careful aim. He could feel himself weakening as every beat of his heart pumped the life blood from his body, but he pointed the pistol unerringly at Keith's heart. His golden-brown eyes glowed like hot coals as the seconds passed, and the silence was deafening.

No one moved or even breathed in the frozen tableau. It was Scott's game now, and what happened next was up to him. Sweat ran in rivulets down Keith's face, dripping into his collar as he stared down the muzzle of Scott's pistol. His discharged pistol dangled from numb fingers and his heart beat frantically, willing him to action. But his honor was at stake and he remained stock still waiting for the inevitable.

Hours passed, years passed with that pistol pointed straight at him. There was a vicious smile on Scott's paling face, a triumphant grimace as he clenched his teeth against the agony of severed nerves and gaping flesh.

"Damn it, Harrington," Keith shouted, unnerved by this cat and mouse game. "Get it over with—shoot!"

The explosion sent the birds soaring upward into the hot, blue vault of the sky, disturbed for the second time on what had started as a tranquil day. This time they circled warily, not settling back into their nests until the intruders were gone.

"I heard shots!" Angela cried, rushing to the window, though she knew she wouldn't see anything. A moment later she began her uneasy pacing, fingernails biting into her clenched hands.

"I wish I was there!" Angela blurted out. "All this waiting is driving me insane."

Every attempt to get Keith to reveal the secret of where the meeting would take place had been in vain. She had teased, coaxed, and begged, all to no avail. "One thing we don't need is two fainting women on our hands," Keith had told her, informing her of the day but not the place.

Idly, Angela had flirted with the idea of following at a distance, but that would not have worked. They would just spot her and send her home. She should know soon what the outcome was, but the very nearness of the revelation agitated her beyond keeping still.

"Angela, please sit down. You are making me jumpy," Jane said looking up from her needlework.

"How can you sit there so calmly when at this moment one or both of them might be dead?"

Jane jabbed the needle into her finger and with an exclamation thrust it into her mouth. "I'm not calm," she replied, throwing the embroidery aside and getting to her feet. "Inside I feel just like you do. Keith is my brother, you know. This," she gestured at the tangled needlework, "helps a little—not much, but some."

"Oh, Jane, I'm so sorry," Angela cried, throwing her arms around her friend and hugging her tightly. "As always I'm not thinking—or rather, thinking only of how I feel!"

They clasped each other for support, and the sound of horses approaching the castle sent them scurrying to the door. Horses' hooves drowned out the whisper of soft kid slippers skimming over the intricate brick design of the drive, and Angela's eyes widened in disbelief as Keith and Scott rode up to the house together.

Keith's face was grim and white and Angela ran to him. "Are you hurt, Keith? You have to be all right!"

"I'm fine—"

Scott's voice cut through the conversation. "I'm not dead yet, Angel—will you finish the job?"

She looked up at his pale visage and the crooked

smiled that was pasted on his face. Those brown eyes that she knew only too well flickered and closed, and Scott slid from his horse and fell unconscious to the ground. The coat he was wearing fell open and she gaped at the scarlet-drenched body lying at her feet.

There was a flurry of activity as the doctor had him taken to his room and Angela followed after them, unwilling to miss a moment of his torment. Neither Jane nor Keith could dissuade her from her impetuous decision. Their arguments fell on deaf ears as she contemplated the defeat of her archenemy.

She stood in Scott's room out of the way of Doctor Wallander and Angus but close enough to see everything. The wound was bad. The ball had entered his side and curved along his ribs, slashing him open from front to back right down to the bone. Angela had never seen so much blood in her life. As the doctor cleaned the wound a crimson tide flooded the white sheets.

He was conscious again and Angela stared into his wide open eyes. He stared back, gritting his teeth as the doctor removed bone fragments and finally began stitching him up. Those aqua eyes were coldly appraising, and a slight smile played around her mouth.

Damn, she was enjoying the whole thing—the pain, the blood, and the fact that he might die! Seeing it all was her revenge for what he had done to her and he couldn't blame her. His pain was her pleasure and in spite of the agony and the fact that he was choking on his own suppressed groans, Scott couldn't help admiring the woman that he loved. Any other woman would have fainted right away but not Angela. She was a blood-thirsty little savage and she was his.

As a dressing was applied Scott gave her what passed for a smile and said softly, "Bitch!"

That only amused her, and he wondered if after all this was over, they could wipe out the past and start over again. Maybe the fact that he had lowered his pistol and discharged it into the ground instead of Keith's heart would help. He knew positively that if he had killed Keith she would have been lost to him forever. This way there was still a chance, a very slight one—if he didn't die first.

"Is he going to die, Doctor Wallander?" asked Angela, not bothering to lower her voice so that Scott wouldn't hear her.

The doctor frowned at her callousness and drew her aside speaking softly. "He has lost a lot of blood—more than I like to think about. He refused to let me attend him until we got here. That, coupled with the risk of infection, constitutes a grave danger. Lord Harrington is very weak now and what will happen I just cannot say. We will have to wait and see."

Angela went over to the bed and stood looking down at Scott. His eyes were closed and there were lines of suffering on his pale face. Very lightly she touched his shoulder with one finger, the scar that she had made so many years ago. His eyes flew open and she smiled cruelly.

"No, you are not dead—yet!"

Every day Angela went to Scott's room to gloat over him. She stood looking at him, unspeaking, and watched as he steadily grew worse. The doctor's worst fears became a reality as his wound grew infected, and she took particular pleasure in watching him change the dressing, which caused his patient excruciating pain. Doctor Wallander was only too glad when he could leave and be on his way from that strange, brooding household.

It was almost as if the duchess was willing the duke to die, and a silent battle was fought between the two, right under his nose. Once he had ordered her from the room to make his patient more comfortable, but the beautiful sadistic lady had put him in his place with just a glance. All that hostility could not be doing the duke any good, yet in some odd way Doctor Wallander sensed that her presence, however disconcerting, gave Lord Harrington the will to live. A lesser man might have died days ago.

A raging fever blazed through Scott's body, and for three days now he had been delirious. Yesterday, as Angela had watched Angus bathe him in cold water, he had raved about a pirate he had carved up, and now he was muttering about her. Warm blushes stained her cheeks at some of the garbled sentences she made out, and she ignored the dark looks Angus shot at her from beneath his bushy brows.

It would be over soon; the doctor was not optimistic, wondering how he had held on this long. His feverish body thrashed around on the bed and Angus leaned over him, restraining his movement. Angela stared, amazed at the bottomless depths of her own hatred, wishing he would live longer and suffer more.

As if the very violence of her feelings cut through his delirium Scott opened his eyes unexpectedly, his gaze fastening on her face. She took a step back, disconcerted at the unmasked emotion radiating from him and touching her like warming rays of the sun.

"Sweetheart," he whispered, his voice a hoarse croak. "Angel, Angel! I love you so!"

"No!" She backed out of the room, bumping into furniture, unable to tear her eyes away from his. Panic tore at her from every side. He was sick and helpless and couldn't hurt her yet those words struck her like blows.

She fled to her room in terror with her hands over her ears to stop his voice from following her. "I love you so!" No—he couldn't have said that! She had imagined it or he had.

"It's not true!" she screamed slamming the door and throwing herself on her bed. "It's impossible!"

Scott was out of his head, raving with delirious dreams—that had to be the answer. A man in love could not do what he had done to her.

"I hate you, Scott Harrington! I hate you!"

Her face was wet with the first tears she had shed since that night, and her fingers slid over her cheeks in astonishment that he could be the cause of her weeping. What was happening to her? A pain more terrible than any he had inflicted upon her twisted deep within her breast, and she gave way to the dam bursting in her.

The next day Angela had to force herself to go to his room, chiding herself for being a silly fool to be so affected by the incoherent ramblings of a dying man. But it seemed he wasn't dying after all, for when she entered the room she found him propped up in bed and as lucid as ever. The fever had broken during the night.

He ordered Angus out of the room and watched Angela looking out the window to the garden below. She wouldn't meet his inscrutable eyes, and now that he was no longer helpless and recovering from his wound Scott's suffering no longer gave her pleasure.

"Well, my little vulture," he began, "I'm not going to die after all. Your vigil was in vain—now you can fly away!"

"Yes, I think I will."

She started for the door, but as she brushed past him Scott's hand shot out grasping her wrist, forcing her to sit on the edge of the bed.

"You are hurting me," Angela protested, surprised by his strength after his bout with the fever.

His grip loosened and he reached out to touch the velvet softness of her cheek. Angela recoiled as if he had struck her, fear showing for a brief moment in her eyes.

"Did you think I was going to strike you?" And then before she answered, Scott said, "I promise, Angel, I will never strike you again."

He put her hand to his lips and brushed a kiss across her fingertips. Angela was powerless to stop him. The depths of his eyes drew her toward him, and she couldn't look away no matter how she tried. It was happening again, the way it had at the lake and countless times before. In spite of his past cruelties he was seducing her with just a glance, making her forget everything but his lips hot against the palm of her hand, her wrist.

"I must go," she managed to say.

"But you just got here, love. You seemed to find me much more amusing a few days ago. Most women would have fainted at the sight of all that blood, but you—I think you enjoyed it."

"Yes, I did," Angela told him defiantly. "I wanted to see you suffer the way you made me suffer."

"But there is one difference between us," said Scott solemnly. "You took delight in my pain—I didn't enjoy what I did to you. It was as if I was doing it to my own flesh." It was out, the closest avowal he had dared make about the way he felt about her. "I won one battle—you the other. Can't we call a truce, sweetheart?"

"A truce is just the suspension of a war—the hostilities always begin again."

Scott placed her small hand on the thick white bandages encircling his body. "So you don't feel I have been tormented enough? All you have to do, Angela, is move your hand just a little. Go ahead—I assure you it will hurt like hell."

His brown eyes searched her face, not missing the quickening of her breath between her parted lips. As she tried to pull her hand away he held her fast, making her lean against him, pressing on the wound.

Scott's face twisted with pain, going white again beneath his tan. His lips clamped together in a thin line and his eyes narrowed to slits, but still he watched her.

"Stop it! Stop!" cried Angela struggling with him, so close she could feel his panting breath on her cheek.

"But you want to hurt me—don't you?"

"No—no! I don't!"

"Why not, love?"

"You said something—yesterday. . ." she gasped, so upset she could hardly speak.

"Yesterday? I don't remember yesterday, or the day before, or the day before that. What did I say?"

"Nothing—leave me alone!"

"But it must have been something," Scott said, grabbing her chin and turning her face toward his, "because you are crying."

"I am not!"

"Why are you crying, my love?"

"Damn you!" she sobbed. "It's all your fault! I always cry when I'm—" Angela caught herself just in time. Another word would have been disastrous. "When I'm upset," she finished lamely.

With a gentle pressure of his fingers Scott led her

captured chin down, until her lips were just a breath away from his. "Just one kiss," he told her softly, "to welcome me back from the grave."

Angela ceased to think as her mouth obeyed his request, soft and tender against his. Scott's tongue gently sought the sweetness of hers, inflaming his senses until he was sure this couldn't be happening. It was one of those tormenting, feverish delusions. But she was real and didn't disappear like a mist as he drew her down next to him.

Her will slipped away as it always did at times like this, and the hot press of his open mouth on hers drowned her in sensation after pleasurable sensation. Scott took his time cherishing her, worshiping her with one kiss that lasted as long as ten others. This couldn't be happening, she couldn't be lying beside her worst adversary, a man she wanted dead, letting him taste what had been granted to so few. She hated him but—oh—he did know how to titillate her, how to transport her to another world where only rapture existed.

Scott kissed her face and neck, oblivious of the pain in his side. When his love was so sweetly yielding he couldn't resist her. He forgot everything but pleasing her and winning her heart. Her quickened breath, the way her lashes moved restlessly against her pink-tinted cheeks, the softness of her breasts against him, all intoxicated him beyond common sense.

"Why is it," she began, then shook her head, dismissing her own foolish speculations.

"What mysterious thoughts are in that lovely head?" asked Scott, tracing the line of her nose and mouth lazily with a finger. "You always manage to elude me, Angel. Why—" He stopped as she laughed, entranced by the infrequent sight that lit her face with radiance and set twin dimples in her cheeks.

"Yes, why? I ask myself a thousand whys every time we are together." Her voice was a whisper, almost as if she was talking to herself. "Why do we fight so brutally? Why do we devastate each other like clashing armies, only to regret it later? Why, when we love, is there a magic that cannot be put into words—only felt? Why is it that when you are here I wish you gone and when you are gone. . ." She closed her eyes briefly, a mixture of pain and ecstasy contorting her features. "Why you?"

"I could answer all those whys," Scott told her, his smoldering eyes searching hers deeply, "but I don't think you would like the answer."

"No! No!" Her expression that had been so guileless and revealing seconds ago was gone, replaced by the usual closed, watchful look he was used to. "I don't want to know—don't ever tell me!"

Angela pulled free of him, heedless of his wound, knowing only that she could not stay within the enchanted circle of his embrace. He had done it again, captivated her against her will. She ran to the door to escape.

"What are you so afraid of, Angel?"

"You! It's always you!"

As she fled from the room Scott called after her, "Could it be yourself that you are really afraid of, my love?"

Angela tore through the hallways, pursued by her own questions—and his. It was impossible for the two of them to live in the same house, even the same town. Something would always happen to bring them together again, either in bed or in combat, and she wanted neither.

"I've got to get away," she murmured over and over again. "I'm going home—home to Windy Arbor."

Chapter Thirteen

Angela hummed to herself in the kitchten, up to her elbows in flour. Everything was exactly as she remembered it, and she reveled in the simple everyday tasks that she hadn't been allowed to do in years. The delicious odor of apples and cinnamon wafted through the air and she smiled contentedly, her mouth watering for the pies that would be ready soon.

She had been up at dawn cleaning and baking, filled with a bottomless reservoir of energy. Life was wonderfully uncomplicated with just Lorna and Molly to share this peaceful interlude, and she couldn't think of why she had stayed away so long. To be home in the summer with the apples and cherries heavy in the trees, to be as carefree as a child again, to be free of all the pressures of money and a title—that surely was paradise and she was glad she had the good sense to know when to get out of a difficult situation.

An annoying wisp of hair tickled her nose, and Angela blew upward at it as it promptly fell back again. Loud male laughter sounded in the open doorway and she jumped, startled out of her skin.

"I didn't know you could cook!"

"There are a lot of things you don't know about me, Scott Harrington—and if you don't get out of here this instant you will find out a few unpleasant things!"

The audacity of the man, following her, spoiling her little retreat with his bold presence! He filled the tiny kitchen banishing her peace of mind, for Angela could not contemplate him for any length of time without finding her emotions and thoughts in a complete jumble. With an engaging grin and sparkling brown eyes he whipped his hand from behind his back and held a bouquet out to her.

"For you, my lady."

"Why, I'll bet you picked those right outside the door—from my own garden!" she exclaimed, half angry, half caught up in his boyish mischief.

"Ah," he sighed, "it seems you know me too well." Scott laid the suddenly forgotten flowers on the table and reached out a hand, brushing the tendril of raven hair from her face.

"What are you doing here? What do you want?" she asked, disconcerted by his possessive touch.

"You," he answered honestly, his hands closing around her upper arms. "The mountains came to Mohammed!"

Scott's lips were alarmingly close and she knew the power they could exert over her—the power to make her forget her resolutions and her agreement with Keith. No, he could not be allowed to touch her under any circumstances.

Angela shoved him away from her with all her strength, and he fell back in surprise. Two small, white handprints marred his black broadcloth coat, and he looked so startled and funny that she couldn't help dissolving into laughter.

"Well, you just so happen to have flour smudged on your nose," Scott said playfully, kissing it off. Then his mouth found its original target muffling her laughter, moving triumphantly as her arms encircled him and the contours of her body molded into his. There was nothing like laughter to overcome a woman's objections.

"Papa! Mama!" Lorna ran into the room beaming like the morning sun, to be caught up into Scott's strong arms. He smiled ruefully at Angela. The timing had been disastrous. If only they had returned an hour later, even half an hour. Not that he wasn't glad to see his daughter but there were times, he had just discovered, when children could be a nuisance.

He had been so close to winning Angela and now he had to start all over again, certainly with more difficulty, since surprise was no longer on his side. Molly surveyed the domestic scene with a sniff, putting her market basket on the table. Angela avoided her critical look, wiping her hands off on her apron.

"I'm afraid my coat will never be the same," said Scott putting Lorna down and shrugging out of it. But he surveyed its ruin with apparent good humor.

"What happened to it?" asked Lorna, brushing at the marks.

He caught Angela's eye and winked at her, not missing the color it brought to her cheeks. "Well, little one, your mother was going to put me into one of her pies and pop me into the oven!"

Lorna hung for a moment between belief and disbelief, her turquoise eyes huge. Then she burst into laughter. "You are so funny, Papa—you are too big to fit in the oven!"

The rest of the morning passed without incident, and Angela was relieved that Molly and Lorna had returned when they did—before she had a chance to disgrace herself again. But Scott seemed disinclined to leave, and the time dragged by as he and Lorna played with the present he had brought her.

The man had no idea of what to buy for a little girl—first a ship and now lead soldiers. But Lorna was delighted with them, lining them up across the sitting-room floor with Scott helping to arrange them.

They lunched together, and then Angela sent a vehemently protesting Lorna upstairs for her nap. Scott disrupted everything.

"I want you to go now," she told him, pacing in front of the chair he lounged in, too uneasy to keep still.

He remained silent, his eyes traveling over her face, down to her bosom, slowly undressing her in his mind. The change of atmosphere had done wonders for her, she positively glowed with health and vitality. Scott noted with a smile that she had gained a little weight. Her breasts strained voluptuously beneath the simple green cotton gown, and he wanted nothing so much as to unbutton her bodice and strip every stitch off her.

"Stop looking at me like that!" Angela put her hands

to her scarlet cheeks. What if he noticed? She had to get rid of him somehow.

"How am I looking at you?" Scott asked, his smile broadening at her discomfiture.

"As if I had nothing on!"

"I've seen you often enough without your clothes. It amuses me to see that you still blush like an innocent maiden."

"This conversation is going nowhere. Leave now! We have nothing to say to each other."

"I have something to say to you." Scott's arm caught her around the waist and swept her onto his lap. She struggled to get up but he held her easily till she gave up and sat stiffly where she was.

"All right—say what you have to and then get out!" Her back was ramrod straight, her body unyielding, and her heavy lashes veiled her downcast eyes.

"I love you," Scott said, his voice soft and charged with emotion.

Angela's lashes flew upward, her surprised aquamarine eyes looked unbelievingly into his. "What did you say?"

"You heard what I said, Angel. I'm in love with you, and I want you to marry me."

All the starch went out of Angela, and she slumped against his encircling arm. But as he made a move to kiss her, she slapped him hard across the face and jumped from his lap.

"Liar!" she screamed. "I know you don't mean it and so do you—so stop playing games. I'm not one of those silly women who can be taken in by a charming smile and a few flowery words!"

"I meant what I said, Angela." Scott's eyes were grave and his tone serious. "I've been in love with you for a long time but was too stubborn to admit it, even to myself. It took a long separation for me to realize how much I want and need you. Angel, love, you're in my blood. You mean everything in the world to me—because without you I want to die. Let me love you, let me show you how good we are for each other!"

Scott rose from the chair and caught her to him, crushing her lips against his. The heat rose in him in spite of her resistance and this time she was too angry to give in. Was he forever destined to have her fight him—to have to subdue her by force? He could take her right here and now but it would only be a temporary victory. When it was over she would feel the same, so there was no point in continuing. To have Angela come to him eagerly and willingly was worth waiting for.

So he released her, catching her arm before she slapped him again. He smiled wryly as her furious gaze took in his condition, clearly visible beneath the tight breeches. That only made her madder.

"I hate you!" She stomped her foot, eyes flashing and hair tumbling in dark disarray. "I know what you are really after—the rest of the inheritance. You want to possess everything your father had—even me. And if it just so happens that you find me desirable, so much the better!

"I refuse to be a. . .possession. . .a meek little wife to sit at home and breed children. I detest you, and I'm going to marry Keith Montgomery!" Angela clapped her hand over her mouth as if to put back the last words she had spoken.

Scott grasped her arm, his fingers almost crushing the bones. "And when," he demanded, "is the wedding to be?" There was a dangerous look in his eyes and his voice was contemptuous.

"Soon," Angela managed to get out, refusing to say anything else.

Scott released her as if she had burned him. "You may have won this time, Angela—but we still have a score to settle, you and I."

On that threatening note he slammed out of the house.

Jane stood back, her eyes sparkling with excitement as she inspected Angela. "Perfect! I'm going to love having you for a sister."

Angela tried to smile, pressing a hand to her bosom to

still the nervous fluttering of her heart. In just a little while she would be married, but she wasn't at all sure she was doing the right thing. Time and circumstance had forced her into a decision that could not be ignored or postponed.

"Are you ready?" inquired Jane, and at her nod she handed her the bouquet of yellow roses and violets.

Her parents were waiting in the carriage, beaming with pride as she and Jane joined them. It was to be a small gathering of only a few friends, an intimate affair in contrast to her first wedding.

Angela was so jittery she felt like screaming, but instead she sat stiffly, forcing herself to study the passing scenery. The sun was warm and golden but there was a hint of bad weather on the horizon. In any event the ceremony would be over long before the rain spoiled the day. But she wasn't concerned about rain ruining everything. It was Scott.

He had done another one of his disappearing acts. Angela hadn't seen him since their argument at Windy Arbor almost three weeks ago. His very absence worried her. If only she had some inkling of his plans, a way to reassure herself that he wouldn't try and disrupt her life again. But she knew better. His threat had been very real, and now he knew she was going to marry Keith. It would be just like him to crash the wedding and make a scene.

The carriage halted in front of the chapel and she was relieved. She couldn't let her own fears wreck this very important day. So she tried her best to push all the bad thoughts aside and forced a smile to her lips. Nothing is wrong—nothing is wrong, she repeated silently to herself, and when she took her father's arm and started down the aisle she almost believed it.

Keith's breath caught in his throat as Angela walked toward him. She was a vision, a dream come true in a delicate yellow dress embroidered with amethyst flowers and tiny green leaves. The smile on her face was fixed, and he knew she was afraid of this final commitment. How naive and skittish she was, so used to being mistreated by men that she distrusted them all. Well, he would prove her wrong and love her so faithfully that her world from now on would center only on him.

As she joined him at the altar he took her hand, and Angela twined her shaking fingers through his. The ceremony began and she released a long tremulous sigh. Nothing would matter now—not the past, not Scott, not her own stupid fears. The whole future spread before her, a long, smooth, easy road. There would be no obstacles unless she herself put them there, and Keith's hand gently squeezed hers soothing away all her worries.

There was a slight stir at the back of the chapel as some latecomers joined the gathering, but Angela ignored the disturbance, intent on the words being spoken. But the rustling and whispering became louder and Vicar Grindell looked up, faltered, and stopped completely, a look of amazement on his face.

Keith and Angela turned in unison, and hot rage shot through her. At first all she saw was Scott's face, darkly handsome with a mocking smile that didn't reach his eyes. He had come! She opened her mouth to utter a protest and he grabbed her, kissing her with a brutal passion that caused everyone to gasp aloud at its intensity.

When he released her Angela was so furious she couldn't even speak, but before she could slap his face Scott spun her around, clamping his arm tightly around her waist. Why didn't someone move? Why were they all frozen in place like icicles? Then she felt the cold metal against her temple and saw her mother crumple to the floor like a wilted flower.

"Don't anyone move," Scott warned in a loud voice, "unless you want the bride to have her head shot off!"

"Keith, help me," Angela pleaded as Scott dragged her down the aisle. She turned and twisted reaching out to her fiancé who stood unmoving with a stunned expression on his face. "Keith—he won't kill me—he's bluffing!"

"Shut up right now, Angela," murmured Scott in her

ear, "or I just might shoot your golden lover instead."

"You son of a bitch!" she screamed trying to grab hold of the pistol. "Bastard! I'll kill you myself for ruining my wedding. I'll. . ."

He started laughing and two dozen pairs of astonished eyes followed them to the back of the chapel. "She is mine," he said, looking straight at Keith, "and no other man will ever have her. Tonight Angela will warm my bed instead of yours, Montgomery—and she will be my wife!"

The sun struck hot on Angela's face after the cool, shadowed interior of the chapel. As she blinked in the glare, Scott hauled her onto his horse and held her tightly in front of him. When she tried to throw herself off the galloping mount he squeezed her until she couldn't breath, and she leaned back limply against his hard body.

They slowed as they neared the cliffs, and as the horse made his way down the path to the beach Angela gaped in alarm. For bobbing on the ocean was a ship, and she didn't need to look twice to know it was the *Dark Lady*.

"No!"

"Yes, my love, yes!"

Angela's hopes sank. If he had spirited her away on horseback then Keith would follow and eventually find them, but Scott had thought of everything. He was going to take her somewhere so far away that they would never be found. A ship left no tracks and they could travel anywhere in the world without a trace. She was lost!

Stopping near the water's edge, Scott handed her down to a scowling Angus who forced her into a boat. The sea was rough and waves slapped against the craft as Scott took his place and the sailors launched them into the surf. Spray soaked her dress as she eyed the distance to shore, wondering if she could swim it. As if sensing her thoughts Scott put his arm around her shoulders making sure she stayed put.

Horses and riders were outlined against the sky at the top of the cliffs. So, Keith had come, but too late to save her, and Angela almost cried in frustration. They were so close yet so far away, and there was no way he could reach her without a boat.

"Scott, please don't do this. Let me go back. We can never be happy together."

"Shut up!" he told her tersely.

"I hate you!"

He grabbed her hair, forcing her face close to his, brown eyes impaling her with their fury. "I don't care if you hate me or love me—as long as you are mine!"

The conversation was closed and she sat in rebellious silence the rest of the way to the ship. When they reached it Angela was hauled unceremoniously up the side and shoved roughly into a cabin. The door clicked from the outside and she was alone.

"Hell!" she muttered, kicking the solid door and then pounding on it with all her strength. "Damn you, Scott Harrington—before I'm finished with you, you'll wish you were dead!"

Now she was a prisoner again, for the second time in her life, but this time no ransom would be asked or given. She was the prize, stolen from under Keith's nose by an unscrupulous rogue who meant to use her for his own pleasure. There would be no escape.

The cabin was small but luxuriously appointed. A bunk took up one wall with built-in cabinets above and below it. Beneath the window was a highly polished rosewood desk and chair, and the whole cabin was paneled in teak. Spirit lamps were fastened to the walls and more cabinets lined the wall opposite the bunk. There was a thick Oriental rug beneath Angela's feet in soft jewel tones of gold, green, blue, and red.

She opened a cabinet and glanced at various charts, books, and instruments. Another one held Scott's clothes and much to her surprise the last door she opened contained some of her own garments. So, everything had been well planned, and his absence had only served to lull her suspicions, while all along Scott had been deviously planning to abduct her. The fact that he had snatched her away from her bridegroom at the altar probably made the venture even more exciting.

Angela kicked the door again in a rage and only succeeded in hurting herself. "If you think for one moment that I will be a meek, compliant companion, Duke of Brightling, then you have another surprise in store!"

The masts and rigging creaked overhead as the wind filled the sails and the vessel headed out to sea. Angela, her anger momentarily forgotten, opened the window and looked out, fascinated by the rise and fall of the dancing waves, the movement beneath her feet, and the salt tang on the breeze. There was a special beauty about a ship, sails aloft, skimming like a beautiful white bird across the water. She longed to be on deck with the wind in her hair and the sailors in a blur of activity around her.

The last ocean voyage she had been on was the return from Italy with her parents. She had been only fifteen then and interested in everything about the ship. Shivering, Angela realized she was cold, and she stripped off the damp dress selecting another from the closet.

Scott chose that moment to enter the cabin, his preoccupation with the embarkation abating at the sight of Angela in her undergarments.

"I see you have made yourself at home," he said nonchalantly, leaning against the door with his arms folded across his chest. A smile played around his mouth as he noticed her sulky expression and the defiant tilt of her chin. She was aching for a fight and he was just the one to give it to her.

Clasping the dress in front of her Angela looked at him from angry, narrowed, aqua eyes. He was so very sure of himself and of her, and she knew exactly what would happen next. Scott would make love to her, consummate the strange new relationship that would begin aboard this ship and end she knew not where. For end it would if she had any say in the matter, and no matter how many times he claimed her body as his she wouldn't let him touch her heart.

"Don't you have anything to say to me? My scheme

went off very well, don't you think? I can still see Montgomery now—"

"I have nothing whatsoever to say to you!"

"Come, come, my prickly little love—you are usually quite verbal on your likes. . .and dislikes." She turned her back on him, but he continued, "I see—the silent treatment. Well that's fine with me because I don't feel like talking either."

In one stride he was beside her, his hands caressing her stiff shoulders. Moving aside the jet-black spill of her hair, Scott placed small nibbling kisses on the side of her neck. Still she didn't move, neither accepting nor rejecting him.

In spite of the wonderful sensations his lips sent through her, Angela made herself think instead of the last time. By concentrating on the brutal rape and beating she blocked out her own sensual feelings and presented Scott with her cold shoulder. She was his prisoner—let him do what he wanted. This time she refused to succumb or give him the satisfaction of her resistance.

He was breathing faster in her ear as he cupped her breast with strong brown fingers. The other hand trailed down over her abdomen doing all the things that usually aroused her. Was it possible that his mistreatment of her had affected Angela in some subtle way? Scott frowned, thinking back. When he had kissed her at Windy Arbor she had responded, and before that in his room he knew he could have taken her if he hadn't been wounded. She was just exercising her feminine wiles on him, and he intensified his efforts.

Turning her to him, Scott kissed her, pressing her close and letting himself feel the wonder of her yielding body. Angela was unresisting, letting him plunder her mouth but she kept her eyes wide open and her arms at her sides, defying him by her very docility.

"I'm not in the mood for games, Angela," Scott told her curtly, stripping off her petticoats.

"Then go away because I don't feel like playing games either!"

Ignoring her comment, he finished undressing her and laid her on the bunk. As he took off his clothes she lay passively, watching him, making no attempt to flee or even cover herself.

Angela almost gave way when his hot, virile body pressed against hers demanding an answering reply, but she steeled herself and remained resolute. Scott kissed and caressed her very gently, taking pains to do all the things that she liked best. And when he pressed a kiss on the mark on her buttock, she jumped as if he had burned her again. Her only other reaction was when he fondled her breasts too enthusiastically, and she cringed.

"Did I hurt you?" he asked, and her only answer was a brief nod. "I'm sorry, Angel—I didn't mean to."

She was so adorable, his obstinate little love, and even though she wasn't participating Scott knew that he had to take her. The downward curve of her mouth, as if she was about to cry, only called up the tenderest feelings in him and he whispered love words in her ear that she didn't want to hear.

Nothing moved her. Angela just lay there inert and indifferent as he gave up all attempts to arouse her and concentrated instead on his own desires. He was careful not to hurt her, but Scott knew he wasn't pleasing her either, and since he didn't have to wait for her, the final rush of passion was over in minutes. It was an empty victory.

"Now you are totally mine," Scott said, stroking the silky black hair that he loved to touch. "Nothing will part us, sweetheart—I will see to that. Angel, Angel, my stubborn little enchantress, my beautiful lover—only from you would I endure such obdurate behavior. But don't think you can keep play-acting forever. I know you too well, my lusty vixen, and sooner or later you will give in, and when you do. . . ." He left the thought unfinished because they both knew what would happen then, and he smiled to think that his words had reached her, for she squirmed against his imprisoning arms, restlessly seeking escape.

Now that some life was returning to Angela he was unwilling to let her go, and she wriggled impatiently against his light kisses and threatening words. She should tell him right now but it was no guarantee that Scott would set her free, so she endured his touch with a wicked plan forming in her mind. When the time was right she would play her winning card, the one that would cut him to the heart.

"I love you, Angel," he said, kissing her ear. "When we are married everything will work out—you'll see."

"And what will you do with a wife that hates you?"

"I'll just have to love her twice as much!"

Angela flung herself from the bunk and under Scott's watchful eyes proceeded to wash every trace of their encounter from her body. When she finished she slowly got dressed, a nasty, triumphant little smile on her lips.

She was up to something; Scott could tell by her attitude and especially by that look. He had seen it before and it always preceded an unpleasant shock. There was no way of knowing what her surprise would be or when she would spring it, so he would just have to remain alert and forget about it until she decided to reveal it.

"We are in for a blow in a few hours," Scott informed her. "There is no danger but there will be high winds and seas, so stay in the bunk and don't light the lamps. There's the danger of a fire if you do."

The sea surged black and oily, broken by whitecaps and flying foam. It seemed to merge with the murky sky, and as Angela looked at the horizon she couldn't differentiate between the two. It looked dangerous enough to her but she supposed Scott knew what he was talking about—hadn't he survived a hurricane in the tropics and lived to tell of it? It seemed nothing could kill the man!

The storm began, tossing the ship like the toy he had given to Lorna just a few months ago. Had the time been that short? It seemed like years. Angela braced herself on the bunk to keep from being thrown across the room. She couldn't risk an injury now but had to keep herself unhurt and alert so that when the time came she could flee from her prison.

The fury of the squall increased and rain burst from the clouds, cutting icily into the men on the bucking deck. Every time the ship plunged Angela was sure it would be the last and they would all end up at the bottom of the ocean, a fitting finale to the disastrous day. She was stiff and sore from crouching in the dark and was beginning to get a queasy feeling in the pit of her stomach.

The *Dark Lady* creaked and groaned in the shrieking blast, and lightning, followed immediately by great claps of thunder, only increased the chaotic turmoil, till Angela thought she would go deaf. Burying her head beneath the pillow she muffled the sounds of the tempest only slightly, but at least those blinding flashes were blocked out.

Nature's assault lasted for a long, sleepless night and suddenly abated as a cold gray dawn approached. Scott opened the door drenched, dripping a puddle onto the rug. His eyes were bloodshot and his lips were blue with the cold.

"It's over," he said, struggling to remove his sodden clothes with frozen fingers. "It was worse than I thought it would be." Having little success with the unyielding buttons, he poured himself a drink spilling half of it on the desk. Grasping the glass with both shaking hands, he raised it to his mouth, and Angela heard it rattling against his teeth as he gulped down the fiery liquid.

She couldn't help herself from going to him no matter what he had done to her. Hostilities were suspended as she took the glass from him and unbuttoned his clothes. For a change Scott was helpless, needing warmth and comfort, and he closed his eyes wearily giving himself over to her tender hands.

They didn't speak as she removed his clothes and dried his lean brown body. He shivered as her hands, like warm flames, touched his chest, his thighs, realizing how cold he really was. The palms of his hands were raw and bloody from clinging to the lifelines, and she bathed them in warm water, tearing strips from her petticoat to bind them.

"You should go to bed. You must get warm." And she put him to bed as if he was a sick child, tucking the blankets in around him.

Watching her undress in the pale, gray light Scott couldn't help but be amazed at this sudden change in attitude, the almost sympathetic treatment of him. He had seen her treat one other person that way—Lorna when she had fallen and hurt herself. Chagrin coursed through him as he realized that at the moment he brought out her maternal instincts. He smiled—what did it matter as long as they could share a moment when she cared what happened to him?

Angela came to him naked, lying on her side and taking him in her arms. This he couldn't believe: the soft press of her breasts against his chest, her hips tight against his, her long smooth legs tangling with his, imparting a gift—the blessed warmth of her body. He held her tightly, and she didn't struggle but smiled into his eyes, her face so close to his on the pillow that he could feel her sweet breath against his lips.

"Thank you, Angela," Scott began, and she touched her lips lightly against his, silencing him with a hot, close-mouthed kiss.

"Shh!" she whispered as his eyes closed heavily. "Go to sleep. The storm is over and we are safe. Everything is all right—sleep."

And Scott felt himself relaxing as she stroked the tense muscles of his back and shoulders, felt the slippery silk of her hair beneath his cheek and her body heating his. His last thought was of her curious touch against the long scar on his side.

The scent of wildflowers and the sea awakened him, and Scott found his head pillowed on Angela's breast. Her gentle breathing rocked him, and he had never been so contented, wanting to stay suspended in this world of warmth, comfort and softness forever.

Angela stirred and turned away from him, reaching for the blanket that had slipped down. Scott drew it back up over them and snuggled her close, content just to hold her in his arms.

"Keith," she murmured dreamily and felt him stiffen. Through barely open eyes she saw a strange room and her dream of waking at Bentwood in her marriage bed vanished.

The dull gray light of day revealed instead a small cabin rising and falling with the motion of the sea. The gentle rocking was soothing but it was taking her away from everyone and everything that mattered. Where were they? Where were they going? What would happen when they arrived and she was forced to meet her fate?

Deep down inside she had known something like this would happen. It would have been too simple if things had worked out the way she and Keith had planned. He had worked out the whole pattern of their lives together and now it didn't exist. It was all so meaningless, the plans and the dreams, all wrecked before they had a chance to begin.

"Where are we?" Angela asked, putting her fears into words.

"Somewhere in the North Sea."

"Where are you taking me?"

"Home."

She turned to him, her face radiant in the light of the good news. "Oh, Scott—you've changed your mind! Thank you."

Dimples appeared and she couldn't suppress them, his changed attitude shattering her suspicions and melting her coldness. Her fingers moved lightly up his chest to rest against his cheek, and in a spurt of gratefulness she kissed the cleft in his square chin, the corner of his mouth and then his lips.

It didn't matter if he made love to her again, she would receive him and please him and herself one last time. Scott was taking her home! Home to Lorna and her parents, Keith and Jane, Windy Arbor and Brightling Castle—home to peace and stability and everything she loved.

"Thank you!"

Hating himself for having to shatter her happiness Scott said, "Don't thank me, love. I'm not taking you back to England. We are going home—to our new home—where we can live forever undisturbed by the outside world."

"You tricked me!"

She was withdrawing from him, hiding herself again in a shell of cool indifference. The change was immediate, and she looked so tragic he almost laughed.

"Not on purpose, Angel. If I had wanted to trick you I would have taken advantage of your good mood before telling you the truth.

"I'm taking you to the Seafield Castle in the Scottish Highlands. It was my grandfather's and now it is mine."

The half-formed fear that he was taking her to Jamaica vanished. Scotland! That wasn't as far from home as she had imagined. It would be easy to get back to England from there.

No man could hold Angela against her will, be he enemy or lover. To exist she had to be free. She would loosen the chains that were tightening around her, fly to safety and sanity, far from the man that would make her his slave. Somehow she would elude Scott. Somehow she must escape.

Chapter Fourteen

A shooting star lit the sky, flashing with the brilliance of a diamond against a moonless sable night. Its ephemeral flight only made it more beautiful and rare, something to be remembered long after it had disappeared.

The heavens stretched forever on the wild, windswept night, presenting a matchless stellar display unequaled in magnificence. Angela felt that if she reached out she could touch those fiery crystals, and though she shivered on the deck she couldn't tear herself away. A nocturnal magic was in the air, an enchantment that pervaded her so that she felt like a part of this land she could not see.

Scotland. It called out to her wild blood, making it sing in her veins, demanding an answer in return, and Angela strained against the railing wishing it was morning so she could see this remote, lonely land. The scents of sea, pine, and an odd pungent tang of smoke entranced her even more. How tiny and alone she felt beneath the vast darksome canopy spangled with stars that twinkled and dipped down to the water to dance on the waves.

And now that the *Dark Lady* rode at anchor in a place Scott called home she could almost believe she belonged there. Could it be her ancestors reaching out from the past to enfold her in her heritage? It was too soon to tell but a profound contentment settled down upon her, the likes of which she hadn't felt for years.

A tall, dark shadow joined her where she stood and Angela didn't resist as his arm went around her shoulders. He was warm and she let her head rest against him with a weary sigh, for once letting herself be lulled into serenity. They didn't speak but Scott stroked her black hair, then her cheek, and for once it felt so right to be with him.

After a while he said, "You are like the night, Angel—dark and secret, too beautiful to describe or ever tire of, everchanging. My dark lady, my only love."

He looked down at her smiling and she tried to see his face in the darkness but the shadows hid his devilish good looks. His head bent closer to hers until she could feel his breath warm against her cheek.

"There are stars in your eyes and they look more fascinating there than where they belong."

Their lips touched, warming each other, growing hotter, opening and seeking an elusive moment, finding it and knowing when to stop. Scott kissed the cold tip of her nose and they went back to watching the million eyes of the night gazing down at them.

"It's magnificent, isn't it?" he asked, not expecting an answer. "I've been to many places in my life but nothing quite equals the Highlands. There is a mystery about it, something in the atmosphere that defies description. You can only see it and feel it and know you will never be the same again!

"Wait until you see the castle and the glens and lochs. Soon the mountains will be covered with heather and the moors. . .but no, I won't tell you. I'll let you see everything for yourself, sweetheart—the way I did when I was a boy."

She could feel the excitement in him, the longing to once again see the place that he loved best. He was preoccupied with his own thoughts and rememberings but still very much aware of her and he drew his cloak more closely around her.

"Darling," he whispered against her hair. "I will never let you go!"

A faint spark of resentment invaded Angela's tranquility and she tried to fan it into a blaze. "Why me? You can have any woman you want, Scott. Why not a willing one?"

He laughed and drenched that feeble spark as he

quoted softly:

"Oh, many and many a young girl for me is
 pining,
 Letting her locks of gold to the cold wind
 free,
For me, the foremost of our gay young fellows;
 But I'd leave a hundred, pure love, for thee!
Then put your head, darling, darling, darling,
 Your darling black head my heart above;
Oh mouth of honey, with the thyme for fragrance,
 Who, with heart in breast, could deny you
 love?"

His strong arms encircled her, pulling her close, broad shoulders blocking out the stars. And Angela could feel the steady beat of his heart and the virile length of him as his hands caressed her shoulders and wandered with lambent touches; one finding the softness of her breast, the other trailing down her spine with delicious ease.

Spellbound! Once again caught in that dark magic that only one man could bind her in. Like a butterfly caught in a silken web, fluttering uselessly against the gossamer strands of passion.

She pushed away from him, grasping the railing hard between her shaking hands, not daring to let Scott know her reaction. Forcing herself to be quiet and still Angela beat back the desire, not accepting her defeat. She would gather all her strength and determination for the final battle to break free, would use her one last weapon with deadly accuracy.

It was barely daybreak but already the ship bustled with activity. Angela was alone in the cabin for Scott had gone before she awoke. She sipped a cup of coffee with her eyes half closed in the dim gray light, and leaned her chin upon her hand gazing dreamily into space. The whisper of poetry still swirled in her mind. Last night had conspired with Scott to be entirely too romantic. But she had proved immovable.

A sudden shaft of light pierced the gloom at the quick opening of the door and Angela put down her cup with a crash and could only stare, transfixed. Scott grinned audaciously, golden flecks dancing in his brown eyes, as he strode into the room and deposited his burden on Angela's lap.

"Good morning, Mama," said her daughter, and Angela hugged and kissed her till she wriggled.

"Lorna! Oh, baby," Angela repeated over and over. "I never knew you were here!"

Scott had backed away and stood in a far corner watching their reunion. That should soften Angela's heart a little, for God only knew it was as hard as steel where he was concerned. But he hadn't brought their daughter along just to make Angela malleable—he had done it for himself too. Already Lorna had him wrapped around her finger.

She was just like Angela! And if her mother obsessed him, Lorna charmed him completely. He had to have them both here at Seafield to complete his plans—and his life.

The scene was charming, and Scott could not tear his eyes from Angela's tumbled blue-black hair that swirled like smoke over her apricot velvet dressing gown; the wonderfully maternal smile that set dimples dancing beneath her high cheekbones; the passionate rose-colored lips that he had dared to kiss just once last night; the eyes, huge and thick-lashed, the exact color of the aquamarines he had given her in April.

Angela was staring at him with unspoken questions brimming in her eyes and Scott said, "Rather an effective coup, don't you think? A triple abduction you might say, although Lorna came willingly enough."

"Triple?" questioned Angela, her dark eyebrows taking flight.

"Well I couldn't leave your faithful maid behind."

"Molly!" Angela gave a little gurgle of laughter and put her fingers over her lips so Scott wouldn't see her amusement. She could just see skinny, middle-aged Molly squawking and flapping in his grasp like a trussed hen as he carried her off.

"Molly's angry, Mama," Lorna informed her. "She hit Papa. Doesn't Molly like my papa?"

The laughter burst forth then, and try as she might Angela couldn't force it back. So that's where the bruises on Scott's shoulder and cheek had come from. She must have hit him with a chair! Not that he didn't deserve it.

He smiled at her, knowing exactly what she was thinking, and said, "Get dressed, Angela, we're going ashore within the hour."

Scott left her alone and sent Molly to her, and by the time they emerged on deck Angela was under control once more. But seeing the Highlands for the very first time sent her bounding to the railing with Lorna at her side.

Angela could only hold her breath and stare round-eyed at the panorama set before her. The waters of the loch were cobalt-blue, and set on the summit of a small, green jewel of an island stood an ancient, gray granite castle. It was something out of a medieval fairy tale or a legend of shining knights and damsels in distress.

The product of centuries of building and remodeling, it had a different innovation from each era: a keep and a tall, slender round tower, soaring turrets and crenelated battlements. A vaulted stone bridge connected the island to the mainland.

Rocky, heather-covered hills curved like fingers into the loch forming a natural cove. Beyond that the mountains were huge, lined with pine, beech, and fir trees interspersed with bright yellow gorse. It was wild, desolate and lonely, and it was the most awe-inspiring sight Angela had ever seen.

Scott smiled at her speechlessness. "Welcome to Scotland, Angel—and to Seafield Castle."

"Oh, Scott!" was all she could say as she leaned over the railing, craning her neck to see more. Her eyes sparkled, and a bemused smile curved her lips like a child that is handed so many presents it doesn't know which to open first.

As they were rowed toward the castle Scott pointed out various points of interest, smiling secretly because Angela's reaction was almost identical to his the first time he had visited his grandfather. She could be so delightfully enthusiastic and childlike, at times just like Lorna.

Bringing her here had been the perfect strategy. He had toyed with the idea of sailing for Jamaica but he had just come from there and had been filled with a terrible homesickness for Scotland. The Highlands were part of him, just as much as the ravishing, black-haired creature sitting by his side.

"Seafield Castle sits at the junction of three lochs," Scott explained. "There's Loch Long on the left, Loch Alsh, behind us where the ship is anchored, and straight ahead, beyond the castle, is Loch Duich."

"You are certainly in your element," observed Angela. "Do you know everything about this place? What is that big purple mountain over there?"

"It looks like part of the mainland, doesn't it? But it is actually the tip of the Isle of Skye. The mountain is Sgurr na Coinnich."

"The Isle of Skye," she murmured. "That sounds so romantic."

"It's not—it is barren and bleak with nothing but mountains, the ocean, and the sky. There are only a few spots on it that could even be called pretty. One of them is a small forest. . .no, I will let that be a surprise. Look we're almost home."

As the boats reached the dock Scott helped Angela and then Molly out, lifting Lorna up into his arms. A tall large-boned woman with a severe face and steel-gray hair waited. She was obviously the housekeeper, Angela observed, noting the bunch of keys at her belt.

"Eilean!" Scott bounded forward, and holding Lorna in one arm he hugged the housekeeper with his other. "Damn, but it's good to be home again!"

"Watch tha' cursing, milord!" she reprimanded sternly, but her features softened with a fond look, and there was almost a smile on her mouth.

Scott only laughed. "You never change—but look who I've brought to meet you. Lorna, say hello to Miss Rannoch. This," he beamed proudly, "is my daughter."

Angela made a face at Scott behind his back. Was the whole world to know the details of her daughter's birth? She watched as Eilean Rannoch fussed over Lorna, a smile actually cracking her face. At Angela's approach she looked up questioningly.

"And this," Scott said mockingly, taking Angela's hand, "is a very important personage—Lady Angela Carlyle Harrington, Duchess of Brightling."

"Welcome, milady," Eilean made a stiff cursy. "An' I never thought to see the day! Ye married and wi' a bairn of yer own."

With an amused drawl Scott corrected her, "No, Eilean—not my wife. Did I forget to say dowager duchess? Angela is my stepmother." Ignoring the dangerous glint in Angela's eyes he plunged on recklessly. "She is my mistress and fiancée and the mother of my child."

Angela couldn't help her outraged gasp, and she pulled her hand violently from his grasp. The housekeeper had fallen back a step in surprise. Scott grinned and gave Angela a wicked wink. Her hands curled into fists, and if the gaping servants and sailors hadn't been there she would have liked nothing better than to pummel the smile from his face.

Pulling herself up haughtily, Angela said, "I would like to be shown to my room—now!" With her head high she followed the flustered housekeeper into the castle with Molly and Lorna in her wake.

Scott watched her go with the dignity of an enraged queen. He should have held his tongue, but he had just meant it as a joke. Now she was furious with him again, shattering the serenity of the day, and he wished he had never spoken those words. But it was too late and Angela was angry.

Angela was so miffed she didn't notice the uniquely vaulted ceiling of the great hall or the magnificent tapestries faded to subdued pastels lining the stone walls. Lorna stared in wonder, getting a fleeting glimpse of a suit of armor and huge branched antlers hanging over a vast fireplace. But she was whisked upstairs by a grim-faced Molly before she could even protest.

The master bedroom on the second floor was a haven from prying eyes. Angela shut the door and threw her balled up gloves onto a chair. It was a large masculine-looking room dominated by a gigantic four poster bed of dark polished wood. Her eyes avoided the bed, knowing only too well what use it would be put to tonight.

The stone walls were whitewashed, lightening the room, and tastefully hung with oil paintings, tapestries, and sconces. Windows, obviously enlarged from the obsolete slits, glinted in the sunlight and she went to look out through the wavy glass. A distorted view of blue waters and distant mountains met her gaze and she opened it for a better look.

Below was an intricate herb garden that lent a tangy scent to the air, and Angela breathed deeply, trying to steady her nerves. Last night Scott had been utterly charming and romantic; this morning he had reverted to the rogue that she knew was the real man. She would never get used to the lightning-quick changes in his personality and didn't want to.

A small village huddled near the base of a mountain not very far away, and she contemplated it solemnly. There had to be someone there that would help her get away. Perhaps she could bribe one of the fishermen to take her to a large city so that she could make her way home. But were there any cities near here? All she knew for sure was that they were on the west coast of Scotland, and she realized her first priority must be to find a map.

There was a sharp knock on the door and she turned to see Scott followed by several servants carrying her trunk. He had thought of everything. Angela ignored them, turning again to the view, her back stiff with displeasure at his presence.

To acclaim her openly as his mistress and fiancée, when both claims were false, was almost beyond her comprehension. Unless—it was another tack to shame her into marrying him. Well it wouldn't work! She had faced up to worse charges and gossip before and could again. Did Scott think he was dealing with a fool?

They were alone. The heavy, carved oak door closed and would contain the inevitable explosion of tempers within the thick walls of the chamber. Scott touched Angela's shoulder tentatively, alert to her every movement as she spun around and faced him like an angry tigress.

"How dare you tell everyone that I'm your mistress and fiancée," she shouted. "You hypocrite! You know it's untrue!"

"It is true," Scott shot back at her. "We sleep in the same bed and make love—that makes you my mistress. And you are my fiancée because no matter what you say now, in the end you will marry me. I want you, Angela, and I will have you."

"Never! I will tell you once more so you can get it through your thick head—I will never marry you. And as for being your mistress," she said with a short brittle laugh, "you will tire of me soon enough. In a few months time I will be as big as a cow and not up to tumbling around in bed with you!"

There, the truth was finally out, and Scott stared at her in shock. That nasty smile she had worn after he had taken her aboard the *Dark Lady* was back.

"Pregnant?" he asked incredulously, and before he could continue she struck again.

"Yes, pregnant—with Keith's baby!"

Her sharp, smug words hit him like a knife in the back, and he gripped the back of a chair to steady himself and to keep from striking her. Keith's! He should have noticed the signs: the swollen tenderness of her breasts and her slight weight gain, her blooming looks and touchy short temper, the sudden burst of tears for no apparent reason and the hurried wedding arrangements.

"How far gone are you?" Scott asked, unable to keep the pain that was twisting inside him from showing on his face.

"Four months, maybe more," Angela said triumphantly, well aware of what her confession was doing to him. Though he tried to mask his feelings she could see right through him and his efforts were worse than useless.

"You could be wrong. It could be mine."

"No!" Angela's voice was adamant. "It's Keith's. I should know—it is happening to me and it's not the first time. Believe me, Scott, the child I'm carrying is not yours!"

She thought he was going to slap her but instead he turned and without another word left the room. Distraught and trembling, Angela threw herself on the emerald-green velvet of the bed, pressing her hot face into its softness. Her fingers nervously traced the gold embroidery and she wondered what would happen now. Would Scott let her go?

She wasn't sure of anything. It was very possible that the child was Scott's. Closing her eyes, Angela had a quick vision of a blue lake surrounded with daffodils. If it was his it had happened then and there. But there was a possibility the child was Keith's, and using that doubt as a weapon, she hadn't been able to resist the urge to hurt Scott for all her past and present suffering.

Turning over, she placed her hands over her face. What would he do to her now? He was capable of anything, especially when he was hurt and angry. Angela could still see his eyes like great dark wounds in his face and hear the pleading note in Scott's voice as he tried to convince her and himself that the baby could be his.

It moved deep within her belly and Angela turned her face to the counterpane and wept.

The simple pink silk dress made Angela look young and carefree, both of which she didn't feel. Her hair was carefully coiffed and she sat fidgeting on the edge of a chair upholstered in blue and green cut velvet. Her fingers closed convulsively around the diamond pendant Percy had given her and she stared miserably at the floor.

What difference did wealth, elegant surroundings, pretty clothes and jewels make when she was so unhappy? Yet, she admitted to herself, she wouldn't necessarily have been any happier with Keith because she didn't love him either. She wondered if she was destined to go through life bearing children for men she didn't love. Well at least she loved her children, and she was growing more and more attached to the new one with each passing day.

Angela hadn't seen Scott all day. She had lunched, played with Lorna, directed the unpacking of her clothes and wandered in the small garden. Then she had bathed and dressed for dinner, positive she wouldn't be able to eat a bite. She looked wonderful and felt awful.

If only he would get it over with and do whatever it was that he had decided upon. The tension was unbearable. Scott was probably off thinking up a newly refined torture to punish her again, and she shivered. Here in this godforsaken place he held the power of life and death over her; hadn't he almost killed her before?

A knock sent Angela bounding out of the chair as Scott threw open the door, electrifying the room with his tense presence. In spite of their enmity she felt that inescapable tug of mutual attraction between them. She couldn't help being drawn to his dynamic masculinity, always more intense when he was angry and glowering at her. And she was glad thay were at odds again, for fear that if they weren't she would give in all too easily to him.

The golden specks in his dark eyes glowed and danced like angry flames, and Angela stood apprehensively, judging the distance to the door as Scott studied her with deliberate coolness. He was impeccably dressed in dark breeches, a snowy, ruffled shirt and a fine wool coat in a plaid design. Angela wondered if it was the Campbell tartan, but didn't dare ask.

Four months. She didn't even show yet and Scott's

eyes narrowed as she blushed beneath his scrutiny. She was becoming an accomplished liar, especially when she struck back at him. No, he was not entirely convinced that the baby was Keith's and he didn't think she was either, but he would play along with her little deception. It was more like three months and that took him to his first day back in England—the beginning of April and their ecstasy among the flowers.

"We will discuss this subject now, for the last time and then never again," Scott said curtly. "My offer to marry you still stands—regardless of your condition. The baby—no matter whose it is—I will consider mine. I will be its father, Angela, and you will never refer to Keith as that again.

"Now listen carefully to what I have to say next because I want you to get it straight. I will not take you back to England to marry Montgomery. You will stay here and if you refuse to be my wife then you will definitely be my mistress—the choice is yours.

"Also you might want to consider this: the decision you make will greatly affect the future of your unborn child, especially if it's a boy. You alone will be responsible for whether the baby will be legitimate or a bastard."

So that was his ultimatum! Angela could tell by his manner and tone that there would be no gainsaying him. She felt like swearing at him but instead remained silent with downcast eyes. Scott wasn't fooled though, for he saw her rebellious mouth and the defiant tilt of her chin.

"Do you understand the two possibilities open to you, Angela?"

"Yes!" Her eyes flared into his. "If I am your mistress. . .if I did it. . .willingly—would you let me go when you tired of me?"

"No," he said quietly, all the more believable because of his understatement. "I promise, I will never tire of you and I will never let you go. Whatever decision you make, you will stay here with me permanently.

"Oh—one more thing. If you think you can bide your time and then escape—if you do manage to elude me—

it will be without the children. They remain with me." Scott smiled at her stunned expression, so positive of success that he added, "In fact, if you still want to leave me when our baby is a year old, then you can go. I will arrange to take you back to England—you will be free."

"And the children. . ."

"You will leave them too—you will be entirely free of all burdens and evidence of our relationship. Do you think I can't do it? Any court in the land would give me custody of them once I proved what an unfit mother you are. It would be so easy, Angela—because you are already an infamous lady."

She was defeated! They both knew it as she quickly turned away so he couldn't see the tears. Scott knew she would never leave Lorna or the baby and had gambled cruelly and won. One way or another Angela was bound to him with ties stronger than chains—the bond of motherhood. He had woven his web with cunning and skill and now she was caught!

The days were tolerable, even enjoyable for Angela, full of new sights, sounds, and customs, but the nights were unbearable. They shared the big bed and Scott's nightly attentions became a battle royal. Her only way of protesting her predicament was by passive resistance and the more she denied him the more he intensified his efforts to break down the barriers she placed between them.

Every night was a struggle against Scott and her own nature, as her body screamed for relief. Angela knew that if she let go for even a second, everything would be lost and the passion held in check for so long would burst out, her traitorous body betraying her as it had done so many times before. So her nights became tense and sleepless as she steeled herself against his insatiable demands.

Scott was not unaware of what she was doing, but in trying to castigate him Angela was only punishing herself. She was becoming as high strung as a purebred horse and the stress was taking its toll on her physically as well. There were haunting shadows beneath her aqua eyes, and she wasn't eating enough. Her belly was rounding out with the baby, but she was losing weight and was pale and listless.

One morning Angela woke rested and refreshed, stretching luxuriously in the sunlight that spilled like warm honey across the bed. Scott had made no demands on her last night, the first time that had occurred since his ultimatum, and she had slept like a baby.

"So you are awake at last," Scott said from the doorway. "Are you hungry, sweetheart?"

Angela glanced up at him, and he stood there smiling engagingly with a tray in his hands. The smell of food made her mouth water and for the first time in almost a month she was ravenous.

"I'm starved," she admitted, starting to get up, but he motioned her back.

"Breakfast in bed, Duchess."

Putting the tray on her lap, Scott sat in a chair beside the bed. They shared a pot of tea and he watched her as she ate, encouraging her to finish every bite. They hardly spoke but when she was finished Scott took the tray away and then sat on the edge of the bed, leaning across her.

"You look rested this morning, Angel. Are you feeling better?"

Angela hesitated for only a moment. "I feel wonderul. Thank you for bringing my breakfast, and—"

"You still have shadows under your eyes," he observed, brushing a stray curl from her cheek.

Scott rested his hand on her shoulder and felt the reaction, her resistance to him. Angela's eyes went vacant and she leaned limply against the pillows at her back, waiting.

"Please, don't look like that," Scott pleaded. "I didn't come here to attack you!" Relief was visible on her face. "Angel—Angel, you stubborn little witch. Don't you realize now that I love you—that I'm not lying when I say it? How can I prove it? What can I do to make you trust me?"

"Scott, please—" Angela wriggled uncomfortably beneath his ardent gaze and the warmth of his words. What was he trying now? She preferred it when he attacked boldly and she knew what direction he was coming from. But this subtle undermining of her defenses left her shaken and unsure of herself.

"I love you," he repeated. "I love everything about you, but especially the way you look in the morning, all sleepy-eyed and tousled. My sweet little beauty, my heart, my soul."

Angela smoothed down her coal-black hair with shaking fingers but Scott playfully ruffled it again and let his fingers curl into the soft, heavy mass. Very gently his lips touched hers and she was totally unprepared.

Scott was caught as much by surprise as she was when her mouth clung wet and scalding, parting under his eager lips. His tongue sought hers and she let him find it, recklessly casting herself into his arms. All her resolutions went up in smoke, and she clung to him as if she was drowning; and she was—in his kisses and the sensations that coursed like pleasured shockwaves through her body.

Scott was the one that pulled away, smiling tenderly into her aquamarine eyes. As rational thought returned he saw the quickly suppressed fear flash across her face. She was afraid of herself! The thought struck him with the force of a cannonball. Angela was falling in love with him and just the hint of it petrified her so, that she fought against him and it as if for her life.

"Don't be afraid of me, love," he murmured. "I'm not going to do anything alarming. I have been very selfish. I thought that our physical union would bring us closer together—but I was wrong. I was sure that eventually you would give in and admit you cared for me but all I have succeeded in doing is driving you away from me and ruining your health.

"I'm sorry, Angel," Scott whispered, his eyes large with regret. "I never meant to repulse you and turn you into a nervous wreck." He rested his hand lightly on the bulge of her stomach. "I care too much for you to jeopardize your health and the welfare of our baby on my own whims. From now on I won't make any demands on you—so you can sleep at night and regain your appetite, and smile again.

"You haven't smiled at me for such a long time, beloved—and you have such delightful dimples. Won't you smile for me just once so that we can make up and be friends?"

The sincerity in his voice told Angela that this was no lie. The long difficult speech was so unlike him—but then what did she really know about Scott? Only that he was a paradox.

"Don't cry, Angel!" Scott gathered her into his arms and held her against his chest. "I never meant to make you cry. Your tears do something to me. . . ."

He rocked and caressed her, whispering soft love words until her sobs ceased and she gave him a tremulous, watery smile that thrilled him more than all the indifferent nights they had spent together. If this was the way to win Angela's heart then he would be patient and understanding. Scott almost dared to hope that he was making some headway.

It was a blessed relief to be able to relax in Scott's presence, not always on the alert for unseen danger. Though they still shared a bed he was true to his word and seemed content with a few kisses, smiles, and touches.

He was probably repulsed by her ungainly shape, thought Angela—but then again he liked to hold her with his hand on her belly and feel the baby's movements. Scott teased her about her increasing girth but at night when she was exhausted and her back ached, he massaged her for hours until she fell asleep.

Sunshine and fresh air were the best medicine, Scott told her, insisting she get outdoors as much as possible. On fine days when the sea was like glass he would take Angela and Lorna out in his ketch, and they sailed around the small islands and into the numerous firths that indented the coastline. They fished from the boat and ate their catch for dinner, laughing over their expertise as fishermen.

At other times they went for drives and picnics or else walked into the village of Dornie where Lorna gorged herself on gingerbread hot from the oven of a small shop. They were becoming a family and Scott could feel the closeness growing day by day.

The roses returned to Angela's cheeks and her health improved under Scott's tender care. She flourished and he couldn't keep his eyes off her radiance and the soft round lines of motherhood. That was something he had missed with Lorna. He had been gone long before her pregnancy had really shown.

After a week of dismal rainy weather that confined everyone to the castle and set their nerves on edge, the day dawned crisp and clear with a tang of autumn in the air. Scott was up hours before Angela, and when she woke late in the morning he impatiently urged her to hurry. When she asked him what the rush was he just smiled mysteriously and replied, "There's something I want to show you."

When she was ready Scott led her through the courtyard to the round tower. With a rusty key he unlocked the door and they went inside.

"The door is a relatively new innovation in the tower," Scott told her. "A few hundred years back someone decided the conventional entrance was too inconvenient."

"What was that?"

He pointed to an opening high over her head. "The entrance is there, about eighteen feet up. The only way in was up rope or ladder. It wasn't good for invaders to gain access, and made a good watch tower and storage place."

They climbed the narrow spiral staircase inside, pausing frequently for Angela to rest. Each story had one window but Scott wouldn't let her look out. "Not yet," he said, "wait until we reach the top. You will be glad you waited."

It was too narrow to walk side by side so Scott

ascended behind Angela, one hand securely at her waist. Finally they reached the room at the pinnacle, right under the conical roof of overlapping stone slabs. Four lancet windows opened to the cardinal points.

Scott opened an iron-studded door and escorted Angela carefully out onto a narrow stone balcony circling the tower. The vista stretched before them for miles. Angela was stunned with the grandeur spread at her feet. Overnight the heather had bloomed, covering the hills and mountains with a purple haze. The whole landscape was green and blue and purple and the shadowed ridges were the color of spilled wine.

"Oh, Scott! I feel like a bird soaring in the sky. It's wonderful—thank you!"

Just the look on her face was thanks enough and they walked slowly around the balcony drinking in the beauty spread below. Angela could see beyond Loch Alsh to the ocean and the misty islands of the Hebrides. And on the other side facing the mainland the mountains rose majestically, layered one behind the other till they blurred and turned a transparent violet at the horizon, blending into the sky.

The sun gilded it all until it turned into an unreal picture, like a half-remembered dream. Gulls and rooks wheeled around, protesting the disturbance of their lofty place and a cuckoo called far below in the forest. In the rarefied atmosphere Angela was perfectly happy, all her cares and worries miles below her on the earth.

"How high are we?" she inquired.

"Oh, about two hundred feet, I would say. Watch your step, Angel, there's a loose stone there."

"Are you sure it's safe?"

"Yes, the balcony is another recent addition. The original tower didn't have it. Maybe my ancestor that put in the door decided on this too. Personally I think it spoils the lines but it does make a convenient viewing platform."

"I wonder how old it is," Angela said, looking at the circle of grotesquely carved heads and curious zigzag ornaments beneath the cornice of the roof.

"I don't know," admitted Scott, holding her tightly. "At least a thousand years, probably more. Some scholars think round towers date back to the pre-Christian era and that they were used by pagans for sun and fire worship. There aren't many in Scotland but they litter the countryside in Ireland."

The vast Isle of Skye was just below their feet, as misty and faded as a crumpled tapestry, and the bare Cuillin Hills looked like mere hills instead of the mountains that they really were. Like a miniature romantic stage, the ruins of Castle Moil appeared near the Kyle of Lochalsh with the ocean on two sides and bounded by the straits.

"I can't believe that this is real." Angela breathed deeply of the sea and pine-scented air and rested her head on Scott's shoulder.

"And I can't believe that you are real and here with me, my sweet little love."

They spent several hours reveling in the dazzling splendor, soaking up the sun of a flawless day. Scott persuaded Angela to go back inside and warm herself by a fire only by promising to bring her back again. He wouldn't let her come alone, he explained, for the stairs were treacherous and she might fall.

As they stepped back into the tower room Angela noticed a large square of tattered, faded silk hanging on the wall. It was old and stained with dirt and blood.

"What's what?" she asked, pointing and going closer to inspect it.

"No! Don't touch it!" There was alarm in his voice as Scott grabbed her inquisitive hands and held them tightly in his own. "It is the Bratach Sith, the Fairy Flag!

"According to legend it was given to Clan Campbell by a fairy who endowed it with magical powers. It was to be flown only in times of desperate trouble and would only work three times. It was used twice and both times it protected the clan from utter disaster."

Angela gazed at the flag spellbound. "Why don't we hang it in the great hall? It would be perfect there."

"No!" he said again emphatically, and she looked at him with a perplexed frown. "There is no one in the castle or in all of Scotland who would dare touch it, never mind move it. The magic is not without its consequences. It is cursed!

"The superstition is that whoever raised the flag or flew it in battle—the one who actually touched the Bratach Sith—was cursed. Their fate, no matter where on earth they fled, would be such that death would be the only release."

"Do you actually believe that?" asked Angela, her wide eyes glued to the flag.

"I don't know but I have never been tempted to try it. Heaven knows, I have enough problems without a curse hanging over my head!"

Chapter Fifteen

She was happy! Angela wasn't quite sure when the transformation had taken place, only that it had crept up on her gradually and quietly, springing a sudden surprise when she realized she was no longer unhappy. At first she had explained it away as the placidness of entering her last few months of pregnancy, but there was something more.

In spite of everything that had occurred between them in the past there was a growing understanding and tranquility between her and Scott. His total acceptance of her child as his, even though she vehemently denied it, puzzled her. The tender way he treated her, the warm looks and loving words, had her half convinced that perhaps he did care about her. Love—it always came back to that, and though he told her he loved her a dozen times a day there were absolutely no physical demands made. Could he be telling the truth?

Lorna was growing like a weed and running wild like a gypsy, with a freedom in the vast Highlands she had never had in England. It would be good for her daughter to have a little brother or sister to share the lavish attention showered on her, especially by Scott.

The only thing that shattered the contented atmosphere was the nagging question in the back of Angela's mind. Should she give in and marry Scott before her baby was born? He urged her to, broaching the subject every few days, but she always rejected it. To be tied to him forever was a big step. But wasn't she already bound to him with invisible ties, some even stronger than a few words mumbled in a church?

She sighed, the question unresolved as always, and Scott reached for her in the darkness, drawing her head onto his shoulder.

"Can't you sleep, Angel?" he inquired, concerned by her tossing and turning.

"No—my mind is preoccupied tonight and I just

can't stop thinking."

"What about?" Scott stroked the curve of her stomach rhythmically, trying to get her to relax.

"You," Angela answered candidly. A month ago she wouldn't have admitted it. "No matter where I direct my thoughts they always circle back to you."

He smiled in the darkness. "That's a good sign, love —because you are all I ever think about! Were you thinking about the question I asked you for the thousandth time today?"

"Yes."

"Well I can wait indefinitely—but our baby can't. In a few more months you might regret your stubbornness. Why don't you give in, you tenacious little vixen? I will get my way in the end."

"Will you?" Angela whispered.

He laughed, suddenly amused, and stroked her hair. "I know I will. There was another bold Scotsman long ago who dared to take what he wanted. He abducted a queen and made her love him—and because she couldn't live without him they married and she lost her throne."

"She lost more than that," Angela reminded him. "She lost her head and Bothwell died insane in Denmark!"

"Give in, my love—before you drive me insane."

"No! It's so. . .so final. I can't, Scott. . .not yet."

"What will you do—wait until the first pain strikes you?"

"Yes," she laughed delightedly. "And you can spend your wedding night pacing the floor and getting drunk!"

"Little witch! You would do it just for spite."

Screams pierced the solitude of the night, reverberating through the room. Scott woke instantly, lighting a candle and reaching for Angela. The baby! She couldn't be having it now—it was too soon!

She lay rigid, her eyes wide open, yet unseeing, and she continued screaming even as Scott shook her gently. At his touch she fought him off, no recognition in her dilated eyes.

"Shh, Angel—wake up! You're having a bad dream." Scott captured her flailing hands and spoke soothingly for several minutes until Angela came back to reality.

She was freezing, shaking all over with uncontrollable terror and Scott held her tightly, whispering and caressing her hair. The warmth of his body seeped into hers, but still she couldn't stop trembling. He was filled with relief that she wasn't having the baby prematurely but frowned with worry at her distress.

"It's all right—everything is fine," he soothed. "I'm here and I won't let anyone or anything hurt you. It was only a nightmare, just a dream. Tell me about it, love —what scared you?"

"Blood!" Angela whispered, her teeth chattering between words. "I was having. . .the baby. . .but it wouldn't come. Days and nights. . .pain. . .I couldn't have it. And then I was lying in. . .blood. . .a pool of my own blood. My nightgown was red. I was cold, so cold. Voices whispering. . .that I was going to die. I don't want to die. Scott, Scott!"

"Be quiet, Angel. You're not going to die. Shh! It was only a dream. You are young and strong and healthy and nothing is going to happen to you. I won't let it! You can't leave me, beloved—I won't let you go."

"It was so real!" Angela murmured, clasping him tightly.

"No, it wasn't real," Scott contradicted. "Don't think about it. This is real!" And he held her, kissing her face and hair and finally her quivering lips.

"Hold me, Scott!" Her lips moved against his. "Tighter—don't ever let me go!"

Angela couldn't seem to shake off the horror of her dream. Had it already been a week since it had happened? It returned at the oddest moments to scare her and when Scott was with her he saw the look and knew what was bothering her.

He planned an outing, hoping to take Angela's mind off her troubles. "The autumn is almost over," Scott explained. "The snow comes early here in the Highlands so we have to take advantage of the good weather while we can."

On an unseasonably mild day Scott loaded Angela, Lorna, and a picnic lunch into a buggy and they began a leisurely drive up Sgurr An Airgid. The mountain road was hardly more than a path but the compact, well-sprung vehicle gave them a comfortable ride. As they got higher her fears melted away and Angela began to relax, safe and secure with a man intent on pleasing her.

At first the forest seemed quiet and still but as she listened Angela made out the sweet songs of invisible birds high in the trees. The breeze sighed softly through the needles of the evergreen trees and a brook near the road splashed, babbling and blending its own music with the other sounds to form a captivating melody. The now familiar scent of peat smoke was in the air and she couldn't think of Scotland without smelling that unique fragrance.

Scott concentrated on driving the narrow, winding road and Angela leaned against his side, one hand resting on his hard thigh. He was very much aware of her touch and the fact that there was a natural spontaneity between them now. The Angela of a few months ago would never have reposed so serenely against him.

"I love this place," she murmured. "Seafield Castle, the lochs and mountains—they are enchanted. It's as if friendly spirits reside in the woods casting spells over mere mortals, to bewitch us and hold us captive in this lovely, lonely land."

"I know," said Scott, "because I feel exactly the same way but it's hard to find the right words to express the fascination. It's like having a love affair with a beautiful woman.

"Many people visit Scotland and never feel the magic in the air—but a few special people recognize it. Maybe that's why it's so sparsely populated. The Highlands reject all but a few." He smiled at her with unconcealed emotions. "I'm afraid you're caught, my love. You are too special to ever let go!"

In a secluded glade they stopped and Scott spread rugs and unloaded the big basket of food. Lorna and Angela wandered among the trees, the rowans heavy with clusters of ripe, red berries. Thrushes and black-birds darted among the branches partaking of the bounty and Lorna gathered pine cones and chestnuts.

They both stopped transfixed to see several red deer drinking from a burn. Quietly they watched the graceful creatures with their large liquid-brown eyes and soft reddish-brown coats. A green woodpecker hammered at a tree and their heads lifted in unison as they realized they were not alone. With white tails waving like signal flags the deer bounded into the forest.

"Papa! Papa!" Lorna ran excitedly to the clearing to tell him what she had seen.

Scott looked up from the fire he was building as his daughter burst from among the trees laughing and chattering. He listened patiently as she tried to explain, his precious little girl that he loved all the more because he had missed her babyhood. How lovely she was, laughing and dimpled, all flushed from her adventure.

"And how many deer were there?" he asked, prompting her.

She held up three fingers. "Three—just like me. I am three years old."

"So you are and quite a young lady. Look what I have brought you to look through."

From the blanket Scott picked up a spyglass and showed her which end to look through, training it on a bird sitting on a branch. She was delighted with her new toy and when Angela reappeared Lorna was sitting on her father's knee completely engrossed in scanning the distant trees with the instrument.

They didn't see her, so wrapped up were they in each other and Angela paused watching them. Even if she couldn't bring herself to believe that Scott loved her there was no doubt at all in her mind that he loved Lorna. Just seeing them together, his patience, the time he took to explain things and answer her every question, the way he looked at her and ruffled her hair—he adored his daughter and somehow that drew her closer to him.

Would he love the new baby as well, not knowing whose it was? From his reactions he already did and this new facet of his personality confused her. "I love children," he had told her one night with his hand on her belly. "You look surprised, Angel. I must admit that it surprised me too. But then, I have never been around them before—how was I to know?" So he was a wonderful father, and though she accused Scott of spoiling Lorna it never affected her daughter adversely. No, just the opposite—Lorna had needed a father.

How could she be thinking like this, was she weakening? Angela remembered the last time when she had been pregnant with Lorna how she had been drawn to Scott when he showed her the least tenderness. And now he was all loving and gentle, wooing her slowly, every moment of the day and night. How could she have forgotten the past—the rapes, beatings, and betrayals? He was wiping them from her memory but she could never allow herself to forget.

"Angel!" He went to her, his bronze hair disordered and glinting in the sunlight. That boyish smile made the memories vanish and he kissed her cheek and whispered against her hair, "Did you have a nice walk? I missed you for the few minutes you were gone, my sweet little love. Has our son been behaving?"

She pulled away from him laughing. That was the first time he had mentioned or speculated on the sex of the baby. So he would like a son. But was it his?

"I gave you a daughter before, over your vehement objections. Perhaps I will disappoint you again."

"Never!" Scott told her taking her hand. "You may give me a dozen daughteres like Lorna and I will be happy. And if you marry me—"

"Please—not now!"

Lorna looked up at her mother's angry words and Angela hurried over to the fire. She hadn't meant to shout, but just then she had been so close to giving in she had frightened herself. Her heart pounded with panic and the baby kicked vigorously and she put both hands on her belly to still it.

"Angela, are you all right?" There was undisguised fear in Scott's brown eyes at her suddenly pale face and closed eyes. A pang went through him, sharp and piercing. Women died having babies and if Angela. . . No! He wouldn't even think it, imagine it!

"I'm fine," said Angela. "I'm sorry."

"No—I'm the one that's sorry," Scott insisted putting his arm around her and drawing her over to the spread rugs. "I shouldn't have upset you. Sit down, love, let me make you comfortable."

He put pillows behind her back and a blanket over her knees with such solicitude that the tension evaporated. Angela touched his lean brown cheek and his eyebrows drawn together in a worried frown.

"Scott, I. . ."

"Yes, sweetheart?"

Angela had his full attention as he knelt beside her and she didn't even know what she had been going to say, only that she wanted things to be as they had been before her angry words.

Her eyes were huge and lucent, aquamarine jewels silently pleading for understanding, and his frown vanished. Scott smiled at what her look told him—he knew! His lips touched hers and his heart drummed loudly at Angela's instant surrender and reciprocation. This was the day! He had known it since dawn, that today he would gain his heart's desire. It wouldn't take much more, just one final, bold gesture, a surprise that would storm her last defense.

"Oh—darling!"

Scott's blood sang in his veins. She had called him darling, the first endearment that had ever passed her lips. He had waited forever for that and it had been worth every second of longing. Angela loved him! She wouldn't even admit it to herself yet but he knew and was content to wait until she finally had the courage to acknowledge it.

They had a long leisurely meal and watched Lorna's antics, content to let the day slide by in a lazy, golden haze. In the afternoon their exhausted daughter curled up like a kitten on the rugs and fell asleep. Angela covered her and kissed her cheek and when she looked up Scott was watching her with such an unusual smile that she couldn't help but respond in kind.

Contentment enveloped them as they walked among

the trees always keeping Lorna in view. They stopped at the edge of a cliff and Angela leaned back against Scott with her head against his chest. His hands stroked her shoulders and a golden eagle soared overhead against the backdrop of a brilliant blue sky.

"It's been a lovely day," Angela said. "Let's do it again, soon. Look—Seafield looks like a toy from way up here. This is the most beautiful place in the world!"

Scott got the spyglass for her to look through and Angela watched the eagle, so majestic as it circled on invisible currents of air. When it flew away she spent a long time viewing the distant islands and a few fishing vessels blown like scraps of paper over the sparkling sea. Cloud-shadows chased one another across the hills in an ever-changing pattern of deepest purple.

Angela viewed the castle, its weathered gray stone an intrinsic part of the scene. She couldn't picture a time when it hadn't existed, so well did it blend into its environment. The spyglass traced the tall slender length of the round tower to the very roof and then stopped. She froze, not believing her own eyes.

"Scott!" Angela exclaimed, her voice thick with disbelief. "The Fairy Flag—it is flying from the tower!" She handed him the glass.

"I know," he said not bothering to look.

"But—but who—why? Everything is peaceful here—there is no war being fought. And who would dare touch it?"

"I would dare!" Scott told her, noting her shocked expression. "Do you remember the legend—to be used in times of trouble to bring victory?"

She nodded speechlessly and Scott grabbed her shoulders, her troubled eyes held mesmerized by his.

"We have been fighting a war of wills from the first day we met, and now it's going to end. I would dare anything to have you—anything! Even defying that ancient curse. I mean to win this war, Angela, and if it takes flying the Bratach Sith to make me victorious—then to hell with that damned curse!"

He dragged her into his arms possessing her mouth

tenaciously, bruising the soft lips that trembled and parted beneath his. Scott felt the shaking of the earth beneath his feet as desire flared quick and sharp, as heady as the pungent autumn air. Their bodies strained together and his hands could not keep still as Angela arched against him.

Her knees went weak and only his strong arms kept her from falling. But then Angela was falling as he lowered her gently to the leaf-strewn grass and lay beside her panting with his efforts to control himself. The trees, sky, and clouds spun crazily overhead and the golden eagle reappeared circling faster and faster until Scott's face blocked it out and he was her entire world.

"Marry me," he urged, with nibbling kisses against her neck and shoulders. "I love you—I adore you!

"You mean everything to me, sweetheart. You are my whole world—the essence of life. Without you I am nothing." Scott spoke between quick hard kisses on her tender mouth. "Be my wife, Angela—be my love. Say yes!"

"Yes, yes, yes!" The words were soft moans against his lips that were driving her mad with delight.

"Yes!"

Events moved as quickly as storm-whipped clouds driven across drenched skies. The brooding solitude of the Highlands yielded to love in spite of the cold rains that swept in from the Atlantic.

"I always get my way," Scott laughed, his eyes as warm as glowing coals.

And Angela usually got her way but Scott was bending her to his will and making her like it. She didn't say anything as Molly helped her dress, and he sprawled in a chair wearing only a robe. His gaze was on her like a caress, possessive and proud, the victor in a match that had been destined to end only one way.

"I think I will wear the green velvet today, Molly," Angela said, not missing the quick look of conspiracy that flashed between Scott and the maid.

What were they up to? She gave him a sidelong glance and found a pleased smile on his wickedly handsome face. Something was in the air and when Molly returned with a dress she had never seen before Scott burst out laughing at her puzzled expression.

"What's going on?" Angela demanded and he came and kissed her with a twinkle in his golden-brown eyes.

"I wanted you to look very special for our wedding."

"Today?" Angela was caught off guard. "So soon—it's only been a week."

"It's not soon enough for me," murmured Scott touching his lips to her flushed cheek. "You aren't backing out, are you love?"

"No, it's just that. . ." She couldn't think of any objection.

"I wanted it to be a surprise," Scott cajoled, "and I have a few more surprises planned before the day is over. The second one is marvelous weather." And he flung open the draperies to reveal sunshine and blue skies where for a week there had been rain. "I ordered the day just for us."

Angela couldn't help smiling at his cocksure attitude and he didn't miss the dimples deepening in her cheeks. "The dress, Molly, if you please, now that the duchess has remembered how to smile!"

It was exquisite, of turquoise panne velvet with a high waist that would easily accommodate her rounded belly. The bodice and long sleeves were embroidered in tiny seed pearls in a stylized flower pattern and it fit Angela as if it was made for her and she had a sneaking suspicion it had been.

"You are as beautiful as a spring flower," Scott told her, observing her from every angle, "and you grow lovelier every day."

She wrinkled her nose at him and said with her hand on her belly, "Some flower! I'm as big as a house and clumsy—"

"Never clumsy, love—you could never be that!" Then he whispered huskily in her ear, "But I do long for the time when our son is born and I have your delicious little body all to myself. Rest up now, Duchess, for you won't get any then. I'll—"

"Scott!" Angela's face was scarlet and she rolled her

eyes toward the maid straightening the room.

He laughed and shook his head, always amused at her flashes of modesty. "I'm sure Molly knows how babies are made—and there is no doubt in my mind that you know!"

"Tease! Shouldn't you get dressed?"

"Not yet. You won't get rid of me so quickly!" Scott produced a satin-covered case and held it out to her. "For you, my radiant little bride."

Fiery opals blazed against the white satin lining, their multicolored brilliance bringing a cry of astonishment to Angela's lips. They were the most beautiful stones she had ever seen; ten of them linked together with minute Celtic spirals of gold.

"They have been in the family for hundreds of years," explained Scott taking the necklace from its case and laying it around her throat. "The opals are always presented to the new Countess of Seafield on her wedding day. They are as fiery as you are, love. The Campbells are not known for marrying docile women—that too runs in the family!"

He left her then, staring at the gift in the mirror, so astounded she hadn't even thanked him. It was all happening so fast and perhaps Scott was right to spring it on her as a surprise. It had left no time for doubts or regrets, no time for her to back out.

England and her life there seemed a thousand years away, a vague hazy part of her past barely remembered in her preoccupation with today. She frowned, trying to recall Keith's face but brown eyes took the place of blue ones, a rakish smile and bronze hair dissolving the image of her golden lover. Scott was everything to her now and suddenly she was afraid, not of marrying him but of something else—a shadow hanging over her happiness.

"It can't last!" she whispered with amazed surety. "And I don't want it to end."

Angela was speechless once more when Scott returned and he cocked an eyebrow at her daring her to laugh. He was dressed in traditional Scottish regalia: a kilt and sporran, Argyle stockings tied with colorful ribbon garters and a coat of forest-green velvet with a plaid across one shoulder. It was all topped off with a tam adorned with the feather of a golden eagle set on his head at a rakish angle.

He looked exactly like one of the notorious robber-barons of the Highlands that her father had told her of years ago. The untamed, savage, desperate men who made their own rules and met destiny head on. Their ancestors who had fought and loved with reckless abandon, trampling underfoot anyone that got in their way. Angela almost expected the whole clan to come marching into the room behind him.

The kilt only emphasized his masculinity and her own wild blood drove her across the room and into his arms. The velvet stretched tautly across his back, warm beneath her fingers and Angela tilted her head back to gaze deeply into his gold-filled eyes.

A mischievous smile curved her lips and at last she spoke, "There is an old question that has puzzled the English from time immemorial."

"And what is that, Angel?" he asked with an amused look.

She leaned closer and whispered in his ear, "Just what does a Scotsman wear under his kilt?"

Scott threw back his head and laughed, then told her devilishly, "Nothing, my love—but his manhood. And if we weren't all dressed and you were not so very pregnant I would prove the fact to your satisfaction!"

They sailed on the ketch through the Inner Sound to the Isle of Skye. During the night the temperature had plummeted and Angela shivered, pulling her fur-lined cloak closer. But the sun was warm and the day was clear and Scott was by her side, unable to tear himself away from his bride.

The wedding party was small—just Molly, Eilean, a minister, and Angus. For once the little Scotsman wasn't scowling and he too was attired in Highland finery with bagpipes cradled protectively in his arms. And the surprises weren't over yet for Scott had planned everything to perfection.

They anchored in Loch Sligachan and a carriage was waiting to whisk them all deep into the center of an ancient forest. There, close pressed by huge dark trees was a tiny chapel of faded red sandstone. It was stark in its simplicity, unique in shape, a forgotten tribute to love all the more precious because time had passed it by.

Sweetheart Abbey. It could have been built yesterday or a millennium ago, for hidden away from the world time stood still. The sun slanted down through the trees in golden rays illuminating the heart-shaped structure built by Lady Mary Macdonald in memory of her husband.

They entered through a small double-arched door and the rose windows set high in the walls cast a kaleidoscope of color across the sheltered solitude. It was simply furnished with carved oak benches and a small altar. Great baskets of red roses scented the air.

"It is said," whispered Scott, "that a marriage performed here will be long and fruitful, and the husband and wife will be lovers for all eternity!"

"It's charming—perfect." Angela looked up at him with wide green-blue eyes and a wistful smile. He might be everything she had ever accused him of being but he was a romantic at heart and his love enveloped her like the heat of a summer day.

"Let's just hope," he murmured, "that the legend of this place offsets the curse of the Bratach Sith!"

The wind soughed through the trees to the accompaniment of bird songs, the minister solemnly read the words, Molly sniffed into her handkerchief, and Angela was totally caught up in the enchantment of the day. Aqua eyes met brown eyes as they repeated the vows and a golden spark of affection blazed between them binding them closer than any words. Scott slipped a heart-shaped diamond ring onto her finger and she met his kiss with a smile.

Bagpipes whined as Angus played a pibroch and a rose-colored aura permeated the atmosphere. They were married, husband and wife joined together forever by God and man as one flesh.

"I love you, Angela—my sweet little wife." Scott's fervent smile melted her heart.